WHAT THE LIVING KNOW:
A NOVEL OF SUICIDE AND PHILOSOPHY

Matthew C. Kruger

NFB Publishing
Buffalo, New York

Printed in the United States of America

What the Living Know: A Novel of Suicide and Philosophy/ Kruger 1st Edition

ISBN: 978-1-953610-09-6

1.Title 2. Philosophy. 3. Suicide. 4. Novel. 5. Social Science.
6. Kruger

This is a work of fiction. All characters are fictitious. Any resemblance to actual events or locations, unless specified, or persons, living or dead is entirely coincidental.

NFB
NFB Publishing/Amelia Press
119 Dorchester Road
Buffalo, New York 14213

For more information visit Nfbpublishing.com

For Kate

and

For all in my life who have died;
“At the going down of the sun and in the morning…”
I will remember you.

Contents

PART 1 - 9

PART 2 - 121

PART 3 - 229

APPENDIX - 341

Part One

"He was, obviously, beginning to experience the revulsion that would force him to look at death as the gratification of his desires, as good fortune. In the past, each separate desire evoked by suffering or privation, such as hunger, weariness, and thirst, had been satisfied by some bodily function that gave him pleasure; now, however, privation and suffering could have no relief, and any attempt at relief evoked new suffering. And so all desires were merged into one: the desire to be rid of all sufferings and their source, the body. However, he had no words to express this desire for liberation, and so he did not speak of it but out of habit demanded satisfaction of those desires which could no longer be satisfied."

Leo Tolstoy, *Anna Karenina*[1]

Chapter 1

"Yeah, he blew himself up last year."

"Oh?" she asks.

"Mmhmm, they just sewed his head back on," I continue. "On to one of his spares, of course."

"Was it a good show?"

"Not really."

"Shame." I'm standing next to a beautiful blonde woman named Cynthia, who I've just met. She is immaculately dressed in a black tuxedo with no blouse. We're discussing our favorite suicides. "If you're going to do something like that," she continues, "you might as well make it interesting for the rest of us."

"It could be better this time," I say, and she nods obliquely.

We're at a party for Phillip George, a friend and former coworker of mine, and the man who exploded himself this past year. No one had ever done it before, he explained, so he wanted to see if he could do it. And he did. But no one was excited as he was—the explosion, too muffled, and though his body was tattered, there was only a little splatter. He knew this, knew he would have to do better, and this time around he's promised an amazing event, something to really break up the monotony of our lives. And though he hasn't revealed whether or not he'll die—whether it'll be a proper death party—it seems a safe bet to guess he's on his way out.

"Tell me about your best death party," she says to me, still with her bemused eyes.

"Hmm, I think my favorite…it was like four hundred years ago. Reynaud Mancini. So he had a laser net suspended between two gigantic pylons that arced towards him while he stood on a platform thirty meters up. The net cuts him into pieces and makes this, like, putty substance with his body, and then his body putty is molded with compressed air and robots armed with spatula tools into a series of sculptures covering all of the best works of the human form for the intervening ten millennia since Michelangelo. And all around him, the whole time, a laser show, and all of it above the fountains of the Madeline Hotel, spraying in time with the music. It was amazing, a singular experience."

She laughs. "I heard about that, I think. I'm seriously pretty sure I remember that."

"Did you know him?"

"No, no," she smiles. "I was in New York at the time. Teaching. That's kind of what I still do, but everyone was talking about it. You must have been very popular to get the invite."

I laugh. "Not really. Reynaud was the son of my fifth wife, so we were friends through that." She nods. "Tell me yours," I say.

"I'd have to think. But I can tell you my worst. It was last weekend."

"What happened?"

"It was in Belgium. Terrible place."

"And?"

"They just used a sword. And beheaded him. In the middle of a park. It was very strange. Just THHHUNNKKK and his head was off and it was over."

"They just cut off his head?" I ask. "Nothing else?"

"Mhmm. Samurai sword," as she takes a sip of her champagne. "I think it was something traditional. Like a family member died that way. But the samurai sword makes no sense in Belgium in a park. And no music, no lighting, no DJ."

"Oh."

"It was just boring," she says. The ennui is strong with this one. But I see in her a respite for the evening. "Speaking of," she continues, "what is taking so long?"

"Phillip has never been on time in his six thousand years of life."

"Is that right?"

I laugh. "I've only known him for a couple hundred. But I still feel confident in my statement."

"I see that you have found a friend," says someone from behind me.

Cynthia smiles and greets him with a kiss on both of his cheeks. "Justinus," she says, "this is Warren."

"Warren Walker," I say, and offer a bow.

He smiles broadly and points in recognition, bowing as he does it. "Dr. Walker himself. I've been hoping I'd run into you."

"Is that right?" I say, looking him over. He is tall, two full meters, also blonde with short cropped hair. He is wearing a black strapless dress with shoulder length gloves patterned with diamonds.

"You are *the* Warren Walker, right? You were the lead singer of the 5th and Independent Songbirds."

I laugh. "That was a while back," I say. About five thousand years ago, actually.

"You were the top act of the 7760s with four number one hits, and you began a renaissance of vintage style electronica."

"You were a fan?"

"Well, not a true one. I wasn't close to being born yet. But I became one when I discovered you. I actually completed my third doctorate a few decades ago on your musical style."

"A dissertation. I'll have to read that."

"Oh, don't bother. It's very academic work, and rather dull. But it did win a prize..."

"Impressive," I say, and the conversation pauses for a moment, because what do you say when someone brags about their dissertation? He has more to say, but I am not engaging with him in the way that he wants, as he expects a person when praised to be excited about it, or perhaps to be flattered. But I can't summon the energy to care about my days in music.

"There's a few other things I wanted to talk to you about, actually."

"Oh, sure. I've got all night."

"We've forever, of course," he says, nudging me with a wink. This is the most frequent joke one hears, but if you acknowledge that it is overused, then someone makes a secondary quip about how "it never gets old," which makes everything worse. "How'd the two of you meet?" he asks us.

"He saw me standing here, alone, looking at the spot where I'd dropped the canapes on my lapel," Cynthia explains. "And then he introduced himself."

"What fortune," says Justinus. "As I was saying..."

Before Justinus can explain himself, we are interrupted. I see Peter, a friend of mine, looking frantic as he winds his way through the last of the crowd to get to me.

"Warren," says Peter. "Phillip wants to see you, now, please."

"Oh," I say. "Really?" Peter nods in quiet exasperation. "Excuse me." I start to walk and realize I'm leaving Cynthia behind, and I don't want to do that. "Don't leave without me," I say to her, and she smiles and mouths "okay."

"Who is the woman?" he says, as we head away.

"Cynthia something. She seems pretty and bored."

"Your type, huh?"

"Well, everyone is beautiful. And most of us are bored. So everyone's type."

"True."

"You know the guy, though?" I ask.

"Yeah, Justinus. Everyone knows Justinus."

"Not me..."

"Are you ready for Morris's death party next weekend?" asks Peter.

"Yeah," I say. "I haven't found a room yet."

"Is that right? Stay with me. I rented a house."

"Of course you did. I'd love to, if you'll have me."

"I insist."

We reach a door at the back of the room behind the center stage with its blast shield. Peter knocks once and then turns the knob. "Phillip?" he says. "I've brought Warren."

"Come in," he says.

Phillip is sitting on a strangely short wooden chair in front of a mirror, his knees wide and rising above his waist. The room is completely empty, bare white walls, concrete floor, no food, no drinks, no drugs. On the way out, most of us choose absolute luxury. Instead, he is fidgeting with the wiring that stretches across his chest and connects itself to a great number of explosives all over his body.

"Is that safe?" I ask.

"Of course," he laughs. "I'm glad you're here. Peter, would you give us a moment?" Peter nods and heads out of the room. "I wanted to say a few words to you before I head out there."

"Phillip, of course."

"I'm going to end it tonight."

I am taken aback, but I play as if he has told the best joke ever. "Way to spoil the surprise! Come on!"

"I can't imagine there's anything new left for you now."

"For me?"

"You're so old, right? Nothing new…" he pauses.

"Not really, I suppose," offering a tepid response. I'm not sure where he's going. "But I still like a good time."

"What can be new for a ten thousand year old man, right?"

"Nothing new under the sun," I say, finishing his line, and curious as to what he's getting at.

"That's right. I'm sorry to do this, but I need to confess something to you."

"Yes?" I ask with a grin. I've never known Phillip to have any sort of depth, so I am rather bemused at his attempt at gravity.

"I've been pretending like I do not want to die. But I want to die more than anything. I'm so excited for tonight," he says, beaming. "I've been alive too long, and now I hate living."

"That's rather common, Phillip, nothing to be ashamed of," I say.

"You have never given in. I don't understand that, and it really bothers me, honestly. Ever since I met you and learned how old you were I've been thinking about it. But I want to ask you before I go if there's something else I should try before I die, something that could make me live. We have one extremely long life to live, so I want to make sure that I haven't missed something, in case I could still survive and be happy. So, am I missing anything?"

"Phillip, I don't know. Have you read Milnius?"

"Yeah, didn't care for him. What else?"

"I don't know that I have a secret or anything. You just need to find joy in whatever you can and kind of work on yourself to be able to do that."

"So, you don't really have an answer?"

I shake my head. I'm not sure what he's asking me for. "Not really, I guess."

"So I can die?"

"Sure, if you want."

"But I have your permission? I won't disappoint you?"

"My permission? It's your life, Phillip, you should do what you want."

"Well, I want to die."

"Okay, then."

"I'm ready. You should get a good seat. It's going to be a much bigger boom than last time. Everyone's going to need ponchos."

"Awesome. I'll go grab one." I walk over to the door and pause as I step out. "Congratulations Phillip. I'm glad that you're excited to move on."

"Me too," he says. "Thanks for being a great friend."

"You, too," I say.

I realized that I am probably the last person to speak to him as he goes to death. We've been friends for a few decades now, but I never thought of us as *great* friends. Then again, an inability to be close to anyone is a symptom of being close to the end of one's life: you run out of friends, as the things which once amused you, including people in general, slowly lose their charm. I start to count the number of close friends I have. But I also haven't been myself recently, I should say. My wife's suicide. It's been a bit hard to keep friendships going when you don't have any desire to be with other people.

After spotting Cynthia in the crowd she offers a subdued wave and wraps her arms around my hand as I take my place next to her. "Thought you'd disappeared."

"Not without you," I say.

"Is this thing going to happen?" asks Justinus. "I've got a dinner to get to."

"Yeah," I chime. "He's finally ready. Says that we're going to need ponchos."

"Is that right?" asks Justinus, excited.

"Really?" says Cynthia. "I don't want blood on my tuxedo."

"We'll be fine," I say.

"You're paying for my cleaning..."

The lights dim and a spotlight appears on the stage. A meter wide hole spreads in the center of the floor, and the crowd leans in to peak down, hoping to catch a glimpse of his emergence. All of a sudden Phillip shouts "Heyyyoooo!!!" from the ceiling of the auditorium, and our eyes dart upwards. He jumps down falling perfectly into the hole in the floor, disappearing, before shooting upwards, completing a triple back flip, and landing perfectly with his arms in victory formation.

He smiles broadly as we cheer wildly and chant "Phillip! Phillip!" He waves a hand to silence the chatter and his face grows stern as a series of instruments emerge from the floor.

"Oh shit," I say.

"What?" asks Cynthia, her attention rapt on Phillip.

"He's going to try match Mancini."

"You think he's going to sculpt himself?"

"No. I don't know. But it's definitely something art related."

She grimaces a bit, but then regains hope and pokes me in the ribs. "Let's see what happens, huh?"

"Okay, you're right."

Phillip carefully measures his position on stage in relation to the instruments. He reaches into the top of his explosive vest and retrieves a trigger switch.

"Good bye everyone! I've loved you all!"

The audience holds its collective breath.

He clicks. Nothing. He clicks again. Nothing. He clicks emphatically now, repeatedly. Nothing. He looks over to a man just outside the blast shield, standing at a control panel. "It's not working."

"What?" says the man.

"It's not working. I keep on clicking it, it's not working."

"You'll have to take it off."

"I'm not taking it off. That'll take hours."

"I don't know..."

Phillip looks up from his side conversation with the useless engineer. "I'm sorry...Turn my damn mic on...I'm sorry everyone. This vest was supposed to explode and my body would be liquefied. And then these jets here, they would have sprayed my body and some paint, and all of it would have made Salvador Dali's *The Red Orchestra* on the wall behind me right there. That was one of my favorite paintings. Should've been pretty cool." He walks to the front of the stage and opens a trap door. "But looks like that's not going to happen. I'm sorry this is so disappointing." He pulls a gun out from a box on the side of the stage, what looks like a vintage plasma baller. "But I don't want to wait any more. So, now...uh...good bye." He puts the gun up to his temple and with an emphatic PHWUMP!!! from the plasma baller the blast shield is hosed with blood and brain matter.

"Fuck," says Cynthia.

"That...wow," says Justinus.

I can't muster a word. What was he thinking? There was no joy in this.

We look in confusion to one another and the murmuring grows in volume. I can't believe he did it that way. My wife did it that…Cynthia grabs my arm, bringing me back. "What was that about?"

"I honestly don't know. He just said that he really wanted to die. I didn't think he'd just shoot himself."

"Poor form," says Justinus.

"Agreed," follows Cynthia. "Guess I've got a new worst death party."

The crowd begins to file out for the cocktail reception, slowly and with much muttering. "Maybe it's a new trend," spits Justinus. "Putting on shitty deaths. Get all your friends all dressed up and shit on their evening with a hackneyed death."

"Tell me about it," she says.

"Not even artful," he continues. "I'm not going to stick around," fidgeting now. "Would you two care to join me for dinner?"

"I can't," I say. "I've got to be here. Friends, you know?"

Cynthia offers knowing eyes to Justinus. "I'm going to hang around for a bit. We'll talk later."

"Of course," he says. "But I would like to see you again," pointing at me. "Have you any plans for tomorrow?"

"I'm hiking, actually."

"Great, I'll join you. Send me the info. Bye, my love," he says to Cynthia, kissing her cheeks this time, "have fun tonight."

We watch as he strides away gallantly. "How do you know him?" I ask.

"We dated for a little while, before he moved here."

"Seems like fun."

"He is fun. And very popular; knows everyone."

"But not for you?"

"No," she says, her eyes intent on mine.

WE'RE sitting at an incredibly long table with the decimated remains of Phillip's death party. The table is set for two hundred, and there are twelve of us. Peter looks at me; he is watching closely. The problem is this: my eighth wife died six months ago. She did not have a death party, as is the custom, as is the polite thing to do for friends and family. She did not divorce me first, either, which is also considered more polite. Instead, she shot herself with an old plasma baller in our living room one night, in the same unexpected and distasteful manner that Phillip just completed his death. Now that we have eternal life and eternal youth, death is a celebrated choice; it means a person has gotten everything out of life that they can and they are ready for something different. It is a happy occasion, but there was nothing happy about her quiet suicide. And now, as I'm sitting at dinner waiting for my next cocktail to be delivered by the robotic wait staff, I cannot remove the image of Phillip shooting himself from my mind. Instead I replay it over and over, only pausing to substitute my wife and our living room.

"You're not yourself this evening," says Peter.

"I suppose not."

"You haven't been for a while," he says. "I'll admit that was a bit off though."

"So is this," I say, gesturing down the table. We are at the end, sitting on glistening onyx chairs across from each other, Cynthia next to me. At the head is a giant throne of the same material, a symbolic empty chair for Phillip, so that we might remember him for the evening.

"Cartagena will be better."

Cartagena is where Morris will be dying next weekend. "God I hope so," I say. "I think we might get going," I say, and then my drink arrives, set down by a prehensile robot arm out of nowhere.

"Can't leave a drink unfinished, can you?"

"No," I sigh.

Cynthia shrugs. "I've still got to finish mine, too." She looks at her full glass of champagne.

"Aren't you upset with him?" I say.

"Who, Phillip?" replies Peter. "Why?"

"That was awful. Wasn't that awful?"

"That was awful," Cynthia confirms. "Really dreadful."

"I didn't say it was good," replies Peter. "Just whatever, he did what he was supposed to do, and that was it."

"Mr. Niemans," I poke at him. "Always so measured. Unmoved. Unswayed by the ways of the world."

Peter's sense of humor isn't the sharpest, and he remains in defense mode. "I don't see why we need to get all worked up about people dying. It's so expensive to throw these parties."

"You're dead," says Cynthia. "You don't need the money when you're dead."

"That's true. But your relatives can use it."

"Says the man who inherited a fortune."

"That's right. And I've always appreciated it. And you, Warren, are not exactly poor, either."

"Ten thousand years of compound interest..."

"Are you really that old?" she asks, and then realizes that might be an odd thing to say. And then, as from the little bit I've come to know of her in the past two hours, she persists. "You do look older. I mean, you're aged up a bit more than everyone else. You have a little silver on your temples."

"That's true."

"Do you dye them?"

"Oh no," Peter laughs. "No such vanity. He is just that old, part of the first generation. And that very first generation didn't age backwards quite so smoothly. "

"Wow. You are actually old."

"Oh thank you," I say, facetiously.

"Come on," she says. "I was ready to go home with you simply because of how you look. Isn't that a win?"

"If that's the only reason..."

"...And your wit and charm," she interjects.

"Now you've got me."

Peter feels that we are not paying enough attention to his concerns, most of which are directed towards me. "Are you asking how I feel about his death because it upset you?" says Peter.

"We stopped talking about that a while ago."

"The question stands," he says.

"I'm having a lovely evening."

"You are not," says Peter.

"I am."

"Only because she's here," he gestures to Cynthia, who looks a bit offended.

"And?"

"And she's very nice, and I can't blame you. You are very nice"—directly to Cynthia—"But there's an elephant in the room. At least for me. Standing on you."

"What's that?" I ask, not believing he would truly be so tactless to persist.

"Your wife died just like that six months ago."

"She did."

"She did?" says Cynthia. "What does he mean?"

"She shot herself," I say looking at Peter.

"Oh. Did she tell you before?"

"No."

"That's horrible," says Cynthia, emphatically.

"It was."

"It was," says Peter. "And you haven't been the same since."

"I'm out, again, having a lovely evening, which you are fully committed to ruining."

"I don't think she minds," he says.

"I don't. You two can talk."

"We don't need to talk. We've covered things."

"We have not," says Peter.

"I'm going to go get something from the drug table," she says. "Anyone need anything?"

"I'll come with you," I say.

Peter remains nonplussed as we stand and excuse ourselves. He is absolutely correct, however, that we have things to discuss. I have been rather absent in my friendship to Peter.

"Sorry about that," I offer to her. Death parties are not for serious conversation.

"It's okay," she says.

"Peter's mostly upset that I haven't been paying attention to him."

"We don't need to talk about it." She says this definitively.

"Good," I say.

"I'll have one of those." Out of the hundred or so pills in their elegant onyx dishes, she has selected a little pastel green triangle. It's an aphrodisiac and ecstatic called Meld.

"Is that right?"

She nods, "mmhmm," but she doesn't smile.

"You're bored," I say.

"No," she says.

"It's fine to be bored."

"I'm not. But I've had enough of this party, I think."

"Me, too." I take hold of her waist and turn her attention my way. She smiles now, and offers a devastating glance of intent. I take a pill and place it in her mouth, and then she kisses me deeply. The first kiss. That never gets old.

"My place or yours?"

"Mine," she says.

We walk to the exit and I avoid eye contact with Peter who remains alone and self-satisfied in his prior position. He will stay until the end of the party, even when all of the other friends have left to do anything other than be there, and he will do so because he is a good friend, a selfless person.

She summons her transport pod, and as it arrives I wonder if she knows my name.

"Warren Walker," I say. "I know you caught the Warren part..."

"I did," she says. "All of it. Cynthia Wellsbottom."

I smirk at her name and she rolls her eyes.

"I'm sorry. Wellsbottom. Unique."

"There's actually quite a few of us."

I try to think of a pun using her name. *Do they all have as swell of a bottom as you?* No, no, that doesn't make any sense. "I bet you have a swell bottom."

"That was the best you could do?"

"I'm sorry I'm so immensely charming. And witty."

I only realize that the pod has stopped soon after my orgasm, the cognition of which coincides with the abrupt exit of the population of my lap.

"I had a lovely time. Please visit soon," she says to me, distantly, from her apartment door.

"What…?" is all I can manage before the door slides shut. The pod starts moving, and flashes my home on the screen. "Computer," I say, "Call Cynthia."

"Did you forget something?" she asks, the interior of her apartment now displayed. She is putting her clothes away, her bare back towards the lens as she tosses her tuxedo jacket across the room into the arms of her robotic closet.

"I didn't have the opportunity," I reply.

"No. Well, no need to rush," she says.

"Is that all that it is?"

"Of course," she says, looking at me for a moment, feigning a smile as she offers the tepid cliché. "We have forever."

I arrive home and throw my jumpsuit into the closet and I think again about Phillip shooting himself and of my dead wife. Gwen. Gwendolyn. Never called her that. We were married only a short time, exactly fifty years, and she ended her life far before any of us we're ready. She was the youngest to die in who knows how long at her fair age of one hundred and forty-seven. People laughed at our relationship, saying our age difference was absurd. And by all practical measures, with me at nine thousand, nine hundred and seventy years old and she at ninety-seven, it was a strange match. She wanted my wisdom, not because she lacked it, but because she wanted to convince herself she did not have the answer. She wanted to find a reason to live and so she came to me, a person who has lived many lifetimes and showed no signs of waning interest in living many more. I couldn't give her this, a simple and straightforward explanation of why it was better to keep on living, why I had lived for so many centuries without opting for the standard course of suicide. There were only about a million of us left from the first generation of those who could live forever, and the weight of the billions who had opted for death pressed on her.

"They'd lived for centuries already," I would say.

"So?"

"They've lived lives. They've experienced things."

"And then they died."

"And then they died."

"And their lives meant nothing," she says sharply.

"Why are you worrying about meaning?"

"Isn't that what matters?"

"Semantically?"

"Right."

"But we have fun," I offer.

"We do."

"That's not enough?"

"But then we die."

"Not necessarily. But yeah, someday. Just not today," I always said.

"Not today," she said.

We cried at her funeral; there were no invitations to her death, and no extravagant party following her peace. For those as old as I, we could remember a time, back to our actual youth, when people died too soon, before they wanted to, when a death represented a tragedy rather than a relief and a party. It felt like that, and I cried for that time long since passed, maybe even more than I cried for her.

I try to think of the most beautiful way of killing myself; the truth is they've all been done before, and there is nothing new under the sun.

Chapter 2

"Thanks for letting me come with you," says Justinus, offering a mini bow from his seat as I step into his pod. "Are we going somewhere nearby?"

"Not particularly," I reply. "Shuttle station please."

"A shuttle flight?"

"It's short."

"They're always short," he says, dismissively.

It's nine in the morning, and he does not look overly pleased to be awake, nor comfortable with the suggestion of heading outside of the city. He wears long white wool robes, with multiple long scarves and belts—the outfit of a philosophical movement from the eighth millennium called the Trusted. His robes are tied incorrectly, however, so it is clear he was never actually affiliated. In fact, I believe he said he wasn't even born at that time. I think he meant to reach out to me by showing his willingness to engage in philosophical pretense.

"What is it you wanted to talk about, oh Trusted one?"

"Oh, these?" he smiles emphatically. "They're actually his robes."

"Whose?"

"The most famous of the Trusted, of course. Grand Master Percival. Died in 7740 while in meditation after setting himself on fire."

"He wasn't wearing any robes? What a scandal."

"He wore special flammable robes that day. Magnesium thread, so that he would die very brightly and quickly. I've been assured that these were his robes by their foundation. Very expensive."

"Have they made you any smarter?"

He sighs with the knowledge that he is being mocked. "They have not."

"Shame."

The shuttle rumbles as the rocket engines ignite and we are pressed into our seats. Justinus continues to speak, however: "Yes, well, such is life. Still, I've been meaning to talk with you," he says. "I used to be married to one of your wives. Did you know that?"

"No. Who?"

"Portia Richards."

"Oh. She died, what, twelve hundred years ago?"

"That's right. She did the whole skydiving into the sun thing."

"That was big back then."

"It was."

"Something to do with her?"

"No, not at all. She told me that you knew how to live. I ignored it at the time, but when I realized you lived in this city, I've been thinking about it more and more."

"It's not that much of a mystery. You just don't die."

"She said you had a sense of humor, as well."

"Justin…"

"…Justinus," he corrects, accenting the I: Just-EYE-nus.

"Yes, right. I don't have any special wisdom. Someone else, of course, has already written down and published every bit of wisdom that has ever existed, so you can just find anything I would say to you in the database."

"Well, it's my contention that you may not be able to speak your wisdom, but you simply live it. So I'd like to spend time with you. And study you. And learn how to do this."

"I'm not the oldest man alive, you know."

"Yes, I know."

"Isn't there a philosopher you could turn to?"

"I've done that." He pauses. His demeanor shifts and he puts his hand on my shoulder, and holds me in place with a light grip and heavy hand. "I am suffering. I'm near the end."

"I'm sorry to hear that. You seem rather chipper."

"Well, I'm on a multitude of drugs right now. A veritable rainbow." He smiles broadly and genuinely.

"Of course."

"And prescriptions. I'm down to my last options on antidepressants. They stop working eventually, you know."

"I know."

"And you don't take them."

"No, not for me."

"I don't want to die, Warren. But there's also nothing I want more." He has the same defeat in his eyes. "So," he says, "I need to spend some time with you. See how you do it."

I consider the offer, although I am without choice this afternoon, since we're stuck together for at least a few hours on this hike. And he is completely insufferable. But I also find myself intrigued, perhaps only because of my desire for novelty, but nonetheless. He is new, or at least interesting, because how often does one encounter a person of his age with such an irrepressibly delusive nature? I think we'll have some fun.

"Let's hang out. I don't think I'll be able to help. But we'll enjoy ourselves in the meantime."

"Splendid!"

As the shuttle comes to a stop after the half-hour ride, I look out the window and see nothing but trees. No buildings, no settlements, not even in the distance. The spell is broken momentarily as you realize you are in a rocket powered shuttle, but soon I will be outside of this contraption and free. Nothing but a sea of green interspersed with stripes and circles of blue.

We are outside the town of Kitcisakik in the middle of Canada. It is a quiet place, and is easily accessible by the all-terrain transit pods currently circling the landing pad. We did not come for the town, however, which has its own dreariness, but the series of paths that circle Lake Agatha. This is where I come when I need a break from the city.

"There's a party tonight," he says. "You'll have to join me. My friend Oliver is having quite an important night."

"Sure," I say.

I pause at the back exit and take in the untamed woods marred by the well maintained hiking path running through its center. To say that Justinus is uncomfortable would be to significantly understate his demeanor. Suspiciously he peers around the woods, listening for wildlife, spotting movement, clamming up and withdrawing.

"Are we in drone range?" he asks.

"Of course we're in drone range," I say. "We just landed at a shuttle port."

"Right," he says.

"You've never been out in the woods?"

"Not like this," he says.

"You've been to Mars," I say.

"I've been to Jupiter, too, twice."

"And you've never gone out to the woods?"

He thinks for a moment. "No, I don't think so."

"This'll be good for you, then. This way."

As we continue up the trail, Justinus is still unable to speak. He hears a branch crack in the distance.

"What was that?"

"Probably a squirrel," I say.

"A squirrel," he says.

"You know what's interesting?"

"No." He stops. "No I do not."

I take his shoulder. "Not fifteen minutes ago you told me how ready you were to die. Now you are afraid of squirrels and checking in to make sure medical drones are flying over. They don't let people die anymore, no matter where you are; you know this. You have to choose it."

"I know." We start walking again.

"And have you applied for death?"

"I have not."

"So what's your problem?"

"It's just unsettling. There are bears out here, I've heard."

"There are indeed."

"See. I don't want to die by bear. I mean, who does that?"

"Actually…" I say.

"No, no way…" he says.

"Yeah, my friend Lili Thomas. Well, it was tigers actually. She wanted to be eaten by a tiger. It's a Buddhist thing."

"Right." He pauses as he thinks of the right way to ask his question. "Was it a good show?"

I laugh. "Kind of amazing. She had them feed the tiger before she went out there, so the idea was that she would have time to bond with the creature, and they would spend a day or two, maybe a week getting to know each other. You know, becoming friends. And then, when the tiger was hungry, she would offer herself up in the sacrifice of a friend, cut off her arm or something and feed it to him."

"Sounds poetic, actually."

"Yeah, it was a neat idea. We're all standing around watching her from about ten meters above on top of a platform. So she walks out into the clearing below—you know, she's got her hands out, like a Jesus pose, or Buddha pose, she has this music pumping in—it's like 'ooooommmmmmm,' all serious and meditative. It's this touching moment, and then, as she's like a half meter away from touching the tiger in their first contact of love, she trips over a rock and stumbles forward"—I'm laughing now—"And she scares the fucking tiger, and the thing reels back for a second, and then pounces, bites her neck clean through. I mean, her head is just off, and she's boom, dead."

Justinus has a hesitant smile on his face.

"It was so funny," I say. "Lili bleeds out in like two seconds. The entire event takes about two minutes. She'd asked us to book an entire week for the festivities, you know, to watch her bond. The trainer, the guy responsible for the tiger, he's no color left in his face at all, he's horrified. My buddy Tim shouts at him from the platform, he goes, 'Guess you didn't feed him enough.' And we all just lost it."

I pat Justinus on the back. He has a restrained look of bemusement, confused at my enthusiasm, I imagine.

"I guess you had to be there. But it was a great party after that."

"When was this?"

"Let's see. The year 2757. Or 2756. I don't remember exactly."

"Ninety-five hundred years ago."

"Or so."

"She was young, then?"

"Like five hundred something, I think."

"And she was done already?"

"Yeah, you got to remember," I continue, "that the first generation, most of us didn't last that long. It felt so unnatural. It messed up our timeline, our life plan—everyone had one of those, and it didn't involve living forever. It made everything pretty meaningless. The boredom caught up with people real quick."

"Approximately 75% of the population was dead within the first thousand years of their eternal life."

"Write a dissertation on this, too?"

"I did, actually. Well, on the second generation. They've done pretty well living."

"Yes, they have. Now, look."

We've stopped on a hill overlooking the lake; there is a point with the brush cleared away which affords a view of the crystalline water. The sun is still low in the sky, the wind is light, and the leaves rustle in the cool air of the early fall. I breathe the clear air in.

"I went to the woods because I wished to live deliberately," I say.

"Oooh, ooh, I know that one. David Thorough. David Thor-EAU."

"Yep, Henry David Thoreau."

"He retreated to the woods to live apart from society, to get in touch with nature and the roots of humanity."

"Yeah, kind of." I'm avoiding eye contact with him, hoping he'll take in the view instead of insisting on himself and his knowledge. Doesn't the view make you feel small, Justinus? Doesn't the wildness surrounding you remind you that existence is untamed and we barely have a place here?

"'Kind of'?" He asks. No, it does not, apparently. "What do you mean by 'kind of'?"

"I mean he lived about a mile and half away from his parents. There were train tracks even when he lived there; he would have heard the train going by, and then he could walk a half mile into town and be back in the middle of civilization."

"Well, you live in a city."

"No shit."

I continue the hike.

"Where are you going?"

"We've got to finish the trail before your event tonight, don't we?"

"Right, right."

We walk a bit further down the trail, turning down the hill. The trail has mostly washed away, leaving a rocky, sandy mess of treacherous footing. I alternate between trees for an additional handhold as Justinus scatters rocks behind me, sending them down slope in my direction.

"So is Thoreau the reason you can live forever without being so fucking depressed?" he shouts.

"No. I don't particularly like him actually."

"Why not Thoreau?"

"Well, he didn't live in the city."

"Right." He stumbles and runs past me, catching his own fall, grabbing a small tree to break his gait, and he swings around the tree to face me. "Who is then?"

"My favorite philosopher?"

"Yes."

"Hmm. Maybe Milnius Severus. You know him?"

"Yes, of course. The first of the eternal philosophers. Lived from 2176 to 3558. Died by taking poison hemlock in reference to the death of the ancient Greek philosopher Socrates."

"That's right."

"Did you know him?"

"Actually, yes. He was a professor of mine in my first grad school. While he was still Charles Milnius. And after that, I was a friend of his."

"Is that right?"

I start walking again. "I quote: The great realization of our eternal life is that our eternal life is completely meaningless. There is no meaning to be found in the work we accomplish; it has already been accomplished before, and will be done again. There is no meaning in the birth of children; we do not die if we do not want to, and they do not preserve us, nor produce anything. They move on with their own meaningless lives. There is no meaning to be found in wisdom; none of us are wise, nor could we ever be. We cannot live for pleasure, as it turns to poison 'as the bee mouth sips.' We cannot live for pain, as it becomes pleasure and fades to nothing. If we wish to live, it must be for nothing, and for no purpose; and then we will live forever."

"What's that from?"

"His magnum opus. *On meaninglessness*. The opening words."

"What can he say after that?"

"He explains for three hundred thousand words why the removal of death has confused the mental structures employed by humanity, which leads to our irretrievable depression, and then our death—if we do not change ourselves."

"He's right, I suppose."

"Well, people aren't sure if he's actually correct about the details of it. And predicting that life ends with death isn't actually that bold. The people who wore those robes you've got on, they were quite insistent about his mistaken presumptions."

"Oh," he says. We're going up another hill, a steep one, and he's struggling in his sandals, his robes continuing to catch on every little bush and tree limb. He pulls his scarf free: "these are authentic robes, you know."

"You mentioned that."

The Trusted disagreed with Milnius because of his contention we could alter ourselves at any point in our lives, suggesting that we were limited by the way we spent our first twenty-eight to thirty-two years, after which we could not alter certain features of our personality. The Trusted argued that early youth was *the* essential point in the formation of eternal persons who could weather the meaninglessness of existence. So, people trusted (hence…) them with their children, who they raised in a strict philosophical manner until they were ready for their aging to stop. The movement lost steam after a few youths raised by the trusted—persons who had gone on to prominent positions in society, as far as those still exist—had ended their lives, something which was not supposed to happen, and certainly not after only a few hundred years. They were supposed to be prepared for existence, capable of withstanding the disappointment when everything you've ever wanted to accomplish has been completed, and the only things that are left are those which you never wanted any part of.

"I heard that your wife died a few months ago," he says.

"That's what you want to talk about?"

"No, of course not. It's just that, sometimes people are depressed when it happens like that."

"I've been better," I say. "And I've been thinking about ways to kill myself." His face pales a bit as I say this. "I'm not there though. I mean, sure, I think about it. I'll try and come up with ideas every once in a while, try to think of some beautiful way to die."

"What are you thinking of now?"

"I haven't found anything that I really like."

"Oh."

He pauses his conversation, most likely to consider his own vision for his death.

"I haven't used my lungs like this in a while," he says.

"Is that right? I try to get them burning every once in a while."

"Burning?"

"That's something you used to be able to do. Now we're all in perfect shape all the time. You forget, or maybe you don't know, that we used to have to work at being in shape. The average man would have quit this hike a while ago, back in my old time."

"Your old time," he says, mulling that over. It sounds strange to me, as well. I still remember most of the way life used to be, as we don't really forget much anymore. "I never studied their philosophy, to be honest," he continues. "The Trusted, that is. I did take a course on Severus. He's very depressing."

"He intended it to be freeing. He freed himself for his own death. Didn't quite free himself from death, though."

"Are there any happy philosophers that you like? Anyone cheery?"

"Of course. But I don't think they're going to be what you're looking for."

"Why wouldn't they be what I'm looking for?"

"All of the happy ones I know have killed themselves, which generally makes them unpopular. Everyone watches to see if they can live forever to see if their philosophy is worth following, and then when they die, argue that their philosophy was never worth following. Epictetus II is still alive. But she's only about eight hundred years old at the moment. And she just pretty much repeats the original Epictetus."

"They all give in and die. And you wonder why I'm here with you, Dr. Walker." I laugh at him using a title. Nobody uses titles anymore. Everyone's been a doctor or something at some point. "I'm here," he continues, "because you are the one with the secret to life."

"I keep saying I have nothing to teach you."

"Fine," he says. He trudges along, annoyed. We're approaching the main overlook point, a cliff about ten meters above the water. I can hear the ducks off in the distance, the squirrels fighting in the trees. This is my favorite place on this hike. But I can hear his thoughts through his body: 'Fuck everything about this, it's so dirty out here, and I'm not learning anything, it's all this depressing philosophy bull shit again. It's just ridiculous.' I am both annoyed and entertained by this man with me.

"Come over here, stand next to me." We're standing on the cliff edge and I attempt to be redeeming. "Kierkegaard says that you get a feeling when you stand on the edge of a cliff. Angst, or dread, or whatever. You have this feeling because you have the choice to throw yourself off the cliff. It's the anxiety of having the power. Do you feel it?"

"All the time," he says. "That's why I'm with you. I am anxious to choose my death at every moment."

"Interesting," I say.

"What do you feel?" he asks.

"The same, I guess. But I don't care about the feeling, so there's not much angst to speak of."

"So I'm screwed," he says. "Because I have angst?"

"Or you're fine," I say. "Always with the drama. Have you tried not taking yourself so seriously?" He doesn't say anything, but continues to stare down to the water. "Come on," I say. "We've got to get going. I want some time at home before we go to your party."

"I choose," he says.

"Don't…" I say, lunging towards him.

Too late. He jumps. But even before he begins to move downward, the drone in the lake has surfaced and hummed in his direction, arriving only a second too late to catch him. It is a Federation TF 4300 Watersafe Drone with four rotors, about eight meters in diameter. Below the rotors lies an entire hospital worth of equipment, including four extending prehensile cable arms to pick up wayward souls like Justinus. He lands partially in the water but hits his leg on a rock at the surface resounding with a loud *crack*. The drone drops two arms while hovering above him, and pulls him free of the water, flying him up to the top of the cliff. It lays him down. He's shivering, but his breath quickly slows—he's already been injected with painkillers and antibiotics, from the moment the drone contacted him.

"What the fuck, Justin?"

"Just-EYE-nus!"

"Well?"

"I chose."

"You sure did."

"If there's a drone here, why didn't it catch me?" he looks around, confused.

"It's not high enough for you to kill yourself here. At least, not easily. They catch you in the city, but only have water drones here, you know, for the swimmers."

"Right. It's supposed to catch me."

The drone has pulled his robes above his knee, set and injection casted his leg, and is now blinking a readout to me.

"Broke my leg," he says.

"That's right. Broken fibula, stress fracture in your tibia. Way to go."

"Thanks," he says, looking a little embarrassed. The adrenaline is gone, the synthetic opioids are flowing now. "I did choose."

"Not really," I say. I turn to the drone, "return patient to the shuttle port, ship #37GF; we're scheduled for two hours out." The drone bleeps a confirmation, and the rotors spin up, carrying Justinus up and away. "I'll see you back at the ship."

By the time I walk back to the shuttle port, he's up and walking around, chatting up the station manager, a person I've met a few dozen times before. A federation employee, he's been stationed here for close to a hundred years, which is deeply confusing to me. It is likely the least exciting station a federation employee could have, and the entirety of his job can be accomplished by computer and robot; at the very least, you could ask to cycle through the very boring placements. I've talked with him several times, he's always eager to chat, but then he has nothing much to say. Perhaps he knows something more than I do.

The sun is setting as it is the middle of the fall in northern Canada. I take in one last breath of non-city air, and head on to the shuttle with Justinus.

"You still haven't told me what this event is tonight."

"I don't believe you've asked," he replies.

"Well?"

"My friend Oliver. He is exiting his chamber of ecstasy tonight."

I'm in my bedroom at the moment, trying on outfits. Justinus is sitting in the next room on the couch reclining, his leg elevated. He is still in his robes, now covered with mud and dirt and pondscum, but has carefully draped himself to avoid fouling the furniture.

"An orgasm machine? How long has he been in?"

"One hundred years."

"Oh. Not bad."

"You must have a story for this, too, I assume."

I peak my head out from my room. "I do, actually."

"Well?"

I step out to face him. "Someone I met once spent a thousand years in one. She came out, lived for about three weeks, and then had herself killed. Had her heart stopped mid-orgasm, so she could die the way she lived." I head back in.

"Amazing."

I step out again, this time in a midnight blue tuxedo with a bit of sheen and a jacquard pattern. White lace shirt, black silk bowtie. Vintage. "Think this'll work?"

"Oh yes," he says, "that's very nice."

"Did you want to change? Have we got time?"

"No. I want to show off how rugged I was today. Look at these streaks of dirt!"

"Your leg hurting? You want a dose of something?"

"It's not hurting, just throbbing a bit," he says. "But I'd always like a dose of something."

I head to my kitchen where I keep most of my drugs. I select one of my favorites—a variation on morphine, synthetic, of course, with a few additives that make your limbs feel detached from your body. It's a very distinctive feeling of floating, where you can see your leg touch the ground, and your body operates normally, but you have no sensation of propulsion through the leg, only a forward movement. I hold out the bottle for him to take, but instead he opens his mouth.

"Under your tongue…no, move your tongue…to one side...keep trying."

I place two drops under his tongue, and laugh at this ridiculous person on my couch.

"Ooooooh, floaty," he says. "I'll have to get some of this from you."

"BLACK marble floors. Three story windows. A pool. The biggest balcony in the city. You'll be impressed."

"Is that right?"

"This is a special place," Justinus assures me. "Huge."

The transport pod doors open.

I follow the white streak in the marble across the floor up to the windows, towering, as he said, three stories up. The marble appears to be one continuous piece. Everything else is chrome—each edge of the wall, every sliding door frame, every table leg and lamp and chandelier.

"He worked for the Federation as an accountant for two hundred years. Retired as CFO a hundred years ago with this apartment and a brand new masturbation machine."

Justinus points across the room to a chrome ball.

"He's supposed to come out in an hour, I guess."

About two hundred persons crowd the floor, men and women in ball gowns and tuxedos and oblong sewings of vinyl and rubber, dressed all immaculately, and my companion in his dirty robes, walking with a slight limp. He has affected this limp; he is quite healed. Just as he has kept his dirty robes on to prove that he has encountered dirt, he will evidence his injury for the benefit of all. There are many faces from Phillip's party the evening prior, persons that I do not often commune with. Many of them are invested in the governance of the Federated Societies of Humankind, and power has never been my thing, so I tend to avoid them. I have, I should admit, lived through a few stints with the Federation myself, and a few rotations among those powerful people, but those were long ago.

"This is how to convince people to be accountants, I guess," I say.

"There's only like two hundred accountants, I think, for everything. But they need some people to double check things sometimes."

"Well, I still wouldn't do it."

"Nor I," says Justinus. "Certainly not."

We head over to the drug and drink table and find Theodore, and another friend of Justinus' named Aurelius. Theodore is dressed in a pink tulle gown, the skirt appearing to have approximately forty layers, all of which floof out from him in massive circumference. It is impossible to stand near him without hitting the skirt. It has a pronounced bodice and a sweetheart neckline, and paired with his white satin gloves and diamond tiara, he does actually look like a princess.

"Does that dress glow?" I ask.

"It does!" he says, excited that someone recognized it. He snaps his fingers, and every seam glows with radiant lighting. "It's not quite your jumpsuit from last night, I was dying over that."

"Oh thanks," I say, "but this is a nice dress."

Aurelius clearly feels jealous that Theodore is receiving all of the praise for his outfit. He is in a maroon ball gown, mermaid cut, made of a stretchy satin nano-material that changes color with movement. They were all the rage two or three decades ago, but they haven't had their swing back into fashion, and they are not old enough to be vintage. It's a poor choice, really, though his curves suit the contours of the dress. Vinyl is in right now, not nano.

I spot Cynthia across the room, and she is in a similar outfit as she wore the previous night—this time, her tuxedo is white. I didn't expect to see her here. I wave to her as she turns my way, and she makes eye contact. She perfectly expresses disdain, registering no delight upon seeing me. Her head shakes and she mouths "Fuck off" in a measured way before returning to her conversation, having an uproarious time without me. She will be fun.

The lights are dimmed inside and out, with only the twinkle of the stars and the residual radiance of billboards illuming the room. Justinus taps me on the shoulder and whispers, "I'm so excited."

Now the space ignites in neon blue as a lengthy glass tube flushes with color. At one end of the tube is a monstrous bulb. On the other end and now radiating with light is the orgasm machine, a chrome ball three meters in diameter with a porthole on each side.

A background buzz hums to life, increasing, and we hear the heavy panting of a man in the midst of sexual pleasure. On every chrome corner and every screen, our worthy host's face appears; he is in the midst of what appears to be the most painful activity ever conceived by the human mind. His face distorts and he is sweating, his lips alternating between a confused grin and a grotesque anger. He starts to moan, focusing his mind, and withdrawing his body from the pain. His voice grows, and he screams in a musical tone. The images flash to different parts of his body, first to his arms tensed and ripping at the handholds, now to his testicles which are disconcertingly massive. This draws a raucous cheer from the crowd.

His voice loses any melodic quality now, only intense shouting. Only silence accompanies his screams. What could we say in a moment like this?

The chamber glows brighter from its thousand miniature lights, and they begin to spiral and rotate, while the view pans back to his face. His eyes are wide now, his mouth askew, and he is only shouting, "OHHHHHHHHHHHHHH MYYYYYYYYYYY GOOOOOOOOOOOOOOOD DDDD!!!!!!!!!!"

He begins to shudder, then to seize, and the flickering lights on the machine pause and then slowly increase in intensity in time as he peaks. The glow of the glass tube swells as its purpose becomes apparent. A flood of semen pulsates outwards, waving its way to the bulb, which is quickly filling up.

"That can't be real" says Theodore.

"I hope not," I say.

"Amazing," says Justinus.

The flow stops. The bulb is almost completely full, and many of us are scared; that was an unnatural quantity of ejaculate.

We cheer loudly, and shout, and clap, and a bold guest walks up to the bulb to tap it and to shake it a little. "I think it's real," she shouts to the crowd. Raucous cheering once more and now the machine is opening.

Cracks appear on the surface of the ball, as the seams give way and the dramatic hiss of gas escaping and steam seeping punctuates our sound. The lights come on overhead and mist appears around the base, encapsulating the orgasm device; a form appears and Oliver Waters stumbles out. He is dazed, as one might expect following the largest male orgasm in human history, at least by volume, but he is smiling the smile of the man who believes he has achieved complete victory. He is also completely naked—he is not a tall man, nor a massive person, but he is immaculately toned, even after a hundred years in seated masturbation. The onlookers rush forward and hug him, his first human contact in a century, celebrating the end of his masterful avoidance of all others.

They lift him into the air, Oliver extending his arms above his head, exalting in the merriment. He signals to come down, and he taps on his ear piece. He is going to offer a speech.

"I wrote this before I began my hundred years. I've thought about it the entire time I remained in my chamber—when I wasn't cumming [raucous laughter]. I believe it has only grown in truth." He pauses for a moment to catch his breath. "Give me some champagne."

"Here's to our civilization!

We have conquered death.

There is no one in poverty, no one in poor health, none who are disabled, none who die.

What have we to fear, we who live forever?

Only the end of our joy.

And yet our civilization provides us with endless opportunity for joy.

Here's to our technology!

We sail to the stars and distant planets, we vacation on the moon, lounge at the bottom of the sea, and circle the planet on our merest whim.

Everything is accomplished for us, and for the little work that is left, those who accomplish it are richly rewarded.

Here's to the gifts we have received!

I have spent one hundred years in this machine, including a full decade in perpetual orgasm.

My mind is expanded now—that's true—and it only makes me appreciate this world all the more.

We all have financial security, a home, and a life to live, and I love it.

Here's, most importantly, to all of you!

What joy would we have if we did not have friends?

What joy would there be if there was no one to celebrate with me?

This is truly a blessed day!

Raise a glass!

Pop a pill!

Share a kiss!

I love you all!"

I am standing at the drug table, flanked by Justinus, Theodore, and Aurelius. In addition to a bartender and sommelier, they have a drugtender curating highs for everyone.

"What's something I've never tried before?" I ask him.

"You are experienced?"

"Of course," I say.

"We've got patches and stands, I could set you up?" He offers.

"Patches and stands! Way too early in the night for that."

"Okay then."

"Let's ease in. Some energy, some giddiness."

"For a man of your taste," he says, "I'd recommend two reds, a blue, and a pink powder straw."

The reds I recognize, I think: "The reds are bowlers, right?"

"Correct. These are sourced from a lab in Cambridge."

"Those college kids. Always a new drug," says Justinus.

"They make some excellent stuff," he replies. "They are faster acting, peaky, you know, you'll go in and out of peak high, but they maintain coherence very well. They're a bit mellow on their own, though."

"And the blues?" says Theodore.

"Jetsets. They're from Oklahoma—before you say anything, I've been to this lab, and they have the highest standards, and these offer something different than your standard Jetset, that's why they're blue. You just can't find this kind of energy, they don't increase your heart rate or blood pressure, like you'll get with a lot of the cocaine simulators. You're just pleasingly awake. You only need one to get you through the night. At least until patches and stands time."

"Oh my God," says Justinus, "I can't wait for patches and stands. You're in right?" he says to me.

"Yes, of course. But not yet. Late night."

"Next are the straws. They're a sensory high. Just take a little bit at a time unless you want to spend the rest of the night rubbing yourself with stuff. But if you just take a bump or two, every touch is heightened."

"Excellent recommendations."

"Oh, no problem," says the drugtender. "My name's Chuck, I'm here till three, so let me know if you need anything. And let me know when you're ready for the main event."

We take our mini shot glasses of pills and cheers to each other.

"Here's to us!" says Justinus. "And here's to the good life!"

"Cheers."

After downing the pills I take a bump from the straw and immediately my skin begins to crawl, then to tingle, and then it feels a pleasure simply to be me. Every movement is like a massage with the contact of my skin and clothing. I can see why you would want to avoid taking too much. I mostly just want to stand here shimmying for a while, but no, we must be social.

I see Cynthia again, this time she's close by, talking to a woman with a severe bob. I first make eye contact with this new woman, giving her my best seductive glance. I steal a glass of champagne from a tray floating past to join her empty hand and make Cynthia jealous.

"I don't know you," I say to her.

"You don't," says the woman with a severe bob.

"You asshole," says Cynthia.

"Oh dear, I didn't see you there." I hand this woman her drink.

"Ha," Cynthia says, "I know you did. I've been watching you." She trips a little as she says this.

"What did you take?" I ask.

"None of your business," she replies.

"You two know each other, I gather?" says the bobbed woman.

"We've met," I say.

"He's an asshole," says Cynthia.

"I've been accused. Never convicted," I say.

"I'd leave you two to talk, but I don't think she can stand."

"No, no, please stay," I say. "I came over here to meet you after all."

"I doubt that. I'm Ryan."

"He just goes around hitting on younger women all the time," says Cynthia. Ryan is confused by this joke. "He's hitting on younger women when he's too old," Cynthia repeats.

"We're all the same age, sweetie," says Ryan.

"No, no," says Cynthia, "he's an original. He'll get the joke. Why don't you date someone your own age for a change? You pig. Half plus seven, that's the rule, I looked that up."

"What did you take?" I ask. "I want some."

"I don't think you do," says Ryan.

"She's having fun," I say.

"You do get it, though," Cynthia says, "right?"

"Yes," I say.

"I don't," says Ryan.

"Before we lived forever you were expected to date people close to your age in years, which doesn't make much sense anymore. Yeah, so I've been reading up about your time," Cynthia continues, "so that I can make jokes with you. But I still don't want to see you tonight."

"That's honestly very sweet," I say.

"Oh fuck you. I said go away." She stands looking at me torn about what do next, and annoyed by that fact that she wants me. I try and play along with her and reach out and kiss her, and she kisses me, and then pushes me away, saying, "No, you asshole, go away." She's smiling, and I go away. "I mean it," she says, "keep walking."

The party blurs, the next several hours spent drinking and dancing to two-hundred BPM pipe organ electronica until there is only myself and Justinus and Theodore and Aurelius and a few others sleeping on couches throughout the apartment. Oliver is nowhere to be seen.

Justinus is complaining again: "He made me go out in the woods."

"It was good for you," I say. "When was the last time you went to the woods?"

"Never like that."

"See, it was good for you to commune with nature."

"Is that what you call that? Hiking and looking at pretty things. What's the difference between that and a museum? Maybe if they put hills and dirt into the museum, you would be satisfied."

Hmm. I hadn't thought about that.

"That's ridiculous," says Theodore. "The wild is the wild. A museum is falsely tamed for our consumption."

Justinus is still in his robes, still covered in mud and pondscum, but they are now splayed even more dramatically, revealing his perfectly shorn legs piled in Theodore's lap. Theodore's dress has ceased glowing, as he's been showing it off all night, and the back has been partially unzipped so that he could continue breathing. Aurelius, on the other hand, has unzipped his two side zippers, though he has left the clasp on at the top, all of which appears decidedly unpleasant, but allows him to maintain his insistent hope that he might receive more compliments. I have undone my top button and my bowtie, but am otherwise fully dressed. I suppose this makes me the same as Aurelius.

"Did Justinus tell you about his little accident today?" I ask.

"No," says Theodore, "do tell." He nudges Justinus.

Justinus gives me a playfully disappointed look, as if he didn't really want to talk about it, but he's actually been dying to talking about it. "I just fell down a hill."

"Jumped off a cliff."

"You jumped?" says Aurelius.

"Kind of. He was being all philosophical and I got worked up."

"So you jumped?" says Theodore.

"And you got caught?" asks Aurelius.

"No. It wasn't a very big cliff. I broke my leg on the rocks below, and then just splashed in the water." He mimes it with his hands, the one hand falling straight down into a clenched fist, and then flailing around in the figurative water. "Then a drone dragged me out and fixed me."

"Water drone," I say. "For the lake."

"That's so hardcore."

"It was kind of awesome," says Justinus.

"You've been dancing all night on your broken leg?"

"Yeah, I forgot about it. Got caught up."

"He's fine," I say.

"So no more philosophical talk for you, then," says Theodore.

"No, no," Justinus says emphatically, "this man is going to teach me."

"I have assured him I will not," I respond.

"Do you know how old he is?" says Justinus.

"No. Are you really old?" says Theodore.

"I'm a little old," I respond.

"He's ten thousand years old."

"You're ten thousand years old?!?!?" Aurelius says excitedly. "How have you not killed yourself yet?"

"I'm ten thousand and twenty. And I guess I just haven't gotten around to it yet. Busy schedule, you know."

"Too many people to fuck, right?" says Theodore.

"Theodore," I say, "I had no idea you were such a whore."

"I've never been married and I never will."

"Well, good for you," I smile.

We sit for a moment looking at each other, trying to think of what to do or say next. The party is quiet now, only a quiet beat of music lurking in moments of silence. Without Oliver, we aren't sure of whether we should stay much longer. But we're also enjoying ourselves.

Justinus stands up at once and takes off his robes, stripping down to a pair of sparkly black trunks. He poses, flexing, and then says, "Underwear! Now! Everyone!"

Aurelius and Theodore stand and obediently strip, while I remain on the couch not overly interested in participating in underwear time. The reason, however, for Justinus' recommendation becomes immediately clear as Oliver strides into the room barely clad. He is wearing pink underwear, lacey, clearly not his. His testicles have not shrunk to anywhere near an appropriate size, and are dangling out of the sides of his bikini bottom. His face is streaky, evidencing recent tears, and he gives a slight sniffle before he says, "Hey, guys."

"UNDERWEAR PARTY!" shouts Justinus, prompting a few of the couch sleepers to wake up, look around, and roll over.

"No, no," he says, "no more party." Justinus gestures to my clothing and then over at Oliver, so I stand and start to drop my suit in a gradual process. "No, really," says Oliver, "just stop. We should go to bed."

"Oliver, this ten thousand year old man has come to your party and is stripping for you."

"You're ten thousand years old?"

"Yeah."

"Wow."

"Isn't it crazy?" says Justinus.

"How'd you do it?"

"The trick is to avoid dying."

Oliver slaps his hands over his eyes, rubbing them, and then breaks down, falling in a heap as his tears return. I take my seat, pants still around my ankles, so I kick off my shoes and sit in iridescent green boxer briefs as Aurelius and Justinus drape themselves over the forlorn man of the masturbation machine.

"I'm so fucking bored," Oliver continues. "Already. It's only been six hours since I came out."

"You've been in there for a hundred years. It's going to take time to adjust."

"I don't want to adjust. I want to go back, but even then, I don't want to do that."

They all, Oliver excepted, look over to me hoping for an answer.

"We have just the man to answer this question," says Justinus.

"You should jump off the balcony," I say.

"What?" says Oliver.

"Seriously," I say, "Give yourself some natural adrenaline, you'll feel alive again."

"I heard you can get fined for that," Aurelius chimes in.

"He can afford it," I say.

"I've never done that," he says, before standing and rushing to the massive sliding door, which retreats at his arrival, welcoming his exit. At full spring he lifts his arms like he's an airplane and soars over the edge. Down, down, down at once, below our line of sight. We've run to the balcony now and as we arrive he is back, a drone hoisting him by the ankle. It drops him on the floor of the balcony, and we see his chest rising and falling with heavy breaths searching for fulfillment.

"Oliver?"

"WOOOOOOOOOOOOOOOOOOOOOOOOOOOOO," he answers. "YES!" He stands up, runs in a circle around his balcony, his massive testicles jangling between his legs. He screams: "I'm alive again! Let's do this!"

I'm laughing hysterically as Oliver disappears inside, and the rest of the group overcomes their confusion at suggestion, result, and aftermath to join me in appreciating the humor of the end product.

"How'd you know that'd work?" says Justinus.

"Remember the lady I knew who was in for a thousand years?"

"Yeah."

"Well, she walked around at her party asking people to slap her as hard as they could so that she could feel alive again."

"You said she killed herself shortly after."

"She did. But at least she didn't do so immediately. She just needed adrenaline to keep going."

Theodore spots Oliver through the window wheeling something around. "Patches and Stands time!" he shouts, and offers everyone a high five.

We gather around him as he attaches all of the feeding tubes. I haven't done patches and stands in a while. It's an odd feeling—you lose most your of bodily control, your arms wave wildly, standing becomes an inexact science, speaking an impossibility, all joined with an absurd and distracting ecstasy in your mind. At the same time, you are completely rational, and you can watch yourself acting in this insane manner without having any choice in your behavior.

"Me first!" Oliver says as he takes a giant swig followed by him immediately projectile vomiting on the floor.

Justinus takes a patch from a small box on the stand, unwraps it from the foil and slaps it on Oliver's forehead. "You forgot the patch, bud."

Oliver licks his lips a bit. His floor cleaning robot hums over and begins to consume the vomit as Oliver moves the stand over a meter or so to avoid his mess. "Thanks," he says to Justinus or the robot. "For real this time." He takes a massive sip, replaces the tube on its hook, and now struggles to stand. His knees bend to sixty-five degrees as he attempts to stabilize himself. He looks over at the couch just a few brief steps away, but flails instead of grasping. He staggers forward into the cushions in a face plant, then manages to roll himself onto his back, descending into hysterics.

We've killed the bottle of patches and stands and moved to something mellower called euphorium. It's a form of synthetic opium inhaled via vaporizer, and Oliver has an eight tube electric hookah he rented sitting now in the center of the room, shining in all its gaudy chrome magnificence. It was a brilliant decision of him to rent it—though I doubt it was a product of foresight—as one literally cannot feel depressed on this drug. You can only feel vaguely happy and contented, with no possible element of sadness or anger, and preventing these feelings will be crucial for Oliver to make it through the next few weeks.

"How are you feeling now?" I ask.

He laughs. "Are you serious?"

"Not like that," I continue, "But do you feel accomplished?"

"Oh."

"Yeah," says Aurelius, "what made you want to go in there?"

"Well, I knew it wasn't going to be a record. I think someone is still in there going on a thousand years."

"…with no plans to come out, I heard," chimes in Theodore.

"…That's right," Oliver continues, "so it wasn't a record thing. It was just, I don't know, I felt like I needed it, like I deserved just pure pleasure for a long time, because life is hard, and nothing ever feels good like this, just purely good."

He pauses for a moment to take another puff from his hose and to reflect on the meaning of life while also stifling a contented giggle.

"I started doing research for this like three hundred years ago after I saw an ad at the free food court. I remember it because I was waiting to meet my date for the evening and it was for the new OGM 11000, and while I'd heard about them before, this time it got me. I thought, I'm just meeting this girl tonight for sex, and I was just meeting a guy the next night for sex, and that's fun and I do it for more than the sex, but maybe I should just orgasm for a while, see what I think about it. So I started researching machines, and kicking it around in the back of my mind and then one day my friend Mike, he has a random friend, might actually have been his son, who has a machine, not the same as the one I have but like it. So I'm like, 'Can I try this? I've always wanted to know what it's like.' And the guy is a little weirded out because I've only met him a few minutes before but he puts it on a cleaning cycle and he's like 'go for it,' so I hopped in right in the middle of the party I was at."

Another puff.

"And it was amazing. And I learned some things. Like his had only a small piece go up the butt, and I wanted something a bit larger, and there's others than can like pinch and shock the nipples, and, like, everything else, but I just wanted the body rubbing. But I also wanted cameras and footage, which you can't get always get good shots on a normal machine, so I had to do some searching until I finally found this glorious device. The Onanator 9000. It's an older model, but easily modifiable, and I had it refurbished to my specifications. I had the glass tube hand blown in Finland, for example."

"So…" says Theodore, "you have video of yourself cumming for a hundred years."

"Yeah, definitely," Oliver replies. "Fred—holy shit, I haven't talked to Fred in a hundred years—Fred, turn screen twelve on."

A screen flashes on across from the couch where we sit.

"Fred, can you give us some pictures and video from the Onanator, especially the orgasms."

"Confirmed," says Fred the computer.

"But also the highlights."

"Confirmed."

A video starts of Oliver first settling in to the device, making some adjustments, adjusting the feeding tube that runs into his nose. It then flashes to his first orgasm about an hour into the process. The date at the bottom of the screen jumps forward three years to his first major multiple orgasm which lasts six full hours (we only see the first few minutes of seizing and ab work). Fast forward now to an abstinence period where there is nothing but sexual teasing (with actual feathers scooching across his body!), his first major effort at this of a week leading to his first giant ejaculation.

"I can't believe how big your balls got," says Justinus.

"I know it," Oliver responds, proudly, "you just train them, and they can get huge. It's going to take a while for them to go back down, and it'll be a bit embarrassing in the meantime, but whatever, I already fucked some girl named Ryan tonight, and she was cool playing with them."

"Are those her underwear?"

"Yes," replies Oliver solemnly, "these are her underwear."

"Neat," I say.

"Fred, show more scenes of my balls at full size."

"Testicles confirmed."

So here we are, five men lounging in our underwear, appreciating images of engorged testicles under the influence of an engaging array of intoxicants. I look around for a moment and mentally acknowledge the situation, but if I pause for too long, I will get lost in the significance of it, and perhaps attribute some falsely grand design to my activities. This, in various forms, has been my life for one hundred centuries—not this exactly, of course, but variations on this. I get dressed up and go to a party.

Perhaps I meet a woman, or perhaps I bring my wife, or perhaps I do both, depending on the wife's state of mind at that point in the marriage. I take some variety of drugs, and drink some variation of a classic cocktail I've always loved, and then I meet new people and have some variation on a conversation I've had once before. In the background a song is playing, and it always sounds like something I've heard before, and the apartment looks like a place I used to go.

But still, I don't see why I should want to die. Even before everything changed, even when my life was temporary, I felt this way when I went to parties or met new people or heard new songs. Novelty disappears quickly when you've led as privileged a life as I have. I do not need something new if I simply remember that I am actually having a good time and that I can actually have fun, even if I have done it before, because I enjoyed it before. If I have enjoyed it before, it can work for me again, so long as I do not let the creeping neuroses convince me that there is no longer any such thing as fun when there is no longer novelty.

After another half hour of the group studying his scrotum and his orgasm tremors, Oliver decides he is truly going to bed for the night. Theodore has fallen asleep on the couch, and Aurelius announces his exit in favor of his bed.

"And you?" Justinus says.

"I was hoping to stay up a bit. I think I've got another hour or so from the energy pills."

"Me, too," he replies. "Let's hit the balcony."

Realizing how cold it is we grab a pair of faux bearskin robes with stuffed bearheads for hoods from a chrome trunk next to the couch and drape ourselves. Even with global warming, the very early morning in October in Maine is still cold. I grab a bottle of wine for us to sip on, as well.

"Hell of a night," I say.

"Quite a day, actually," he says.

"Agreed." I pause for a moment, and then continue, "And look, we ended up in robes together."

"That's right," he says. "Look at us, two philosophers dressed as we should be. Masters of the intellect and guides to the good life."

"We certainly do pretend such things well."

"Who can stop us from pontificating?"

"Who would dare?"

"Not a soul."

"Not a one," I say.

We smile for a moment, enjoying our bit of chemistry.

"You are a philosopher, though," he says, "I mean that, I have learned things from you."

"I keep on saying that I'm the wrong one to turn to."

He chooses his words carefully this time. "Do you think you can't help me because you're ready to die now? Like, I just came to you at the wrong time, now that your latest wife has gone, and it's been hard, and now you're just done?"

"I'm not sure about things now, I admitted that to you."

"I will celebrate you," he says. "But I want you to continue."

"Thanks for that," I say, and I do appreciate it, even if I do not know how far it will take me.

"And not just for myself," he continues "we all love you. But mostly for me."

"Well, if it's for you, Justinus, then, well, I'll stay alive for fucking ever." We laugh, but I continue, "I have moments, I do," I say, "I have moments where I'm down and then I have nights like this, where I have great fun, and you know..."

"I do."

"It's not complicated."

"But you do miss her?"

"My wife?"

"Yeah."

"Yeah, I miss her."

"And you've had eight wives. I was married to Portia."

"You mentioned."

"And you miss them all?"

"Sure."

"And friends?"

"Sure."

"That's it," says Justinus. He seems disappointed. I'm not sure what he's thinking about. Then he says it. "Oliver's next, huh?"

"We don't know that."

"You've pretty well said as much. The one thousand year orgasm lady lasted three weeks. What does that give Oliver? Two months?"

I hand him the bottle of wine and think for a moment of how to answer his question. It's a legitimate concern. Oliver will be entertainment deficient for the rest of his life, probably. He's been sitting in the highest form of human pleasure for a full century, or second highest if you ask the monks who contemplate. Everything in life will be deficient and gray in comparison. He will have to relearn fun and to adjust his standards, while also dealing with dramatic imbalances in his brain as his body adapts to a new environment once more.

"Tell him to go the therapist tomorrow. One who specializes in chemistry, preferably. I've got a name if you need one."

"Drugs are the answer?"

"Well, for now. They don't work forever."

"They don't," Justinus confirms.

"But he's just going to be dramatically depressed for a while."

"I don't want to lose him."

It's an interesting thing for Justinus to say. He hasn't, as far as I understand, spoken to this person in a hundred years. And still, they are friends, and they pick up as if nothing has changed; and still, devastation would result from his permanent absence. You would think that without death we could avoid loss but it is just the same. A friend moves away, a marriage ends, a child moves across the solar system. Sometimes, a friend dies. Sometimes, your wife shoots herself in the head splattering her skull across your living room. We have thousands of years of these losses, and they are not forgotten, but accumulate until one can only expect further loss, or effectively pretend that the rule of life is not actually loss, but some sort of singular gain.

“He’ll make sure that you don’t. Got to zap his brain with the drugs until his chemicals come back on line.”

“Right.” He sighs heavily. “But you should tell me if you’re upset.”

“Are you going to save me?” I ask. “Be my rescue philosopher?”

“Didn’t you see my robes earlier?”

“Yes, yes, you looked stunning.”

We hear the sliding door to the deck recede and find Oliver trotting his way out once more in his—her—underwear.

“Freezing out here,” he says.

“Hey, we thought you were asleep,” says Justinus.

“I was, but I can’t sleep.”

“What, are you too depressed?” Justinus follows, inappropriately.

“No, no. I think I just have to fuck something. Ryan’s completely asleep. And my balls are killing me right now.” We laugh, and Oliver gives a half chuckle, indicating that he is in fact in some degree of pain. “Either of you want to have a go?” he continues.

Justinus looks over to me, and puts his hand up in a polite offer of the first round.

“Oh no, none for me,” I say. “You two enjoy.”

“Well, then” says Justinus. “A nice way to end the night.”

He walks over to me, and gives me a deep hug. I shake Oliver’s hand and exchange a bow, and watch as Justinus throws his blanket around Oliver’s shoulders and they head away to a bedroom. I wait on the patio until the sun is all the way up and the noise has returned in the streets below and I fall asleep in my pod on the way home.

Chapter 3

As I sit in the tub slowly recovering after only a few hours of sleep, my computer announces a call.

"Cynthia Wellsbottom for you."

"Put her through. Hello?"

"It's Cynthia."

"Hi there. What's new?"

"Not much."

"Well, I've had the most interesting evening," I say, and it still feels like understatement.

"Uh huh," she replies, sans interest.

"You called me, right?"

"Yes, of course. Don't you remember?"

"I do. But you don't seem to be interested."

"I'm not particularly," she replies, sharply.

"We don't have to talk."

"We don't?"

"No, no. Just grunt to each other."

"Just breathe into the phone," she plays along.

"You've got it."

"Grrnrrnrnrn."

"(breathes heavily into phone)"

"Okay, that's enough," she says.

"That's enough?"

"Uh huh," she says, "You want to go to brunch?"

"Now?"

"No time like the present."

"You're a sweet kid."

"I am actually. I will make your life worthwhile."

"And I yours."

"Is that a yes?"

"Sure."

"12:30. The Old Salt."

"That place?"

"Yes."

"I'll be there."

"Call is disconnected," says Meredith.

"Drain the tub, Meredith."

As I step into another jumpsuit, this one pink, I try and understand Cynthia. It's a common tactic to violate etiquette when attempting to date someone. It's done because it's out of the norm, given the current culture's emphasis on manners. Even as it grates it intrigues, and you are drawn in because of the mystery of it. I must admit that I have used this tactic before.

But there is something that gives me pause about the thought of Cynthia doing this as a tactic. It seems more likely that she will be chronically impolite, that she simply finds something more truthful about being callous. She may have earned this disregard through a difficult life. She certainly has some history to her, something she carries around but does not speak about. Mostly she's just lovely.

"I'm sorry about being so drunk last night."

"That's okay."

She smiles as she apologizes. "Ryan gave me a bunch of neutralizers and put me in my pod."

"That's great."

"Yeah, I needed to sleep, and then I felt embarrassed about what happened."

"It's really not a big deal. Should we get a table?"

"Oh, right, of course," she says.

A line on the floor illumines and we follow it to our table. They don't even have robotic waiters at this place. Not my favorite.

"I love eating here," she says.

"Oh?" I smile. "Why's that?"

"It's so terrible. And run down. They actually spray fake dirt on the walls to give it this feeling. Because they have to clean it for code, but they want it to look like this. Like it's old and before technology."

"Is this another thing about me being old?"

"What?!" she laughs. "No, of course not."

"I get it."

"No. I really just wanted to apologize about last night. And see you again."

"Well, it's good to see you."

"I can't believe how I was acting in front of you. And Ryan. You remember Ryan?"

"Of course."

"She's pretty isn't she?"

"Are you fishing for compliments? I don't believe you're insecure."

"I'm not."

"Good. She's pretty, but I'm here with you. Besides, she spent the night with Oliver."

"Really?" says Cynthia, with genuine surprise. "She's not usually like that."

"You mean likely to date someone?"

"She usually only sleeps casually with women, and dates men."

"Does anyone really follow rules anymore?"

"You do, don't you?"

"I mean, I guess. Not really rules."

We order something off the touch screens in front of us. Coffee appears in porcelain mugs from the dumbwaiter in the table. It's terrible.

"See," she says. "Authentic coffee."

"This is disgusting."

"I know. It's amazing here."

She is feeding off of my reactions to the place. Even as I work to conceal my disgust, she sees it in my movements. But I am, in turn, enjoying her joy at my discomfort. Is there a word for that?

"So," I say. "How long have you been in Portland."

"No," she says. "No. None of that. I have questions for you."

"And your questions get priority?"

"Of course."

"Okay then."

"Tell me about your ex-wife."

"Which one?"

"You know which one."

"I don't."

"You're in so much denial. The one that just shot herself in the same way that Phillip George did last night."

"That one."

"Yes, that one."

"Not much to tell. She was very young and very lovely, but totally, helplessly depressed. She was in no way fit for life. Not because of her genetics, though. They did a review of her genetics and she was not any more disposed to suicide than anyone else. I don't know if I believe it. But she was so young, so they did one anyway."

"How old was she?"

"A hundred forty-seven."

"Wow. I was still figuring out what I liked in bed at that time."

"What, leaving immediately after sex when your partner is in a state of confusion?"

"Exactly."

"So, yeah, that's about it. It was very sad."

"That's all you have to say about it? A medical report and that it was 'sad'?"

"What else would you like to know?"

"You didn't want to die with her?"

"Something in between, I think. Which is why Peter keeps bringing it up. I mean, I'm ten thousand years old, I can't tell you how many deaths I've lived through."

"But when you're not ready, it's different."

"Is that right?" I ask, prying. She is speaking from experience and not admitting it.

"Am I wrong?"

"No, you're right. It was different. I can't stop thinking about it and her and I can't stop thinking about a way for myself to die. It's loss. It's death. It's a different death, but it's still death, and I've seen so much death."

"You have?"

"I think so."

"Interesting," she says and sips her coffee.

"You don't believe me?"

"No," she says. "Pancakes!" Breakfast has arrived. "I think you're in denial, that you can't admit the terrible pain you're in because you've never felt something like this before, and that it will come out before long. That's what I think."

"Oh. Are you going to help me out?"

"I can't help you. Let's eat." She starts pouring syrup on everything. "Seriously, enough heavy stuff. You can ask me about my life now. But nothing serious."

"WALK me home?" she says.

"Of course. I'm unscheduled."

"Going back to sleep?"

"I think, yes."

She smiles at me and we continue our walk.

"Warren!" A familiar voice calls out to me. I can't place it. I look around for a moment or two only to find Cynthia with a heavy frown on her face as she points to a beautiful blonde woman standing almost directly in front of me.

"Helen," I say.

"Warren," she says. And seeing Cynthia's cold response. "Dad. Good to see you."

"What are you doing in Portland? Last I heard you were on an asteroid near Jupiter."

"Yeah, I left there about twenty years ago. I've been doing a lot of traveling since then."

"Oh. That sounds nice."

"Yeah, it's been great. Who is this?"

"Oh, right," I say. "This is Cynthia. Cynthia, this is my daughter Helen."

"Pleasure," she says.

"Likewise," says Helen.

They don't seem to like each other. "What brings you to Portland?" I try again.

"I'm here to see you, of course," she says. "I was going to show up at your door, quite honestly. Surprise you. Because how often do we get to have surprises anymore?"

"Well, it's still a surprise," I say. "And a lovely one. Will you stay with me?"

"If you'll have me."

"Of course."

I can feel Cynthia chilling over as I say this. "Looks like you two have some catching up to do," she says.

"It was so great to meet you," says Helen.

"You, too."

"I'll call you," I say.

She nods and strides purposefully away.

"She seems lovely," says Helen.

"She's a fun bit of mystery."

"She's not your wife though. I remember your wife looked different in the wedding announcement."

"Oh, right. Gwen. Yeah, Gwen's dead."

"Oh," she says, noting my tone.

"Let's go home."

We change directions and start walking towards my place, her luggage floating behind us.

"So a surprise visit?" I say.

"Yeah."

"Have you seen your mother recently?"

"No. I'm visiting her next. Do you know where she is?"

"We can check. I'm not great at keeping track of people."

"I know."

"Yeah, it's been a while since we've spoke."

"I think it's been about two hundred years."

"Really?" Even if it's hard to always be in touch with your children, most people do better than I have.

"I haven't called you either, Warren."

"Right."

We arrive at my building and take the elevator up.

"You can have the guest room," I say, as we step into my apartment. "To the right, down the hall there."

"Nice." The luggage is still following her.

"I'll be on the couch."

I head to the kitchen where I mix a cocktail and take a synthetic opioid. Just a little something to take the edge off the conversation. We have always loved each other, I think. But we haven't always agreed. I think we were just very much alike. She was just like her mother, Addison, and her mother and I were perfect for each other but also perfect for fighting with each other. And so it was with our daughter. There was a point where we didn't speak for two thousand years or so. I never forgot that she was my daughter, but she certainly did not occupy my mind in the same way.

I take my seat on the couch and she emerges a few moments later, changed. She is wearing a tight gray and orange workout outfit, her hair pulled back.

"It's good to see you, dad," she says.

"It's good to see you, too, daughter," I say.

"I guess that you've gathered I'm here to share some news with you."

"I was hoping it was just because you loved me."

She gives me a look. "You know I always love you. Even when I tried not to love you, you are my parents and I love you."

"As you should."

"I know. But what I wanted to tell you is that I've decided that I'm ready to die. It's been a long time coming and I've felt it coming for a long time. But I'm ready. And I've been going around visiting everyone and it feels right."

"Oh," I say. It hits me the wrong way. She seems so alive. Her smile is still so alive. I don't see her as dead. I know I'm failing in my response. The custom, upon hearing of a person's decision to die, is to celebrate their decision, and to provide only words of support. I am failing.

"I'm really excited about it!" she continues, smiling broadly. She's trying her hardest.

"About what?"

"Dying! I just said that. It's really time for me. I'm tired." Still smiling.

"Wow, Helen. Good for you."

"Not everyone's like you, Warren…Dad. I've had enough, like, over seven thousand years, that's a long time. Jesus, I didn't come home for the judgment, you wonder why we haven't spoken to each other in centuries."

"I don't wonder that," I say, and then remember to add, "I don't mean it like that." I try a third time. "And I'm not judging you either."

I sigh heavily and sit back on the couch. She doesn't know what to say. I don't think she expected me to be this upset about it. People aren't usually upset when you decide to die, they usually are a bit jealous that you can admit you're ready.

"I need another drink," I say. "Want anything?"

"Sure."

I mix another cocktail and take another pill.

"Want one of these?"

"No, I'm fine. Just the drink."

"Good."

"So, really, what happened with Gwen?"

"Yeah. Gwen. She died."

"You mentioned that," she says. "When was it?"

"March."

"Is that why you're like this?"

"No, Helen. I think this is just how you react when your child tells you they're going to die."

"That's not true at all," she says. "Wait, wasn't she really young?"

"A hundred forty-seven."

"Oh, dad! I didn't know." She looks genuinely upset—not to the point of tears, but she can imagine my pain, at least.

"I know, kid. Just been a tough year. And now you're here to say goodbye."

"Yeah," she says. "But you have lived longer than I, and I know you've been through this before. I know because I've been through it before. How many of the people that you grew up with are still alive? How many friends do you have from the beginning?"

"None. They're all gone."

"That's why I'm going, dad. I'm so tired of burying my friends. Everyone dying or disappearing all the time. They die, I move to a new planet or a new city and I start a new life over again, and I pretend like I haven't lost too much. I've lost too much now. But I've lived so much more than a human should. I watched the sunrise from the edge of Jupiter. I traveled to Proxima Centauri and back, stepping foot on a new planet, building a colony, coming back home. There was nothing there when we left, now a hundred million people live on this planet in a different solar system! I don't want to do anything else now. All those moments, are just 'tears in the rain. Time to die.'"

I sigh again and lean back on the couch. I normally would have something reassuring or comforting to say, or at least have acknowledged her reference, one of our rare shared pleasures, but I'm not in the right place to do that.

"Have you told your mother yet?"

"No. I'm staying in Portland for a few months and then going to see her."

"So you haven't talked to her?"

"Not since I left for the asteroid." She looks around the room hoping to find a more active conversation partner than her depressed father. "You're not saying anything. I'm so tired. I'm done. I've lived a wonderful life, and I'm just sad all of the time, now, and I can't fall in love anymore, and I can't make friends anymore, because I know they go away eventually."

I look over at her and see her dying and I see her still as she came into the world. We were so excited to have a child. We applied in our first year of marriage, and it took another forty-seven years before we were approved. With the total human population capped at ten billion, it is a novel feeling to be rooting for more death so that you can bring a child into the world. On the other hand, the whole thing takes so long that there were multiple times we forgot about children entirely, forgot that there was something new potentially coming into our life. And then Addison would blink into a crazy smile and brightness in her eyes and she would say, "we're having a baby someday." And we would hug and kiss and maybe have sex, though that's not the way it's done anymore, but it seems right at the time, at the time when you are talking about having children.

Of course they warn you about it; that your life will never be the same, that you'll have to sacrifice more than you ever thought possible. The rumor is that when they do the video call to confirm your date they're actually reading vital signs and imaging your brain to make sure that you are actually excited about the prospect of children. I've never heard of anyone rejected after the call, though, so this may be a falsehood, but then who would admit that they were rejected? Perhaps they did measure such things in the old days, the first few centuries. But they must have realized that there is no one who has lived for several centuries who can avoid excitement at the news that they will have a new child. It *is* exciting, and always maintains this power, even while almost every other aspect of life becomes routine and uninspiring.

And then one day you're at home and you receive the call from the Office of Children and you feel elation you have not known in centuries. Your mind thrills and spins through all that you'll need to know for the time to come, and all the research you've already done—of the three cities for raising children, we chose the extended peninsula of Singapore, since it has the highest reputation for academic excellence.

This means, of course, that we had to move, to give up our jobs, and to sever ourselves from our friends. We had a lovely home inside the city walls of Cartagena, Colombia, and Addison was quite attached to her job designing transport pod interiors, something she was thriving at. I worked at a hillside hydroponic coffee mill, optimizing production for a mass producer of mediocre coffee and I was ready to do other things, perhaps nothing for a while.

We would move a few weeks before the baby finished its incubation into a high rise filled with people within a week of our timeline. They would be our neighbors for the next twenty-five years, in a city filled only with parents of children growing up in a world that no longer ages. The children start their lives in tubes from preserved and genetically perfected eggs and sperm and are watched even before the moment of their 'birth' and all through their first thirty years. Parents are corrected if they are causing any adverse harm to their children—even emotional harm; you cannot get away with teaching passive-aggression to your children, or parenting through your own insecurity. Agents of the Office of Children will requisition the child until you have completed further training, or have been sufficiently medicated as to capably raise a child without inflicting your psychological anxieties upon them. You will watch them as they complete, at the very least, a master's degree, but more commonly a doctoral degree in whatever they like, along with extensive general competencies.

Helen completed her doctorate in the art of the 35th century and started a master's degree in electrical engineering before she turned twenty-five. At this age, parents are removed from the city, and we returned to Cartagena. We'd had years of preparation for this enforced time apart; starting at twelve, Helen would go on trips, first for a week to see a new place, then for a month for a summer sailing excursion or an archeological dig, and then away for a full semester as an undergrad.

The great challenge of raising children in this situation is helping them to create separate lives and identities from their parents, and doing so in a way that is destructive for neither parent nor child. It is tremendously confusing to look at your parents, as you age, and see that you are quickly approaching them in appearance. In no time at all, for these children, they are thirty and their parents are thirty, at which point the dynamic is broken. You are no longer the wiser but now weaker parent, the one who raised the child but is now aged and in need of care and ready to be supplanted. Instead, you are the same, and this in more ways than one. Personalities quite often repeat, and appearance, selected for greatest beauty, leads to frequent nearly identical resemblance between parent and child. Not that children are prevented from freedom, as they are encouraged to wander around in jungles and to make new friends and to experiment with drugs or art or carefully defined deviant behavior. But there is no criminal element for them to fall into, no friends incapable of academic achievement or brilliance in some way or another, no depression or anxiety or lack of attention from parents, no dearth of financial opportunity, no paycheck to paycheck existence, no family strife over finances or employment or the questions of how to raise a child. All that life could once do to tamper with an ideal upbringing has been removed. Stress and sadness must now be manufactured for children, something accomplished through competition and time away from one's parents. Athletics, academic competitions, poetry competitions, book awards, all with great fanfare and prestige for the victors. Yet by the age of twenty-five, everyone has won something once, and lost something several times. They know disappointment and difficulty, and they know how to live without a family.

Helen is beautiful. One point eight meters tall. Blonde, with wiry limbs and long legs and perfect proportions and a magnificent smile. When we met with the genetics lab before implantation, the scientists who managed her genes and saw the outcomes of all children in the world each stopped to tell us how beautiful our child would be. "Perfect beauty," they say. And Addison says to me "Helen," and I agree, because who better to name a child after than a woman so beautiful that it was plausibly said she caused a massive and eternally memorable war.

She is precocious and artistic and from the age of five she spends hours daily alone in her room on the Barbie® fashion simulator designing outfits. She prints them and wears them and we all agree that she has remarkable taste for a five year old. Her teachers encourage her to send her designs off to fashion studios around the world. As parents we think this is a questionable idea, but her teachers ask us what she has to lose, so we go along. Her portfolio is universally rejected and elicits even a nasty video message or two questioning our wisdom in wasting the precious time of artists as significant as they. So now our dear Helen has learned disappointment and failure, but also resilience and that most important fact that most of the world is filled with people who won't be proud of you simply because you asked. She grows in that moment, and she will be prepared for life.

She has been many things. I have always watched her grow, even when I was not involved, just to see what she was doing, just to remember that I brought her into this world, and maybe to console myself with that. She has been married fourteen times. She made it as a fashion designer, and the Helenika, which has recently re-ascended, stood among the elite designer brands for several decades. And then it began to fade; your level of taste may stay the same, but you run out of ideas eventually, and then you can longer innovate and be the new. She left the public world at that time, and we did not hear from her for four hundred years. She had changed her name and became a man, speaking only Neo-Mandarin and living in the Chinese section of the Martian colony on Olympus Mons. Of all her lives, that was the longest, and I wonder if it is because she was happiest there, or because she needed all of that time to mourn the life and creativity she had when she was younger.

She found new inspiration after this time designing electrical systems for interplanetary shuttles before becoming a lawyer and then a chef and then a television screenwriter and then a professor and then a doctor and then for a long time doing nothing at all but socializing and enjoying marriage and relationships before working for the past few centuries in asteroids and the outer planets.

She has had a full life, and I have no reason to feel sadness for her. But I do not want her to go and do not want to admit that she may be right to go.

"So what do you want to do tonight?" I say.

"You're so weird."

"Well?"

"I've got drinks in a half hour with a friend, so I should go soon anyway. But let's do dinner later. I've got a reservation for two at Miyake, and I'm only one."

"I'll be there."

"Good," she says. She stands up and then leans over and kisses me on the lips in an unexpected way. "Good to see you, dad."

"You, too."

As soon as the door slides shut and her pod is away I walk over to my pill cabinet and find another opioid. I put it on my kitchen counter and crush it with a cutting board into a fine powder. I don't bother to cut it into lines, but simply snort it up in a disorganized fashion leaving my nose a powdered donut. I take a swig from the bottle and then flop face first onto the couch. Someone calls, of course.

"Call from Justinus," Meredith says.

"Answer," I say, my face in a pillow. "Whaaatt?"

"Oh, hey fella, you still sleeping?"

"I was, and then my daughter stopped by."

"Oh, nice."

"Not really. She's killing herself, too."

"Oh."

"Yeah, quite the year."

"I'm sorry to hear that. I was just calling to say that Oliver's now in therapy at the person you recommended. He says he's feeling much better. Doesn't actively want to die anymore."

"Great."

"It really is." Justinus expects me to have more to say and so he pauses for a few beats, but then realizes I have no interest. "So we're heading out tonight..."

"No, thanks, man, I'm okay."

"Later this week, then?"

"Maybe."

"What about this weekend?"

"I'm going to Cartagena for a death party."

"Morris?"

"Yeah." Of course he knows him.

"Fun. But I'll see you when you get back."

I swipe my hand to end the call.

"So what was Gwen like?"

"Are you interested in that?"

"I know I didn't come around, but that doesn't mean I didn't care," Helen says, a little annoyed. "I was on an asteroid for the wedding."

"Fair."

"So, what was she like?"

"She was young and beautiful and idealistic. A little dark, a little punk. When we started dating she was only ninety-five, and she was just starting to settle down."

"That's really young."

"I know."

"I don't even remember that," Helen says, though I'm sure she does.

"I remember you at that age."

"Yeah. But you, now, go on."

"She was young, or she appeared young. I should have noticed it sooner, but she had these two sides. All I saw at first was this impetuous and lively person who wanted to live so deeply. But then she would withdraw and it was clear that she wasn't satisfied."

"Not satisfied?"

"Like, she was trying to live, and wanted to live, but she was trying so hard only because she was trying to justify living at all."

"And then?"

"And then she couldn't. So she killed herself."

"I'm seventy-five hundred years old. How old was she, again?"

"A hundred forty-seven."

"A hundred forty-seven. Jeez." Helen pauses for a second, looking into my eyes. I know what she's going to say next, and she knows I know what she's going to say but she says it anyway. "It's not the same for me, dad. I've lived a full life, and I'm not just killing myself because I'm dissatisfied."

"Fine. I don't want to talk about this."

"Fine."

"You're just like your mother," I say, knowing this will enrage her.

"And you're still an asshole."

"Fine."

"Another drink," says the waitress, avoiding eye contact with both of us.

"Yes, please," says Helen, "the same for both of us."

We're drinking Martian wine punch from mini punch bowls which require two hands to lift their little golden handles, this being my drink of choice these days. Miyake has been around a very long time, using human labor since well before it was considered a special treat to do so. Robots and computers can cook you anything you like with exacting precision, and it is, according to several studies, literally impossible to tell if your food has been cooked by hand or by technology. Still, every city has a few of these restaurants that make everything from cocktails to desert by hand, claiming to offer a deeper connection, or a more human experience than can be had elsewhere.

"Aren't you done yet?" she asks impatiently.

"I've been miserable, I admit. But not yet. I want more life. I'm not done."

"You're the Nexus Six," she smiles.

"Sure."

"But you don't have to die. You haven't run out of time."

"No."

"I have to die."

My throat clenches a bit. She puts her hand on mine.

"Did somebody die recently or something?" I ask.

"No, nobody died. I haven't buried anyone in a long time."

"That's good."

"You would think. But no, it's not any better. People don't die that often, but we just change. I know you know what I'm talking about. I know because you didn't mention that stage of my life."

"I didn't."

"And I'm still upset about it, however many centuries later."

"You can't get over it?" I take a sip of my punch. "They can teach you how to get over things."

"Not that. It's not that, I'm over it, really." She smiles, but still looks like she is only ninety percent over it. "They always said in history class how sad it was that people died so young, that there were so many great minds that existed and are now lost forever. *If only, if only* they could have lived in our time, and then Newton or Jesus or Ngakoue, they would have lived forever, and we'd be benefiting from their minds today."

"I think they've stopped saying that so much."

"I know they have! Exactly!" I look meekly in her direction. She continues: "I was a great mind, once. In fashion, but still, my designs are in museums. They still hold exhibitions on my work."

"You were an amazing designer."

"That's it—" she points at me emphatically "—you nailed it. I *was*. I *was* an amazing designer. Same human. Same person. But I'm not anymore. I can't do any of it anymore. I could try and design you a dress: it would be nice, but it wouldn't be fashionable or innovative or legendary or stand the test of time. I had a window in my life, maybe thirty years, and now for the rest of my life I have never been as good at anything else, and can never be as good at anything else."

"You've had lots of careers."

"And I've been okay at them. Still not the point. The point is that even though we keep living, we're still dying. We die with every new career and every new friendship, and that's it, that's enough, I'm done." She takes a big sip of her drink and looks around, maybe attempting to calm herself. "They stopped talking about this because they realized that if Jesus had lived to be two hundred years old, he would have run out of things to say. He would no longer have been an innovator, at least not in his job as Son of God. Maybe he could have started over and gone into, I don't know, automotive design, and made a few breakthroughs. But after that peak," she starts her hand up high and crescendos, "it's all downhill. Forever."

She pauses again for a moment, looking around, looking back at me as I sit in semi-stunned silence. I don't want to play this game with her; I certainly couldn't convince her that she was wrong, because she is, in fact, right. We live forever, so we all have time to find out the thing we can be truly great at, but there's generally only one thing, and we keep on living, never as good at anything as we once were.

"So what's new with you?" She changes the subject.

"You don't want to talk about this anymore?"

"No."

"Seems like you've got a lot to say."

"No. Let's talk about something else."

"The weather?"

"No, dammit, not the weather. You're always talking about the weather."

"Fair enough. There's just not that much going on in my life these days. Besides getting over my recent widowing, you showing up, going out partying regularly."

"Are you working?"

"No, not for a while now. I've been writing. General memoir type stuff, some philosophy thrown in."

"Oh, neat."

"Yeah, but I think everyone in the world has actually written a book."

"I've done three."

"Same."

WE'RE walking home now, quietly, unsure of the next steps. She might have plans, or may feel obligated to spend more time with me, but I couldn't guess at her feelings. I've known her for seventy-five hundred years; we've been close for about thirty, twenty-nine of those being the first years of her life. You'd think...you'd think that since we are now rid of the anxiety of death and of being replaced by our children, then we could have a normal relationship, but it never works out that way. There is, I suppose, still the anxiety of being your own person, and the person who comes out of you is always a reminder of everything you could have been or done. I don't know. I don't know that it's anxiety between us.

"I want to ask you something," she says.

"Sure," I say.

"You're sure it's okay that I live with you for a couple of months?"

"Of course." I'm deeply flattered that my daughter might want to spend time with me.

"I don't have to...."

"I didn't think you'd want to. I'm thrilled that you do."

"You're still my dad. I wanted to come home before the end. Bookend my life. I'm lucky to have both parents still around."

"I guess so."

I turn up the street and smile for a moment until my eye catches the brightly lit sign of a boutique about fifty meters away. "HELENIKA," glowing in pink on the screen, flashing a model posing a new pose every other second. I turn and say nothing, but my silence gives me away and she spots the sign herself.

"It doesn't matter," she says. "I see them everywhere. 'Brand expansion'"

"You still get any royalties?"

"Fuck, dad. Don't."

"Okay, let's head home, I'll make you a drink."

"I'm actually supposed to meet some friends tonight."

"Oh, of course. I'll head home and make up the room for you."

"Okay," she says, smiling. "You can come if you want."

"No, no, go have fun with your friends."

"You sure?"

"Of course."

"Okay, see you in a bit."

She gives me a hug and a squeeze and turns and walks back the way she came.

I stand bewildered for a moment. This is a new experience, I suppose, and I should probably be thankful for it because how often does the ten thousand year old man have a new experience. And yet, I have never been one for a new experience simply because it is new, and the fact that this experience is the first experience of my child's oncoming death, I think I will be forgiven for my hesitance to seize the moment. I can't tell you how many deaths I have celebrated, how many times I have laughed and sang a friend to their death and reveled in the parties that followed. I have competing inclinations now. Now with Gwen, now with Helen.

I look around. My building is just around the corner, hence our decision to walk, but it seems premature to head home. I'm on the fourth ground level, so I can see the towers reaching into the sky, feel the hum of the transport pods on the tracks below. There is an incredible tension in my chest. Realizing I'm standing in place as people make their way around me, I choose a direction and head for the docks. As you walk out onto the piers, which are designed to look like those from the 19th century, they have broadcast a residual light blocker, which rids the space over the water of light pollution from the city. The stars shine there, and I imagine I could use the space and the reminder now. I feel myself starting to cry, though, as I think about the stars, and I do not think I am ready for them. Forgetting about the docks I turn home, and walk straight to my guest room and take a set of sheets from the cabinet on the wall. I could just have automation set up the room, but it feels right to do this. I made the bed for her when she came home from the birth center almost seventy five hundred years ago. I can do it now.

I learned the art of Zen interior decorating at that time. To have a peaceful room, to secure the space for the new child entering the world, to cozily wrap her up in the comfort of a blanket set in the logic of the place of nothingness. This would help her, I thought, if she could know tranquility.

Fukuzawa Itagake was the founder of the Zen Interior Decorator School, and a particularly famous philosopher of that period. The final significant member of the neo-Zen school of the 5th millennium, his arguments eventually developed into his own eponymous school. The Fukuzawa School argued that there was no more philosophy to do—in the sense that, humanity, in the seven thousand years since Socrates and Confucius and Isaiah, had expressed every possible form of philosophical understanding and approach to life and reality. There was no more philosophy to do, at least now that he had invented a patently ridiculous (his words) system of interior decorating in a philosophical manner. We've written every range of emotional response, denied the possibility of writing, turned to poetry, turned to fiction, turned to science, denied the purpose of living, affirmed the purpose of living, and even folded our sheets a certain way, every single possibility, he argued, has been covered. He set his graduate students upon proving this, and they devised a computer program that read and categorized every philosophical outlook from every possible source of data that could be found, and in fact, confirmed that this was the case.

There were, of course, skeptics of this argument. *There have yet to be an infinite number of people, thus there has yet to be an infinite number of ways of life, thus not yet an infinite number of philosophies.* Or, perhaps more damningly: *Categories? There is nothing more artificial than a category. How could one possibly think it accurate to categorize to the various ways of living, or even to categorize expressly documented philosophies.*

In their defense, they used ten thousand categories to describe the vast variations in philosophy; and it is not so unreasonable, when you think of it, that there would only be ten thousand categories, as they were all answering the same question: "How ought we to live?" That there are ten thousand answers to one question seems fitting. Perhaps there are more, but the vast number of these are unconsidered in an indefensible way, as even if we find some virtue in the unconsidered life, it is still, on average, disastrous.

But regardless of whether one were to quibble with the minutiae of the argument, Fukugawa's discovery resounded throughout the intellectual world. The worlds of music and art had already experienced their own "vintage reclamation" movements in the centuries prior, and these efforts to recreate the aesthetic of prior generations were interpreted as an indication that we have run out of ideas for new art: they were already smearing feces on canvases in the 1900s, and they were likely smearing feces on cave walls ten thousand years before then and appreciating it in the same way. How many more surfaces are there to smear feces on? In how many different patterns? Is it ever actually new after someone has done it once before?

I fluff the pillow once, twice, throw it down on the bed, bow to reverence the Buddha of the sleeping time, fluff the pillow once, twice, throw it down once more, square the edges, pull the case tight and finish the stack. I'm supposed to burn some incense now.

Out to the hallway closet in search of incense, and I pause and wonder why she never had children of her own. We never had the best relationship with each other but she always assured us that the reasons for this were entirely from her own concerns. She felt we did a violence to her simply by existing, that she always had to measure herself in terms of us, and therefore she could not be herself when there was an implicit pressure from us. So she had to distance herself, and she had to hate us, to give herself something to respond to, to build from.

Aha, the incense.

Chapter 4

The café is crowded and smells of roasting coffee beans, the acrid smoky taste mixed with the promise of the beloved high and the pleasure of warm porcelain in the hand. The man I will meet, he is my friend, I have known him for many years, and I am hoping he will save me from the madness of my life.

The city of Cartagena is one of my favorite places on earth. The old walled city, because of its status as a "world heritage site," has been perfectly preserved since even before my ten thousand years. I am transported in walking down streets older than myself, in seeing buildings older than myself. I am transported, as well, as this city will be the death of my dear friend Morris.

As I step into the café, I spot Peter, looking the same as last week, as he always does. He is sitting alone, reading on his tablet, most likely the news, as he is wont to do, fidgeting with it really. He is a bit of a nervous person, quiet; his hair is longer these days, parted and brushed to the side, a golden brown, and though he is handsome—no one is ugly—he has never been about appearance. His clothes are plain, grey techmesh shirt, long, draped, matching sweats, matching sneakers, a black watch on his wrist over the top of his long sleeve shirt.

I have much love for this man.

He sees me and stands, we hug, and take our seats.

"Justinus called me," he says.

"Oh, what about?"

"He's worried about you."

"Huh."

"Says you are thinking about killing yourself."

Peter seems very unhappy about this idea. "Not really," I say, not even convincing myself.

"You know what a poor choice that would be."

"Are you going to have this conversation with Morris tonight?"

"No, of course not," says Peter, confused.

"Why not?"

"Because he should die. He's been working on this for decades."

"And me?"

"You're going through something."

"I'm glad you're so confident in me."

"Where have you been these past few years?"

"I guess I haven't been going out much."

"No, you've been pretty much absent."

"Well, I had the wife thing going on."

"You guys spent a lot of time with each other."

"Yeah, mostly me saying, 'hey, don't kill yourself.'"

"Yeah, look I'm sorry we keep talking about it. I'm sorry again this happened to you. We do have to keep talking about it, though."

"I get that. I appreciate your concern."

"So yes, Justinus called me…"

"Right. To say what?"

"That I should watch you?"

"Watch me?"

"Because of your daughter."

"Sure. But watch me for what?"

"I don't know him well, he's a very popular, social person, and I am not. But I know that he cares for you, and I think he says 'watch' but he means 'love,' that is, love you in his stead, because he cannot be here, because he did not get the invite."

"Oh."

"So I offer you my affection."

"I appreciate that. I didn't know that you had affection within you." I smile as I say this so he knows I'm joking. "Though I have not kept up my part in a long time, I have always valued our bond."

"You had reasons."

"I still don't like that I failed us."

"I know."

"I'll have a coffee, the medium blend, thanks," I say to the robotic waiter. "And a pain au chocolat."

"The same," says Peter.

"I've got all sorts of things to say right now, I'm just…well, a mess."

"Speak," he says.

I look around. "I don't want to pour my heart out in a coffee shop."

"We can head to the house. Can you wait?"

"Of course," I say.

"I just wanted to get a pastry."

"It's fine. Anyone else there yet?"

"Jason and his wife should be there."

"Oh my God, I haven't seen him in years."

"And Regan Smithson. Do you know her? She arrives later tonight."

"I don't know her."

"Works with me. She's very lovely."

"Nobody else will make it from our little crew?" I ask.

"No. There's not so many of us left."

I came to Portland to complete a doctorate in nano-camera programming about two hundred years ago. There were eleven of us who started that year. Peter, who is with me now; Morris, who is killing himself; Phillip George, who began this week with a bang; and Jason Maynard, whom Peter mentioned. Besides them, there was Alex Watson, who announced their intention to begin a completely new life as a woman in Singapore, with a new identity—we were not invited to this new life, and have not heard any update since; Andrea Green, who moved to Mars to implement this technology for mining purposes; Vitruvius Huxley, who moved to an asteroid with a population of two, himself and his wife, again for mining purposes; Jane Reynolds, who killed herself by compression on the way to the bottom of the ocean (not as bad as it sounds); Eric Wythe, who wingsuited into an erupting volcano; and Timothy Richardson, who died quietly in his sleep while dreaming of electric sheep.

For the first twenty years or so, we were inseparable; everyone found work nearby after completing the degree, and we made sure to live in the same building and hold grand parties that we forced Peter to attend. Alex moved first, then Vitruvius. Jane announced her death, followed by Eric, followed by Timothy and then Phillip. I fell in love with Gwen, and my attention to the remaining group faded. Andrea left, divorcing her wife, who I always liked more than her anyway, and we stayed something of friends—perhaps she will be here, though I think she moved to Honduras. Jason, well I don't think we ever actively disliked each other, but we were never as close, and with everyone else gone, gone was our reason to remain friends.

This is the nature of friendships, as I know so very well. I remember most all of them, but I could not honestly tell you how many people I have known and loved in my time.

"Think we'll see Willa?" I ask. Willa was Andrea's wife.

"You always had a thing for her, didn't you?"

I laugh. "Not the reason I asked the question. And I think she's pretty committed to women, isn't she?"

"Not always," says Peter, before catching himself, "not that I'm saying I know. I had a friend who knew her before her Portland days, said she was a bit freer then."

"So, is she coming?"

"So I've heard. Bringing a plus one, though, so you'll have to fight through that."

"That's too bad. But hopefully we'll see her anyway."

"Agreed." He sips his coffee and thinks for a moment.

"Who are you dating these days?" I ask, picking up on his pause.

"A nice man, named Nigel, who did not make the trip."

"What's he like?"

"As I said, he's nice. You can meet him when we get back to Portland."

We finish our afternoon pastries and head over to the casa, my luggage floating behind us. As we walk through the streets, the memories crash in. Addison and I used to eat at the restaurant there, our friends Chloe and Soon-Yi lived in the house with the great balcony up the street. We arrive at the house Peter has rented.

"This used to be a hotel."

"That's right," he says.

"Not anymore?"

"No, you just rent the whole thing now. I've got it for the week."

"Addison and I stayed here when we were looking for a place to live."

"I wonder if it's changed."

"Looks just the way I remember it."

We step in through the gate into a long hallway. There is a pool at the end of the hall, open to the sky through the atrium three stories tall. There is a bedroom beyond the pool which has its own private place to dip; Addison and I stayed there.

"Pick whatever room you want upstairs. Sheets are on the beds."

"Will do."

"I'm going to contact the market to see why we still do not have food or drink."

I walk up to the third floor remembering the space and my eye is drawn to a small room to the front of the house. It's set apart, not near any of the other beds, and has an adjoining sitting area. It's a strange little room; there are two beds, set back within the corners of the space, little twin mattresses and stucco walls and no windows. The bathroom has the only window, and it goes straight up into the air as a skylight, with no covering, letting the leaves in from the bushes on the roof, creating a little pile of decaying matter on the floor of the shower.

As I hop in the shower, I appreciate the light. The sun shines differently here, of course; and with everything painted a brilliant white, the glow is intense, even in my dark space of a shower with only natural light. I head up to the rooftop patio and lay out on a deck chair in a pair of swim trunks. My mind wanders and I start to fall asleep, only to be roused by voices.

"Warren!" I crack my eyes open. "It's been too long."

"Jason," I say. "How are you doing?"

"Wonderfully, thanks."

"Is this your wife?"

"No, no, she's downstairs napping. This is Regan."

"Oh, of course, Peter mentioned you."

"Very nice to meet you," she says. "I've heard a lot about you."

"About me?" I say. "It's all false, I assure you." We stand around momentarily looking at each other, unsure of how to proceed. "I'm sorry I'm so scantly dressed, wanted to get some sun."

"It's a good choice," follows Jason, taking his shirt off.

"I'll burn," says Regan, settling herself on a lounge chair. "This sun is intense."

"I could use a cocktail," I say. "Anyone else?"

"Oh yes," she says, "whatever you're having."

"Seconded."

I order a few caipirinhas from the rooftop counter and they are delivered by robot as we sit.

"So where are you these days, Jason?"

"Still in Portland, actually."

"Are you serious? I'm....I'm..." I'm too embarrassed to speak. I was sure he had moved away decades ago. "I'm sorry we haven't kept in touch."

"Yeah, well, I heard about your situation," he gives an understanding smile. "I'm very sorry for you."

"What happened?" asks Regan.

"His wife died very young."

"A hundred forty-seven," I say.

"Oh, my. When was this?"

"A few months ago," says Jason. "But a long time coming."

"Incredible," she says. "I can't even imagine."

"Yes, well, life goes on, I suppose," I say, trying to save the conversation from bogging down in pity for me. "Regan, Peter tells me that you work with him."

"I do. I work on a research team with him. I moved here from Proxima about twenty years ago. I was born there, lived there for my first thousand years."

"No kidding," I say. "What do you think about earth?"

"Honestly, the scenery is different, but it's exactly the same. Exactly."

"Really?"

"Seriously. Exactly."

Peter walks upstairs. "As soon as I get back from the market with limes they are sucked into the counter and cocktails are being made. I know who is responsible for this."

"You actually had to go to the market?" I say.

"It's across the street. A few of their robots are down, so I carried the groceries across the street."

"How vintage of you," says Regan.

"I know. I see you have all met."

"We have."

"Is this one complaining?" Peter asks of me.

"No," says Regan, "I brought it up."

Peter looks disapprovingly towards me. "We're all here to celebrate Morris, so we're going to do that. Especially you."

"I think you could use a drink more than me."

"You've already got yours."

The robot wheels over to him and hands him a caipirinha.

"Very funny."

He sits down with his drink and sighs heavily.

"Are you all worked up from having to fetch your groceries?"

"Yeah, I suppose." He thinks for a moment. "And I'm annoyed that we're here two days early to pray with Morris. It's just his death, what are we doing here?"

"I think he wanted to share it with everyone else," says Jason.

"I swear, we are all becoming so dramatic about death. You, you excepted, I guess, you get a pass for a little while, because that was dramatic. But I know you've had plenty of death in your life, and that you get it. And I know your daughter is going to die now and that can't get to you because she's seventy five hundred years old."

"It can still get to him," says Jason.

"I think it should," says Regan.

"It is getting to me," I say.

"It shouldn't," says Peter.

"It's still his daughter, and what if they were close?"

"They're not close."

"We're not."

"You still love her though."

"I really do," I say. "I don't want her to die."

"No one wants anyone to die," says Peter. "That's not the question. Just...everyone dies. It's a fact, no need to kvetch about it."

"I've got a few downers in my bag downstairs. You look like you need one," offers Jason.

"I'm fine," says Peter. "I'll sit down."

"Are you going to be nice to Morris?" I ask.

"Of course I'm going to be nice to Morris."

We step outside of our casa, the streets now lit by "gas" lamp and projected torchlight that, I have to say, looks authentic. The shadows play on the streets before us as we walk in a leisurely procession to Morris and his introspection. He is in the Church of the Most Holy Trinity, la Iglesia de la Santisima Trinidad, a "very old church," they tell us, that he has rented for the end of things. There he is attended to, there he prays, there he readies himself for his death, his very own chosen death.

We pass the Cathedral on our way and Peter announces our presence at the "*domus dei*," as it says, written in Latin above the door.

"House of God," he says.

"Seems a little quiet in there," says Jason, only to be met with quiet disapproval. "Jeez, I didn't mean metaphysically. It's just empty."

"This isn't his church," says Peter.

"I know that."

Further and now to the city square where animatronic horse drawn carriages await your direction. There is a garden and a piazza and the streets full of life, the early crowd, headed to dinner—the city will resound tonight.

Through the city walls now, we walk through the park and turn right, following another narrow cobblestone road lined with walled casas until we come to a little circle in the road punctuated by a church. The church is a dark ochre color, matching the glow from the pseudo flames and yellow bulbed lamps. Standing outside is a man dressed as a priest, long black cassock and cope and white collar, though I'm sure he's not.

He greets us. "Welcome," he says, offering a bow, "Morris is expecting you." He gestures and the doors swing open, powered by two more men dressed as priests. It is a colonnade style church, white columns supporting ochre walls and ornate tilework on the floor. The altar glows with a bright white light, decorating the head of the church, layered in flowers on its sacrificial plane and all surrounding. Morris sits in the middle of the floor on his knees, a Bible in front of him, open. He is in a long tan linen robe, bare footed, his dark skin standing out against his setting. His appearance is legitimately biblical, a seeming manifestation of the divine; maybe an angel is more fitting.

He is not alone. Standing beside him is a nun, and she is joined by four others in the front pews kneeling in prayer with him. They are not your typical nuns, however, and they all wear shiny black vinyl habits. Morris, it seems, could not resist the parody even as he wades towards the end.

The nun next to him holds a jug in two hands, presumably of water, presumably to keep Morris alive in his fast. She sees us, and leans in to whisper to him. He nods slightly and bows his head to the floor, returns to his knees and crosses himself, before standing and turning to us.

He is draped in a long gray robe, tied with a plain rope with three knots. Perhaps he took his vows this week: poverty, chastity, obedience; then again, he may not know what his robes mean.

"Good evening," he says. "I'm so glad to have you join me."

"We aren't interrupting, are we?" I say.

"Not at all. It's perfect timing actually." He guides us over to a side chapel, where the pews form a square facing each other, and where hundreds of candles flicker. He takes a casual seat on the pew, decorously arranging his robes—it is clear that he's not wearing pants.

"Beautiful space," Peter breaks the silence.

"It is," he says. "In Gethsemane," he laughs and points, "and I've got my little garden. I'm very happy with it, which is a funny thing for me. I was sure I would waver."

"Not in the house of God!" says Jason, glibly.

"Never in the house of God," says Morris. "But seriously, I haven't... when's the last time you've taken something seriously?"

"Not since I left my parent's house," says Jason.

Morris looks over to me. "Hasn't been that long for me," I say.

"Well, maybe it comes back around," Morris replies. "But I feel good here, honestly, I do. I'm reading through the scriptures, I'm praying, *lectio divina*, and such. It's a good time."

"And the nuns," says Peter.

"They're good to me," says Morris. "But no sex. No drugs. No rich food—until tomorrow night, at least. Just living. Being embodied. My knees fucking hurt, I've been sitting in prayer for so long. Remember the last time your knees hurt?"

"No," says Jason, "I guess I'm missing out on things."

"You really are," says Peter.

"How did you even come up with this," I ask, and Peter looks over to me, concerned, as if I was now looking for ideas.

"It's all an artifice," says Morris.

"What do you mean?"

At that moment, he is handed a bowl by one of the nuns.

"Not water," he says. "Vitamins and electrolytes and essential nutrients."

The nun carrying the jug walks over and fills the bowl. Morris drinks deeply.

"You've got to stay hydrated for your death," replies Peter, smiling.

Morris flashes a smile, but his face turns serious once more. "More than this, though. More than this." He smiles again, but there are pools in his eyes; in each corner the thousand candles reflect into a thousand points of light. He keeps it in, but it's a strange thing to see in this place, so serious and somber and pure of intention. Perhaps he's just being authentic, and crying in the Garden, but he's a night early to be doing so. "It is an artifice." He speaks quietly now, restrained. "Life, that is, I know this, we can only gesture and bow and reverence and revel in it, but never understand or grasp or complete. I have loved it, and I love it, and I love this moment where I am coming to my end, and I will love my end. It will be beautiful, it has been beautiful, I am fulfilled, I am happy, but there is no authentic thing that I can do to show this. I'll imitate the man who gave up his life most beautifully for all humanity, and I'll do it for you all, and for myself, but above all else, I do it to show my love for existence." We sit for a moment, unprepared for that weight to be placed on us. Jason looks away at the altar; he will play the part of the skeptic amongst us. "I know it's odd to tell you how I love the life that I am ending, but I am truly grateful." He smiles to himself. "We always have these parties, you know, and we all cheer; we all went to Timothy's last party, what a fucking show that was. I got so high," he gestures to me with his eyes.

"Me too," I say, playing embarrassed.

"They were going to call a medical droid for you," says Peter to me.

"Yeah, yeah, be careful what you mix," I continue, "like you all were in fine shape."

Morris laughs. "That's the thing, fellas, it's been good. It's been good to me. I don't want to go out as an art piece, though. Let me go"—in this moment he turns, his anger turns—"let me go out, all beautiful and shit, and not knowing, still not knowing what it's supposed to be. I still don't fucking know how to do it. How many years do I have to live to know it? How many years..."

"I don't know," I say.

"You've got like what, six thousand years on me. We never fucking know."

"We see now through a glass darkly," says Jason, "or in a mirror dimly."

"Font of wisdom, Jason, look at you," says Morris, appreciating the reference. "I'll have to read that shit again later."

Peter crosses his legs uncomfortably, and I follow his eyes as he looks over to the nuns praying in the pews, and the woman with the jug looking off into space. I imagine he's thinking back to our conversation earlier this evening—he doesn't understand the hand wringing that's going on, and doesn't much care for it. You live or you die, it's your choice: what are we crying about?

We pause for a moment, Morris still looking serious, absorbed, the nun with the jug turns her attention to him once more, concerned. She wants to keep him on message, I think, the faithful guide for the imagined flock.

"So can I ask the elephant in the room question?" I say.

He looks a little confused, but nods, "Sure..."

"You aren't going to crucify yourself, are you?"

Everyone looks expectantly to him, a bit of a grimace buried in their grins.

"No way, man," he laughs, "No way. That's not for me."

"Oh thank God," I say.

"I told you," Peter says. "He's taking a pill."

"Yeah, I'm going to take a pill that works slowly. So I'll gradually go out."

"Well, I just wanted to make sure that you hadn't changed your mind. I don't think we really want to see a crucifixion."

"Neither do I," Morris says, "but it's still Jesus inspired. It's just more the path leading up to it. I'm going to carry a cross from the Plaza San Pedro

Claver, out beyond the walls, and to the water. And, I think it's timed right, so I'll be dying as I reach the ocean, I'll put the cross in the water and lay on it and fade away out to sea."

"That should be nice," says Jason, longingly.

"I agree," follows Peter.

"I'm glad you're happy with this," I say, "and happy now."

PETER and I are sitting at lunch at the Café del Mar, a bar perched on the edge of the city walls overlooking the ocean. It is not an exceptionally beautiful coastline, but it injects one of my favorite feelings, that of being at the edge of the world and looking out over the expanse. It minimizes you for a moment, internalizes the cosmic.

"The food at this place is always so bad," I say.

"I know," says Peter. "And I don't understand it."

"Why not just update your robots, right? They aren't that expensive."

"I think they want the food to be bad here. It's their identity."

"*Café del Mar: we're so popular that we don't want you to actually enjoy coming here.*"

"Sounds right," he replies, before his attention shifts. He gives an odd look over my shoulder. I turn to spot Willa, and I smile reflexively. To her right, however, and looking directly at me, is a confusing sight. It appears to be Helen, but Helen would never wear head-to-toe khaki. Her mother, however, would do exactly that. And I realize that it is Addison, my third wife, the mother of my first child. She looks as she always does, blonde, tall, beautiful, with a radiant smile.

"What the? Addison? What are you doing here?" Confusion. *What is she doing here?*

"Good to see you, too," she laughs. "I'm here with Willa, her plus one."

I stand and we hug, giving a quick kiss on both cheeks.

"Oh." I look over to Willa, trying to imagine them as a couple.

"Not a date: we live next door to each other in Honduras."

"In that case," I say, reaching out and giving Willa a suggestive hug and kiss on the cheek.

"Oh, good to see you, too," replies Willa, feigning shock.

"She told me you were always into her, trying to break up her marriage" says Addison, laughing at my attempt at drama.

"What are the odds?" I say. "I can't believe you're here."

"And I knew Morris. Before you knew him. But I didn't know that you knew him until like three days ago. Small universe, huh?"

"So true."

"Well, I wanted to come and see you, and this is as good an occasion as any, right? A death party in Cartagena?"

"Yeah, it's good to see you. I'm sorry, my mind is just blown. I actually just saw our daughter. She's living with me for a bit."

"Oh. Wow." Her face blanches.

"Yeah, it's been interesting," I say. "You two still look exactly the same."

"Oh, well, no aging, I guess. Anyway, I wanted to surprise you here."

"It's good to see you," I say. "Won't the two of you sit down?"

"We can't unfortunately," says Addison, smiling at Willa, and jabbing me. "You'll have to flirt with Willa and ignore me later. We're doing a quick scuba thing this afternoon, before the 'Last Supper.'"

"That sounds wonderful," chimes Peter.

"We'll catch up," Addison says to me.

"I look forward to it," I say. I do not. I'm suspicious of why she made the trip to see me, and I do not feel good about it. "But I'm more looking forward to spending with time with you." I point to Willa, who laughs.

"I know all of your moves, Mister Walker. I'm ready for you."

They turn and walk away, and I watch them as they go. Addison looks beautiful as always, luminous and tan in the glowing noonday sun. And I've always had a thing for Willa, her form and movement strike when I watch her. But still, but still, the odds of these two figures—Helen and Addison—from my deep past resurfacing in a week, it's a strange thing.

"Did you know she was coming?" I ask Peter.

"No, I honestly did not."

"Strange."

"It is," he holds eye contact. "Are you okay?"

"I'm fine. A bit overwhelmed."

"What should we do with our afternoon?" he says.

"Why did she want to surprise me?"

"I'm sure she'll tell you tonight."

"Maybe we should join them."

"I'm not scuba diving."

"I'll wait until tonight."

Peter simply looks at me, quietly; he has concerned eyes for me now.

Morris is seated to my left, or more appropriately, I am seated to his right. It is the seat of honor, I suppose. I am playing the part of the disciple that Morris loved. I'm not sure that we ever taught each other anything, but we were quite close once upon a time. Peter sits next to me, and to his side is Regan.

Candlelight and white stucco stained yellow; the walls layered, crumbling in moments, dotted with yellow lamps with ancient bulbs casting their oddly tinged glow; crucifixes, the dying Christ, and centuries past paintings of the stations of the cross; we sit at a long white table-clothed rough-hewn wood slab tabletop, brass candelabras with true candles dripping wax, and all with smiles and festive sociality, all life, no tinge of death.

Around us a multitude of robotic wait staff roll to and from the table, while a group of five nuns, including the jug nun, stand quietly behind him.

"I'm so glad that you all have joined me tonight," says Morris, standing and beginning his speech. He is still dressed in the same robes with flowing sleeves that drape and cover his hands, forcing him to readjust moment to moment. "It's an exciting time for me. I first decided I was ready about twenty years ago, and since that time I have been carefully discerning how I wanted to go. So I began to look for a sign, and to think through a solution, and it was one special day, like five years ago, that I saw, I think, five crucifixes. You just don't see them much anymore, and it's not like I was running around a convent." (polite laughter) "Not like I am these days. So it struck me, maybe there's something to going out like Jesus. We both are *choosing*. Choosing to die. With time to say goodbye to friends, to spend time in prayer and preparation. To ready ourselves for the end. It feels good to have the Christ as a model."

He looks around for a drinking glass and the jug nun nods to another nun standing nearby. She produces a wine glass and pours from the communal wine on the table, serving Morris. He looks excitedly towards what I imagine is his first wine of the week.

"Have to be authentic after all," he says, holding the cup in front of himself. He holds his right hand over the glass and speaks: "Take this all of you; this is my blood, given in thanksgiving for life. Whenever you drink of it, do so in thanksgiving for your own." He sets the cup down on the table and reverences it. He then picks up a loaf of bread, holds it above his head for a brief moment, and then brings it down to the table once more to break it. He holds the two halves and says: "Take, eat; this is my body, broken in thanksgiving for life. Whenever you eat of it, do so in thanksgiving for your own."

Morris passes the glass of wine and the loaves of bread down the table, each person taking a sip from the cup and a little piece of bread. Though Christianity has persisted to this present moment, the observation of organized religion is not a particular commonplace; engaging in rituals, on the other hand, we do that all the time. Solemnly sip, solemnly nibble, pass with the appropriate reverence for the moment, speak the words, wait in silence.

The elements finally reach me and I hand them back to Morris, completing the circle. He elevates the remaining crumbs on the plate and the last few sips of wine in the cup before handing them back to the nuns behind him.

"This is my last supper," he says. "I will miss you all."

We sit, still silent.

How many times have I shared a last supper with someone on their way out? I honestly do not know, and I do not know if I care to count. It's not a sad thing, right, not a sad thing at all, because every one of us has lived a blessed life, and when they are ready to die, they move on to something better for them. We have not lacked opportunity or privilege or even love—everyone who has lived at least five hundred years has experienced at least one tremendous love, they've done studies to confirm it—all of these things, which make possible an excellent form of life. We have lived the beautiful life, and now it's time for the next step, the next thing, the only thing which is truly something new. We've tried life, now we'll try death.

But if I'm being honest, my wife has completely ruined death for me, and by extension, ruined life. She went and she shot herself and now I no longer want to party and celebrate the glorious experience of a life fully lived. I want to hold on to life and not let go of anyone, but all this does is put me in greater pain. I feel this pain in my chest. I'm looking at Morris and I feel a tremendous weight because I do not want him to die. It is a general desire, not specific to him, because I know it is better for him to die, but I do not want him to. I do not want this pain anymore.

Ten thousand years, and now something new. The death of a beloved always felt ambivalent, like the feeling of a friend moving away for a great opportunity. You are excited for them, and you know they have to do it for their own happiness, but you wish you could still have them stay nearby. Still, you know they must go. I am doubting him now. I wish he'd decided something else.

"I want to remind you all to celebrate me, and not to miss me. Well, maybe miss me a bit. But mostly, celebrate. 'Rejoice always; again I say, rejoice!'[2] I read that this morning. I love that passage. We know what Paul was going through when he wrote that, too. He was in prison and swimming from shipwrecks and rumbling through earthquakes. We don't even remember what it was like to have the actual threat of injury and death as a constant thing. There was such terror. And yet he says, 'rejoice!' Now that we always have reason to give thanks, we perhaps forget to do so. I have so much gratitude, and I want you to do the same. I want you all to do the same."

As he says all of this, he is forgetting to do the rejoicing himself. He smiles, but there is a palpable sadness to his movements that we are willfully ignoring.

He takes a sip of his wine and steadies himself. The jug nun puts down her jug and waves over another nun, who turns around before her presenting her back. Jug nun unzips her vinyl habit, revealing her bare skin and a handwritten piece of paper. She peels it from her back and presents it to Morris, returning to her place once she is rezipped.

Morris takes a deep breath, and looks out at us. "My final words," he says, and smiles. "'There is a time for everything under heaven, and a season for every activity. A time to be born and a time to die,' and it is my time to die. 'Whatever is, has already been, and what will be has been before, and God will call the past to account.' I have studied the world, and I have gained the wisdom of the ages, and I have learned what we can know. I have loved, and I have lived for love, I have seen it grow and seen it fade, and it is lovely. I have worked to be good, and I have been good, and I have helped others be good. And now, and still, 'all come from dust, and all return to dust.'"[3]

He pauses again, fiddling with his paper. "I cannot express to you the excitement I have. I firmly believe for the best and worst of reasons that there will be something after I close my eyes, that I will awaken to something new, and be restored. I have never believed in Jesus, and sometimes even struggled to believe in God, but I have an unspeakable certainty that there is something next.

"Jesus said to his disciples, 'Do not let your hearts be troubled; you believe in God, believe also in me. My Father's house has many rooms; if that were not so, would I have told you that I am going to prepare a place for you?'[4] I am going to the prepared place. I will wait for you there. I will see you all again. Live; rejoice always; give thanks. We will meet again. Thank you."

We applaud him, which is perhaps inappropriate, but he accepts it. The wait staff brings out the food for the appetizer course, and conversation begins.

"Well done," I say to him. "Nicely composed."

"Thank you," says Morris. "I had some time to work on it. Been doing some fiddling, trying to find the right words to say goodbye. A happy goodbye."

"Nice. Well, that was the right way to do it."

"Thanks," he says, and takes a bite of his salad. "What do you think happens when we die?"

He says this casually, but it is clear that he is not asking casually. "What the fuck?" I respond. "Why are you asking now?"

"It's not a big deal," he says. "I wanted you to sit here. I know you are wiser than most of us."

"I don't understand why people keep saying that."

"That's what makes you so wise." He pokes me in the ribs. "So, as a parting gift, before I shuffle off this mortal coil, answer my fucking question."

"Well, you know I don't know, and that nobody has ever known, and that nobody will ever know until they die."

"Yes, yes, suitable caveats for human ignorance."

"It's a brutal question and I stopped worrying about it a few millenia ago. Some early Sufi writer that I was reading at that time, he was like, the time after death has no significance. You can't do anything about it, God will decide, and God will do the right thing. There is something or there isn't something, and you have nothing to do with that. God, by definition, makes the right decision, so trust that God has made the right decision."

"You're avoiding the question."

"Well, I think you have to."

"But, say there is something, what do you think it is?"

"Only because you're dying. I think our current existence is the closest thing we can have to heaven, and even now, most of us don't want to stick around for eternity. So I would guess for there to be a heaven it would be something entirely different."

"Like the beatific vision?"

"Sure."

"Okay."

"Or maybe just reincarnation."

He offers me a partially disgusted look as he takes another bite of his salad.

"That's all you wanted to hear?" I ask.

"Yeah. That's what I think. I'm ready for something different, too."

"You're not doubting everything at the last moment?"

"No, no. I am going to miss you all, but it's good. I feel good."

"Good."

I look around and notice that jug nun is staring at me intently. I turn back to Morris and whisper in his ear: "Jug nun is staring daggers at me."

"Yeah, she's worried I might back out. She told me to watch out for you. I keep telling her I'm fine. It's her job to make everything go smoothly, so I have a good out."

"Oh, she thinks I'm corrupting you?"

"Ha, yes, corrupting me with your constant living. She's a total pill."

"I can see that."

"I think I might have her blow me tonight."

I laugh. "I thought you were giving up sex."

"Yeah, but it might be worth it, just to see what it's like to get that from her."

"It would be a singular experience. In the chapel."

"Of course it would be in the chapel. Right on the altar. I'll drop my pants and hoist myself up. And then...my dick in her mouth."

We are gathered now in the noonday sun in the Plaza de la Aduana, a few hundred of us, including dozens who simply came out of their houses to witness the show. Morris is kneeling in the middle of the square in long robes, a shiny chrome crown of thorns for his head with blood trickling down. On the ground next to him is the cross, a massive crossbeam of rough planed wood. The nuns are standing around him, including one with a sponge on a stick, waiting to provide him with vinegar and opiates to drink in case he needs it. In successive rings, the crowds are kneeled, some in prayer, some in quiet patience towards the religious ritual occurring around them. My head is bowed, but I am watching Morris, waiting to see what he'll do next. It's been several minutes now.

Finally he stands, and we remain seated. The jug nun, now armed with a tray, approaches him, joined by the sponge on a stick nun. She offers him what lies in the middle of the tray, and my breath catches for a moment. Peter is next to me, and he puts a hand on my shoulder; he is still watching me.

In the middle is a little pill, some fancy poison that Morris has recruited for this adventure. He holds it up for all of us to see, and without hesitation he places it in his mouth and swallows it. He holds out his tongue for the jug nun to offer proof, and she kisses him on both cheeks and bids him on his way to death.

Morris takes up his cross. In front of him, the nuns—there are eleven of them now—form a procession. We all stand at once and retreat, forming a path for the procession, and then falling in line behind it. Peter and I are at the front of the line, just behind the cross, as Morris has requested. He wants us close, he says, he wants us to walk with him.

We begin, heading through the streets deeper into the Old Town to stop at the Cathedral, where Morris will receive his final communion before heading to the ocean outside the city walls. As we reach the streets, Morris turns around and smiles at me, offering me a reassuring wink. The jug nun frowns.

He pauses for the first time. A woman standing on the side walk approaches him, embraces him, kisses him, and returns to her spot.

Again he pauses, now at the next corner. A man walks from the side of the road and wipes the sweat from his brow, and then whispers in his ear.

He pauses for the third time now, outside of the Cathedral. He turns to me once more, and staggers momentarily. The poison is working too quickly, it seems. The nuns are startled, and Peter and I jump forward, together catching him and his cross.

"I'm okay," he says. "Let's go inside."

The procession waits for him, and inside we are greeted by an empty church thick with incense. A priest stands illuminated at the altar, holding his chalice and paten with a single wafer of bread in the center.

"Wait here," Morris says. He walks up the aisle. Peter kneels and bows his head to the floor, and when I notice he is on the ground, I follow his lead. But I can't avert my eyes. I want to watch him.

He kneels before the priest, and he receives the bread and the wine. The priest then anoints him with chrism and breathes inaudible words of death before saying for all of us to hear, "Benedicat te Deus Pater, sanet te Dei Filius, illuminet te Spiritus Sanctus. Corpus tuam custodiate et animam tuam salvet. Cor tuum collustret et te ad supernam vitam perducat." He offers the sign of the cross.

"Amen," says Peter.

"Amen," I say.

Morris rises uneasily to his feet, and he comes to join us. "The moment is coming," he says with a quick smile.

As we exit the cathedral, the crowd has once more formed a circle around the doors. The cross stands in the middle, supported by the nuns, while the jug nun holds her look of concern.

"I am ready," he says, and tries to take up his cross once more.

I feel my mind come back to me as he falls to the ground. His knees buckle and the cross thuds on the pavement. I have not been able to think until this moment, caught up in the rush of watching my friend walking to his death. I should stop him, I need to stop him, push the cross off his shoulder, put my finger down his throat and force him to expel his desire to end it all. I know, however, I know, that I don't wish this for him.

Peter taps me on the back, summoning me ahead. Morris is standing, but he cannot walk, cannot proceed forward, and the nun is waving us to her. We stand next to Morris, and he says to me, "Take my cross." He turns to Peter and says, "Take me."

The cross is unpleasantly heavy, and I understand now why he is struggling. We move again, Peter carrying him, the jug nun standing on the other side, worrying, waiting.

I see his legs trembling with each step on the stone pavement. His toes drag, his arms hanging limply on his friend. I can hear him breathing heavily now. His face wracked with concern and committed effort. It is taking all his strength to stay alive now.

With his first step onto the sand he falls. He is lying down, and I push the cross onto the beach and stride over to him. Peter, the jug nun, and I gather around him, and there is little chance he will make it.

"You're so close," says Peter.

"I'm fine," he says. "Let me catch my breath for a moment."

"There's no time," says the jug nun. "You must move now."

"We can carry you," I say, and he waves his hand at me.

"No, no," he says. "No, my friend, I've got this." He pulls himself up on our arms and stands upright.

The jug nun steps in front of him and offers an ear-ringing slap across his face. "Strong for the end," she says, and steps back. I pick up the cross, and Morris takes his final steps towards the shore. It's not far now, just a few more paces to the water's edge.

He covers the first few easily. He looks over to me as I struggle in the sand with the cross on my shoulders. "I love you," he says.

"I love you, too."

"I love this," he says.

I can't speak.

He pauses, the water touching his feet now.

"Time to die."

He staggers two steps forward, falls to his knees in the sand, and now he takes his last breath.

I throw the cross down into the water and wave to Peter to come and help me. He was supposed to make it to the cross on his own, but now he is just lying there, the waves lapping at his face. Peter jogs over and I notice the crowd behind him, they are talking now. The feeling is confused; there should be joy, the party is supposed to start, we were supposed to celebrate his death. I see the jug nun, on her knees, sobbing; what was she to him, or he to her? Why the tears?

I cannot cry but must jump into the water to retrieve the cross, now floating away, I bring it back to Peter, and he has a grip on Morris's body, on his shoulders. I grab his legs and we awkwardly heave his body onto the beam, balancing him, stilling him in the water, and set him sailing. Peter joins me where I stand in the soft waves, putting his arm around me, and we watch him float away.

Behind us, the music starts. Drinks are passed out, and people start to eat. The beach fills in as people mingle on the sand. The conversations grow louder and the laughter begins and life goes on as it always has and always will.

"Let's get you a drink," Peter says, and we walk up to roaming waiter with a tray of bubbly, its wheels struggling slightly in the sand.

"Thank you," I say, as I take one.

Peter takes his own.

"To your health," he says.

"Salud," I reply and down the glass in one.

"YOU'VE been avoiding me," she says.

"Maybe," I reply.

"That was nice, wasn't it? A beautiful way to go."

"A bit heavy for my tastes," I reply.

"You with the puns, you kidder. That cross was big."

I smirk. The pun was unintentional.

"Why are you avoiding me?" Addison says, "I'm here to see you."

"I'm a little concerned about that."

"Been too long?" she asks.

"No, not that," I say. "I just don't really want to know why you're here."

"I'm just here for a bit of small talk, then," my third wife says.

"Oh, I love small talk," I say. "Just small talk."

"Me, too."

"Let's talk about the weather."

"It's getting colder these days," says the mother of my first child.

"I've heard that."

"But it was nice today."

"It was."

"Do you think it will get colder still?" Addison asks.

"I've heard it gets colder this time of year."

"Oh yes."

"And, also, it gets colder the further you travel north."

"What are we avoiding?" she asks.

"Please don't tell me," I say.

"I've never seen you like this. I thought you were crying over there, I couldn't believe my eyes. When's the last time you cried?" I don't reply. "Well, I don't know what's gotten into you. I'm happy to see you. Why won't you ask me how I've been? Why don't you ask me where I've been?"

"It's been an interesting year for me."

"See, that wasn't that hard. Mine's been interesting, too. I've been living in Honduras the past two years, met Willa there, and I found out she knew you, and she caught me up to date on your life. I've been traveling around for a while now, about twenty years straight, and I knew you would be the next one on my list."

"Don't," I say.

"The last one on my list." She beams with great joy, as she lifts the weight off of her shoulders.

"I can't," I say, and I start to walk away from her.

Addison has never been one to give in, and she chases after me until we're standing in the street, away from the party. "What the hell are you doing?" she yells.

"I know what you're going to say, and I don't want to hear it."

"What do you mean?" she says, confused that anyone could be disappointed with what she's going to say. "I came to see you. I want to stay with you in Portland. I want to say goodbye to you before I die."

Chapter 5

Up with the sun. The hotel is quiet. I beat everyone home last night. All things considered, I put on a good show. I stayed, I partied, I even danced for a few moments, a hollow dance, but it convinced suspicious Peter who smiled at me as he awkwardly swayed. All night I pictured Morris saying to me, "I love you." It's the first image in my mind this morning as well. Then I think of Addison.

I put on some swim shorts and head down to the pool at the back of the casa. Nothing feels better the morning after a party like an early swim. Keep the mind clear for a moment or two. Dipping a toe in the water, and it's cold, so I lay in the warmth of the early morning for a moment to prepare, a towel over my face. The palms hanging over the walls sway in a mild breeze and make their wonderful sound. A faint humming of the filter, the distant hum of the city, and just me.

"Warren," a voice disturbs my peace.

"Come on," I say.

"Can't escape me now."

"Who said anything about avoiding you?"

She pulls the towel off of my face. "You're a bad liar."

"Yep."

"Can we talk?"

"Why are you awake?"

"I knew you'd be up."

"Fair enough."

"Because you snuck out early."

"It was two in the morning."

"Like I said."

I sigh. "What is it that you wanted to talk about?"

"You ready to talk about me dying?"

I look into her eyes. They are so pained and I immediately sit up and take her hand and bring her in for a hug. She melds into me, and we balance on the overburdened lounge chair.

"It's time for me to go." She starts to cry.

"Okay," I say, holding her. She sobs into my shoulder.

"I can't do it anymore."

"Okay," I say. "That's okay."

It has to be okay, doesn't it? She needs me now.

"I'm sorry. I'm so sorry. I'm disappointing you."

"Don't worry about that," I say. "Don't think about that."

"I can't help it. But it won't stop me. I'm sorry it won't stop me."

"I know I can't stop you."

"I love you still, you know it," she says. "You were my one, my life changer, everything is before and after with you. I still love you but even that doesn't matter anymore."

"I know."

I squeeze her. I want her to be okay with silence for the moment. She doesn't need to say anymore, and every word breaks me further.

She leans away, pushing me back, hands outstretched. "You have to let me go!"

"I said okay, I said it."

"You don't mean it. I need you to understand it. You mean too much to me not to understand it."

"Addison. Please. Come back to me." She relents and I hold her again. "I promise I'm okay with you and I'll be okay. I mean it. I'll be with you every step of the way, right until the end."

"You can't avoid me anymore. I can't handle that. It makes me feel so wrong."

"I won't. We'll stay together. I'm with you to the end."

"Promise."

"I did. I promise." I'm crying again.

"Okay."

"Okay."

We sit quietly for a few moments.

"When are you going to Portland?" she says. She was always concerned about practicalities, and now even in death.

"This afternoon."

"Okay. I'm coming tomorrow, okay."

"Good. You'll stay with Helen and me."

"Right," she pauses. "Were you going to go swimming?"

"Uh, yeah, I guess."

"Let's get in. I want to watch you swim. You always loved it so much."

THE house is still quiet after my morning dip. I grab some coffee from the kitchen and I am folding clothes when I hear an old fashioned knock echoing on my wooden door.

"Who is it?"

"Hi, Warren, you don't know me."

A woman's voice.

"Would I like to know you?" I ask, heading to let you in.

"I'm so glad to hear you be a little funny."

"Well?"

"Someday I'll be the most important person in your life."

I open the door. I study her. I cannot place her. But then, she smiles and in that smile, and in the fact that she is not bundled into a vinyl habit, I see her as she is. The jug nun. Stunning. My breath catches in something of a novel feeling, something I know I've felt centuries before but which I am now privileged to feel as new again. Beauty is universally shared, but we all still have our type, and there is that significant alternative category of charismatic beauty. She has a presence—sexual, yes, but also tortured, also creative, also mischievous. Her blank face is more compelling than the average person in the most dynamic moment of their lives.

I noticed her before, but not in this way. I do concede her current outfit may be a factor. She has dropped her habit in favor of one of the more overtly sexual outfits possible in an unencumbered society, silk thigh highs, garters to a lace and mesh bodysuit, tall patent high heels, mesh gloves, a choker, all in black, her hair up high in a tidy bun; far from depriving it, her revelation inspires the imagination to new heights.

"I did not expect you to be here," I say.

"I'm sorry to intrude."

"I thought you didn't like me," I continue. "Felt your eyes on me, whenever I was near Morris."

"Yes, well."

"Yes?"

"I was concerned," she looks around, stuck as she is in a narrow hallway. "Can I come in?"

"Of course. I'm delighted to see you, actually."

"Delighted?" she says standing shyly, at a distance.

"I've been wondering what happened to you. Such an enigmatic presence. We were all curious—'who is this lady? Who is her crew?'"

"Well, I'm here."

"Please, come in. Have a seat." My tiny room has no furniture, only a pair of twin beds head to head in a corner. She curls herself onto a bed. "Drink?" I continue. "You can have my coffee, I guess, or I only have beer and aguardiente."

"Beer, then," she says. "Thank you."

"So…who are you?"

"Well," she pauses. "My name is Rose."

"You don't normally tell people that, do you?"

"Not that one," she replies. She shifts on the bed, trying to get comfortable without laying down or uncovering too much. I'm reminded of the 8400s when the entire world went through a sex crazed cultural shift and ensembles such as hers were the standard for everyone. It was an exhausting time.

She looks expectantly to me. "You were explaining why you don't like me," I say.

"It was never that I didn't like you, silly, you have to understand what I do. You were going to mess it up. Morris was supposed to die, and you are life, you are compelling."

"Hardly," I say.

"Shut up, everyone tells you all the time," she smiles. "You were going to make him reconsider. I know what he asked you. He would have stopped, if you had told him to. If you had told him there was more for him to know."

"I wasn't going to do that."

"Yes, but you could have. And he needed to die, I think you know that."

"But why is it that you are here?"

"Well, you found me compelling, no? I find you compelling."

"Is that it?"

"No, much more. I needed to see you again. I hope that's okay. I've been a disaster since he died. It wasn't supposed to be like that, and I don't think that anyone else really noticed what a disaster it was. He was supposed to go in this beautiful way, and it was beautiful, I think—wasn't it—oh, whatever, it was what it was, I guess, and to me, it was beautiful but also terrible. It was so tragic. And…"

"Why was it tragic to you?" I interrupt.

"…it was…oh. Right. I don't know. Wasn't it tragic? You could see it!"

"Yes, but he was my friend. Was he your friend?"

"No. I just met him. And he was not really friend material to me..."

"So why? You cried."

"You did, too," she says, with accusation. I raise my eyebrows to confirm my prior explanation. "Oh, right. Look, this is what I do. I've done this for like thousands of years. I help people die, help them celebrate their deaths."

"You're a death planner?"

"Yes. And it means an immense amount to me."

"I noticed."

"I want a perfect resolution. A spiritual resolution. Morris almost missed that."

"He seemed happy. I think he got what he wanted."

"He did," she says, taking a deep sip of her beer. "You gave it to him. I failed him."

"Huh?"

"You did. You tell him 'I love you,' and you freed him. He looked to you, his friend, his wise and loving friend, and you confirmed him. He took something from you though. I know he did that. I saw it happen. So I cried because of what he was doing to you, what he took from you that I didn't give, and it broke me. And I cried for what you did for him, that you gave him his death when it was the last thing you wanted."

Huh. I've been holding the bottle of aguardiente for a few moments, since grabbing her beer, intending to pour some in my coffee. Instead I take a sip from the bottle. "I don't know that he took anything from me..."

"He did," she interrupts.

I can't disagree with her. I start and stop a few times before deciding on a sentence. She waits patiently. "...I've had a rough stretch. My wife killed herself a few months ago, and she was way too young to go, and she didn't tell me. And just before going to see Morris die, my eldest daughter arrived, and she decided she was going to go, too. At least she gave me a warning, I guess, but it didn't make anything better. And at the party for Morris, my wife, her mother..."

"I know," she says, again correcting me.

"You know..."

"I do."

"...my story?"

She nods with her eyes as she finishes her beer. I grab another from the fridge and hand it to her.

"I'm glad it's public knowledge."

"It's not, don't be silly. I want to help you. I owe you. Not this one time, either, forever. I'll always owe you."

I smile at her. "The idea that you might forever be in my debt is not something I would ever dismiss, but that does seem a touch dramatic, wouldn't you say?"

"Well, we shared something. I know you recognize it. I'm just saying it."

She is so straightforward and dominating. She sits coyly and meekly but she is directing us to our end. I am playing as if I'm not convinced, or as if she is not in charge, but she is, we know that she is.

"We did. What do you owe me?"

"I will take care of your daughter and your ex-wife. To start with."

"You'll convince them not to die?" She returns my suggestion with a look of disapproval that matches my mother's. It takes me back. "I know," I say, "there's no stopping them."

"Nor should you want to," she says.

"Nor should I want to," I agree. "Well then," I raise my glass, and she meets mine, "here's to death."

She smiles at me directly for the first time, her eyes in mine, only for a moment before she regains herself. "May it be ever beautiful," she says.

"And until it comes," I continue, "may we live beautiful lives."

We clink our drinks.

"I should go," she says. "I'll be in touch."

ALMOST ten thousand years ago, I worked for the government of the federated societies in the Department of Transition. My job, along with many other committees and sub-committees, was to make life as happy and joyous and perfect as possible. So many policies—so many choices we took away, because humans were always making bad choices about how to live and how to treat each other and it would lead to injustice or self-hatred or unremitting pain and then to death. That is what I wanted to avoid.

I'm on the shuttle now, leaving Cartagena. Peter is next to me, sitting quietly, but watching me, ready to chew me out if I show my depression. I am in a place I did not think I would ever find myself. It reveals my deepest hypocrisy, and I am ashamed at myself.

But it is as he predicted it. Wilbur Reils. A name you don't hear so often these days, but a very personal one for me. I met him only once for a brief few moments, tasked with interrogating the leader of a rebellion, one which sought to undo the very thing I was working towards. Reils was an unremarkable and rather boring man. He did not have tremendous achievements or great talents of any variety. But he did find that one thing he could do, I must admit. Before Reils, death is outlawed; there is no dying, except for the very rare accidental variety. After Reils, after his revolution and his movement, there is death for anyone who wants it. That is the victory he wins.

We outlawed death. Not as a formal policy, really, but as a logical consequence of our technology. There was no need to die, so why would we want a world where there was death? Suicide was just mental illness, and we could treat mental illness. Sickness, war, violence, all things we had cured in our world of unlimited resource. Humanity had worked against death for so long, the fight was always against death and disease and dying. So why keep death around?

This was the revolution that Reils brought. The right to die. The right to kill yourself and not be revived. Not because of any difficulty in your life, we'd taken care of all of those. Unlimited energy, a simulated economy which makes everyone rich, the destruction of bias and racism, genetically enhanced humans who are all talented and beautiful with an unending world of opportunity before them. And yet, he didn't want to do it anymore. Just didn't want to keep on living. I didn't get it, I had such disdain for him, confounded by him. But now, but now, here we are.

I bring up the video of our conversation. I want to relive the moment.

March 2, 2460 CE
Undisclosed location
Vicinity of Washington, DC
Transcript of interview

Session 1

Warren Walker: Good afternoon.

Wilbur Reils: Is it?

WW: They told me you were humorous.

WR: When you say it like that I sound like a loser.

WW: Quite intentional, I assure you.

WR: You are my interrogator?

WW: Not at all. I don't know what we would interrogate you for.

WR: And yet, here we are.

WW: Here we are, indeed. Tell me about your mother.

WR: I've already been through so much therapy.

WW: What did you discover?

WR: I wanted to fuck her. And kill my father.

WW: Interesting.

WR: It was very productive.

WW: And now you want to die?

WR: Not as bad as I want to fuck my mother, I guess, but yeah, seems like a good idea.

WW: Have you considered buying her dinner?

WR: (laughs) She actually died a few centuries ago. But you knew that.

WW: I did.

WR: Why would you say that, then? Other than for laughs?

WW: For laughs. And to see if I could get a rise out of you.

WR: And you wonder why I want to die.

WW: I do.

WR: I won't have to deal with you ass-farts any more.

WW: Right.

WR: You don't believe me?

WW: That's not the real reason. You could avoid us quite easily.

WR: If I didn't try to die?

WW: Of course.

WR: Crafty.

WW: I think your honesty is worthwhile in this moment.

WR: Why on earth would it be worthwhile? I said I wanted to die, and now I'm in jail.

WW: True.

WR: So?

WW: Well, you're here anyway, you might as well explain yourself.

WR: Explain how?

WW: Why on earth do you want to die? Are you missing something?

WR: I don't want to live. It's not complicated. Just let me die.

WW: Well, the scientists we have working on this, they suggest that there are essentially no creatures that, when healthy, will choose to die. You are healthy. Not conventionally depressed, no terminal illnesses; you haven't lost any loved ones recently. You have sufficient possessions and access to meaningful work. We're confused. Give us something.

WR: Give you what?

WW: Just a brief explanation. A few words. 'I want to die because…'

WR: I want to die because I want to die. I suppose it's an incomplete logic for your elite minds.

WW: Quite sure that you are smarter than that.

WR: Are you?

WW: This is fun, isn't it.

WR: Not really. Compared to therapy, I suppose.

WW: Yeah, therapy is brutal.

WR: Tell me about it.

WW: I work with the Department of Transition. We want to know what we're missing. Now that people have eternal life, we want to make sure that they are provided with everything they need to thrive. You are not thriving, are you?

WR: I'm doing just fine, actually.

WW: You have attempted suicide thirty-five times in the past two weeks.

WR: That many?

WW: Indeed.

WR: Maybe I'm just frustrated. You guys keep stopping me.

WW: There would be a prior issue, of course, where you are desirous of ending your life. So, I must ask again, what are you missing from your life?

WR: Hmm. Perhaps I am missing the possibility of dying.

WW: You say that as if it is so profound, and it is likely the tritest thing either of us have said today.

WR: You don't feel like we've messed with human life a bit too much?

WW: What do you mean?

WR: I've got a six pack. I've never seen a situp.

WW: Do you wish you were fatter?

WR: Not the point I'm making. This isn't natural.

WW: Natural is a constructed term, meaning different things in different contexts and to different people. All it means in its best sense is things that occur according to the laws of nature. Human perfection is following all the rules of nature.

WR: And yet…And yet…

WW: And yet, what?

WR: Someday it'll hit you.

WW: What will hit me?

WR: You'll want to kill yourself.

WW: So, why do you want to kill yourself?

WR: There's no point to living this long.

WW: Ooh – a moment of honesty.

WR: How long do you plan on living?

WW: I suppose I haven't thought of it. I believe the general answer is forever, and I haven't considered the alternative.

WR: Well, that just sounds awful.

WW: This is the reason you've started a revolution, with many of your followers attempting to arm themselves? Because it sounds "awful."

WR: I'm not some great thinker. I just don't want to live.

[There is a knock on the door, audible on tape. WW turns his head towards the door, at which point WR breaks the ecoplastic chair he is sitting on, shattering it into a few sharp pieces. He steps back, then forward as if he were about to grab a sharp piece. The guard at the door runs toward the chair, as does WW. WR takes two quick steps to the door, wedges his head in the door frame, and snaps his neck.]

WW: What the fuck?

Guard: Turn it off

<End of transcript>

"Someday it will hit you," he says. Here we are, at that day. I can't do it yet, can I? I have to live through two more deaths, my wife and child. Two more death parties.

What a tremendous prophet. And utter simpleton. Why does he have to be the one who is right? It's so depressing to be defeated by the non-philosopher, the non-thinker, the person who wants nothing to do with life. He just wants to die, for no reason at all. And that is it, that is the end of our lives. I've spent so much time pursuing the wisdom of existence, the wisdom to live and to live well. And "has God not made foolish the wisdom of the world?"[5] Foolish, I am foolish. I am foolish for thinking I could always live.

It was nothing so aspirational. Just day by day, I would wake up and see the sun and maybe catch a glimpse of the stars at night or watch the waves roll in, and I would want to live that day and find enjoyment in that day. It was enough. But it seems so naïve, so protected, and all I needed was to be disrupted by some tragedy and then I would lose it all.

He won, of course, obviously. Reils. After his death in the interrogation room, we quickly legalized death. Billions would die over the next few centuries. And I started, with the rest of the world, attending death parties and enjoying them and watching approvingly as everyone around me, all my friends, my family, chose to go to their death. It was never for me, I was never interested in dying, I didn't get what they wanted from it. But I gave them my blessing and enjoyed watching as they came up with ever more creative ways to die.

I give Peter a hug as we step off of the shuttle and into our separate pods. He is quiet, always quiet, measured. I don't know what more I could say to him to draw him out. Nigel must be the one, his fiancé I've never met. He must be the one who can bring him out of his calculating self. I've only ever broken him a few times, my favorite times with him of course, but only deep into the nights of the deepest party.

Not that I've ever shared all of myself with him. Bared my soul a few times, of course, and more regularly than he has, but never everything, right? Never everything. Not now, certainly, I won't say anything to him. Milnius says "Kierkegaard says suicide is solipsistic." Yes, it was, it was once upon a time. He never stopped talking about it at the end of his life. I think it was a last shot for him, a last evaluation of his philosophy. If he talked about it with others, it wouldn't be the solipsistic error he thought it might be. So he spoke of it all the time and shared with anybody who would listen. He was like Helen, like Addison, just ready to casually discuss their plans and what sort of death they were leaning towards. It was no longer a private decision for them, these selves reduced to nothing, I suppose.

"Were you going to say something?" he asks.

"No, no," I say. "I'm surprised you're letting me go home alone."

He laughs. "We're never as alone as we think we are. Go, get some rest, and we'll talk soon."

JUSTINUS is sitting on the couch when I enter my apartment.

"Warren!" he says. "What brings you here?"

I can't help but laugh. "Just in the neighborhood," I say, "thought I'd come by."

"I'm so glad you did. Cocktail?"

"Of course." He pours me a gin martini from a shaker. It's something Gwen gave me, a Boston shaker, engraved with a short toast she wrote:

Because we are together under this sky,
I drink a toast to you, my love,
Because we are together under this sky.

It has always sat idle in favor of my counter, who makes pretty good drinks, but also because I cannot stand to touch it. But I am glad it is put to use. "You've made yourself quite at home."

"All jokes aside," he says, "I hope you don't mind. I spoke to Helen before coming, she's out with a friend for the day. Peter has permissions, you know, which he passed on to me, so Meredith let me in."

"It's fine, of course. Peter's been watching me like a hawk. I should have been more suspicious when he let me go home alone."

"Yes, you should have."

"What are we doing tonight?"

"Dinner?" he says. "No real plans. I've got a new restaurant I'd like to try, if you're game."

"Sure," I say. "I'll just get washed up. Like to get a shower in."

"Of course."

I walk into my bedroom and start to undress. I can't believe he was just sitting on my couch. I can't even muster any upset. It's hilariously intrusive and I'm happy to see him, I can't resist it.

I turn on the shower and step in.

"So how was Cartagena?"

He's behind me. Holding the shower door open and shouting into the water.

"Oh, fine," I say.

"Peter told me about Addison."

"Yeah," I say. "Not great news."

"No," he says. "But he said she's not doing well."

"No, she's not. Any other time, I think I'd be just fine."

"Just feels a bit different now?"

"It does." He pauses, so I change the subject. "How's Oliver?"

"Thriving, actually. Seeing some new people, feeling much better. He's got life back in him, zest again. Loves that therapist you recommended."

"I'm glad to hear that. Will we see him tonight?"

"No, no," says Justinus. "He's at some orgy or something."

"Of course."

"It'll be dull. Very dull. Not where I want to be at all."

"You don't need to hang out with me," I say.

"Surprisingly enough, especially to me, I would rather be here, invading your space."

"Lovely."

"Do you think you have had every variety of food that exists?"

"I doubt it. I think you'd have to be intentional about that."

"Completist, right?" he says. "That's not for me."

"Nor me," I say. "But I have traveled well, and always try to sample what is local. So who knows?"

He smiles and looks around the restaurant. "Well, I honestly wish I hadn't had this variety of food." He's right. Not that it's a specific regional cuisine, just a chef who is creatively combining distinctive methods; sometimes it works, here not so much. For that matter, the décor is equally pastiche, connected by the theme of black lacquer, yet the result is a sense of sterility.

"My dinner was pretty good. Fish perfectly cooked."

"Sure, of course," he says. "But the appetizers, weak, and my dinner, you tried it, honestly terrible."

"It's a new restaurant, they always have to work out the kinks, find out what works."

"I'm glad we haven't spoken about death for the entire dinner. Peter told me you were very dour."

"He is very sensitive about my emotional state."

"You seem okay to me."

"I'm enjoying your company these days, I admit. But don't get too attached to me. I don't know if I believe in my own story anymore."

"Too late for that, Warren. Well past attached at this point."

It's a mistake to be attached, I think to myself. "Helen and Addison together, I think it might ruin me."

"I don't believe it," he says. "You'll make it through."

"I've been hit though. Hit hard. We don't always make it back from this." He grimaces when I pause. "And here we are talking about death. Let's talk about other things, at least for tonight."

"I've tremendous gossip, if you're so inclined."

"Please. I don't care at all, but please, go on."

Justinus tells me of the lives of several people I've never heard of and have no interest in meeting. One has successfully been dating four people, despite making purely monogamous agreements with each, and spending a surprising amount of time with each. He just told them he was touch averse, except during sex, and then would run a hologram with predictive responses from a device he set up in the different apartments, including his own. Took four months for someone to bump into his hologram and catch him in his lie.

"I think he just wanted the challenge," says Justinus. "Wasn't about sleeping with four different people or, you know, an inability to decide who he should be in a relationship with. Just the difficulty of living that life like that."

"It's honestly amazing," I say. "I don't know that I've ever felt the need for that kind of challenge."

"Yes, well, that's what makes you special."

"Is it?"

"Don't you think?"

"No, I thought it was my gray temples."

"Speaking of, have you called Cynthia yet?"

"No."

"Maybe you should."

"I don't want to do that right now. She's been through a lot, don't you think?"

"You could help each other," he says. "She's in a similar place, I think."

"Has she been struck, too?"

"I guess."

I pause, swishing my drink.

"What are you thinking about?" he asks.

"An article, to be quite honest."

"Hmm."

"Yeah. By Veronica Freedberg."

"Still alive?"

"Oh no. Long gone. But my mentor, Milnius, he hated this article. I never paid much attention to it, though I knew it well because he talked about it all the time. Just never understood why until this weekend."

"Oh," he said. "Right, then. I'll have to read it, I suppose."

"If you've got the patience for it. I'll send it to you." Because it's about being hit. Concussed, really. And now that you've been hit, Freedberg says, you can't escape it. And here I am. "Someday it will hit you," Reils says to me. Here I am.

Part Two

Aph. 341 The Greatest Weight.—What if some day or night a demon were to steal after you into your loneliest loneliness and say to you: "This life as you now live it and have lived it, you will have to live once more and innumerable times more; and there will be nothing new in it, but every pain and every joy and every thought and sigh and everything unutterably small or great in your life will have to return to you, all in the same succession and sequence—even this spider and this moonlight between the trees, and even this moment and I myself. The eternal hourglass of existence is turned upside down again and again, and you with it, speck of dust!"

Would you not throw yourself down and gnash your teeth and curse the demon who spoke thus? Or have you experienced a tremendous moment when you would have answered him: "You are a god and never have I heard anything more divine." If this thought gained possession of you, it would change you as you are or perhaps crush you. The question in each and every thing, "Do you desire this once more and innumerable times more?" would lie upon your actions as the greatest weight. Or how well disposed would you have to become to yourself and to life to crave nothing more fervently than this ultimate confirmation and seal?[6]

Friedrich Nietzsche

Chapter 1

The Marithe Francis Wilkinson Celebration House is the best known building in Portland, ME, and perhaps the entire east coast. It is a massive structure, intended and ideally fortified for the spectacular festivies which routinely occupy its space. The main room is circular, expansive, capped by a revo-art-deco dome—in style two thousand years ago when it was built, but enduring—a hundred meters across. The room is spacious and beautiful, yet somehow confining and intimate enough to support familiarity among its guests, a necessary ingredient for an unfettered merriment. The floors are a digital marble mosaic, moving faces of the lives celebrated in this room. They rotate, slide, smile, blink, and then they are gone.

It is empty now, the celebration has left and I am sitting in a side room, the sunlight from the dome filtering into my space apart. The light touches Addison and Helen as they lay nearby. The rest of the space is dark—maroon oriental carpet and chestnut stained walls and bronze fixtures patinaed away from their shine. I sit in a chair on the far wall behind my wife and daughter, waiting for the possibility of movement or decision.

My ears are warm, flushed, the feeling one has when they've been caught. Like a child sneaking away from his parents, I have been caught. Addison and Helen are dead now, the party has come and gone and I am sitting alone lost, lost without them.

We have been taught to turn to philosophy in these moments; in fact, I was one of the people most vocal about this practice. There are masters of every form of thought available, there is someone who can think you through every situation and bring you to contentment. I say to myself, who can match my anger? Who will provide satisfaction in the moment of utmost pain and the immediate confusion of death in a deathless world?

On the wall to my left there is a painting, a fitting painting for a house of death. It is of a philosopher named Willoughby Stark attending a funeral, and the first thing I notice is that he is well dressed in a charcoal suit and mauve tie. He gestures aggressively towards a man across from him, and the man peers back, confused, offended, from where he stands hunched over the open casket of his wife. Stark is laughing at him, and calling him an idiot. I have seen this painting many times before, as it is quite famous: *The Laughing Englishman.*

Stark was an odd combination of things. His primary philosophical influences were Diogenes the Cynic and Guo Xiang's commentary on the *Zhuangzi.* Comically atheist and a fervent denier of most social norms—except clothes; he liked fashion—Stark was often found at funerals banging a drum and laughing; or, conversely, wailing in mourning at weddings. Either way, he was never invited to these things. He simply looked nice enough to get in.

Stark's philosophy consists of one book [title: *You fucking morons*] and about a hundred hours of his street preaching, rantings in public places on the imbecility that defines the vast majority of humanity. His text, however, was a formal refutation of the concept of causality paired with a denial of the possibility of meaning. In particular, he cited Guo Xiang's concept of spontaneity, the idea that there is no overarching cause or prompt to the movement of all things, but that they simply occur spontaneously. As support he cited Neil DeGrasse Tyson Watkins of the 28th century, whose work provided an expanded understanding of quantum spontaneity and the cause/non-cause of the existence of things, though, to be fair, Watkins' work maintained a role for causality.

The concept of spontaneity struck a nerve, and Stark became an intensely popular and famous philosopher, transcending the fame of Milnius and Stendahl, an unfortunate fact for him as he was hoping to mock and deride, not be adored as a diversion from monotony. He became increasingly aggressive in his scorn of civilized society, an activity which did nothing but increase the desire in the populace to be the recipient of his taunts.

In this painting, the figures and the casket glow, the background black and empty. The pointing hand of Stark cuts the distance, illuminating the opposite poles and arguments. Stark's face glories in his humor, the mourner languishes in sadness and offense, and yet there is no victor in this work, only balance, because the mourning is pure, the death is honest, and so is the objection.

"Why do you cry for your dead wife?" he says. "There was never anything to do for her. There is never anything to do for any of us."

The deceased woman in the painting, Vana Marsten of Parkhurst, NJ, was one of the last accidental deaths to have occurred in modern civilization. Her sous chef robot burnt through its primary arm motor, leaving it deficient in its chopping skills, unable to finish the preparation of her endive salad. She takes the knife from the robot in a huff, trips over her semi-domesticated ring-tailed lemur clone and falls miraculously forward onto the blade, cutting her heart into two neat pieces. The sous chef robot would normally be able to respond, but one arm is not enough to sew a heart back together, even temporarily. The robot's override system in the face of danger to humans attempted to elicit motion; its damage sensors prevented it from action due to the risk of further danger to the human in its debilitated state, leaving the machine in a microloop of movement towards aid and away at the frequency of twenty hertz. The house security system, which would typically alert authorities and additional robots of a life threatening accident, was in the midst of a software update at that precise moment, one which, due to some faulty code, led to a need for a manual reboot, accomplished, typically, by the sous chef robot.

Kevin Marsten arrived home to find his wife very dead in a massive pool of blood accompanied by the loud humming noise of a robot locked in repetitive indecision. Her brain matter had long since decayed, removing the possibility of revival.

Without this coincidence of cascading causes, Vana would have been fine. She had no fewer than five spare hearts in storage at her local hospital. In storage in the basement were an additional 12 units of her blood sitting in a cooler next to the medical robot, waiting patiently for notification from the house computer to spring into action. For her death, many things had to occur in succession, presumably from each prior cause leading to a subsequent effect and culminating in the unfortunate result of Vana's death.

I wonder if, when she was dying, she felt any terror. To die in that way was unthinkable after the first five hundred years. Too many redundancies, too many systems, too much protection. Death only came in a grand voluntary form, not as the result of a small primate's mislocation. She was perhaps confused, perhaps entering into shock, but she most likely passed away calmly, without any concern. How could she have feared death, when it didn't exist? Or, at least, it should not have...maybe at the last second, a bit of panic crept in as everything went black. Or when a light appeared at the end...

Enter Willoughby Stark proclaiming the spontaneity of the universe. "The shadow does not depend on the light, the footprint does not depend on the foot. It always only happens. There is no connection, no reaction, no action shared between anything."

Kevin looks confused.

"She dies. You cry. You cry. She is alive. She cries. You die. There is no connection. What are you doing? Why do you resist? Did you believe that you could control anything?"

Kevin simply puts a hand over his eyes and rubs his temples, and his brother in law martials a robot bouncer or two to forcibly remove Stark from attendance. Stark stands outside and finishes his speech. Kevin stays inside and continues to mourn, but he is not the same after this encounter.

So now I think of this and I am caught.

WE'RE all together in Manhattan for the weekend, heading to stay at one of Addison's former wives' apartment on the two hundredth floor of the New Freedom Tower. As we walk from the pod to the elevators in the back of the building, I interject.

"So I'd really like it if you would both reconsider dying," I say.

"Oh, sure," says Addison, "that'd be convenient."

"Just go around to everyone we invited, 'just kidding."

"But..." I continue.

"Oh, shit, you're serious..." sighs Addison.

"I knew you were upset," says Helen, "but I didn't think you really wanted us to stop."

"I'd like you to stop."

Addison laughs out loud, and Helen offers me a patronizing glance and then smiles.

"You're a nut," she says, "what's wrong with you?"

"I don't think I'm a nut."

"Hellee, I think he's been having a tough time recently. With his friend dying. And his wife."

"Yeah, we talked about your wife, dad. We're not your wife. We're old."

"So old," says Addison.

"Wait, did you just call me Hellee?"

"Yes, sorry, oh my," replies Addison, genuinely ashamed. "Hellee" was our nickname for our daughter in her early walking days. She did not behave like a dignified Helen, but more like an unchained hellion. Hellee seemed like an appropriate compromise.

"No, it's fine. I just don't think anyone's called me that since I was five."

"Actually," says Addison, "I called you Hellee whenever you talked back to me when you were a teenager. And you didn't like to be called Hellee then."

"I do remember that actually."

"So I didn't mean to bring up stressful times."

"Oh God, mom, I'm over it now. Seven thousand years later, I'm okay. With some distance, I realized that you guys were actually good parents."

"Did you hear that?" says Addison, sliding her hand onto mine. "We were good parents."

"Not that you would have won any awards," adds Helen.

"No, no," says Addison. "We loved you, and we were happy."

"We did," I say. "We were happy."

"Well, dad, you've got two more kids and six more wives. Who knows how many more you'll see in your life. Who knows how much more happiness you could have."

"Both of you could have the same, then, right?"

"No," says Helen.

Addison shakes her head.

"It's too late now."

We arrive at the door of her former wife, which slides open.

"Addison!"

"Jane. Thanks so much for having us."

"What a treat. This has to be your daughter."

"Helen," says Helen.

"Of course. And you're the husband."

"That's right. Warren."

"How wonderful. Come in, come in!"

She's a bright and bubbly woman. I can't see Addison being married to her, or even enjoying her company, but one can marry all kinds in nine thousand years. I have loved many strange people, many who I should not have, but can you really say that you should not have loved anyone? I didn't lose anything but time, really. I've got that.

"Take a seat." She gestures to a set of couches sitting before the two story floor to ceiling windows overlooking lower Manhattan and actually most of the city. It's a stunning view. We are one point two kilometers in the air now, clouds are passing by, seems like we are floating. "So, I understand that the two of you are dying soon?"

"That's right," says Addison.

"We're meeting with a planner," follows Helen.

"That's wonderful. You are both excited?"

"I really am," says Helen. "And it's made that much better to go out with my mother. I didn't think it would work out like this."

"That is really sweet," says Jane.

"It worked out beautifully. Makes sense that we would go at the same time. We were always so similar. Too similar."

"And you Warren? Are you going anywhere?"

"No, no. I'm doing fine."

"Warren has always had a strange predilection for existing," explains Addison.

"He's first generation," says Helen.

"Is that right? You've outlived them all."

"Not all of them."

"Most," she says.

"Yeah." I look over to my wife and child. "I guess I just never saw the point in dying."

Jane grimaces. "Have you found a higher purpose in life?"

"No," I smile. "No point in living either. It just happens to be what we're doing."

"He just asked us not to die," says Helen, smiling.

"It's very precious," says Addison.

"Oh, Warren, you know better. The ten thousand year old man should know better."

"I do. Deep down, I do."

If you really think about it, the arguments against causality are pretty compelling. For any one event to happen it requires thousands of proximate causes—if you are analyzing an actual event, so long as you are not simply engaging in an artificial thought experiment ('Watch me drop this pencil.') You need gravity to be itself and existence to continue and you need every individual atom and molecule to persist in its activity. And then you need actors, the choices that need to be made to actually precipitate the event, and these must go back many years. A person decides not to go to the bar that night and they do not meet their future wife and then life is completely different, if you accept the causal chain, which maybe we should not. If there are ten thousand causes to every event, can you say which one in particular caused that event to happen? Can you say which of the ten thousand causes, if left out, would actually lead to a different outcome? If there are ten thousand causes, and none of them, in particular, causes or does not cause an event, is there any particular cause to the event?

There are too many different outcomes, too many different possibilities. It seems life, for the most part, does not follow any plan or course. It is compellingly random, and in the confusion that follows we only grasp for the causality to explain away our lack of control and our accompanying fear.

And if life was simply random, pure spontaneity, wouldn't that be an interesting thing? Wouldn't it be a compelling thought—you are not bound, but always spontaneous, the free action of the ten thousand things in existence, the free action of the infinite acting in alignment with the Tao.

"HELEN," I say, "I didn't expect you back so soon."

"Addison, actually," says Addison. "You still can't tell us apart?"

"I mean, I never could. Are you wearing her clothes?"

"Oh. Yeah. Why?"

"No reason."

"Is that how you tell us apart? Our clothing?"

"She may have better taste than you."

She provides a questioning glance and sets her things down on the console table. I stand up from where I've been sitting on the couch. "Is that right? Is that what you would say?"

"Yes, *mhibu*."

"Oh, wow, pulled that one out of the old days."

"I think people still say that."

Addison notices what I was watching before she came in. An interview with a member of the Universal Government Coalition on education policy and possible changes in the genetic manipulation requirements.

"What have you been doing all day? Watching this drivel?"

"No, no. I did some writing today. Most of the day actually."

"Writing your life out? Giving an account of yourself?"

"I was writing our love story, actually. And how great you were in bed."

She walks over to where I'm standing and gives me a playful push onto the couch before she sits down next to me, leaning into me. "I *am* good in bed. Millennia of practice. God that's still weird to say."

I smile at her, and wrap my arm around her shoulders. We sit peacefully, quietly, for a moment, her eyes are closed as she leans on my shoulder, and I tune out the noise of the words being shared.

"Do you remember?" she says.

"Of course; we don't forget."

"You know what I mean, don't you?"

"I do."

"I sit with you and I remember it now. Seven thousand years later." She laughs at the insanity of life and she smiles as she speaks. "I sit next to you, we think of Helen, we talk about her, the world goes on, and we are happy."

"In this moment, and in the moment that has passed."

"In the moment to come?"

"Not for me," I say.

"Oh, stop," she says, thinking of more joyful things than her oncoming death. "How old was Helen when you started to confuse us with each other?"

"Fifteen," I reply. "I think she turned fifteen and her boobs really came in and then there was hardly a difference. If you both were dressed up, then it was impossible."

"And she dressed better than me even then. From like age five, right?"

"You said it." She hits me lightly in the chest. And then she leans in and kisses me lightly, quickly.

"I miss that time," says Addison. "I miss you and I miss when she was small and I miss me when I was that young."

"I don't know that you've changed too much."

"Neither have you. Except you're a little more depressed."

"I think I have reasons."

She turns and stands up and walks over to the kitchen.

"I thought we were going to make out for a while," I say.

"Oh, no," she says. "I'm thirsty." And then, "What are we going to do tonight?"

"Helen comes home in a couple of hours, and then I thought we'd cook dinner together. Family meal."

"So we do have the house to ourselves."

"Yes, we do."

"And you think we should take advantage of that?"

"I don't know, yes, of course, I do, but I know, it's not really a good idea, necessarily."

"Do you still like me?"

"Of course I still like you. We didn't break up because we didn't like each other anymore. Well, not really, it was just the exhaustion." I stand and follow her into the kitchen.

"*The exhaustion of marriage*. What a brutal movie. Mfune is so intense."

"It's truly a depressing film."

"We weren't depressing together, were we?"

I spin her around in an impromptu dance. "No," I say. "We were beautiful together." I look plaintively towards her as we dance and she knows what I'm going to repeat to her, so she places a finger on my lips and then kisses me.

"That's why I came back to see you," she says. "Because I loved you the most out of anyone in my life. Such a crazy thing," she smiles at me, but her expression is quickly lost. "You don't need to say that you loved me most."

"You and Gwen," I say. "The two of you have messed me up the most. Truly."

"Good," she says. "That's why you're upset with me."

"I wish you'd change your mind."

"You don't really want to stop me," she says.

I'm taken aback. "Of course I do."

"You do. But you know it wouldn't work. I'm already dead, just still here. You'll see it in me soon enough."

I hold her and resume the waltz.

I have touched each of their cold faces in turn to confirm they are dead. Just to make sure, I guess. It is supposedly important to familiarize oneself with the dead bodies of your loved ones, such that you now actually understand they are dead, and then one can begin the grieving process.

I have done this many times before—buried loved ones, that is. I should be better at it by now. Somehow mourning does not seem like a truly developable skill, as if further practice would increase the efficacy of the dismissal of pain. The pain of missing is all it is, an internal pain, and effectively a choice, something we decide to feel as a way of honoring the person who once was and now is not. We do not need to feel pain at a funeral, in the same way we do not need to love or even like other people. We do not need to do these things, but for some reason, we continue to do them. Because what would life be without that pain?

The funerals for my grandparents were for me, in typical teenager fashion, non-events. I knew these people, but not in any significant way, and certainly not in a way that would lead me to a dark place. Death was a new thing for me at that age, but I believe that I knew enough about it in some way to restrict my affection for this older group of people who moved in fragile motions and could not lift me up into the air.

My parents straddled the transition. My father died three years before of a particularly malignant version of colon cancer, which was rare in those days. The processes of extending life had not yet been perfected at that time, with life expectancy around one hundred and fifteen years, and though cancer and heart attacks and strokes and aneurysms were lethal only about five percent of the time, they were still lethal five percent of the time. My mother was devastated, and from the moment my father died she wanted to die.

This was a trying thing to hear a parent say. I had heard it from others before; generally the widowed will express something like this: *I have been married for fifty years, and do not know what life is without my beloved, and I do not want to know life without my beloved. So I wish for God to take me.* God generally seems to take his time in getting to these widows, though some do catch pneumonia and die in a way that profoundly confuses the doctors—"Her body just gave out, and she's signed her DNR, so...."

So yes, my mother wants to die, but she is waiting patiently for death. And they have now announced that there is no longer any death, well, not if you don't want it. Just sign the dotted line, we'll inject you with some stuff a few times over a few years, nano-molecules and nano-robots to correct the aging process, to perfect and maintain the DNA and RNA replication processes, to ensure that cells remain perfect and, most importantly, that your collagen tightens, your muscle tone returns, your vocal cords sharpen, the thin lines on your face disappear, and your old age recedes. You are a young person once more—well, younger. Gone is your back pain, gone is your knee pain, gone is any physical limitation. Your mind is sharp, your energy high, but there is always a catch. You know things now, and you have experienced things, and you are not the same as the young person you once were.

The system is not perfect immediately, and the early years see a number of deaths. During this time, perhaps my mother can be defended for not rushing to adopt her eternal life. I did not do so either, for that matter, for some ten years or so. But twenty years on, thirty years on, she still refused, and at thirty years later, she is sick and she has the choice of whether or not she wants to live forever or whether she wants to die. The injections will cure her, but she cannot be otherwise helped. She cannot continue aging with her disease.

We have the discussion.

"Mom, I think it would be better if you would continue living."

"Oh, Warren, no thanks."

"Really. You don't want to see the future?"

"I want to see your father."

"I know. But I'm sure he can be patient."

"Sure. He's fine. I'm not. I've lived long enough, I'm happy to go."

"I love you, mom."

"Enough of that. I love you, too. I won't be going far."

I think I could have put up more of a fight. I could have pushed her, or made a scene. I could have had her declared mentally incompetent and taken over as her medical proxy, and then assigned her eternity. In this moment, that would seem to be the worst curse I could have placed on her. So I must say that I do not, I cannot regret not pushing her further.

Who am I to stop anyone from dying?

Rose came to see me, angry but contained. Disappointed in me for resisting.

"It was the same with Morris. You could have hurt Morris, I saw you thinking about it. Every time you ask them to reconsider, you do nothing but hurt them," she says. "You must see it by now. You must see their empty eyes."

"I'm trying."

"I know," she says, and hugs me. It is unexpected. She is wearing more clothes than our previous encounter, a simple black silk dress, mid-thigh, and underneath a silver fishnet bodysuit, her hair bound up in a ponytail. "You still need to do better."

"Weren't you supposed to be meeting them now?"

"We had to talk alone." Before I can hug her back, she lets go of me and points to the couch. "Over here."

"Yes?"

"What are you reading these days?"

"Oh man, nothing good. Reread Stark. Freedberg. Taking a look at some Milnius stuff."

"That sounds okay."

"You're not worried about me reading all of the suicide stuff?"

"I'm not worried about you right now. You'll keep it together for your family."

"Of course."

"What did you do when your mother died?"

"Ha. Hmm. Cried. But not too much. The narrative, you know, it was still set then. Live till a hundred and then you die. Age and get old and fall apart and die. Have a career, do something, retire...you get it. It feels controlled when it goes according to plan. Not enjoyable, but not as hard as it could be."

"Not as hard as it is for you now?"

"No."

"Do you see what I'm saying?"

"I see what you're getting at."

"Good."

"She didn't have to die, you know?" I say. "She could still be with me now."

"You wouldn't be together anymore."

"I know. She was done. Once my dad died. The same eyes."

Rose stands up. She straightens her dress, which clings to her bodysuit underneath. "They will have beautiful deaths. A truly beautiful celebration. So many friends and lovers are coming. A true celebration."

"I know," I say.

"I mean it, Warren. They have lived beautiful lives, really. I don't say that lightly. There are many who have wasted it and lose their chance; then again, maybe they were never really so capable. But remarkable people. You married a remarkable woman in Addison, and gave birth to a remarkable woman in Helen."

"I get it," I say, my throat dry.

"Let them go. Let them GO! See it with me, with the same eyes that I see it, Warren." She walks over to me and kisses me on the head. "See you next week."

Which is more comforting? That life is a ten thousand year long series of coincidences, each not coincidental in an accidental sense, but all profoundly caused by prior events; or, that there is no causality and no order and that life simply occurs spontaneously? There is, of course, no demonstration of any of these ideas that is possible, a statement which drove the physicists insane through about the year 7000, at which point they boldly claimed a new discovery, that no demonstration of the nature of the universe was possible. They'd just discovered it, you see. They scanned for the smallest of the particles, and beneath every particle, another smaller particle—turtles all the way down.

Though no answers are available, we tend to cling to some vision of reality narrated by ourselves to ourselves, and we tend to correct and attack those we find unappealing. The primary approach of Willoughby Stark's detractors was through a pursuit of his history. There must be some terrible trauma in his personal life to explain his odd behavior and his unappealing philosophical outlook. Why shout at people at funerals? What an odd thing to do.

His biography was permanently sealed for several centuries. His estate—of course he fucking killed himself—ensured his privacy after his death, which occurred centuries after his popularity vanished and his preference converted to quiet anonymity in the Lake District. I like to think, and rumor suggests, that he spent the remainder of his days slowly chipping away at his life by means of laudanum, increasing the dose each morning, which would explain his increasing calm and reluctant rejection of societal shouting matches. I think he would enjoy a vintage death of that sort, romantic and poetic cynic that he was.

And then, on his death bed, he would shout at his friends or the doctor or whoever was nearby, "It's not the drugs that are killing me. I am dying on my own. I am dying spontaneously. All things move on their own, and my movement to death is my own."

"If your tolerance for morphine wasn't so high, you'd have died months ago."

"And here I am, aren't I? Because I am dying on my own, you ignoramus, nothing is causing it. You deny the truth when it's shouting in your face."

THEY died together in a circuit cloud—a field of electricity that stops all cellular activity in the body instantaneously. They walked into the center of the theater holding hands and waved to the thousand or so spectators standing around them. A glowing blue orb ensconced their waving figures as a platform lifted them into the air. Addison said something to Helen, and Helen hugged her and smiled. The platform stopped, and then receded, leaving them floating, tending upwards, until well above the crowd. They waved one last time, raising their hands high.

The blue orb turns green and they fall in place, still floating; the orb turns opaque, and collapses in on itself, and they are gone.

It was a beautiful way to go. It was Rose's idea, I was told, with a few choices made by Helen, always the designer, always with her eye for the lovely. She was the jug nun, and then Rose, but she told Helen and Addison to call her Izzy. Asked for further clarification, she said it was short for something which both heard as "Israel," and figured she was one of the few remaining people who identified actively with Judaism. I'm quite sure, however, given her "z's," that she was going for "Izrael," a slightly prettier variant on the name of the Archangel of Death. It seems like something Rose would do. Even her namesake rose is a funeral flower, though it is also a great deal more.

I watched their death from a back room, on a screen, standing next to Peter. I asked him to be with me, and I held his hand the entire time. I banned myself from the mainstage, remembering Socrates' admonitions to his mourners to quit their public whining and keep their tears to themselves. I did not want to disturb them; in hindsight, of course, I realize that I simply did not want to listen to them as the crowd cheered and waved excited goodbyes to the people I loved. Their disagreement with my position was too much for me to publicly stand. How could they be excited? How could they not listen to me?

I held his hand and watched and could see nothing else and think of nothing else. My knees went out in time with theirs, and when the orb turned opaque I turned away. Peter consoled me, he held me at that moment, and for a few moments more. Then he took my lightly crying face into his hands and told me to stop.

"What must you do now?" he says.

"I must be a proper host," I reply.

"Sure, I guess. I think that's taken care of. Just stop crying and go say 'hi' to everyone. Just for a while. Then you can crash. So be nice."

"I can do that," I say, and I wipe my eyes on the sleeve of my suit coat and ready myself to smile and be friendly.

As I think of what I've just agreed to, a pit of nausea greets me and I feel inclined towards the bathroom. I tell Peter I'll see him out there and stand in front of the sink. After a few controlled moments of breathing and splashing water on my face, I have convinced myself not to throw up. I look in the mirror and practice smiling. My eyes are red still, and sad, and tired, and defeated, but the rest of me is as bright as I can be.

This is what I will do for you, Addison, Helen, for both of you. I will celebrate your lives with your friends. I will do this for you.

I am home now, a week after the funeral; I have stayed in my apartment with no visitors and no interest in anything and no desire to leave. I cannot stop thinking about what has happened.

Before she died, Addison said, "We'll see each other again soon." It has bothered me for reasons I can't quite figure out, as I accept that it is a bit of a platitude, more something we say out of courtesy, and things said out of courtesy are not offensive. It is, in fact, the last thing that she said to me.

We were standing in the waiting room in the Wilkinson Center, just the three of us at that time.

And then Helen said to me, "We won't be going far."

It is, of course, what my mother said to me just before she died. I don't know if she knew that; if she did, it may have been an attempt to remind me of maternal comfort. I accepted my mother's death, perhaps it would work to have me reminded once more of that acceptance.

It does not work, however; it shatters me. All that I think of this is the ten thousand year distance between myself and my mother. I have not seen my parents for ten thousand years—is there a greater distance? *I won't be going far.* My mother, I think she meant to say that she would remain within me, within my heart. That all that she has given me in raising me, all the genetic gifts, all these things live on in me. Or it was a religious reference, that she would be in the non-spatial dimension of heaven, always near, always different, but always with me. Regardless of these things, she is too far away now. I couldn't even tell you if I have elements of her still remaining within me. I have changed in all my time. I do not know where she persists. I do not remember her in every step of my day. I am sure that I have gone years without thinking of my family, without thinking of the parents who raised me. How significant are those days anyway to me now?

Helen and Addison, then, when she says this, I know they will be going far from me. Every day, they will be further away from me. Each day they pass further from my mind and from my being, farther from my actions and my thoughts. I will cease to know them eventually, only my misremembering of the fondest moments of our lives together, this will be all that I have left. I will lose them each day that passes. I cannot preserve them, cannot preserve their memory perfectly, cannot preserve their life. They are passing away from me. They will not be near me. The days will pass and they will no longer be near me.

I hug them both and I hold my tears in. Addison gives me one last kiss and they turn away from me. The jug nun nods to tell me I've done well before she walks to the controls. It will be over soon.

I am sitting in the corner at the funeral, off to one side, avoiding the noise and confusion of the raucous party occurring in this beautiful space. One of Helen's friends approached me, I think it was her ex-wife, actually, from when she was a man, and I do not feel like speaking to her. She is quickly dismissed because I do not want to talk to anybody.

Peter arrives. He has watched the whole of the previous conversation.

"What the fuck is your problem?" he says.

"Pretty apparent," I reply, sharply.

"Oh, your nine thousand year old ex-wife and your seventy-five hundred year old daughter died? What a surprise!"

"Fuck you."

"That's right."

"You want me to celebrate? Go do some drugs, maybe get laid?"

"Isn't that what you do with your life anyway?"

"Again, fuck you."

"Oh, you act like you're so fucking cursed. You live for ten thousand years, you're probably going to have something like this happen at least once. In your next ten thousand years, it'll happen again. So don't act like you're special. Don't act like this is so terrible. This wasn't just reserved for you."

"I don't even get a day?"

"You've been like this for months. Always moping. You need to stop."

"Fine. I'll work on it. Why don't you go and bump an upper so you're not so cranky?"

"Maybe if you do the same." He pauses for a moment, his façade of righteousness cracking temporarily as if he might feel somewhat mixed about cursing at me for mourning at ma funeral. "Look…I'm getting married in February."

"You're getting married?" I say. "Who are you marrying? I haven't even met this mystery person you're dating."

"It's—well, his name is Nigel, Nigel Hawes. I told you that. You'll meet him. You'll get it."

"Okay."

"And you're coming and you're going to be happy, okay? Happy for me? None of this woe is me shit. None of it."

"Fuck, Peter, okay. I'll be happy."

PETER's words are ringing in my ears as I sit and think in my apartment. I was not yet ready to leave them that day; I wish they were here now, even in death. They were living once, but they were empty bodies; now they are dust, poured into the dirt, gone from their form forever. But when I see a movement in the corner of my eye I think it must be them. Even with their empty bodies in front of me, I would be looking for signs of breath, as if their deaths were only for the show and in secret they will come back to me.

She was right, though, about being dead. Addison was truly dead. We played, we had fun, but then the fun was gone and she was a glass with one last lingering drop, waiting to be tasted. I did not have to work to spot it; the pain that life now caused her was easily visible. Even Helen, who herself claimed the pain, did not feel the way that Addison did. This served only to strengthen Helen's conviction, of course—'look what I would become. I will be just like my mother, a stale husk, trudging through life.'

Who am I to stop them?

I loved them, and that is why I would stop them. But I hear Milnius now, not Stark: "We cannot live for love simply so-called."

As I prepared myself to leave, I walked over and I put my hand to their cheek—first to Addison, and then to Helen. They were still cold, still dead.

"Helen," I said. "I'm very angry with you now, but I want you to know that I know what a lovely life you have had. I met many of your friends and lovers today, and they were wonderful people.

"Addison, I'm even angrier with you. You have led a beautiful life and you shared so many hundreds of years with me, but your friends were so boring, dear, how did you put up with them?"

I smile for a moment thinking of how she would respond to me.

"But I have spent hundreds of years without the two of you before, and now I will say goodbye, and for the last time, and my life will be empty of you again....I want you both to know how much I hate this, and how much I wish that you had just become well-disposed to yourselves and to your lives. More than anything, though, I love you both. I will miss the two of you always. I will never forget. Good bye, my darlings."

This is when I left, when I stood up from my mourning and took myself home to collapse in sadness. So now I sit here having moved only for the basic necessities of life. I sit and I cry and my tears come, and I cannot bring myself to move on, only to silently cry and drop tears to the floor as I hold my head in my hands. I'm not thinking much now, just loss, just anger, just a terrible feeling of dread, as if now, I, too, must die, because what else is existence attempting to say to me now? Shouldn't I die?! Everyone is leaving me. Isn't this what the universe is telling me? Isn't this all where the cascading series of causes will lead to? I can cling to spontaneity but I cannot defeat the nagging feeling that the meaning of all of this terrible pain is that I should die.

I have so much more to say to them. So much more to ask. We did not have enough time together, there was never enough time, and they didn't want any more.

Chapter 2

I wake up on my couch, the screen still on showing the end of a twelve hour Wyman film. I stretch and walk to the bathroom and then to my counter and think about having coffee. Today, I feel different. They are farther away now, and I am forgetting, and I am getting back to life. I think of this and then I no longer feel ready to do anything, but I know that this is not what they wanted for me. They do not want me to sit and pine for the dead.

I have my counter make me an egg and cheese sandwich and then drink my coffee and convince myself to accomplish something today. Walking into my bedroom I have my closet pick out an outfit, a suit. I look at the suit and the cravat and decide I am not ready for clothing so I retreat once more to the couch to sit and do nothing as tears well in my eyes. It may be time to watch something new to distract myself, so I put on a cartoon and sit for the next few hours until lunch chuckling to myself and I get up and eat and then return to my spot doing nothing but waiting for time to pass more quickly so that I can get through this day and the next one.

At three I stand up and get a cocktail, at my established starting time, and then I lounge some more and think of what I should be doing today instead. I open up my writing station and a keyboard floats over to me as I sit. I look at the words of the last chapter I've been working on and then think of them dead once more and lose what I had to say.

I read Freedberg again:

> "Specters of Reils"[7] Published in *The New Derridean*: 20:3 Fall 2470, Professor Veronica Freedberg, New York University.

The title of this lecture would commit one to speak first of all about Reils. About Reils himself. About his teaching and its legacy. About his ghost, which, upon his death, we have enacted, seemingly in perfect tempo, the process of imagining that it is no longer still present, haunting us with its insistence.

The death of Wilbur Reils is now proclaimed, with absolute consensus, as a glorious victory for a new way of life; his existence dismissed and, we insist, to be forgotten. The footage of his death is published, easily accessible, to remove all doubt. We see him, still human, in three quick swings, crack the lone chair in his prison cell. We see him, then, still human, patiently wait for the instantaneous response of his imprisoners. He welcomes them, and they move to secure the chair, concerned that Reils will use the serrated pieces to end his tedious existence. In their haste they ignore him; he wedges his head in the easement of the doorway, now withdrawn, and using his own momentum, cracks his neck for spectacular death.

We have ensured his burial, as we are wont to do with corpses, ensured that he will not come back to life. His body is embalmed according to his wishes, and he is placed in a coffin, all filmed, to prove his death. His corpse decays. The United American Governments insists on formal procedure, but is there really such a need? Have we not killed all of his followers? They wish to prove his death is not only bodily but normative, that his politico-logic is extinguished.

Reils, though denial persists, now enters the phantomatic mode of production. His Holy Spirit now infuses his followers! They have hidden his crypt! But they will not stop, because the ghost continues his production, and his answer to the injustice of existence now activates in his particular *techne*. He is the evidentiary moment of the greatest trauma inflicted on human narcissism. In these past one thousand years, we suffered the *cosmological* trauma ("The Copernican Earth is no longer the center of the universe, and this is more and more the case one could say as to draw from it many consequences concerning the limits of geopolitics"); the *biological* trauma ("The animal descent of man discovered by Darwin"); and the *psychological* trauma ("the power of the unconscious over the conscious ego, discovered by psychoanalysis"). The publishing of the death of Reils is intended as a means of denying the trauma he has inflicted on our narcissism, the idea being, which is as now denied, to bring his objection to silence, and compel the biopolitical moment of eternal life.

The Reilsian trauma will carry on and carry past in the exceeding of the life of Reils himself, now as a ghost, a ghost which will not share the secrets of his reflections, not in full, at least, but in part, and only as a violence. He is reborn in death, *revenant*, and his work, no longer his but that of the spirit, continues:

> The century of Marxism will have been that of the techno-scientific and effective decentering of the earth, of geopolitics, of the anthropos in its ontotheological identity or its genetic properties, of the *ego cogito—and* of the very concept of narcissism whose aporias are, let us say in order to go too quickly and save ourselves a lot of references, the explicit theme of deconstruction. This trauma is endlessly denied by the very movement through which one tries to cushion it, to assimilate it, to interiorize and incorporate it. In this mourning work in process, in this interminable task, the ghost remains that which gives one the most to think about—and to do.[8]

The GHOST, ah yes, the ghost, this is what we are called upon to consider. It is only a trauma, perhaps the final, the most irresistible, with no means of cushion or assimilation. That we have no means of incorporation is perhaps demonstrated already—the persistence of Maximo Lopez, unmatched in our world, in his pursuit, and unintentional extermination of

The specter of Reils: the specter is the trauma, the trauma which acts to dominate the ego of humankind. It is this: we counter the *cosmological*—in short order, masters of the universe, space travel unbounded; we counter the *biological*—descended from animals, perhaps, but no longer animal, now eternal. We are GODS! It is an irresistible conclusion; we counter the *psychological*—well, we are so high on the first two, could we even acknowledge a third? But yes, some among us, and these scientists have reworked the genetic defining of humanity to exclude the worst aspects of our self-damaging behavior. If we are subject to the unconscious, it is only barely the case. So we have countered these traumas; and what does Reils do?

Reils is the trauma that given the offer of perfected and unending human life, *we do not want it!* It is so unpleasant to live with ourselves that we would actually prefer to die. He is only the first, certainly, the first of a Holy Spirit invited on this day of Pentecost; we are baptized in the name of our chosen death; *in nomine mori*, specifically my own.

This Holy Ghost indwelling, as we say, as is to be told, will now forever remain, an incorporated feature of our society, always haunting. Those that pronounce this ghost will be chased—where is undefined—even to acknowledge its presence is too much trauma. Haunting, haunting. It is the final stroke, the masterful disadjustment of the human calculation of predicament. But it will be denied that this ghost can ever have been, that its vocalizations ever formed a challenge, ever indicated a possible conviction. Nonetheless, this ghost persists; it will not return, it persists; it remains; in every chosen death, *Epi-phane*, the divine presence (revealed!) of our true God, the death we have always denied worshiping. With the death of Reils, the mass of humanity breathes a false sigh, and the illusion persists for them, that no one might ever again choose death, that the impenetrable dominion of life persists.

Wilbur Reils never wrote anything; eschewing literary possibility, his composition occurred *in re*, his literary masterpiece his fractured C1 via door sill. Possible to capture his argument otherwise…certainly not *le mot*. We will be quiet, hush, hush, and then a death—another death! Who would choose to die? How can this be? We live forever! We no longer fear death! But what if we never did? What if we always loved to die, to be rid of corpor-reality? Reils says yes, we have always loved to die, we have always been the Manichees, the Gnostics, the vegetarian Pythagoreans desiring release. Hush, hush, deny the death, I choose LIFE! I swear it.

And then the holy infusion, the imprint of the character, the operating grace becomes cooperating grace, the noose is tightened, the affairs ordered, and the liturgy has ended: Go in peace.

Following the progenitor of this speech, I will add this qualification: "the specter first of all sees us…it looks at us even before we see *it* or even before we see period. We feel ourselves observed, sometimes under surveillance by it even before any apparition." It comes in a moment, a sense, a touch. It is not truly present then, but only the sense—only our own manifestation in our own thought. One considers the universe, one passes the mausoleum—'what was this building before?' 'A hospital, I think'—one slips and falls, one remembers that they must shit. The universe, it regards me. The former, it regards the current, reminding the current that the former once was, and the current will become the former in due course.

In the prior age, the *memento mori* formed a medicinal practice; now it is concussive. Death haunts by its non-appearance. We experience its view, the gaze is cast, the sense possessed, and the specter, it may even appear before us, but not of necessity. It was a true thing once, and thus will always be a true thing. The death we avoided inevitably arrived, and the death we deny—haunting.

No one in civilization dies. The specter still haunts. Now Reils dies. He is the first. The first now. The first of this time. He is death. He was not haunted, he pursued and chose and desired. Now, however, he is the omnipresent ghost by the communication of idioms. His body, everywhere present, his body everywhere broken. His spinal-injury eyes watching, regarding, convincing: 'Make my ghost appear once more.'

To hear the name is to be concussed. A reminder: you are not satisfied with your existence. You will be Reils soon enough. It will only take one more event; hear it once more, and you will go; you are ready; "Reils."

And then the holy infusion, the imprint of the character, the operating grace becomes cooperating grace, the noose is tightened, the affairs ordered, and the liturgy has ended: Go in peace to your death. You have waited so long and now the time is given. You deserve it.

MEREDITH offers a "bing" and announces "Oliver Waters and Justinus Perriman."

"Tell them to go away."

The door opens anyway. Meredith has been worried about me.

Oliver and Justinus in matching green lamé dresses with fur bolero jackets and veiled fascinators step into the room. They walk over to me and stand me up, each grabbing a shoulder and hoisting me to my feet. I move to speak, to explain myself, but Oliver holds up a tissue and gestures to my nose. To blow it. I do so, and compose myself, and he snatches it back, disgusted, and throws it to the floor.

Justinus walks over to my closet and says "Tuxedo—the blue patterned one." My tuxedo kit pops out and he says, "dress." I follow his command, as he appears to be very upset, and I do not have any interest in disagreeing. He turns back to my closet. "And some clothes and a bag for the weekend." My overnight bag pops out.

"Much obliged," he says.

They turn to the door, now each locks his arm in mine, and we pace out into the world.

"They told us you were still in there and I couldn't believe it," says Justinus, finally composed enough to speak to me.

"We had to come and get you," says Oliver.

"Had to," follows Justinus.

"You look so dreadful right now," says Oliver. "You've been crying. Here, have a drink."

He hands me a glass of champagne.

"Cheers," he says, and clinks my glass.

I take a sip. We are in a transport pod driving out of the city. Snow has begun to fall lightly, unexpected in late November, but it is just dusting the streets. It will stick in the mountains.

"Where are we going?" I ask, recognizing the formality of our clothing. Oliver sits back and lights up a valcigarette in an old fashioned cigarette holder, takes a deep drag and sighs.

"It was supposed to be a theme party," says Justinus. He crosses his legs in his dress.

"And I ruined it for you?"

"Oh, no, of course not," says Oliver.

"Yes, actually, you did," says Justinus. Oliver smacks him on the knee, but Justinus is unfazed and sits up a little straighter in his chair. "You need to stop being so morose. Oliver and I have been thriving recently, and your little funk is bringing us down."

"I think…" I start.

"Not that you don't have reasons," interjects Justinus. "You have reasons, legitimate reasons. We're just going to coax you along."

"Fine. Where are the drugs?" I ask.

"In the camper," says Oliver.

"You got a camper?" I ask.

"There was going to be a party," says Oliver.

We ride for another half hour in silence. They do not know what else to say to me, beyond their magnanimous action of saving me from myself, so we simply sit and drink champagne, refilling each other's glasses. Justinus opens a new bottle half way through our trip, its festive noise providing us with a reflexive joy which quickly fades as we remember our collective discontent.

I feel the champagne warming me, warming my soul. I still would rather cry, and I still feel the knot in my throat, but I can hold it together. I really should be fine. I have lived long enough without them before.

We arrive at a massive building and the pod drives us in through the garage door where inside is found the camper. It is a ten meter long cabin-like pod sitting on top of two pairs of triangular tank treads, paneled in dark oak wood, with a sheen from a recent polishing, giving way to tinted windows arching over the top. A fold down staircase like the entrance to a shuttle sits open, beckoning us in. Justinus says nothing, but gestures for Oliver and me to make our way.

Oliver hikes his dress into his hand to mount the steps and I follow behind him. It is a generous cabin, about three times the size of my living room. There are couches lining the walls, which are all finely finished teak and brass and gold as a proper land yacht should, with white roping, navy cushions. A lavish spread of food and drink sits on the many small tables abutting the seating areas. There are five people in the room, three whom I do not recognize. Justinus enters the cabin behind me and explains.

"This is Fred, his wife Paula. You know Peter, this is his fiancé Nigel. And you know Cynthia."

"I do."

I shake hands with Fred and Paula. "Enchanted," I say. Fred is dressed in a white dinner jacket and bowtie, Paula in a dress that matches Oliver and Justinus, but she has a fur scarf instead of a bolero jacket. I make my way to Nigel, who claps his hands together excitedly.

"So great to meet you," he says. "Peter said I couldn't meet you at the funeral because you weren't being any fun."

"That's true, actually. I'm much improved now."

"Well, I've heard so much about you."

"I'll have to check your facts."

Nigel is a fluff of a human to Peter's cactus. I have learned quite a bit about Peter in this moment, I think. They stand together in emerald green tuxedos made out of some unidentifiably fancy and advanced material. Down to the placement of their glittering bomber scarves, they are matching.

Peter notices my once over of his outfit, and his eyes move slightly as if to say, "I'll explain later."

I move to greet Cynthia, who remains seated. "Evening." She is also in a long lamé dress. I apparently missed the notice on that one. Her hair is shorter, now, or perhaps just more curled and styled than it usually is. With her blonde twists she looks like a movie star from a long lost era.

"They told me you were depressed," she says.

"All lies," I say. "I'm my usual chipper self."

"That term never applies to you," she replies, "'Chipper.' Ha!"

"Good to see you," I say.

"It's good to see you, too," she says, standing now, she hugs me and gives me a quick kiss. "How are you?"

"A fucking mess," says Oliver. "He was still crying."

"I'm fine," I say. "Just give me the—"

Justinus tosses me a bag of pills. "Happy painkillers," he says.

"Thank you." I turn back to Cynthia who is offering me a concerned look. "See, I'm fine."

"I'll get you a drink," she says.

I sit down in Cynthia's spot and realize now that the door to the cabin has been closed and we are starting to move.

Oliver and Justinus are sitting at the other end on a couch next to each other. I shout to them. "Are we meeting the others there?" I say.

"No," says Oliver.

"Nobody else is coming?" I ask.

"No," says Justinus.

"I thought you said this was a party," I continue.

"We canceled it for you," says Oliver.

"Oh, thanks."

"But we kept the costumes," says Justinus.

The floor of the transport tilts back as we begin the climb through the woods, up a former ski slope to a lodge on the side of the mountain. The treads of the vehicle are self-leveling, up to a point; when the hills get a bit steeper, the lean comes through. Still, the ride is smooth as we slowly cruise over the uneven trails of the ski slope.

It used to be called Shawnee Peak, before it was renamed Meridius Mountain in 3300, after Jonas Meridius, one of the first men to colonize the planet Seven orbiting Proxima Centauri, and the first to die there. I have been here several times before, though never for skiing. If you can travel in thirty minutes—less time than it took to get here—to Antarctica or Switzerland, you will choose those places for your skiing and boarding, not the deficient snow of the northeast.

Peter and Nigel are snuggling in the corner. Fred and Paula have now joined Oliver and Justinus in conversation and drinking. They appear to be sniffing some sort of drug WHICH THEY SHOULD BE SHARING. But no, but no, I don't need anything else. Whatever they've already given me is enough, and I feel energized and a bit happier than the moment before, which takes me one step above desirous of immediate death. I notice Cynthia is still sitting next to me, stilly, keeping me company. It is a sweet gesture, and I am moved by it, as I would not have imagined her to have such a care within her repertoire. She is far too self-absorbed, isn't she? Far too broken inside to care for the broken?

"Are you enjoying yourself?" I ask.

"I am," she says, and offers a smile.

"Sitting in silence, all dressed up, with no party to go to?"

"The party has gotten smaller," she says, "but it has not gone away."

"I always find you so intriguing. So curious."

"Oh, you can speak now? Hold a conversation, perhaps?"

"Yes," I say, "sorry. I've been a bit morose. I'm not sure if you've heard the news…"

"I was at the funerals."

"Of course."

"And the deaths," she follows.

"Yes, me too."

"What more is there to say? It was a beautiful death for both of them. Beautifully performed. And you know they were ready…"

"I do," I say.

"I know nothing will satisfy right now," she continues, "but let's not talk about this anymore. I've been where you are, well almost. Talking will not help you, not talking will not help you, being with people, being alone, all *psshhh…*"

"Is that right?"

"It is," she says.

"So?"

"Time maybe? Either way, I would prefer if you would be enjoyable company for me tonight. You are off to a good start. You're very attractive, and you are charming when you are participating and not moping in the corner."

"I can do that. You look beautiful tonight, too."

"I know," she says, deadpan, then smiling with self-approval.

The transport flattens out and slows, and soon we arrive at our home for the weekend, a restored ski chalet from the days when people would still travel to this mountain. We pull up directly to the balcony and are lifted up to match the four meter height, stepping across to the giant log cabin sparkling with fresh snow and crowded by evergreens.

Polar bear heads and elk heads and moose heads. There were never any polar bears here, of course, but it certainly does set the tone. Nostalgia. Remember polar bears? Rustic charm. An actual fire burning in the fireplace! The smell of toasting wood and the faint tongue-feel of smoke greet us as we walk through the door, even with the fully automated and double-smoke collecting robotic fireplace.

"Your room is upstairs at the end of the hall," says Justinus.

I reach my room and set down my coat, and take a minute to make sure my closet packed appropriately. Then I sit down on the bed and sigh. Fucking Addison. And my baby girl. In one day. My seventy-five hundred year old child.

Cynthia peaks her head in: "No," she says. "Let's go."

I follow her out to the fireplace room.

I fetch the freshly opened bottle of wine from the countertop and pour Cynthia a glass. She smiles as I take my seat at one end of the table, across from Justinus.

"A toast to our hosts," I say, gesturing to Fred and Paula.

"Not at all," says Fred. "We're just happy we managed to get people to come here."

"Oh," says Cynthia, "this is lovely."

"It is," says Paula, "but Banff is nicer. Antarctica is nicer. Mt. Erebus is stunning this time of year." Fred looks annoyed. "I told him it was a stupid decision to purchase this place. I mean, we love it."

"We do love it," says Fred.

"But we saw a few lovely properties elsewhere."

"Well, I'm happy to be here," I say.

Paula begins, "I knew your wife—"

"No," says Justinus.

"No?"

"No discussions of the deceased. He's healing."

I smile demurely.

"Fair enough," offers Paula, pointedly. "What should we discuss?"

"They're decommissioning the Federation Cathedral next week."

"Is that right?" says Oliver.

"Yes, it's been quite controversial."

"Controversial?" asks Fred.

"They plan to use it as a death house," Cynthia continues, "and there are those who imagine that the priests and bishops would be offended if there were still any of them around."

"Are there any?" asks Paula.

"I don't think so," says Justinus. "I feel like I would have met one."

"There were some at Morris's funeral a few weeks ago," says Peter.

"I'm pretty sure they were all fake," I say.

"Oh," says Peter.

"But there are some real ones out there," I say, "Not a full time job anymore. But there are some still alive who are ordained, a fair number actually."

"You've studied this?" says Paula, impressed, but also confused as to why someone would have such knowledge.

"Yeah, a bit." I'm met by expectant faces when I say this—*why would anyone ever study this?* "During my last stint for the government. About a thousand years ago. They wanted me to examine the active religious institutions. We're not very institutional anymore."

"Agreed," says Oliver.

"For good reason," says Nigel.

"I heard," says Justinus, "from a very trusted source, that one of the genetic manipulations the UAG pioneered was to make us less tribally-minded."

"If that's true," I reply, "they never made it public. And I worked on it, so I think I would know. But it is a point of emphasis for the education system. To make us less tribal."

"But not less religious?" asks Paula.

"We're still religious at the same rate—in the sense that we still believe in all sorts of things. But the Pope thing really messed everyone up, organized religion wise, I think. I don't think any of you were alive for this, so let me tell it. The Catholic priesthood had been in decline for a few centuries by the time of the transition. After it, the situation grew dire—though they still wouldn't let women in. But it was one thing to give up sex for fifty or sixty years, it's another to live a celibate life for a thousand years, or forever. So the pope, after being a priest for two hundred years and pope for fifty years—this is like three hundred years after Reils—Pope John the 26th, kills himself. Just takes a government approved cocktail. Doesn't resign. Doesn't become Pope Emeritus first. Just straight up kills himself. He could have at least released an encyclical first explaining it, but no."

They're all listening to me. These details aren't common knowledge, though everyone knows the basic story. The history of the transition is generally covered in required courses at most all institutions of higher learning.

"After that, and the backlash, there weren't so many people wanting to become priests. It signaled an exodus—religious officials who participated in the transition quit en masse. They'd been priests or ministers or imams for four hundred years, and they were sick of it. And who would replace them? They saw the pressure placed on religious leaders and they saw the religious leaders rush to get away now that the seal was broken."

"They just wanted to be free," says Nigel.

"I think that's right," I say.

"That must have been something," says Cynthia. "When they all quit."

"Yeah," I continue. "They had a really hard time electing a pope after that, and then a while after that they changed policies, and there was no longer a pope. And they sold Vatican City."

"Amazing," says Peter.

"Did you know any of these people?" asks Fred.

"I did, actually. I knew one of the popes— he served like two hundred years after the Papalcide, and he was pope for thirty six years, and then quit everything. I met him, when was it, around the 6430s, living in Mexico City. He was married to three men, all engineers, and they manufactured dance club reality stages—the things that make the scenery change inside the club. Hugely successful. I don't know where he is now, but I think he died a few millennia back."

"What a life, though," says Paula. "To be pope, and then gay, and who knows what else in between."

"I don't think those have ever been exclusive," mutters Justinus.

"That is quite a life though. Quite a title," says Peter. "I wonder if his husbands called him 'your holiness.' 'Your holiness,' dinner is ready."

"Dinner is ready, actually," says Fred, and the table begins to distribute plates from the middle doors.

We all sit for a moment and watch as our plates glide across our table, dropping silverware and a napkin from their side as they reach their destinations in front of us. Filet mignon, heirloom potatoes, a side of confit leg of duck, figheads and Romanesco in sauce bercy.

"I just want to say," says Nigel, "that being religious is just too constricting. I can't blame all those priests, all those popes. I can't tell you how many different things I've tried, and I just can't be happy unless I'm free. Un-en-cum-bered."

"That's right," says Peter, patting him on the hand. The Peter I know is very much encumbered by rules and concerns, but I am glad he is in love.

"Totally agree," says Paula. Fred looks uncomfortable.

It was a funny thing to live through, I must admit, but I remember it so fondly. We acted so normally for so long, as if nothing had changed, and then everything changed. Reils kills himself and everything changes. Decades of constant societal upheaval and confusion. We ran around with our heads cut off for the next five hundred years until we got used to the idea of eternity. We got used to it, that is, or we killed ourselves, and then the world leveled off.

"I think," beginning my speech, though no one asked, "that it's not that religion is too constricting or has too many rules. The reason that organized religion decreased so dramatically, and that religious thinking has changed so dramatically, is that most everyone approached religion for its utility. They expected it to fulfill a basic need, which was to provide some degree of strength or logic to face the difficulties of the world. Do you get what I mean? It was, life is hard, how do I get through the day? How do I explain the sadness and suffering of the world? We get rid of death, and boom, there goes the biggest source of anxiety that there ever could be. And then we have these people living for centuries who never expected to do so, and instead of wanting to avoid death, they start to crave death—what does religion have to say about this? What does religion have to say about the creeping disease of boredom overtaking life until they find that nothing satisfies anymore and they want to fucking die? Religion gave purpose to a fucked up world; now there are no poor to feed, no needy to clothe, no one in prison to visit, no sick to cure. 'Those also serve who do but sit and wait' and all, but nobody ever really believed that. The way religion was practiced by the masses, it had nothing to say to help them, even most of those priests, even that pope. It was like: 'life is a gift, life is a treasure, and certainly never take your own life.' But then when you die inside, to keep on living is nothing but constant torture."

"So," says Nigel, "the reason that I don't like religion is that I have no use for it?"

"Well, do you?" I ask.

"What would it do?" follows Cynthia.

"Yeah, well, there are more reasons for joining religion than its utility. But I've always thought that the effectiveness of religion is in the perspective that would enable us to keep on living without constant pain."

"How's that working out for you?" says Justinus.

Oliver grimaces: "That was in poor taste, even to me," he says.

"Apologies," says Justinus. "But the question stands."

I smile at the impertinence of his query, but it is a fair point. "I acknowledge I'm in terrible pain. That I have spent the past week alone crying and generally feeling screwed by the universe. And that I have since rallied enough to sit here, aided by narcotics, and enjoy a delicious dinner with a lovely crew, all of you. And I'm a mess, and I'm seriously questioning whether I want to live or not, but I don't even believe myself when I feel that way right now."

"So, religion is helping you not die?" says Justinus, with genuine interest now.

"I wouldn't say it like that," I reply. "It's just what Peter said to me earlier—"

"—oh gosh—" says Peter.

"—was right. He's right. I'm feeling sorry for myself, but I don't really have any reason to do that. It's not like this was a curse sent upon me by a malicious God or universe. Just a passing thing, and not a real reason for me to give up."

"It doesn't matter to you?" says Cynthia, offended.

"No, it does, I'm a mess. But I just don't think of it as a real reason to kill myself. Do you think I should give up?"

"No," she says. "I guess not."

"So if it isn't that—isn't a reason to quit—then what else can I do but live?"

We finish dinner, and the table has now distributed digestifs. Fred is passing around a small mirror of synthetic cocaine with a golden straw. Addison used to love cocaine. I bet Helen did, too, during her fashion days. I miss Addison. She used to love parties like this, just people chatting, saying smart and witty things to each other. I think of her for a moment and remember it has not been long since she died. Since they died. I know enough about mourning not to make myself feel guilty for having distracted myself and gone about life these past few hours. One ought not spend the entire day crying, even if one would prefer to.

Justinus takes a bump. “Oof,” he says, “good stuff. What are we going to do tonight?”

“Now that there’s no party,” says Oliver.

“I knew you’d come around,” Justinus replies.

Nigel speaks up. “I don’t know about what to do, but since there’s no party, do you think I could change?”

I’m confused as to what exactly he might mean and I look to Cynthia. She knows I don’t know and rolls her eyes.

Paula follows: “Me too!”

“Count me in,” says Fred.

“Sure, why not?” says Justinus.

Nigel runs upstairs; Fred and Paula follow in a more measured manner.

“What is this about? He really doesn’t like suits?” I ask Peter.

Peter laughs. “No, not really. He’s an animorph.”

“Isn’t that…” I begin.

“Yeah, it’s illegal,” says Peter. “But only in cities. And certain areas. You can do it most of the time elsewhere.”

“Like here,” says Cynthia.

“So…what is he?”

On the couch next to me is a sheep. Peter has his arm around the sheep, who is quite fuzzy and fluffy, and generally a pretty sheep with a pink bow. She is also an exceptionally large sheep. Sitting a bit awkwardly on the opposite couch is a llama, and next to the llama is a gorilla. Justinus is leaning on the llama, resting his head a bit, and petting the llama every once in a while. Oliver and Cynthia sit in chairs alone, without the joy of an animal next to them.

I knew this technology was popular in some sub-circles, but I had yet to meet anyone in those circles, and never suspected that I would. Maintaining the novelty of sex is difficult, especially when one has lived for a thousand years with free love constantly on offer; thus, some have to resort to things considered ‘different’ to keep interest up.

I have a glass of milk-plus in front of me. Not like the original, this one has a synthetic heroin which will knock me unconscious in short order and allow me to sleep a sound and expansive sleep for the first time in weeks. The rest of the crew has turned down my offer, but all have acknowledged the wisdom in selection of intoxicant given my mental state. There isn't much better for misery than to completely remove one's sense of time, space, and order; the complication in waking up to the same reality remains, but that will be tomorrow. That is an issue for then, and I will play with this solution for now.

"How's your milk?" says Llama/Fred. The llama lips move like people lips.

"Really tasty, actually. I feel good."

"You sure you don't want any of these?" he replies.

"No, I think it's too late for me now, anyway." I do not know specifically what those pills are that he gestured at, but I have the sense that things will become quite odd in this room in short order. Given the way that Justinus is petting the talking Llama, I would guess that he's just taken a combination of upper, ecstatic, and aphrodisiac, which will all kick in sometime in the next two hours, and at which point, very fuzzy sex will occur.

I believe Cynthia is thinking the same thing.

"You have to explain to me," she says, "how these things work? I can pet the llama, and he feels like a llama, but he's still Fred."

"That's right," says Gorilla/Paula. "It's a force hologram, just like most home porn, but these are wearable units, not attached to VR rooms. They're really amazing."

"And expensive," chimes Nigel/Sheep.

"But *so* worth it," says Peter. It's the most sexually forward thing I've ever heard him say.

"So," Cynthia continues, "what if I put my finger in the llama's mouth?"

"Try it," says Fred.

"It's not like your ass, though, right?"

The llama remains silent, mouth agape.

"Fine," she tries it. "Ew, it's like a real mouth, all wet. But oh, no spit. It just feels like that. So weird. Was that your mouth?"

"I feel it in my mouth, but it's not all the way up there."

"Now try the llama's ass!" Sheep/Nigel shouts. "Bet you've never done that before."

I take a deep sip of my milk plus.

Justinus catches me. "What a prude you are, Warren. I had no idea."

Cynthia stands and places herself in my lap. "He's just saving himself for me," she says proudly.

"That's right," I say, a bit dizzy now. I'm almost sure that my eyes are not quite focusing, but I'm still here. I just feel light. High. She rubs my chest and I smile at her, and she makes a subtle wink with her eyes and my gears click together and I realize she means she'd like to get out of here before the animals start to mount each other.

"Grab my milk," I say. "We're going upstairs."

I stand up and drop Cynthia to her feet.

"That's the ticket," says Justinus. "Fuck him senseless."

"Good evening," says the llama.

"Have fun, you two," says the gorilla.

We make our way upstairs, Cynthia leading me by the hand. We reach the bedroom and she says "strip," so I do.

"You don't need to sleep with me tonight," I say, "just because I'm having a rough week."

"Rough year?"

"Yeah, that's it."

"We're not having sex. You're about to pass out."

"Maybe," I say. "I could have sex though."

"Just take your socks off and get into bed."

I do as I'm told. She sits at the edge of the bed next to me. We hear someone run upstairs and run back down, followed by some animal noises.

"I don't even want to know what they're doing to each other," Cynthia says, looking horrified.

"I know what's going to happen," I say, smiling dumbly.

"Look, tomorrow you'll tell them that we had sex and feel asleep together, okay?"

I nod.

"Drink another sip," she says.

"You are good to me," I say.

"I am," she says, and kisses me on the forehead. "Sleep now. You deserve it."

My vision blurs...

THE sun is peaking through the curtains and drawing lines across my body, the warmth touching my face. I roll over momentarily, but then acknowledge that I am awake, and then I remember why I slept so soundly and why I needed to.

Those jerks. Leaving me here. Such an inconvenient time for them to die. I could use a drink, I think, but not really. I don't really want to drink the entire day, or spend the day in a thick haze. The nights are fine for that, but not all day. I'll go make some coffee, try to hold off on drinking until at least after breakfast.

I shift in the bed and it releases a hint of perfume. Cynthia. Gone now, I remember her tucking me in last night. I walk down the stairs and in the living room there is a grizzly bear lying on the couch, snoring loudly. I see her standing in the kitchen, staring out the window.

"Good morning," I say.

"Morning," she starts as she notices me, but composes herself. "It's beautiful out there."

I stand next to her. "So it is." I look around the vintage countertop and locate an input.

"There's a grizzly bear in there."

"Justinus," she says. "They had a couple of extra morph belt things."

"I need some coffee."

"You'll have to do it yourself."

"Really?"

"Yeah, it won't make coffee. There's a machine over there."

"Oh. You want any?"

"I'm partial to methee."

"I still can't believe they called it that."

"Well, it's a little more of a boost than coffee."

"True."

I walk over to the machine and attempt to figure it out. Turns out it only requires the push of a button, which is still more than I'm used to. Cynthia gives in and requests a latte when I tell her it's automatic.

We stand for a moment in the kitchen, sipping our coffees and looking at each other.

"Let's go for a walk," I say.

"A walk?"

"Of course."

"Fine," she says. "I'll get my boots."

"I'll take Fred's."

We step down from the deck. It is back above freezing, the sun is low in the sky, but shining strongly, brightly, and the drip-drip-drip of spring is sounding in this late fall. The shallow snow will not last much longer, but while it does, the scenery is rather stunning.

"Are you feeling better today?" she asks.

"Yes, I think so. It's good for me to have some distraction."

"And a heavy dose of milkplus."

"I don't think I would have slept otherwise."

"True."

"I'm okay. Another day to make it through, you know. And you? You seem your usual withdrawn self."

"Oh thank you, so nice of you to suggest."

"You always look gorgeous, of course."

"I know what you mean."

"Traumatized by the animal sex?"

"Oh, God," she says. "No, it's fine, but also no thank you."

"You didn't want to get in on that?"

"Did I want to get in on that? No, I am not having sex with animals. That whole thing…too fuzzy for me."

"Did we?"

"No, you were asleep. And I'm not a rapist."

I smile. "You did help me last night," I say. "So, thank you. I can listen to you now, today. You can explain your dourness."

"No, thanks."

We blaze a path through the two inch deep melting snow, elbows locked down the slope to a flat section populated by a grove of trees. I find a boulder and hand her my coffee before hoisting myself up and standing in dominion over my prey.

"Impressive," she says with no coloring.

"I am king," I say.

"Of what?" she laughs. "Anything in particular?"

"No, nothing at all, really."

"The king of nothing."

"Nothing!"

"Of course." She sighs and looks around.

"What keeps you interested?" I ask her. "I can keep you focused on me for about ten seconds before you leave again. Where are you heading off to?"

"You are really prying today, aren't you?"

"Aren't you interesting, though? Who can blame me?"

"I can."

"And do."

"I do," she continues.

"So?"

"No!" she says, and walks away.

I'm momentarily concerned but she looks back to make sure that I am following her. At the end of the grove there is a small wooden structure, a lookout point of some kind. She walks up the short flight of steps and I follow her there.

She stands at the edge, again staring off into the distance.

"You know," I say, "when I was up on one of these with Justinus a few weeks ago, he jumped off."

"I thought that was a cliff," she replies.

"Well, this is still a ways down."

It is something of a cliff. We are about ten meters off the ground, overlooking the beginning of a particularly steep ski slope. We see the lake at the foot of the hill, and the trees stretching out for miles after that. No real signs of civilization to speak of, other than the bit of a structure we stand on.

"Why did he do that?"

"We were talking philosophy."

"Oof," she says. "I'd jump, too."

"How do you know you wouldn't like a little Kierkegaard?"

"I know. I went to college, too."

"Yeah, yeah."

"But why did he jump?"

"I was just explaining anxiety to him. The feeling you get when you are standing on the edge and have the inclination to jump. The dizziness of that power."

"And?"

"And he wanted to show himself powerful. So he chose to jump. I'm pretty sure he expected a drone to catch him, not wait for him to hit the rocks and the water below."

"Ha! Justinus…"

"I know."

"I usually want to jump," she says. "But today I don't."

"Well, I'd really prefer if you wouldn't."

"I know. Because you like me."

"I do."

She turns to me. "I do know what you're going through," she says.

"I guessed as much."

"You are handling this better than I did, though."

"Really? I've been laying on the floor of my apartment in darkness and silence for a week. Still feel like doing that. I've been moping for weeks leading up to this, since it wasn't a surprise. Justinus and Oliver don't want to hang out with me anymore."

"They brought you here."

"They did. Reluctantly."

"Justinus loves you, stop being silly."

"He does kind of, doesn't he?" She nods. "Well, I am deeply entertained by him."

"Do you need any drugs this morning?" she asks.

I'm not sure where the question came from, but no, I'm good. I shake my head. She turns and walks down the steps from the lookout point.

"Where are we heading?" I say.

"Back to the deck. I want to sit down."

We walk quietly back to the house, where there's a bench.

"I'm jealous of you," she says. "You've pulled yourself together already. You're strong enough to be nice to people."

"I wouldn't say that."

"When my husband died, I couldn't see anyone. I punched my best friend in the face when she tried to take me on a vacation. Six months after he died."

We're walking up the hill from the grove back to the house, the snow now all slushy in the morning sun, the grass poking through. The way is treacherous, and we hold on to each other.

"Well, I'm sure she forgave you."

"No," says Cynthia. "Nope."

"So what happened?"

"Not much to say. We were married for a hundred and thirty-six years. And then, one day, he divorced me. I came home, and he looked me straight in the eyes, and he said, 'I don't want to be married to you anymore.' Caught me completely off guard."

She sits on the bench.

"I remember the same thing happened to me with my sixth wife," I respond. "Well, she left a note, actually, and an interactive program with her recorded explanations. So I just sat in the kitchen debating with a computer program until I came to terms with the fact that I wasn't actually speaking with her and she was gone."

I sit next to her.

"That's awful," she says.

"But you were saying," I offer.

"Yeah, so he divorced me. And he left that day, and I was devastated. I just had such an attachment to him, and I don't know how long the longest marriage ever..."

"...something like seven thousand years..."

"...but I didn't think he was ready yet. Wait, holy shit, seven thousand years? Yeah, we weren't going to last seven thousand years, but I felt that way at the time. I didn't want anything different and then he left."

"What a loser," I say, supportively.

"Right? And then he killed himself."

"What? Just then?"

"No. It was like three months later. I guess he told his friends he waited until he thought I was over him. Waited until I had moved on. I had a one night stand with some random person just trying to feel normal again and that was his go-ahead, go-ahead and kill yourself. Like I had given him permission."

"Not at all. Not your fault."

"I know, whatever, his fault."

"How'd he do it?"

"He didn't tell anyone he was going to do it. Like your wife. It's so much worse that way, when you don't make a show of it. You've got to make a show of it, it makes it just that little bit easier for anyone who isn't ready to let go. He just did it in his country house, in the tub. Slit his wrists and then took a hot bath. It was just weird."

"That's the way Seneca went."

"Who the shit is Seneca?"

"A philosopher."

"What the fuck?!"

"Maybe it was a reference," I offer. "Though, I don't get it."

"Well, I didn't get it either. He could have at least said 'Seneca.' But, what would I get, anyway, the only question was with me or not with me.

Nothing he would say would make me happy again. We were in love and married and full and then he was gone from me and then he was gone from the world."

"Absence."

"No, he isn't just gone. He broke things when he left. Fragmented."

"You're not broken," I say to her.

"I am. I was on anti-depressants for like forty years. I've stopped now. I don't think they were doing anything."

"And now?"

"And now, I don't know. Like I said, most days I want to jump. Not anxiety though, I just want to die, I think."

"Well, don't."

"Yeah, fine." She thinks for a moment. "But what you said last night, that you might feel like you want to die but you know that you don't really want to. I think that's what I feel most of the time."

"Life is complicated."

"It is. We are such weird things, aren't we?"

"What do you mean?" I say.

"That we have these beautiful lives and then so many of us don't want them anymore. I mean, I have everything I could ever really want. Except my husband. But what's that? I'm still here. I was happy with myself beforehand, why not after?"

"I'm sure you can find something again."

I put my arm around her and she leans into me, her head on my shoulder.

"I don't get it," she says. She sighs heavily, and puts both of her hands onto my leg, clutching it. It is not suggestive, only to be close. "It was good to say that to you. I think I've said it before, but not to someone who actually understood what I meant."

"I do know what you mean."

She looks up with a flurry of compassion, straight into my eyes. "You do." She kisses me on the lips. "You're going through it now." She realizes she just kissed me, and that the timing is perhaps inappropriate. "I'm sorry," she says, as she turns away.

"It's okay," I say. I wrap my other arm around her, and I'm clutching her to my chest now. She is peacefully held, breathing deeply, softly, allowing me to feel better for the moment. I'm struck then by a desire to have her. Perhaps it's been too long since I last slept with anyone, but I have no power to resist now. I place my hand under her chin, and tilt her head up, and she looks at me once more, her eyes full of affection. She closes them and I kiss her; she responds zealously.

"Let's go inside," I say.

"Okay."

We head upstairs.

Cynthia and I have spent the morning in bed. Sharing her story of her husband apparently triggered something in her, an aphrodisiac. To be honest, it worked on me, as well. Having her give something like that—especially when I could understand so much of what she was going through—it opened me up, left me raw and together we helped each other.

It is later in the morning now, and much activity has happened in the house below us. I lean over and kiss her, and she is roused from her sleep.

"Hi, there," she says.

"How are you?" I say.

"Good," she says. "You?"

"Good."

She smiles. "What time is it?"

"Eleven."

"Oh, no, I should get up." She rolls over and kisses me quickly. "I need a shower."

"Should I join you?"

"No. Save some for later. Go and be social, it's good for you."

"Kiss me again."

She kisses me, but bounds quickly away. I watch her spring lithely away, her figure lingering in my mind. I lie back down on the bed and realize that I'm smiling like an idiot. I should get up.

I find Peter in the living room alone.

"Peter, what a day! Sun is shining!"

"You're smiling!"

"For the moment, yes, I am."

"The post-coital smile. Irresistible."

"Well, what can we say about you, sharing my joy with a smile of your own?" I continue. "Post sheep-fucking high?"

His smile vanishes. "Oh, quiet down."

"What? Is the menagerie nearby?"

"No, they're all off hiking."

"So, what's the deal? Is he always a sheep?"

"I like him that way. And he likes it that way. It works."

"How did you even meet? How did you find out you liked that?"

"Justinus knows people." He looks at me, and then leans in to announce we will be having a particularly serious exchange. "And—okay, time for honest conversation here—you've been around for a lot longer than I have. Why aren't you seeking out animals for sex?"

"What?"

"How have you not gone through the strangest pornography and sexuality possible?"

"Who's to say I haven't?"

"Are you marrying a sheep? No, I'm the one marrying a sheep."

"That you are."

"Before I even left home, I'm hiding in my room from my parents, coming up with the craziest sexual scenarios. Just weird things."

"Yeah, well, I was like twelve hundred years old when they invented the VR masturbation room. And it was a thousand years after that when they did the full-on force hologram."

"I grew up with that. So what did you do?"

"I mean, I had a sex robot. I think everyone still has a sex robot somewhere."

"Yeah," Peter agrees.

"Can I just say how much I am enjoying this conversation? I didn't even know you liked sex."

"I do," he nods, reddening a bit.

"With holographic sheep!" I add.

"You do need to be mature about this."

"I do," I say, "I will be."

"So, you were explaining how you have avoided my situation…"

"Oh, right. So, it was actually Jen Holt, she was a friend of mine who studied masturbation, along with other things. But she did a study on pornography use, and she was like, 'The *things* I have seen…what you need to do is to find a way to remain satisfied with the things that you once found satisfactory. I don't know how you do that, but you need to do that.' So it's just like you need to remember that you found it interesting, and maintain the interest you have in it. A life practice, actually."

"Well, that hasn't worked for me."

"I mean, I've done different things."

"Not sheep, though."

I hold a straight face for a moment before I crack. "I'm sorry," I say, "maturity." He's right though, I have not moved on to animals. When Jen did her study, she was not young, but she was apparently innocent. She asked to quit twice, and asked two of us on the committee with her to take over her study, despite the fact that we had no expertise in studies of any sort, which she did. What she discovered was that those who chronically used pornography felt the need to alternate interests as they aged, which has long been known to be true. But three hundred years into a habit of inventive pornographic consumption and the choices of what to engage in sexual congress with become more and more erratic. At that moment in history, even without a completely developed interactive form of pornography, visualization-animation processes were quite exceptional, such that if one could picture it in their mind, a movie could be formed and watched from the comfort of one's own home. Jen had the unfortunate pleasure of watching and summarizing these films, at least until she was able to recruit the hundreds of interns necessary to write descriptions for her.

The end of creativity strikes eventually. After visualizing and participating in a one-hundred dancing clock orgy, where the movement of the minute hand into an orifice in time by each participant is the fetish and orgasmic trigger, where does one go? Tables, trees, animals, imagined aliens, scaled down buildings, all these things after the more standard fare of midgets, amputees, BBW [all vintage or imagined, none of these exist anymore] urination, enema, the full variety of BDSMs, peggings, through every race, and creed, down to the beginning of a woman or a man by themselves, perhaps fully clothed, smiling suggestively.

The cure is to not use any devices anymore, but to engage in actual sex with people, a task which isn't theoretically a challenge, with everyone being relatively beautiful and no fear of disease or pregnancy. If not this, as some beautiful people are still awkward in conversation, then one must turn to their sex robot, and only engage in vanilla sex until one finds a way to make it pleasurable once more.

Jen's recommendations and practical cures were not born from an inclination to inhibit the wide range of human sexuality, but the unfortunate realization that if a person loses the ability to find pleasure in sexual activity—the inevitable outcome of the track outlined above—they desire death. Sexual desire is such an intrinsic piece of humanity, and lacking the ability to at least temporarily satiate this desire leads to a desire to leave the world. If you have a strong sexual desire but there is nothing that can meet it, it leads only to disaster. This is why I mock Peter, but I do not condemn him; more to the point, I am concerned about him. I hope he has found something that will satisfy him for a long time.

"I know it's ridiculous, but I don't care. The sex is incredible, and he's hilarious. He's hilarious as a sheep. And so cute. And I've heard of stranger things. Stranger ways of getting married."

"Hey, Oliver sat in a ball for a hundred years. Some people don't ever leave their house, just do their sex robots or hologram porn all day. You, you at least made it to the..."

"Don't—"

"...farm. Couldn't help it. I'm happy for you."

"Good."

"So...Justinus was a bear last night."

"Yeah, you missed out."

"I guess I did."

"I'm glad you're here," says Peter, "and I'm glad that you'll be at my wedding."

"I wouldn't miss it."

A bit later in the afternoon when everyone has finished a brief nap and the snow has melted, Fred summons us to lunch. As we sit at the table, I look around and notice the strange silence and realize they are up to something. I eye Justinus, and he avoids my gaze and begins to speak with great weight: "Oliver thinks we would all share about someone we've lost. He believes that it will help with the healing process for our dear friend Warren."

"I do," Oliver follows.

Paula grimaces and I continue to offer a questioning face to Justinus who continues to avoid me.

Fred begins to speak: "My ex-wife, before Paula here—"

"Stop," I say. "I don't want to hear this."

"No?" says Oliver.

"I thought it was a bad idea," says Justinus.

"Look, there's no need to do this. I don't want to bother you all with anything. I've got people I trust that I can speak with and who can help me through everything. No need to bring down a nice vacation weekend away."

"You don't trust us?" asks Oliver.

"That's not what I was saying," I reply.

"I agree, I think this would be terribly awkward," says Cynthia.

"I just feel better having some normalcy, some casual conversation about Michelangelo, you know the sort," I continue. "No need for anything serious now—I'm in that place emotionally where if someone offers something they think will relate I'll simply reject it out of hand as totally different from my experience and continue in a spiral of self-congratulatory pain Olympics."

"Pain Olympics?" asks Justinus.

"I'll explain later. Quick, someone, give us a topic."

"Religion?"

"No, we just talked about that."

"Politics then. Have you seen the finalists for minister of space?"

"I have. They're all incompetent," says Cynthia.

"Is that right?" says Oliver.

"Absolutely," Cynthia continues. "Complete amateurs. They can't find anyone qualified who wants the position because it does actually involve a tremendous amount of responsibility."

"It only seems like it has responsibility since the last minister fucked up so terribly," says Paula sharply.

"I don't think it was his fault," Cynthia replies.

"What happened?" I ask.

"Where were you?" says Justinus. "They lost the megacruiser heading to Cadmus 1. Nobody died, but it happened because they followed the new route recommendations from the minister."

"When was this?" I'm surprised I missed news of this magnitude.

"Last March," says Peter. "When your wife killed herself."

The room is silent. Peter has been sitting there peacefully, quietly, but also without satisfaction. I imagine he agreed with Oliver, and that he thinks I should be doing more sharing, more processing, revealing my pain instead of doing things in the way I'd prefer to be doing them.

"Ah, yes," I say. "I didn't watch much news or speak to anyone for a while around then."

"Want to talk about it?"

"Oliver!" Cynthia objects.

"No, not really."

Lunch pops up from the table and our plates are distributed. Sandwiches of some kind. I take a look and decide upon an approach vector and then begin to eat lunch.

"Delicious," I say.

Peter shakes his head and follows suit.

It is a quiet lunch.

As soon as I am finished, I excuse myself and step out to the back deck. Justinus follows me out.

"Sorry about that," he says.

"It's fine. You just want to help."

"We do."

"I just don't want that kind of help."

"Sure."

"You've done enough bringing me out here, making me be social. I am really doing all right. I'm still pissed—if you want to hear me share, here you go—I'm still so angry at Addison and at Helen, too, but I get it, they're dead, nothing I can do about, nowhere to direct my anger so I might as well let it go."

"Good."

"And you've put Cynthia on me, and she's wonderful, and she's been through something like me, too, so we can talk to each other."

"Yeah, she's a bit of a mess," he says. "But a good mess for you right now. You can help each other out."

"That's right."

"We do care about you," he says.

"I know you do."

We turn upon hearing a window creaking open on the second floor. Cynthia leans out and says, "come and visit me upstairs."

"Okay," I say.

"Can I come too?" asks Justinus.

"No," she says.

"Sorry, bud."

I walk upstairs and find Cynthia in a little one piece swimsuit holding up a pair of trunks for me.

"Where did you get those?"

"They were in a drawer in my room."

"And where are we swimming?"

"There's a hot tub here, apparently," she says. "On the upstairs patio."

"A hot tub?"

"I think it's like a massage pool, but older."

"Oh."

"Supposed to be romantic," she continues.

We walk into the room with the hot tub, and it does look precisely like a massage pool but without the established chairs. The entire room is a strange setting—red clay tile with gray grout and wood paneling on the walls—wainscotting?—and a distinctly dingy feeling.

I shrug to Cynthia and step into the still water and nothing happens.

"Is there a switch or something?"

"I don't know," she says. "Settle in, I'll find it."

The water is rather hot, and I suppose this is pleasant enough, though the seating is not particularly comfortable and nothing is happening. I spot a small white nob with no markings on it of any kind. Cynthia is still looking along the walls for a switch and barking commands at whatever might be inclined to listen: "On"; "Bubbles"; "Hot tub."

I decide to crank the nob out of curiosity. Immediately there is a tremendous hum and a vibration throughout the room. Cynthia looks to me with a what-have-you-done face but then smiles as the still water of the tub turns frothy.

"You figured it out!"

"I did," I say.

There is now water shooting out of jets in all directions in the tub. None of them are aligned to any particular cause, it seems, and they do not do much of anything but move the water around.

Cynthia steps in and floats over, aligning herself across my lap. She kisses me and then turns.

"This is awful."

"It really is."

"I'm just being battered. They don't massage at all."

"Yeah, I don't get this." Let me turn it down a bit.

"That's better," she says. We resume kissing.

"You found the hot tub," says Fred, in a startling appearance.

"I hate this thing," says Paula.

"Oh yes," I say. "I hope you don't mind."

"Not at all," says Fred. "Thing makes a racket though."

He's dropping his pants. As is Paula. They strip naked and step into the hot tub with us sending the water level up to the top.

"Crank that thing," says Fred.

Cynthia and I exchange a confused look. I turn the nob all the way up and the water froths and the hum turns into a noisy breathy moan.

"I bought this ten years ago. It's an original, refurbished from the 1970s. That's older than even you, I think."

"That's right," I say.

"I love it," Fred continues. "I feel such a connection to the past—like I was lounging in the American Empire, enjoying the fruits of my labors."

"Not this again," says Paula.

"I'm at the height of comfort, and meanwhile war, famine, disease, oppression, everything surrounding me, and I am sitting on the edge of a ski slope in this noisy contraption draining away the stresses of the world. How fantastic is that. "

"Pretty morbid," I say.

"Yeah," says Cynthia.

"That's what makes it great," says Fred.

He leans back and settles in.

"I know you two were making out," says Paula. "So feel free to continue. We're not even here."

Cynthia smiles and takes a seat next to me. She is not an exhibitionist, and the mood has certainly passed.

After extracting ourselves from the hot tub, after a quiet dinner apart from the animals who confirmed they could be animals in the water, we have shared a bottle of wine in front of the fire and now, when we are both a little drunk, it is time for bed. I invite her into my room.

As we lay in bed, she looks over to me and asks, "What do you think of me?"

"Dangerous question."

"Yeah. I'd still like to know."

"No avoiding it then." I hoist myself up onto an elbow. "I've found you intriguing. I find your casual malaise particularly enticing, for better or worse."

"Have all of your wives been malaisical?"

"Is that a word?"

"I'm sure it's not."

"No. Addison was not like that. She was ambitious and corporate and I suppose she would be conformist. She was never skeptical of life in that way."

"I am skeptical of life?" she asks, genuinely curious.

"Aren't you?"

"I don't know what that would mean."

"Eh, fair enough. When I first saw you, you were studying your lapels for food or for their shine or something."

"In my tuxedo..."

"Yeah. Standing by yourself at a big party. There were people around you but you did not care about them."

"Those people suck."

"See, Addison would never say something like that."

"Oh."

"It's great. We were talking about how I was attracted to this. And Addison is dead."

"Yeah, your wife is dead."

"And your husband."

"And my husband. Actually, my first two husbands are, too. But I didn't give a fuck about them after we split."

"Same for my first two."

"I think it might take a thousand years to actually figure out who you are," she says, hopefully.

I laugh at the suggestion. "That seems right," I say, because I think it's what she wants to hear, even when I know she doesn't believe it. We both know that you never know yourself because you are always changing and always acted upon by the world. There's no true self to get to know, just an ever shifting locus of thought and activity. I don't know what to expect from myself after ten thousand years.

She leans over and kisses me. "Are you really doing okay?" she asks.

"I am," I say, only half lying now.

"I want to spend more time with you."

"Okay."

"I feel good with you," she says. "I haven't felt good like this in a while."

"Haven't met the right person, then."

"You are very compelling. And you know that about yourself."

"Is that how you would describe me? Since we're being honest and describing each other honestly?"

"Dangerous question, right?"

"I can handle it."

"You can't even pretend to be insecure. My opinion of you doesn't really matter to you; besides, you know that I like you, and you know all the reasons why I like you, and part of it is that you are so confident that I will like you that I simply must."

"That sounds right."

"But I don't believe that you're really all right."

"Well, not completely."

"I want to see you get that back."

"You're going to help me?"

"I want you to get over your wives and your daughter and be all that I think you are."

"I want that, too."

She nestles herself into my arms, the little spoon. I hold her.

"I still need to brush my teeth," she says. "We can't sleep yet."

"Okay," I say. "But I'm very comfortable."

"Can we spend more time together? I really mean it. I don't want a day without you."

"I mean it, too. I would like it. Every day, let's be together."

"Okay," she says.

Chapter 3

Sun is streaming in. I forgot to shut the blinds all the way, and Meredith did nothing to help. I remember why I didn't remember, and she is sleeping next to me. She stirs, looks up, and smiles. We kiss deeply, and I slide closer beside her.

"We finally got to sleep," she says.

"We did," I say.

I clutch her for a moment and then lie back, my arm still under her.

"You have such a stupid smile on your face," she says.

"I know."

"Are you in love with me already?" she asks.

"I'll deny it.

"You will?"

"No, I'm totally in love with you."

"It's been a week."

"It's been a good week."

She pauses. "It has."

She nestles in.

I'm in the kitchen, waiting for my countertop to produce the batter for my French toast that I will prepare for Cynthia this morning. I will cook for her because I feel she needs a special gesture. She is starting her new job today. The first time she has worked in four decades.

She steps out of the bedroom wearing only her techsilk bodysuit, her brief hair pulled up tightly into a miniature pony. She spots me, and skips on by and jumps into my arms and I hold her.

"How's my love?" I say.

"So good," she says.

"Me, too."

"You're cooking?"

"It's your first day."

"Oh, sweet of you," she says. "I'm actually nervous."

"No you're not," I reply.

"No," she says. "I don't care. I have you."

"There she is."

She comes down out of my arms and walks over to the counter to request her morning Methee. Her to-go mug pops up from the counter, and she pats the counter and mouths "thank you."

"But I am actually excited," she says. "I'm excited to do this again."

"I'm happy for you," I say. "Maybe I should start working again, too."

"You're writing, aren't you?"

"Slowly."

"Well, finish that. Then I can get you a job teaching with me, and we can get dressed together each morning."

She's guest lecturing at the Manhattan University of Ongoing Education. "On the history of interplanetary travel with specific attention to the intricacies of psychological and sociological considerations undertaken in the 9th and 10th millennia, now standard on such spacecraft." In a past life, Cynthia was one of the best known historians of psychology, she tells me, and has had a standing offer to teach one of these courses for the past four hundred years. Now she's ready to take it on.

She disappears with her coffee into the closet, and emerges wearing a skirt and blazer over her bodysuit. Tweed. Noisy.

"Do I look professional?"

"You look exceptionally professional," I reply. "And professorial."

"Exceptionally," she says.

She kisses me once more and we hug and she heads out to the door off to the shuttle and I feel a sudden emptiness.

I've come down to the city as we've decided to spend the weekend in Manhattan. We're seeing the new Muhammad Malcolm film, premiering this week.

The film is a revelation. It is sheer beauty.

"I worship the Goddess of Love," I say.

"What are you talking about?"

"This movie. I'm inspired at the moment."

"You are all swept up."

"You aren't?"

"I can see it," she says, "see the sweeping…you know what I mean. I know you can. We've done this before."

"Sure, but right now it doesn't feel like I've done it before," I reply. "And I think that's what makes this whole thing amazing."

"Oh?"

"I feel alive. You feel alive, don't you?"

"Actually yes."

"And it's because we love each other, right?"

"True."

"It just feels so simple right now. I forgot it."

"You forgot to love? What a romantic you are."

"I know."

She pauses us as we walk, scooching us to the edge of the street.

"Don't make a mistake," she says, with gravity.

"With you?"

"Yes. No. It's the last thing I want."

"I know the risk," I say. "We must always take the risk."

"That's such a stupid thing to say."

"Too dramatic?"

"Yes."

"Are you planning to abandon me?"

She has little tears in her eyes. "No!" she says.

"Well, good then."

"But that's not the way this works, you know that. It ends, it fucking ends. They don't show the end in the movie, they show the beginning."

"We'll come to that someday. We're happy now, right?"

She smiles a little sadly, but with my words defeating her resistance. "Yeah, yes, fine, you're cute."

"I am dashing, I'd say. More than cute."

"And arrogant."

"Expressing the virtue of megalopsychia, the mean of vanity and pusillanimity."

"And a nerd."

"I'll take that."

I kiss her, and she kisses me deeply back, as if she needed me more in that moment.

"I do love you," she says.

"I love you so much," I reply.

"Take me home."

"You don't cry for your wife and daughter anymore?"

"No, I guess not, not for a few days."

"It hasn't been so long."

"Three weeks."

"Right."

"You don't feel sad about them?" she asks.

"I do. Something Addison said to me, though—she said that if she could still feel she would still be alive. I still feel."

"You do?"

"I do. You saw me, I cried for the month leading up to their death and then I had tears for her and Helen. And now I feel something different with you, for you."

"Good," she says.

"And that gives me permission not to cry for two people who wanted to be dead anyway." I pause. "Well, three people, really."

"Your most recent wife?"

"Right."

"Good," she says. "You shouldn't cry for them. You shouldn't cry for people who choose death."

"Well, mourning is always about crying for ourselves."

She pauses. I don't think she likes that answer. "Still," she says, "screw the people who do that to us."

I think she's talking about her husband.

"I think Gwen was wired incorrectly, that's what I've decided. That those masters of genetic manipulation made a fundamental error when they put her together."

"Hmh," she replies.

"That, or she just was smarter than all of this, and realized something about our existence that is taking the rest of us a longer time to figure out."

"Which is?"

"Suicide. The 'fundamental philosophical question.' She answered it. And she was really fucking smart."

"Well, let's hope she's wrong."

"When I'm with you, I have no doubt she's wrong."

"What about when you were with her?"

"The same, I suppose."

"What does that mean for your answer?"

"I'm not really sure. But I don't see how it's an answer when I remember the best part of existence."

"Being in love?" she asks.

I nod.

"You're such a sap."

"Maybe love generally?"

"Maybe."

I run across the room to where she's standing and I scoop her into my arms, lifting her feet into the air. I cradle her and she wraps her arms around my neck.

"Tell me you don't believe it to be true," she says, with weight.

"When I'm with you. And in moments like these."

"What else can we do?"

"I don't know if you'll like him," she says.

"Why?"

"He's very different from you."

"Justinus and I are friends. Peter and I are friends."

"You all get each other," she says, "it's different."

We're heading to meet her son and his husband for a Christmas lunch. The air in Houston is thick and excessively hot for the brief moment we step outside the shuttle station before entering the pod for the ride over. We hold hands as we walk and as soon as we sit down in our seats I lean in and kiss her. I cannot resist her presence now.

"You don't stop, do you?"

"Do you want me to?"

"No. No, I don't," she says. "But we are not having sex before we go and see my son. I want to look dignified. I haven't seen him in years."

"What does he do?"

"I have no idea."

"Who would choose to live in Houston?"

"It's for work. I know that. I don't know what kind of work, but it's for work."

"Okay, I'll have patience."

I sit back next to her on the bench seat and look around at the city for a moment. She shifts in her seat and my attention is back to her. Her hair is getting longer again, she's been letting it grow. It is still blonde, and she looks lovely today, a flowing gray jumpsuit, satin techmesh, she glides and glitters when she moves.

"Is your son like you?"

"I don't know."

"You know."

"He was. I haven't really seen him since before my last husband. Well, he came to my husband's funeral, but then I was a mess and he didn't stay."

"Well, I'm excited to meet him."

"It will be good to see him, I think."

Cynthia returns to looking out the window, and I settle in close to her, my head on her shoulder, and we're still holding hands. I close my eyes and center myself, breathing deeply. I want to breathe her in even more. I want to make sure I appreciate this moment and keep it for my memory.

"You're missing the city. I can't believe this place now."

Houston has greatly reduced in size since its heyday millennia ago. It is now far too sticky for the average person, its legendary heat and humidity increasing to unbearable levels in the late 3000s. In the spirit of environmental efficiency and in a vain attempt to reduce stickiness, the city moved to an elevated grassland concept for the buildings, leading to massive renovations over the past thousand years. None of the offices or apartments stands taller than fifteen stories, therefore, and all of them are woven together by massive strands of grass and garden sloping up and over like the green hills of some more pleasant destination. Each of the hills has pitted flat stone patios and is speckled with windows, the apartments built into the hills.

We exit off of the highway and pull up to the side of one of these great grassy mound buildings. To our surprise, the pod hops the curb and begins to drive up the side of the building stopping at the edge of a patio.

"This is odd," I say.

Cynthia points to another pod nearby where people are stepping in. "I guess this is how they do it here."

"Neat."

We step into the blistering sun onto the numbered ledge and the gate buzzes open. Immediately Cynthia's son strides out and welcomes us.

"Mom," he says.

He is handsome, maybe pretty, and looks a fair amount like his mother. But his hair is black, his skin darker. She kisses him on both cheeks and he smiles broadly, genuinely pleased to see her.

"This is Warren," she says.

"Pleasure," I say. "Heard lots about you."

"Emmit," he says. "Welcome to my home."

We walk into the house and another man greets us. "This is Arthur," he says.

"Nice to meet you both. My husband has told me all about you, Cynthia."

"Wonderful," she says.

"We already opened our presents this morning," says Arthur. "Sorry, it's tradition."

"Not at all," I say. "We did the same."

"Get anything good?"

"An exceptionally rare cognac for me," I say. "I got her some clothes."

"Don't be modest. He got me a stunning tuxedo," she says. "Custom printed for me. It's really incredible."

"You still love your tuxedos after all this time."

"It's kind of my signature," Cynthia replies.

"Please, sit down," says Emmit. "I'll get some wine for everyone."

There is a small Christmas bush, a little round false-leave bulb with a million sparkly points on the surface of everything green which sparkle and flicker. There are two presents sitting suspiciously beneath the tree. We have, thankfully, brought presents, just in case, but they are still in the pod. We'll have to summon it at some point. But then again, I see no tags on these gifts, so perhaps they would only have given them to us if they saw we had presents in hand, in which case, perhaps it is best not to summon the pod and give them presents.

"So, how long have you two been married?" I ask.

"About fifty years now," Emmit replies.

"Fifty wonderful years," continues Arthur, who receives an affectionate look from Emmit.

"That's outstanding," I say.

"That might be the last time we really spent much time together," he says to Cynthia.

"I know," she says. "I'm really sorry."

"It really is okay," Emmit offers, "I wanted to get that out of the way. I get why it's been so hard."

"My last husband. He's just taken years of me working through things to start to get over it. Don't abandon each other," she says.

"I can't even imagine it," says Arthur.

"Well, neither could I," Cynthia nods.

"Why Houston?" I ask, changing the subject a bit.

Arthur shudders a bit, "I know, right? Tell them, Emmit."

"I can't apologize enough to him," he laughs. "My company builds these buildings—the grass slope buildings. Super efficient, extremely high satisfaction rate. Much higher than the high rises in Portland, actually."

"I love my house," I say.

"I don't," says Cynthia. "I think I need more of a yard."

"Well, exactly," Emmit continues. "We're going to do this in Dallas next, but we're completing a longitudinal study about satisfaction and wear and use and all of that. Another ten years and we'll be free."

"To move to Dallas?" Cynthia asks pointedly.

"Yeah. But Dallas is better. Better weather, at least."

"You must truly be in love," I say to Arthur.

He smiles. "We are."

"Should we have lunch?" asks Emmit.

We arrive back from the shuttle stop and she looks at me expectantly. "Did you still want to call your children?"

"Oh," I say, having forgotten. "We could try. I don't actually know where my daughter is. We've been out of contact for a long time. I think she's on one of the outer planets. I'm pretty sure about that. Meredith, where's Diane?"

"Proxima C," says Meredith.

"Okay, so she's out. What about Henry?"

"Henry is in Boston."

"Oh, shit," I say. "I had no idea he was so close. When did he move there?"

"Twenty-two years ago."

"Oh. Meredith, why don't you tell me these things?"

"Apologies."

"She doesn't sound sincere," says Cynthia.

"I agree."

"I'm sincere," says Meredith.

"Okay, well, let's call Henry. Meredith, video call."

Cynthia looks panicked, "What? Why video?"

"You don't want to be in it?"

We can hear the ringing.

"You should be in it," I say. "I'll introduce you."

Henry flashes onto the wall screen. He is immediately recognizable as a relation to myself. But he is also like his mother, a fair number of her features. We are told not to take this too personally—the people who decide these things do so for the purpose of developing an ideal genetic form, not simply pure physical beauty, although this is a central concern. So the fact that his mother was so differently featured meant the possibility of genetic hylomorphism which is very useful.

"Henry, it's Warren. Merry Christmas."

"Hey dad. Good to hear from you. What can I do for you?"

"Nothing in particular. Just wanted to check in. Are you busy, I can call back?"

"No, we've got a few friends over. Here, you remember Noma, don't you?"

"Sure. Hi, Noma. Good to see you."

Noma is Henry's wife. She's lovely, as I remember her, from the last time that we spoke. "Hi Warren!" She says; she's carrying a tray of some food, and is quickly moving out of frame.

"You're hosting dinner," I say. "Good work."

"What are you doing? Who's this?" he says, gesturing to Cynthia.

"This is Cynthia, she just moved in with me."

"Oh, nice to meet you," he responds.

"You, as well," says Cynthia.

"We just visited her son and we're feeling nostalgic. So…indulge me. How are things?"

"Lovely, really. You should come visit. Noma and I have moved recently, and then we just got news that we've been accepted for a child. So you're going to be a grandfather. Or are you already a grandfather?"

"Yeah, I'm already that, your half-sister, but that's really exciting. Congratulations! Where will you be?"

"Havana. And before you say anything, I know it's not Singapore, but they've made some great investments in faculty and curriculum here in the past fifty years, so it's not the same situation."

"No, no, your child. I've heard the same, that it's improving and all. And Havana is a beautiful place."

"I was honestly expecting a lecture."

"I know."

"Helen came to visit me about six months ago."

"She did?" I say, genuinely surprised.

"She was saying goodbye. Stayed with us for a week. You know, some kind of step-sibling bond, I guess."

"Oh, yeah. I guess the funeral was almost two months ago. And her mother, too."

"Oh, really? She didn't mention that."

"I don't think she knew then. Yeah, Addison, third wife."

"Wow, Warren…dad. I didn't know, that's a lot."

"It was. And…" I start to tell him about Gwen and Morris, too, but decide that there's no need to share this with him. It would be too much. "…It's been an interesting year. A difficult one, for sure, but the new year is looking up, I'd say."

"Glad to hear that."

"So, Cynthia, what are you working on these days?" It's a polite way of asking about someone when almost seventy-five percent of the population does not work.

"I'm a professor at Manhattan Ongoing. Well, I start a full semester in a couple of weeks."

"That's wonderful."

"History of Psychology," she says.

"Cynthia Wellsbottom," says Henry.

She smiles demurely. "Oh."

"I finished a doctorate a few hundred years ago in the history of psychology. You were one of my primary interlocutors."

"I hope I fared well," she responds.

"You did," he says, smiling, "I copied my interpretive framework from your work on the UAGS Nebuchadnezzar's thirty year mission."

"*A model enterprise: sociality and social misunderstanding with the resulting revolution in starship design.*"

"That's the one."

"That book was such a slog," she says.

"Well, it was enjoyable to me." He turns to me. "Well done, dad."

"Thanks son," I say. "I've still got it."

A timer goes off in the background. "I've got to grab that. Well, let's catch up soon."

"Sure. I'll come down and visit."

"That would be great."

"Merry Christmas."

"Merry Christmas. Lovely to meet you."

"Bye son."

We hang up and she has a tear in her eye.

"What is it?" I say.

"Nothing," she says, walking away.

"Are you crying?"

"No," she says. "I'm fine."

"Why do you think we are so crazy about each other?"

"I don't know," I say. "We match each other's needs right now, probably."

"What does that mean?"

"We fit each other. Personality. We share an experience."

"Loved ones dying, and our sadness about that."

"Most of the world doesn't give a fuck about people dying."

"I don't think that's true."

"I know it isn't true. But it feels like that when someone dies on you."

"True."

"And we have had a particularly miserable time of things," I continue, "and we have suffered differently."

"I know," she says, and she pauses. "Does that mean we won't last?"

"What?"

"When we are better, will we be done?" she continues, looking away.

"You are worried about the future always. Too much."

"My past hasn't been good to me. It's been the same for me, I expect something different, to feel different, and be better, and it doesn't ever come."

"Nothing ever comes to us just like that."

"Right," she says.

"You'll have to work at it."

"I know."

"We can do it together."

"WILL you read this?"

"Oh," she says, "Sure."

"You don't have to."

"No, you've just never asked me to."

"I know. But I am curious. I'm happy about this."

She holds up her tablet and I slide the file over to her.

"It's about your wife?" she asks, concerned.

"Yeah, my sixth."

She puts down her screen and looks at me. "Why do you want me to read about your ex-wife?"

"It's my memoir. It's about me, not her."

"'Euphrosyne represented for me everything about classical Greek ideals—our lives together a perfect harmony.'"

"Ha! Are you jealous? We divorced three years after the story that I'm writing about."

"So why are you having me read this?"

"Why are you so suspicious?"

"Why are you being such a jerk?"

"Why can't you accept that I love you?" It sounds so suspiciously romantic even as I'm the one speaking it. Her face is scrunched in anger. I walk over and stand face to face, moving my nose ever closer to her until we boop. And smile.

She cracks.

"You jerk."

"You said that," I remind her.

"You're being silly and I'm serious, though. What is this?"

"It's not a test. I just want to know if it's interesting."

"No, have someone else read it. I don't want to know about your life before me or what you've done in the past. I don't care about any of that, and I don't care about any of my life before you and I don't want to dwell on it. I just want this."

I kiss her quickly and then hug her as tightly as I can. She kisses me back and then sneaks away running with her tablet to the couch.

"'Our life together in that time represented an enviable form of perfection, a combination of numerous predicaments and the odd game of chance that had brought us together.' What the fuck are you even talking about?"

"The whole book is pretty much just me saying that kind thing. All the latest memoirs have taken on this indirect language."

"It's tedious. 'The machinations of our minds stood to indicate the deep passion which held us in constant union.' Ridiculous. So you want to write about how you used to love someone?"

"You're getting jealous again."

"Fine. Answer the question."

"I don't know. I do this. I'll write, every once in a while, a sort of stylized memoir. I encounter myself that way, or at least the version of myself that I'd like to present. Or the version of myself that I was. It puts the old life to bed."

"In the grave?"

"So to speak."

"Maybe I should write a book like this."

"You should. I would read about how much you loved your husband."

"How do you say that without jealousy?"

"I'm jealous," I say feebly.

"You're not. You don't feel threatened, nothing. I know I will never live up to any of your past wives."

"We're not even married. Why can't you just let things come?"

"No."

I went sailing today with Peter and Justinus, a quick daytrip to Mexico for a few hours on the water, and also to pick up some Mezcal. Cynthia is working, lecturing in New York, and will be gone for the night, and I was finding the Portland winter tedious.

As we return to the dock, I see a woman standing on the end of the pier. Though I can't tell who it is from this distance, I know who it is, because who else shows up like this? Only the jug nun.

"Ahoy there, Rose," I say. "Care to come aboard?"

She nods her head, hands on her hips impatiently, waiting for the boat to be tied up.

Peter and Justinus wave hello and she holds up her hand to dismiss them. When they do not immediately walk to shore, she speaks: "I need to talk with Warren. Alone, please."

"Of course," says Peter.

"Right, right," says Justinus.

"I feel like I'm in trouble," I say.

"How are you doing?" she says, disarmingly, once they are fully gone.

"I'm great. Really."

"Really?"

"Yes. Why?"

"How's Cynthia?"

I smile and pause. "I didn't know you knew about her."

"Of course I know about her."

"We haven't spoken in a while."

"You didn't answer my calls," she says, accurately. She called a few times the first few days after, and I wasn't in the mood to speak with her then. "So I gave up. Thought I'd give you some space."

"That first week was tough," I respond. "It was too soon to talk with you. I would have answered now."

"Well I didn't want to give you the choice. And I've been checking up on you."

"That's a little strange," I say. "But please, come aboard, let's sit down."

"Thanks," she says, following me. I'm dressed for yachting, white polo, short white swim shorts, white deck shoes. She is dressed for something else entirely: black tube top, black leather gauntlets, baggy pants, studded everything, finished with black clunky sandals.

"Okay. So what have you heard that brings you out?"

"Cynthia."

"What about her?"

"She's wrong for you and you should leave her." I pause. Where is this coming from? I admit we shared a mutual interest, but we never consummated anything. And after killing my wife and daughter, I'm not overly interested in her. And I'm in love with Cynthia. In love with her. Rose sees my face contorted. "I'm sorry for saying it this way. But she's headed in one direction and you are headed in another."

"How can you know that?"

"You know what I do for a living and that I'm very good at it."

"Still, this is bold."

"Yes, I know." She picks her next words carefully. "She may also have made some inquiries. Not to me, but to others in the field."

"About dying?"

"Yes."

"Ridiculous. She would tell me."

"No, she wouldn't," Rose says definitively. "You don't know her Warren."

"Have you ever even met her?"

"Yes. But that's not why I'm saying what I'm saying."

"Look, Rose, thanks for coming to see me. And I admit we—you and I—share something. Got a little connection going. But I don't trust you. I don't trust you like I trust Cynthia right now. I'm in love with her....We're in love. We're in love! You need to accept that."

"Warren, fine. Make your own mistakes."

"Oh, fuck off. I'm finally feeling good for the first time in years, literally years, and you're trying to take me back down. I haven't thought about killing myself at all in weeks, and then you, death lady, you catch wind of it, and your like, hmm, that's wrong, he should be more miserable."

She is genuinely pissed at my words. I think she would have let me vented for any other reason, so long as I left out that accusation. "Don't be so fucking dumb! So stupid! That couldn't be further from the truth."

"Whatever," I mock a glance at an imaginary clock on the wall. "We've got a shuttle to catch."

"It leaves in two hours, you're fine."

"Fucking hell," I say, "I've got to get your connections, always know everything all the time."

"Look," she says, "fine, you don't want to see me now. You don't believe me. You will. You call me when you need me. Promise me that." She is pleading with me.

I see her eyes and I see she is serious. "If I ever think I need you, then I will call you. I can promise you that. But you are exactly who I do not want right now."

"Fine, Warren. Fine." I think she's going to tell me to go fuck myself, but she resists the clear urge. "Call me."

A small motorboat pulls up to the back of our boat as she says this, driven by anonymous man with large black sunglasses dressed in black. "What's this?" I say.

"My ride," she explains, and hops in the back. She takes a seat and watches me as she motors away, haunting me.

The fuck was that? I've got to call Cynthia, she'll never believe this story. And I'm not going to let it get to me, we've only got two hours to run and get the mezcal, and I'll have fun with Peter and Justinus, and I'll be happy and in love, nothing can bring me down, she'll see.

"Are you packing?" she asks.

"I'm just thinking," I respond. I'm standing in the closet, looking at row upon row of clothes.

"We're weeks away," she continues.

"But I like to plan things out. Plan out my outfits."

"Meredith," she says, "would you pack a bag for me for Peter's wedding? Whatever I need for a week in Hawaii."

"Of course," says Meredith. Cynthia's side of the closet starts moving.

"Hey, so guess who came to see me yesterday," I say.

"Who?"

"The crazy lady who organized my wife's death."

Cynthia gives a confused look.

"Yeah, nobody, but she's a death planner," I explain. "And she told me to leave you."

"Huh," says Cynthia. "Are you going to?"

"I don't think I ever will," I say, smiling.

"Why did she say to leave me? Who is this lady?"

"She said you had made some inquiries. Into dying."

Cynthia laughs. "What? No, that's weird. I really haven't Warren."

"I know," I say. "Don't worry about it. I trust you. I just thought it was funny."

"It's kinda weird. Maybe don't hang out with her."

"Don't worry, I'm avoiding her."

The closet produces a small suitcase on a hook.

"See," says Cynthia, "all done. You don't need to think about packing because Meredith just does it."

"Meredith doesn't even do it. The closet does it, he's a separate thing."

"Why are they separate?"

"They still talk to each other, but the closet has dedicated software for picking things out. He's a bit more advanced than Meredith in that regard."

"Is that right," she says, skeptically. "Meredith, is the closet really better than you at picking out clothes?"

"It is an arbitrary and incalculable difference. It is not objective."

"Yes, well," I say, "subjectively, which is all that fashion is, the closet is better at picking things out."

"Do you think this wedding is just going to be a bunch of animals running around? Should I wear a bunch of leather and leopard print?"

"Just to piss everyone off?"

"Yeah."

"You contrarian."

"Do you think Nigel will be a sheep when they do the ceremony?"

"Oh God, I don't know. Probably."

"We should get a pool going. Take bets."

"We should."

It's just been, it's been like a dream, honestly. The past few weeks. Decades since I've felt this way, maybe since the first years with Gwen. I've barely had times when I can form a thought, when I can really consider what's going on. I'm always in the moment, always smiling, always thinking of her and being with her and feeling excited about things.

We're in Thailand, on a little island for the week. Mostly on the beach, in the sun, lounging. Justinus and the whole crew are here, staying in the expansive villa we've rented. It's been a lovely week.

As the sun sets we are on the patio, playing a game of dice that requires copious drinking and little talent.

"You are terrible at this game, Warren," says Justinus.

"Honestly," follows Oliver.

My teammate Aurelius defends me. "He's streaky."

"I'm streaky," I say. I bounce the dice off the table and into the bowl and roll a nine. "See! Drink!"

They shrug and take deep sips from their giant mai-tai's.

Cynthia comes up the steps, returning from an evening walk by herself.

"You're playing this again?"

"Yes," I laugh. "You'd prefer a different game?"

"No game at all," she says.

She continues walking. Not upset, but brusque, which means secretly upset. The rest of the players look to the ground, knowing that I need to continue the conversation, so I follow her inside.

"What's wrong?" I ask, following her into our room.

"Nothing," she says, smiling. She kisses me lightly. "You can go play."

"I don't believe you."

"I'm just going to sit inside with the ladies again. I actually kind of like Oliver's date, we've got things to talk about."

"Really?"

"Yeah," she says.

"You went to bed early last night."

"I did."

"Are you going to do that again tonight?" I ask.

"Probably," she says. "Don't worry about that, it's nothing."

"I don't need to play the game. I want you to be happy."

"Warren, I'm fine," she says insistently. "I'm going to go split a bottle or two of wine with them and once I'm tired I'll go to bed. I'll look forward to you coming in and falling into bed again," she smiles now.

"That only happened once."

"I know," she says. "Go, play, have fun."

"Okay," I say. She does seem okay. "We'll hang out at the beach tomorrow."

"THESE people, Warren," she says. "I can't stand these people."

"What are you talking about?"

"I quit today," she throws her bag down. "My job." She's just stepped through the door, furiously. I try to catch up to her pace.

"What happened? What do you need?"

She sees my energy and catches her own. "Nothing. Nothing," she says.

"I just couldn't do it. They were trying to change my schedule again this semester. And add another course, too."

"Sounds like they like you."

"That's not the point. I don't need that right now. I'm just supposed to teach a course, one course, and now they want to add all of this stuff, so no, no thanks."

"Okay," I say. I'm disappointed in her. She is so remarkable and I think she'll do an amazing job. It's a great opportunity for her. Teaching jobs like the one it sounds like they are lining up for her are rare, since all of us are overqualified and self-congratulatory.

"They're like, hey, supervise these dissertations, maybe? Advise some graduate students? No. No."

"That's fine. You don't have to do any of that."

"I don't want to do any of that. It was a mistake to come back," she says. "I thought I wanted to teach and be back, but I don't. I don't care enough about it, really, I don't."

"You're doing so great," I say. "You've been studying hard for weeks. Last week, on the beach, you were reading the whole time. You have been so invested."

"No," she says, shaking her head, "just no. No." She's crying a little bit.

"Okay, you don't have to all of that new stuff. How much longer is your course? You're like halfway through the semester, right?"

"I quit it, Warren, I said that. I'm not doing it."

"I feel like that's not the right thing to do."

"What the fuck? Don't take their side. I told you I don't want to do it anymore."

"I'm not taking their side."

"What did you just say, then?"

"I said you shouldn't quit the class you've already started teaching. You've been having a great time with it."

"No, I haven't Warren. Fuck this."

I hug her, and she leans into me. "Whatever you want to do," I say. "I'm here for you."

"I don't know what I want to do," she says, standing up. She kisses me on the head and heads for the shower.

"WHAT are you doing?" she asks me, seeing me typing away.

"I'm applying to a job," I say. "I thought it was time for me to get back into things."

"Oh," she says, "good for you. That sounds great."

"You don't mind, right?"

"What, since I quit mine?"

"I was thinking more about me being out of the house more often. Like twenty hours a week. This one's in Boston."

"No, that's fine," she says.

"It's a creative writing job," I say. "Teaching."

"Oh."

"You don't think it's a good idea."

"Going to teach the world how to write about their ex-wives?"

"I put that book aside, you know that."

"Whatever," she says.

"Why don't you have drink? Relax a bit? We're supposed to go out with Peter and Nigel tonight."

"I'm fine. I'll be fine. I can fake smile better than anyone."

I laugh because I think she's joking. "So you really don't care about me applying to some jobs?"

"No, Warren, I couldn't care less."

I step through the door, returning home from a long day of interviews.

"Warren," says Meredith. She never uses my name. "There is a note from Cynthia on the counter."

"A note."

"Yes."

The note is on the counter. Handwritten. Where did she find a pen? It's on the floor now, discarded. *Sorry. I tried. You were great. It was always me I couldn't live with. Love.*

"Meredith," I shout, "Call Cynthia."

"She asked me to prevent calls to her. And she told me she won't answer anyway."

"Call her anyway!" I hate when I shout at Meredith.

"The call is blocked on her end. You are concerned, Warren, but she is still alive. You'll just have to use another phone."

"Call Justinus."

The call buzzes waiting for him. I stand in a state of panic waiting for a response.

"There is no answer," says Meredith.

"Dammit, Meredith. You're sure she's alive? Can you find her?"

"She is still alive. I think she just broke up with you, Warren."

"Oh," I say. "Can you bring me a scotch?" I sit down on the couch.

"Call from Justinus."

"Justinus," I answer. "Have you heard from Cynthia?"

"Warren, right, sorry I missed your call. Yes, I've talked with her. She's just at her apartment."

"She's okay?"

"She's okay."

"Good."

"Are you okay?" he says, with concern in his voice.

"I thought she was going to kill herself," I say.

"Not today, Warren," he says. "But I think it's best if you do what you can to forget her."

"Did she tell you something?"

"Just to make sure that you forget her."

"Did you tell her that was stupid?"

"I did. But really, Warren, she's just breaking up with you."

"Okay. If you're sure."

Justinus and I are enjoying a cocktail and discussing my musical days as we sit on couches overlooking the water of the harbor.

His phone buzzes and his face blanches.

"Yes," he says. "That's…that's not what she said was going to happen….I understand that it did. Dammit, Peter, why did she call you?...I know you don't know....No, I'm with him. We'll be right over."

"What's going on? Was that Peter?"

"We've got to go somewhere," he says, standing and gesturing for me to head to the door. I grab his arm as he walks by.

"What happened?"

"I'll tell you on the way."

We walk outside to his waiting pod. "Now. Tell me now!"

"Cynthia is dead."

"Fucking of course," I respond. Justinus is watching me and I feel him watching me. He knows, he must know how furious I am. I told him this would happen. I told him what was coming.

"I'm angry, too," he says.

I still don't respond.

We arrive outside of her apartment and Justinus moves to go inside.

"I told you," I say. "I told you she would do this!"

"You changed your mind."

"Only because you insisted. You kept on saying, she won't do it. She won't do it. She knows what you've been through, she's fine, she's seeing someone else, she's still teaching. Didn't you say all those things?"

"They were all true. Mostly true, really."

"I keep on letting myself be misled. I don't understand why I keep doing this. Why am I trying with you?"

"Don't say that," he says. "Let's go inside already."

Peter is there along with a few government medical drones. He points to the bathroom.

She's in the tub with her wrists slit, floating in red water with a few pink bubbles left over. I take her broken hand as it lies over the edge of the tub and I sit down next to her. I don't know what else I am feeling other than the deepest possible confusion. *How did I not know her better?* I kiss her hand as the lead robot pauses at the door, lending me a moment of privacy. I stand and let them do their work. Her life is over now. Eleven hundred and twenty-two years. I suspect mine is, too.

Chapter 4

We make attachments, and they are severed. And with each loss, we are fragmented. Once upon a time, life was about family, and when we fell in love our family grew and grew. There can be no family any more, not in the way it was—it is too much to be together for so long. And so we are left with those we fall for; but this is the same, for it will always come to an end, and we always end in pieces. You may think you have avoided the pain, but it will come. Addison and I were apart for thousands of years. But still I lost her and still she left me broken.

Ask the question: what is it that you live for? You may struggle for an answer, but the answer is in front of you: it is everything that you have made your life, the structure you have given it. The way your life is now is the realization of what you love. There are many mistakes I have made in life and perhaps the greatest was to have loved Cynthia. I don't know that I feel betrayed now. I don't think I would say it like that. Just numb. Just as if they had been right all along, and I just found out about it. I just had the answer presented to me, the answer for all of life's questions. And it was in the severed connection of a love destroyed in a moment by a selfish act.

This is something the great philosophers tend to ignore. Except for the celibate ones, of course; they know that there is no greater pull or power in life than to be in love and to be loved, that it changes everything. The non-celibate ones tend not to talk about these kinds of things, and then have all sorts of disasters in their personal lives because they do not apply their philosophical reasoning to their relationships. Or, better yet, they cannot. The relationship simply destroys the order of one's universe and remakes it into the universe of that love. This is not hyperbolic; if you've loved, surely you can recall the unwise things you've done in the name of love. Love takes us outside of ourselves, because this is the nature of love.

This is what Cynthia has given me. I tell her, "I worship the goddess of love," and she laughs at me, because she knows what a foolish devotion that would be. There is nothing eternal in the love that is shared between humans. Not because we die, but simply because we are unreliable, and love is fickle, and it fades and changes and we do not adapt. One loves, the other changes, their love fades, and the one who loves is left behind. Left holding nothing. Left empty. Who can worship the goddess of love? She will leave you soon enough.

I don't feel sad any more. I feel dead. No tears, now. Only defeat.

The great benefit to this is that I will not be such an outwardly dour presence at Peter's wedding.

"What are you doing?" says Justinus.

"What?" I ask.

"You okay?" he says.

I realize that I'm standing in the middle of the floor in the shuttle station thinking about things.

"I'm good. Let's head to the party."

Lightning flashes—
Close by my face,
The pampas grass!

Basho[9]

WE'RE a day late to the wedding. I don't want to talk about why that is the case, but it took me some extra time.

The Niemans Estate is a former resort now owned by Peter's extended family. He owns, as I understand it, a ten percent share, but rarely lives there. The rest of the estate is occupied by some fifty affiliated Niemans or their families, all of whom have decided that Hawaii is an ideal destination when you have a sprawling property with three quarters of a mile of private beach.

Our transport pod pulls up to the residence as dusk is settling in. It is an ancient, massive cobblestone drive way ending in a covered cul-de-sac, lined by torches along the way. The pod has stopped on a red carpet, and we step out in our matching black cassocks with tweed copes and long golden chains. Justinus felt it would help me if we matched, and he felt that perhaps, after my own comments, it was more religion that I needed. Cassocks have actually endured through multiple fashion cycles, however, so we do not look like priests, but more like high fashion urbanites making an ironic reference to a previous existence

"Look at this place," he says. "Who knew Peter was so rich?"

"You're rich," I say. "I'm very rich."

"Do you own a one hundred and fifty bedroom estate?"

"I do not."

"That's right."

"God, this place is ridiculous," he says, laughing at the tiki torches lining the red carpet, interspersed with robotic trays offering welcome cocktails. He fetches two coupes of champagne for us.

"You aren't even laughing anymore," he says, "You could at least laugh."

"I just don't have it right now."

"Cheers," says Justinus.

I offer my best smile and he scoffs. "Cheers."

It's the night before the wedding, after the rehearsal and the dinner, and we have arrived just as the cocktail party begins. Oliver sent urgent texts the night before, describing the insanity of the previous evening, something which Justinus complained about bitterly the entire thankfully brief shuttle flight. Again, I just couldn't make it in time.

The red carpet runs through the building under the glamorous marble archway fifteen meters in height. As we step through the setting on the far side is revealed and momentarily I am forced to marvel. It is a jungle paradise spotted by pools and fire pits and lounge chairs and the sun setting in the ocean in luminescent pink. The open flames flicker bringing a transporting glow to the faces of the crowd and sending shadows dancing on the palm trees. In the center is a dance floor circling an immense pool, both densely populated.

"A lot of Nigel's friends, I guess," says Justinus.

"Huh," I say.

There are almost a thousand people here, and a good portion of them are animals. There are sheep and tigers and bears and all sorts clutching glasses and making small talk.

"This is going to be an interesting night," says Justinus. "I think I'm going to try and fuck that gazelle later." He gestures towards an attractive looking gazelle standing upright a short distance away. She spots Justinus, and looks spooked, as if a lion has entered her field of vision.

"Do what you gotta do," I say.

"You need to enjoy yourself," he says. "I'm sorry and all that, but I believe that you can pull it together."

"Yeah," I say.

I agree but I'm not sure how. The truth is I want to die. I see the mass of humanity doing meaningless things for a meaningless celebration—marriage does not last, love fades, and the loss destroys. I see the skulls and the skeletons, the bodies moving devoid of flesh—this is what they are. The Death's Head meditation, this is what I am doing, a Buddhist practice, but I am not practicing, this is what I see. The wine you drink drips through to the ground, to touch another is to grind bones together, and conversation is just the wind blowing through the gaps in our skull.

A robot wheels its way up to us. "Justinus Perriman. Warren Walker. Please take the keys to your room from my tray. Room five-oh-eight."

"Thank you," says Justinus.

"Cheers."

The robot wheels away.

"Nothing is better than the personal touch, right?" says Justinus with a smile.

"Please don't," I say.

WE step into our room after unlatching the door with an actual honest to goodness grooved metal key in a functioning lock. It's a quaint touch in a building dating from a few millennia after keys were replaced.

I step into the bathroom to relieve myself, and to fix my hair, only to find a terrible joke. There is a robot attendant filling the tub, a massive glass bowl matching the one in Cynthia's apartment. It, in fact, appears to be the exact same tub, with the same entry steps. The robot turns at my arrival to greet me.

"Warren Walker: message from Peter Niemans." It switches to Peter's voice. "'What, are you going to be afraid of tubs your whole life? Take a bath and relax."

"What an asshole," I mutter.

"I'm sorry, sir, I did not recognize your request," says the robot.

"Oh, nothing," I say. "Thanks for the bath."

I look around for a moment, unsure of how to proceed. A bath doesn't sound like the worst thing in the world. The alternative is to pee and return to polite society for a night of heavy drinking on the eve of Mr. Niemans' wedding. But there is no need to rush into this.

I drop my cope and begin to unbutton my cassock, heading over to the toilet to relieve myself.

"Your bath is drawn. Anything else I can provide for you?"

I finish unbuttoning my cassock as I pee.

"No. Well, maybe a cocktail. Something fruity?"

"Of course, sir." The robot wheels away.

I remember when robot attendants and waiters looked like people. They had to change them to oblong machines on wheels because they were treated better. Fewer people tried to have sex with them, fewer people abused them.

I step into the bath, the warmth. This is what she felt when she got into the water. That, and, I imagine, a stabbing pain in her wrists from where she was actively bleeding. I guess she took a pill, too, so maybe she didn't feel any pain. That's what the report said. It's funny to me to worry about her pain in that last moment as if the pain of the previous forty years and likely her entire life did nothing to trump a few minutes of dying. She suffered, and then she suffered for a moment more, and then she suffered no more. I imagine her happy in that moment, really, once I push past my own horror. I imagine she felt connected with her husband, who she truly loved, and who had taken life away from her. She had it back in that moment of connection with him, bleeding from her wrists while sitting in a warm bath, waiting for death to come.

I lean back in the tub, waiting for the itchiness of the heat to subside before sinking all the way in. The robot waiter wheels back in with a cocktail on his tray, which he politely hands me. "Singapore sling."

"I truly appreciate this," I say to him.

"I am at your service," it replies. "I have been assigned to your person."

"Oh. Wonderful. Would you let Justinus know that I'll catch up with him?"

"Of course, sir." He wheels out.

I sip my cocktail and then set it on the edge of the tub. Taking a deep breath, I submerge myself fully, remembering that my mess of a mane is what brought me into the bathroom in the first place. I pause underwater for a moment, and I think about drowning myself. Just taking a deep breath of water in, keeping it in, repeating my breath, holding myself under the water until blackness comes.

I don't have a no-contact, however. My new friend the robot would be forced to drag me from the tub, and he would be disappointed, I imagine, if he had feelings. I emerge from the water, and wipe the bubbles from my face with my hands. I find Justinus staring at me as he sips from a moai mug.

"Searching for treasure, are we?"

"Fixing my hair."

"Well, compose yourself. Don't drip on the tray." He's brought a chair into the room, a large comfy chair set up next to the tub, and he's holding a golden tray with little pink lines on it and a golden straw.

"Please," he says. "Please have one."

I point to a hand towel, which Justinus offers. I dry my face and push my hair back, removing all the drips before throwing the towel across the room. I take the tray and do a line and my face is flush and instantly numb.

"Oh my," I say. "What is that?"

"Special occasion," he says.

"Ooooh," I start to giggle. "Seriously," I'm trying to get words out, "are you…did you take that?"

"I'll do one with you. Half, maybe." He does part of a line. "You've been through some tough times. This is the heavy duty stuff, because I'm here to help, so you'll be happy tonight."

I smile stupidly at him. My mind is conflicted, recoiling at the insistent happiness of this drug competing with my decided and established conviction towards depression.

"You know, she died in a tub," I say, smirking.

Justinus looks disappointed. "I know, I saw her too."

"Just like this one."

"You're giggling a bit," he says.

I am. "Well, that's your fault. But it really is the same fucking tub. What are the odds? Did Peter have this tub brought in?"

"That would be dramatic," says Justinus.

"He did have a bath drawn for me, though," I reply.

"No, he didn't. Peter...."

"He really did. Ask the robot. Play that message from Peter."

The attendant is standing in the door. "'What, are you going to be afraid of tubs your whole life? Take a bath and relax."

Justinus' mouth falls agape. "Peter has some style."

"Style?"

"Balls?"

"Balls. I'll grant that. He's marrying a sheep after all."

There's a buzz at the door.

"Oliver Waters," says the attendant.

"Let him in," says Justinus.

Oliver steps in the door and finds us in the bathroom. Appraising the scene, he kicks off his loafers and steps over to the tub. Evaluating further, he loosens his suit pants, and they drop to the floor, leaving him free to step up and into the tub with his feet and sitting on the edge. He has kept on his suit coat and tie, and his resulting appearance is a bit unsettling with his divergent ends.

"Bubbly," he says to the attendant.

"Please," I say.

"Please," he says.

"He's a friend," I explain, and Oliver nods.

"Enjoying a bath?" he observes.

"I am. Per Peter's recommendation."

"He's a smart man," says Justinus.

"He is," says Oliver.

"I'm glad that your balls are normal size again," I say.

"They are indeed, thank you. But how are you doing my friend? You seem chipper."

"He snorted fairy dust," explains Justinus.

"Oh, God, why did you give him that?"

"I think he can handle it."

"I can handle it," I say, straightfaced, and then I snicker slightly.

The attendant returns, and now that everyone is suitably cocktailed, Justinus offers a toast: "To the groom, Peter Niemans!"

"Peter Niemans!" we say.

"Peter Niemans," says the attendant.

Justinus offers a confused glance, "He's here?"

"Yes."

"Get him in the tub," I say.

The door opens and Peter walks in, looks into the bedroom and notes it is empty before being directed by the attendant to the bathroom. He shakes his head and laughs.

"Inseparable. Oliver, I'm sorry, I should have put you in this room with everyone. I figured… separate beds for each of you, but maybe that's too far apart."

"We're fine," I say.

"We are fine," says Oliver. "I'm just next door."

"Warren wants you in the tub," Justinus explains.

"Oh. Maybe I'll follow Oliver, then." He starts to kick off his shoes and struggles to roll up his pants.

"Off with the pants," says Justinus. "It's your final day of freedom."

"I think that would be a good reason to keep my pants on."

"Don't be lame," I say.

"Ohho," says Peter, "that's a bit pot-kettle for you these days."

I ignore the comment.

"How's your fiancé handling everything?" asks Oliver.

"He's excited," says Peter, "He's really thrilled, actually. I…it's his first wedding, and so he's all jittery."

"It's your first wedding, too," I remind him.

"Yes, but I'm not a jittery person, am I?"

"No. But you should have a drink though."

The attendant wheels in another glass of champagne. "Cheers," he says to the attendant. "That's my favorite robot," he says. "I hope you appreciate him."

"We do," says Justinus. "He's quite good."

"Another toast!" says Oliver. "To the sheep!"

"To the sheep!" we shout, with Peter abstaining.

"The groom," says Peter.

"May he be ever groomed," follows Justinus.

"His fleece as white as snow," I say.

"That's enough."

"We are seriously thrilled for you," says Oliver.

"Thrilled," says Justinus.

I blankly nod, and Peter knows my absence. "And you?"

"I'm very glad for you," I reply.

"That's all you can muster. Even on whatever drug has you snickering."

"It means very much to me that you are happy," I say. "I just can't muster much at the moment."

Peter grins wryly and takes a deep sip from his flute.

"It feels like a mistake," I blurt out.

"What?" says Peter. "Don't be a prick."

"I don't mean it that way. I've just been burnt recently. You're taking a risk feeling anything for someone."

"The risk that makes life worth living, I think," responds Peter. "You said that to me once, didn't you?"

"That solves that, doesn't it," says Justinus, betraying his discomfort with my faux pas.

"What do you have planned for us tonight?" asks Oliver.

"What do you mean?" asks Peter. "There's a party downstairs. We're all in the tub missing what I've got planned for you."

"So nothing special," I say.

"Nothing special like…" follows Oliver.

Pause. "PATCHES AND STANDS!" shouts Justinus.

"Fuck, no" says Peter, "No patches and stands."

"Patches and stands! Patches and stands!" We chant.

"Absolutely not. I don't even have any, and I don't know where you're going to get them tonight."

"I've got a guy," says Justinus.

"No, no, you will not be the anti-social heavy drug people off in quiet rooms failing in social responsibility. Especially you," he points at me.

"You know, I'm in this bath because of you," I say.

"Well, I thought you'd be getting here earlier. But are you enjoying it?"

"It's very nice."

"See. And now you're no longer afraid of tubs."

"I don't know that I was."

"Doesn't matter," Peter follows, "You're not."

"It's a brilliant strategy, I must admit," says Justinus.

"See. Well, shall we head down to the party?" Peter continues.

"Nigel Hawes," says the attendant.

"Uh oh, Peter's grounded!" yells Justinus.

"Let him in," I say.

Peter stands, pantsless, and waits for Nigel to step through the door. As we anticipate his appearance, I quietly bet with myself whether he'll be a sheep or not. "Nigel, dear, in here," says Peter as he reveals himself. He is a person. How disappointing.

"Oh my, my, my, what a party going on in here." He walks over to Peter and gives him a kiss. "And why are you the only one actually in the tub?"

"I'm not sure actually. I was here first, I guess."

"Is it still warm?" he asks.

"Yes, quite," says Oliver.

"Great, I could use a dip." Nigel begins to disrobe, and then turns to Peter, "with your permission, darling."

"Please, come on in."

Nigel does not stop with shoes and pants like the others, but fully disrobes, and slips into the massive bowl, stepping across from me with a few firm plantings on my legs hiding beneath the bubbles. "Apologies," he offers.

The attendant brings in another tray of bubbly, and a new sling for me.

"To the happy couple," says Justinus. "We wish you many years of happiness and good fortune."

"Cheers," we follow, clinking our glasses.

We quietly sip.

"You seem to be doing all right," says Oliver, lighting his valcigarette.

"I'm not."

"But you aren't acting out," says Justinus. "You are still behaving."

"I suppose."

"But you did leave early last night," Oliver offers.

"I did. I wasn't much in the mood for partying."

"I had a friend," Justinus continues, "he broke up with this guy—they're not even married, only been dating for a few months. Or having sex for a few months, really. And he lost it. He tried to take a wotshot bat to the guy's apartment multiple times, each time he ends up restrained by the guys cleaning robot."

"Getting smothered by the vacuum hand," laughs Oliver.

"That's right," says Justinus.

"Well, I'm keeping it together in public. But I'm not really prone to outbursts. I'm too old for that, I think."

"You are too old," says Justinus.

I give him a mock dirty look. "But I did yell at my countertop the other night."

"What?" says Oliver.

"Yeah. I was sitting there on the couch, and I ask it to make me a cocktail, and it tells me that it's out of whatever I wanted, some kind of vermouth, and I lost it. I don't even remember what it was."

Justinus is smiling. "What did you say to your countertop?"

"Well, I was pissed at it. I still am a little. I'd just been acting all passive-aggressive towards it, which is the most ridiculous sounding thing. But the countertop is where Cynthia got her knife. Her countertop, of course. She just walked in there and said 'give me your sharpest knife,' and he popped it right up for her. So I blamed my countertop."

They sit for a moment, stunned. It is hard to predict where a conversation will go sometimes.

"I'll take a cigarette," I say. Oliver lights one in his mouth and hands it to me. "I haven't had one of these in a while."

"And what did your countertop say back to you?" asks Oliver.

"He didn't say anything," I say, "He just popped out a proper Mai Tai with all the fruit in a tall glass with two straws. It's one of my favorite cocktails. I was completely disarmed."

"That's incredibly sweet," says Justinus.

"It really is," says Oliver.

"I know," I say. "I told him I was sorry."

"And it accepted your apology?"

"He gave me a little cocktail umbrella for my drink."

"That's ridiculous," says Oliver.

"And then, when we were out of ear shot, my computer Meredith told me how mean it was for me to yell at the countertop. She's like, 'He just does what he's told.'"

"She's right," says Justinus.

"I know. I apologized. He's being professionally cleaned and refurbished this week while I'm gone."

They both pause as if I've said something momentous.

"What is it?" I ask.

"We've been worried about you," says Oliver. "That you would give up."

"That's why it's good to hear you fixing up your apartment," Justinus continues. "You're talking about the future, like you'll still be around."

"We're having a nice morning," I say, "No need to burden ourselves with such unpleasant conversation."

"But you're fine, right?" says Justinus, pleading restrainedly.

"I'm fine," I say. I don't believe that.

Our breakfast rolls up, and I look in vain for an ashtray. They haven't sat on tables for millennia, even if valcigarettes have been trendy a few times over the centuries. Justinus offers his water glass.

I'm having French toast. I likely ordered it as a means of further punishing myself.

THE sun is setting, and the earth is cast with the grandiose glow of an irrepressible Hawaiian sun. We assemble at the edge of the property, a rock outcropping overlooking the ocean. Thousands of white chairs, a thousand visitors immaculately dressed and smiling happy smiles of a meaningful life.

Justinus bounces along, holding hands with Oliver who notices my forlorn gaze and throws his free arm around my shoulder. And so we bounce together, my body moving with their engaged and lively procession to the place of vows.

What a silly thing this is. Not that the institution of marriage was ever really about forever, but the effective divorce rate of one hundred percent should give us pause "until we are parted by death." Nobody says that anymore anyway.

The greatest excitement I have is still whether or not Nigel will be a sheep when he is married. I know that he will be one for the honeymoon, but it is difficult to predict for the wedding. Peter is certainly on board with the marrying a farm animal thing, so I do not think he'd have any strong preference about who he exchanges vows with. Perhaps it would be more honest to have the sheep respond to him.

We find our seats reserved for us in the middle of the fifty chair first row. Seats of honor for the very many honorees.

At the front, alone, stands an actual clergy person. Peter found our conversation at Fred and Paula's so intriguing that he decided he would like to find someone who was still a minister to perform the wedding ceremony. And Nigel agreed after finding out what Unitarian-Universalist ministers actually stood for, which is generally friendly and expansive minded.

The music begins, and a dirge-trance remix of Mendelssohn's "Wedding March" resounds as the people rise to their feet.

Justinus nudges me as we stand, and I'm confused as to why he's doing that. "He's not a sheep," he says.

"Oh," I say. "I can't see him yet."

Peter is walking up the aisle with a woman. I think it may be his mother, but I'm not sure of that. Maybe a sister. There is some familial resemblance. She takes her seat in the front row on the opposite side of the aisle from us, Peter dropping her off and taking his place next to the minister.

Nigel comes into view, escorted by another woman. It is impossible to tell what relation she may be, if any, since her hair is pink and she is quite a bit taller than him and her features are much softer. Still, she escorts him all the way to Peter, and he greets her and thanks her and takes Nigel by the hand and they stand together in front of the minister.

I have stopped paying attention now, and I am only thinking about Gwen. She laughed at how stupid it was when I asked her to marry me.

"We don't do it because it means something in itself," I say. "It just makes things easier for a while. Clarifies things. Tax purposes and inheritance and medical decisions. We know what we are to each other, now formally."

"We know what we are to each other."

"Tell me, then," I say.

"You are my reason for living. The only thing in the world I don't hate."

I smile at her. I am moved by how much she loves me but terrified at what that might mean for her.

Nigel and Peter look lovingly into each other's eyes and they begin to recite their vows as they grasp hands. They are heading to where I am standing now. Their love will fade and die. It has to, it is what always happens, what always will happen. We are too fragile, too weak, too temporary. Our affections are the shifting sands hidden beneath the waves. Then it is too late, you have run aground, and you are stranded now.

After the wedding, during the cocktail hour, I retreat back to the room with Justinus and tell him that I'd like to have his most intense combination of drugs for the evening. He hands me a single pill and tells me to take one of those, that I likely won't remember anything at all, but I will have the best time in the meantime. I immediately pop one and wash it down with a glass of rum brought by our attendant.

"Why are you going so hard?"

"I'll be fine."

"I know that. You're going to be a blast to party with."

"Good."

"Do you even want to know what you took?"

"I trust you."

"You probably shouldn't with those."

"Still, I trust you."

I haven't mentioned it, but I've obviously decided it's time to die. Once we head home from the wedding, I'll call Rose and have her plan a beautiful death for me, because it is a question I still can't answer. They are right, that I have had some enjoyable moments, but everything has been tinged with sadness and it has made satisfaction impossible. There is no happiness, no light to my soul anymore, and there is no activity or person who reminds me that I am alive. I am simply dead already.

Why should I go on? Why should I even bother?

I have debated whether I am simply being dramatic, or even that I have simply experienced something so profoundly new and unexpected that I am reacting in an unfavorable manner. I have been divorced seven times, widowed three times, so I have ended relationships. I have lost count of how many significant others I've had, and certainly no idea of the number of sexual partners. I have buried parents. I even buried a child, though this quite recently.

The death of my ex-wife was difficult for me, I admit, but she is not the first wife I've lost. My first and second wife are gone, though they died long after we split up. It was an amazing thing to bury them, as I had expected to remain forever with both of them at one point in my life or another. We could still operate under such an illusion. And then, they end up dead, unable to go on living. For both, I was happily committed to my next wife and then to Addison, respectively, and I was not destroyed or even overly emotional following their deaths. In fact, I celebrated them as I have celebrated so many deaths before. I went to the party and kissed them goodbye and waved and laughed and went home and made love to my subsequent wife. Their deaths were so freely chosen, and I had moved on absolutely from each, that there was nothing for me to endure. I received it as good news; I was happy for them, that they had reached the point where they had lived life to its fullest and they were ready to let go.

I can take solace in that. I have never hesitated to live. I did not spend a thousand years in an orgasm machine, nor did I live my life as if the goal of existence was mere pleasure. This was not my end—not the clean, not the straightforward, not the transparent. Always the difficult, the nuanced, the complex, the tangled. This has made it harder and made it better and brought me to this point where I don't feel anything any longer. I have no desire to do something next, no places to visit, no people to meet, no life to be shared in the love of friends and the higher love of marriage or the highest love of God. Instead, I will sink into the nothingness of the divine abyss and live so comfortably there in the authentic form of the beginning and end of the universe.

I have objected to myself, of course. I did not arrive at this decision without consideration of the fact that it may be simply an emotional mistake, resulting from a broken heart. Gwen dies, and she offers me a new trauma. The death of my previous wives did not have such an impact on me, nor did their effective death in the form of unpleasant divorce and relocation. I weathered them. I knew that the real love, the shared quiet desperate attachment of centuries shared is not dismissed without the excavation from oneself of all that one has become in that time together. But I lived, and lived on, and I fell in love again, and then I came to truly love once more, and to live my life fully and beautifully.

So why now? Why is this different?

I don't know that I need to be able to express it, but I am in pain. Perhaps there is no logic to it, and I have never been one to believe in the dominion of logic. I just hurt, and there is no desire in me for anything. I do not need anything. My life is now full, and I need to go.

During the course of his wanderings Basho was obliged on one occasion to pass the night in the wilds. A sudden flash of lightning in the dark showed him that he had taken to bed in a meadow, with the pampas grass alongside his face.[10]

When I woke up this morning, my first thought was of my head sitting freely in the bed, unattached to my body, and no longer living. The poet Basho wrote the haiku as an acknowledgement of the true status of existence, that we are all already dead, and everything we perceive is an illusion from this reality. The lightning strikes, and he sees himself as he is in a moment of pure reality. The pampas grass is the field. "Death's heads all over the field." *Let the field stand for Ginza or Broadway: sooner or later the time will come when they will turn to grassy meadows... We can look at the living as they walk full of health down the Ginza and see, in double exposure, a picture of the dead.*[11]

This is supposed to be a moment of enlightenment, but there is nothing of that sort. Or, better yet, there is in fact a crucial revelation, and that is the revelation that I need to die. I have lived the past month devoid of any true joy, and even before then, only in the illusion of happiness that is the nature of the temporary things.

With a single thought, ten thousand years. And with ten thousand years, a single thought.[12]

I have lived ten thousand years, and my life is now but a single thought. A moment. In another moment, I will be gone.

Heading to brunch, I am filled with purpose. I find Justinus and Oliver, a seat open between them, across from Fred and Paula. The table is almost a hundred meters long, a great proportion of the guests of the wedding now at a single table for the morning.

Peter makes a brief speech.

Nigel makes a brief speech.

A friend stands up. Peter introduces him. "I know many of you know Valance DiMattio. He's been a friend of mine for many years. He'd like to share an announcement with us."

"I'd like to take one happy occasion to announce another. I will be dying in six months' time on this very island." Raucous applause. "Volcano diving!" More applause. "I hope you'll join me for the party."

"I plan to be dead soon, too" I say.

Justinus and Oliver look askance towards me.

"What the fuck?"

"You will not be dead."

"I think it's time," I say.

"It is not your time," says Justinus.

"That's right," says Oliver. "You're not done. Not now."

"Wait, why is it wrong for him to die?"

"It's not right," says Justinus.

The person sitting next to Fred interjects, as well. "Why are we stopping him?"

"He's not doing it for the right reasons," says Oliver. "He's not actually dead, just a little depressed. You're not even on anti-depressants, and you never have been, right?"

"True," I say.

"Why don't you try them?" says this random man.

"I'm not interested in that," I reply.

Random man shakes his head. "Valance, up there, he's been planning his death for twenty years. That man is a waste of space at this point. And even then, he's barely ready. Why are you rushing?"

I look around at the expectant faces of the immediate group of our table.

"Can we talk about this later? It's not like I'm going to do it tonight, okay? I'm just done, but we can talk about it later. It seemed like we were all announcing our deaths."

"This is ridiculous," says Justinus.

"Pissed," says Oliver.

"Don't make a bad choice," says the random man, his wife shushing him now.

"Peter will not have this," says Oliver. "At his wedding, too. Shame. Shame on you."

I am hiding out on the roof of our building where there is a little garden with wooden benches and a trellis entwined with a flowering vine. It is a beautiful setting and I stand near the edge looking out over the ocean. I do not want to see anyone. All they want to talk about is what I said this morning.

My momentary peace is quickly broken. "There you are," says Justinus, walking briskly across the rooftop. "I can't believe you're saying this," says Justinus. "You didn't even really love her. You know what a real relationship is. I do, too. Why give up over someone so temporary?"

The party has started again and there is music and dancing below us in the courtyard. It's day four of the five day party, but Justinus and Oliver have no interest in participating anymore. Instead, their concern is in convincing me to give up my decision. That there is no reason for me to give up now, as if the situation I'm in is somehow different or more challenging than it was before.

"Yeah, I think that's what everyone is."

"What?"

"Everyone is temporary."

"Yes, of course," says Oliver.

"That includes me," I say. "I'm just accepting that."

"You are not," replies Oliver, "you're just upset, weirdly upset over people dying. It doesn't impact you at all."

I give him a disdainful look in response. His words are incalculably out of touch.

"Not the way I would have said it," follows Justinus, "but he's completely right. You are fine, and if you don't rush off to death, you'll be better in short order."

"You don't kill yourself because you are upset. You do it when you are too empty to find anything fun. Or if you're younger, because you hate yourself and do not know how to change or come to tolerate yourself."

"I don't want to do anything else right now. I certainly am not enjoying anything," I say.

"I don't believe you," Oliver says. I'm surprised how upset he is with me. He is not one for these sorts of arguments.

"Death's heads all over the field," I say.

"Is that a reference to something?" asks Justinus.

"Yeah," I say. "It explains what I'm seeing."

"This is ridiculous. You're just in the midst of something. Can't you see it? Can you not see where you are?"

I start to cry a bit. "I can't do this anymore. I don't want to talk anymore."

"You're going to be fine. Let us help you."

"I don't want that."

"Why don't you want help?"

"I want to die. I want it be over."

"You can't do that."

"Tears in the rain," I say. "Time to die."

Part Three

Though thou shouldst be going to live three thousand years, and as many times ten thousand years, still remember that no man loses any other life than this which he now lives, nor lives any other than this which he now lives. The longest and the shortest are thus brought to the same. For the present is the same to all, though that which perishes is not the same; and so that which is lost appears to be a mere moment. For a man cannot lose either the past or the future; for what a man has not, how can anyone take from him?

Marcus Aurelius – *Meditations,* book two[13]

CHAPTER 1

***Principia Moribunda:* A lecture on the goodness of dying**
Hans Svendsen
2967
The Gifford Lecture Series at the University of Edinburgh

> *Foreword: This lecture given by the famed scholar of Wittgensteinian logic* Hans Svendsen *is one of the most widely discussed pieces of philosophy from the third millennium. It also served as the final words of Svendsen, who managed therein to leave an enduring mark on the history of philosophy.*

BEFORE I BEGIN to speak about my proper subject, I will have to offer a few words of qualification. Even after several hundred years of use, though this is something I do not really have to mention, my use of English lacks the precision and expansiveness of expression that is particularly desirable. I ask you to work on my behalf to come to find the meaning behind my words through your additional effort, a burden, I know. The second complication is that I will not be lecturing on the subject that many of you have expected me to lecture on, Wittgenstein's logic and my own versions of this. Your chair, when he asked me to speak, indicated only that I should speak on whatever I would like to discuss in a half-hour's time. I am truly honored that he even asked, and so I pursued a topic which I believed could be communicated to you within this timeframe of a half hour. To take up the lecture on logic, I say, would be a false venture—it is my life's work and I cannot convey anything substantial in such a time. My only goal in lecturing on such a subject would be to convince you that you do not know anything about it, and to study more. So I chose this topic because it will fit into a half hour without any falsehood or false claim of knowledge because it is new.

To begin my lecture, I will speak about something different than what we tend to discuss in philosophical circles like these. I will speak about what I think should be identified as the *principia moribunda*, the foundational principles of dying, if you will. And I will be speaking on Wittgenstein's view of suicide, proposing this lecture on the ethics of death from his lecture on ethics. My reference may be apparent to many of you, and I hope this is welcome.[14] Death, as we all know, went away for a time, but has now returned. It is no longer sufficient to discuss the good in the way that we have done as a result of this. This is why I propose the *principia moribunda* as a matter proper to philosophy generally and in particular to ethics. In this way, to provide a preliminary definition, I take the *principia moribunda* as the general inquiry into a good death.

This is a comically imprecise statement, as you have well noted at this time. We should, in particular, ask for precision into these words, none more so than "good." We are now five hundred years beyond the death of Wilbur Reils, and in that time a little over three and a half billion persons have chosen to end their lives. It is said in the next five hundred years that another three billion persons will choose to end their lives, including some of those born after the transition. So we need an inquiry into the "good"—I should say that this is the classic domain of ethics, an inquiry into what is good—we need an inquiry into the "good" because we have a completely new paradigm for what goodness is because we have a new paradigm of existence. Life is good for a time, and then it is no longer good, and it thus becomes good to die.

We need to talk about ethics as a result of this problem of a purely voluntary existence. Let me quote to proceed:

> Now instead of saying "Ethics is the enquiry into what is good" I could have said Ethics is the enquiry into what is valuable, or, into what is really important, or I could have said Ethics is the enquiry into the meaning of life, or into what makes life worth living, or into the right way of living.[15]

If we say that all these provide some greater depth to "good," and speak to what ethics as a whole is, then can we include these questions in the Ethics of Death? There are ways that these questions still obtain in the matter of death, and I will say a few of them.

First, if I say a good death, I do not know how all of you will respond. The Pope's suicide a few centuries ago is still debated—can he still be Catholic? He lived, from what we know, a saintly life. He was "good," at least Roman Catholic good. His final action we do not know if we would say it was "good." He did much to preserve life in his time, guiding the expansion and adoption of the transition in countries staying behind and showing resistance. He did much good in saving life. But then he chose to die, the rumor being by a government pill of all things. Not the first Catholic to die, but the first to die who we can safely say possessed a firm and public notion of Catholic Good.

In what way was his death a good? To have a good we must have an end, a *telos*. And an end is outside fact, so we never have end as fact, since it is not scientifically verifiable or possible to objectively realize, and therefore we do not have good, not absolutely, but only arbitrarily—the arbitrarily predetermined end. The good road is good if we know the end to which that road leads and it is good. The end chosen by Catholics was life, absolute life—the culture of life, it was called. The pope himself once spoke for the culture of life, and later he offered caution and compassion to those who chose against it. Wittgenstein when he died was buried with a Catholic funeral. He was not, himself, Catholic, but buried in the Catholic style and he may be said to embody certain of the Catholic values. He also faced suicide, though he decided against it—he faced his own suicide after three of his brothers chose suicide and left this world. One of his favorite influences, Otto Weininger, killed himself after determining it was the correct philosophical decision, an argument that Wittgenstein loved to discuss, if only to mock, but likely something more. But in one short span, one brother committed suicide, his uncle died in an accident, and his lover died in a plane crash. He has already completed his *Tractatus logico-philosophicus*. The final proposition: "*Wovon man nicht sprechen kann, darüber muß man schweigen.*" What one cannot speak of, of that one must be silent. At this time in his life, Wittgenstein loved to speak of suicide.

This sixth proposition he applied most directly to ethics. And to God and religion and metaphysics. He said it was a tendency to "run against the walls of our cage," but one that he would never mock. This is the absolute hesitation of the early Wittgenstein, an inability to see beyond the cage and into what ought to be. This is the "*muß*." This "must" is that which can always be removed, because there is no sublime, important or trivial. There is no must without an end. There is no *telos* in the world of fact. One must take this road—one must only take this road if one must go to some end. There is no end which one must go to, it is all nonsense and nonsensical.

In the course of my over six hundred years of life I have taken many roads, and each time I have ignored the nonsense of deeming one road better than another. I have now come to this point where I deem there to be an absolute end and a good road, and this objectively realized. This would make ethics possible, and it makes the ethics of dying possible. To be precise it makes dying ethical; death is the ethical act. Nothing else comes with this declaration of ethical dying into ethics. Ethics is still nonsense in its essence, but the ethics of dying is no longer nonsense. Ethical dying, in particular, suicide and the selection of death are the correct response to a question which can in fact be expressed. Live or die? No. Rephrased. Live(?) "As in death, too, the world does not change but ceases." Further, "The solution of the problem of life is seen in the vanishing of this problem." Is life a question expressed? The experience of it indicates to me that it must be, and the solution to this question is found in the vanishing of this problem, one which ceases and with it the world with the ceasing of myself.

I know that you did not come here expecting me to announce my suicide. But I will be heading home after I take a few questions. My husband of the past four hundred years, Tomas, he should be dead by now—he told me he wanted to die first, and that he didn't want me to see. I think he is dead now. He was supposed to take a pill while I was here. So I will go home and find him dead and then I will follow in the path he has taken.

I do not like my message. I have found it truly horrifying and disgusting when I came to this conclusion. I wanted to dig my way out of the facts, but there was no logic to defeat them, and the logic I used led me to a conclusion. Life is a problem to me as I have now experienced it and it needs its solution which is found in its end. The great problem of this lies principally in the fact that if this is the proper end of life, as I have argued in arguing for a *principia ethica moribunda*, then it has always been the proper end of life. Wittgenstein delayed death until sixty-two despite it approaching him much more forcefully at an earlier date. This was his mistake, in not choosing to end his life earlier. It has been my mistake in not seeing this earlier, as well, being now as old as I am, but it has now been clearly and cleverly demonstrated that there is nothing more to do. This has always been the absolute end, and it is the one assurance, the one truth, the one sublime—the end of life. Not life itself, but its end, this is the constant and the revelation—it is the metaphysical as fact. I have to accept it as nothing else.

So this is the status of things. The critical mind comes to the conclusion that the answer to the problem of life is death, that to choose death is the result of the proper and objective observation of the phenomena of the world. There is nothing else I can do. My affairs are in order, have no fear, and I'll be glad to take some questions and I will willingly mingle at the cocktail hour if you'd like to say goodbye. I've said my goodbyes to my family and everyone else, do not worry.

By way of concluding, I want to say how I feel now—I feel that a weight is lifted from my shoulders. I feel, also, confident in the truth in a way that I have never before. It is, I think, the feeling that those who are religious understand, the peace of dwelling in their God who is Truth. I am in my greatest comfort now, and I come to my rest.

It feels a fitting note, a good justification for where I am, this piece from Svendsen. I have never been a Wittgensteinian, of course. But the logic is compelling.

Milnius did write a response to that piece. Next to *On meaninglessness*, the most important thing he ever wrote. I have no interest in it at the moment. Maybe if I survive myself, I'll read it again.

Time to move. On the way down I peer out the porthole window and spy the second-rate city surrounded by desolating plains. Cheyenne, Wyoming, why would anyone ever come here? I make my way to the pod rental kiosk to arrange for my transportation. There were three of us on the shuttle, but the others have quickly scattered leaving me lonely in the shuttle port. It is a small space, a glass dome on top of gray metallic pillars, surrounded by a few offices and restrooms. I look to the timeboard and see that there are only three more flights scheduled for anywhere today. It is nine in the morning.

I have avoided these parts of the world quite intentionally for most of my life. These parts, to clarify, are areas of low-rent housing. Far from being a classist statement against those who are poorer than I, these communities cater to persons who have committed their lives to virtual worlds, and have generally rejected what we generally call "reality." I believe myself to be as skeptical as the next person, and to greet the reality I face with sufficient hesitation. I understand the limits of human society, its failures, and its false pretensions. My appreciation for the eventual torture of human life is what brings me here, after all, so I do not offer this statement in direct judgment. But those who engage only with the virtual world fail to live in such a radical manner that there is nothing I can do to support their form of life.

I step outside and the cool winds of late winter greet me. I wave my hand to the short row of pods out front of the shuttle station, striding onto the pavement, and searching for the lighted response from my designated vehicle. There are no multi-level roadways here, only a single paved street stretching to and from the downtown area. As far as I can see are housing blocks, low apartment complexes with no balconies or outdoor spaces or trees, few windows, and no lights.

The virtual world was one of the first features of reality to be condemned with the development of the UAG code, and then, later, by the Federation. No one is allowed to play any virtual game (virtual forms of pornography are permissible, as Peter experienced—can't repress sexuality) until they have left home. The allure is simply too strong. Human life, even with the endless possibilities of eternal life, is inherently limiting. For some, it is too far deficient to justify living there.

Imagine, if you would, that you have always wished to have wings, and with that, the ability to fly anywhere that you wanted to. In your world, you now have them, and an unlimited reality from which to choose. One can live in the world of the twentieth century, or in ancient Greece, or the distant planet Cadmus I. Not only do you have wings, you are also irresistible to women, or men, or both. You have programmed your reality where there is no one who will refuse your charm.

Or better yet, if you have no interest in wings, you are a great warrior, fighting with an unconquerable troop of samurai, or space marines, or galactic bombers, or maybe you are a wizard, or a knight slaying dragons. Or, as the studies indicate, many of the visualizations are nothing so exotic, but rather more mundane activities. Always wanted to open a restaurant?

Why risk the possibility of failure in the real world when one can guarantee a riotous success in simulated form?

It all feels the same, after all, to the person. You feel every menu that you pick up as you work an extra shift as the hostess for that evening when your maître d robot is on the fritz. You feel the warmth of the ovens as you step into the kitchen, you taste the richness of your house specialty béarnaise, you grasp the hands of the grateful patrons as they thank you for the wonderful meal, you feel all the elation of actually succeeding.

And then, one day, there is a power flux, or maintenance needs to replace a breaker, or something in your computer burns out, and your simulation ends. You wake up to find yourself in your simulation chair, a feeding tube connected to your stomach; the room is dark, poorly lit, but the glimpse of actual light brings the novelty of true pain. You are filled with an unspeakable rage when this happens. The illusion is broken and you sit in a squat apartment building in Cheyenne, Wyoming, not the beautiful place of perfection you once inhabited. You never venture out, never attempt anything more than an imitation of life in the superficial form you have deemed ideal.

The first few times this happens, perhaps the person can survive it. They are not so immersed, or not so convinced of the new reality they have experienced. Most of these virtual persons will switch between games for the first few years, finding what they really like, finding a community of fellow participants to match their interest and enthusiasm. They will likely start with a foot in both worlds, splitting their day between realities. Then they will grow in their commitment, spend all their time in the reality which is the most satisfying, as the life most of us live is filled with disappointments.

But it never turns out perfectly. And as much as one works to convince themselves that it is acceptable for the simulation to end, no matter how briefly, this conviction is lost the further one becomes embedded.

So you try again, a new experience, a new life. And then, one day, you realize that you are becoming bored. Your time as a Zulu warrior was enjoyable, so you move on. The next time, however, as you learn Kung Fu as a Shaolin monk with special sexual privileges, you find you are not quite as satisfied. Some years later, you try again, and once more, and once more, and once more, until you realize that nothing can match that initial high.

The Federation released a statement of warning some millennia ago that the average time to death after a person begins spending one hundred twenty eight plus hours straight in a virtual setting is two hundred years. For most, two hundred years feels like a long time, and besides, they can stop when they want to. But the allure is too strong and too easy. Yes, it is risky, but so is life, so why not risk having the chance to perfectly realize all of your visions for yourself, if only for a little while? So what if it results in absolute boredom and your inevitable death? We all die, but not all of us have spent twenty years as a blue whale.

I tried to have time limits on virtual living placed while I was a member of the Federation. Each time I was rejected of course; too much of a restriction on human liberty. "This leads more directly to death than almost anything else we have in our world." "It isn't our job to prevent chosen death, as much as we would like to do so." They were right about the need for liberty; this doesn't change the extent to which it is a poor choice.

What great weakness this is, to choose to live a false life because it is easier! Why risk meeting a person and falling in love—simulate the ideal relationship. Why risk moving to a new city, making new friends, trying a new job, studying a new thing—simulate a new place. It is a cowardly way to live. There is no boldness in coming to a place like this and sitting in a simulation room forever. No greatness to it, and nothing positive that comes from it but a waste of an opportunity. It is all an act, all a method of avoidance; they do nothing but pale from the greatest challenge of existence, to come to terms with oneself, and to truly embrace what we are and what we have done and what we are capable of. This what it means to live. To be able to spend time with yourself, and to feel comfortable in that reality.

All of the things you have done in your life, you have done them. You have made those choices, and these are now the consequences that you face. We distance ourselves, perhaps, but that only denies what we have been capable of, and thus, what we remain capable of. The human can expand in every different direction, and it requires constant training to become someone you want to exist as, to become a person who can stand themselves as that person. The one who avoids this in life through choosing the simple, the easy, the superficially entertaining, this person is worthy of condemnation—no matter the condemnation, they die anyway.

This is, at least, the way I used to feel, as I must remind myself. I have come to Wyoming to procure a weapon for my death, and in that fact, I am required to acknowledge that this means I have given up my pursuit of the risk of life. I am called upon, further, to acknowledge that perhaps my conclusions regarding the better form of life have been misguided. The choice of the virtual world leads to death; my choice of a bold life is bringing me to the same place.

So my previous judgment may have been in error. Perhaps I have been mistaken in my choice of life. I did not set out to accomplish anything greater than contentment with myself, and from that first achievement, to live a varied life amongst the people, interacting with all that the context I find myself in has provided. And I have always felt comfortable with myself, knowing the errors I have made, and will make, and the pain that I have caused others, and myself. I know these things, and I have made them a part of myself, and maybe this has been the reason that I have been able to survive this long. But now, it seems so meaningless that I at one time accomplished that lofty goal of knowing myself and being okay with my strangeness and now I want to die.

At least, however, I'm going to die in a mildly creative manner. I'll be driving up to the Cody Firearms Museum, formerly the Buffalo Bill Historic Center. There they have the shotgun of one of my favorite writers, Ioan Aaronson, who died in 4652. Perhaps I was a bit inspired by Morris, to follow someone else's fame on my way out. He chose Jesus, and I turned to the literary figures who gave me so much to think about. Aaronson. Ernest Hemingway. Hunter S. Thompson. Kurt Cobain. Alfred Littlewright. Frederick Marsted. Jim Weiland. All dead of a shotgun blast to the head. The only shotgun I could find was Aaronson's, and the staff have assured me that it is in working order, except that I will have to locate the proper shotgun shells, though they, again, have assured me that I will be able to do so, as they haven't been trying particularly hard to get them.

The ride will take several hours, as there are very few shuttle stops in Wyoming as a whole, and especially in the portion I am traveling to. Cody, Wyoming sits close to the edge of the Yellowstone Volcanic Area, and it is considered a minor risk to fly in that area. I can certainly handle a few hours of comfort in a transport pod. It is, after all, time with myself, and I have indicated that I can handle that with the utmost aplomb—ten thousand years, and I am not yet sick of myself.

After a brief trip through the city, through cold apartment block upon apartment block, the pod locates the interstate. I recline my seat a bit further and settle into a comfortable position. I could put on music or a movie or read a book, but I want to sit with myself, and sit with my decision. I don't want to enjoy this trip.

Outside of the city, the empty plains roll on, a great flat expanse of nothing. I have never enjoyed these parts of the world; I prefer the ocean, or at least a body of water. Trees, even, would be nice. There is nothing here but flat grasslands and maybe, every once in a while, some foothills or a mountain.

Much of this used to be farmland, I believe. Now, we grow our beef and our plants are farmed in ultra-efficient high-rises. Farms in the middle of nowhere are incredibly wasteful.

What am I doing here? I'm thinking of nonsense as I roll my way across empty terrain to pick up a gun to shoot myself with. Am I just going to avoid that issue?

I put on a show, something familiar. It's a sitcom from the 2400s, when the DT in its infinite wisdom decided to intervene in the modification of culture. They saw it happening already, very quickly after the transition, that as culture moved on from the older population as they aged, they would become deeply alienated from society. As part of the program of educating youth, a series of movies, serials, and books were offered as standard. If you were educated in the traditional manner, as 99.9% of the population is, then you have been raised on the same collection of media as everyone else in society. It was a brilliant method to keep language from transitioning too dramatically, and to keep cultural norms within a certain framework. Everyone can make a reference to *Decimus' Place*, and we'll all get the joke.

My first time through the show was voluntary, I should say; I simply lived through it, and watched it because it is genuinely one of the funniest productions in history. Such a brilliant and beautiful collection of actors. Decimus (Dex) was played by Arthur French, a perfect goofball. The man could fall in the most ideally silly manner—even the intelligentsia who scoff at physical humor and accept nothing less than Malick or Schoenhof are forced to laugh at the way Decimus rolls down the flight of stairs. Universally beloved and universally desired, universal appreciation didn't end well for Arthur. Even within the first few years after the selection, with the events of Wilbur Reils and his friends, he wanted to die. We approved massive surgery, the construction of a completely new identity and appearance. It helped for a while. He moved to Mars, and he found peace for a time. But every reference to that silly Decimus would stir something in him, and he could not escape his character.

He killed himself before the end of the millennia, along with those few billion others, along with almost every actor, director, and writer selected for cultural core education by the DT. It is one the most painful aspects of my life, the knowledge that the unintended side effect of maintaining a relatively static cultural base was the mass death of those who made the culture worthwhile. It was too much for them—having their work perpetually discussed and perpetually referenced by every member of the society for all eternity. I left the government, and had no interest in returning for a few millennia after that. And it took me many years to truly come to terms with myself as the murderer, as the proximate cause of the end of so much life. It was my idea, after all, to include Decimus.

On screen, Decimus falls and spills a coffee on Hypatia (Hype), the woman he is always trying to date but can never quite convince. I let out a reflexive snort of a laugh. I know that I can't be blamed for my suggestion. This is just good stuff.

THE pod lets out a muted "Arriving at your destination," and I am snapped back from my haze. There is a parking lot with a single pod sitting nearby, and a man standing out in front of the museum. He waves as my pod comes to a stop next to what I assume is his.

"Welcome," says the man. He is tall, with a pointed goatee and mustache. His stature screams military. He is thin and muscular, with perfect posture, dressed in a gray urban camo cassock, topped with the somewhat cowboy-like hat of the UAG from the 31st century Holt's Rebellion, where religious extremists attempted to end the system of eternal life completely. The conflict lasted almost two years, but there was very little violence, and the use of drone technology effectively ended the possibility of meaningful armed conflict. The government of essentially the entire world at that time will always be able to produce more drones, and these drones will always be more effective than humans with hand held weapons. It is the last armed conflict in human history, and there are no prospects for a new claimant to that title. What would be the point? One would lose before beginning.

"Hi," I say. "Warren Walker." I offer a bow, but he waves it off and shakes my hand. "I knew it was you. Not too many people out here this time of year."

"You are Timothy Street, correct?"

"That's right. Welcome to my museum." He gestures to the door, so we walk. "I was excited to get your message. We don't get visitors at the museum so often, especially not since the collection was put into the reality synth a few centuries ago."

"Well, I wanted to see things in person," I say.

"It's always better that way," he says.

"And to see that gun I asked about."

"I've got it for you," he says, as we walk through the sliding doors at the entrance. "I'm happy to get it for you if you're in a rush."

"Not at all, no shuttle flights for a while. Not much going in and out of Cheyenne."

"I noticed that in your message. Why didn't you fly into Billings?"

"What?" I ask.

"Billings. It's a few hours closer. A lot more flights, too."

"Shit."

He laughs quietly. "You haven't spent too much time out here, huh?"

"No. I like the ocean."

"Not for me," he says. "Give me the plains any day. A sea of grass."

"All yours."

"Well, if you've got time, I can show you around. Some good stuff here."

"Sure. And you'll have to direct me somewhere for lunch."

"Hell, I'll join you for lunch."

"Excellent," I say. Seems like this man hasn't seen another person for a while.

As we enter the museum, we walk past a front desk lined with kiosks—a ticket booth, I think.

"Do I need a ticket?"

"Ha, no. No, no, you're all good with me. The exhibits are this way."

The first room is filled with weapons from the 19th century, from the original museum, from Buffalo Bill Cody, a figure I've never heard of, but whose image is plastered on every surface in this place.

"Muskets, rifles, our Gatling gun, from the 1860s. Here, you should check this out." We walk over to a small display case and there is a hand sized weapon looking back at us. "The Colt revolver. The weapon that changed the world. Mass produced, easily affordable."

"Everyone used to have a gun, right?"

"Not everyone, of course. But if you lived out in a part of the world like this back then, you needed one. It was a different thing."

"I remember knowing some people like that."

He looks at me deeply for a moment. "How old are you?"

"Pretty old. Some old gun culture was still around when I was growing up. But they all refused the transition."

"You *are* old. I'm not even that old, and I'm old."

"Were you in that war?"

He looks confused.

"Your hat?"

His cheeks tinge only the slightest.

"Most people don't recognize it. No, I'm a few thousand years too late for war. I was a space marine for three hundred years, so I feel like it's okay if I wear the uniform. Even if we never found anything to fight."

"Of course," I say.

He keeps walking, and we move on to the next room, this one filled with weapons from more recent centuries. In particular, there is a giant cannon looking object, with a back pack attached to it.

"What is that?"

"That is a plasma shotgun. Works in space. When they thought they had found intelligent life, it was commissioned, just in case, you know?"

"Yeah," I say.

"Never used in battle though," he laughs. "But I've shot it a few times."

"Is that right?"

"Oh yeah. Man, at full power, you could blast the biggest boulder and it just melts away. If you're trying to kill yourself, this would very much guarantee your death."

I smile at him. A delightfully gross suggestion.

"You don't think the shotgun will be enough?"

"No, no," he says, "that'll work just fine. Just in case you wanted a show."

"I'm okay with the gun. Sentimental reasons."

"I like Aaronson's work, too. *Moon Sickness*, in particular."

"It's a brilliant book." *Moon Sickness* was about the peculiar form of depression prone to strike the first few thousand moon dwellers. It was also a bit of a love story, and a murder mystery, but the reason it endures is because of the way Aaronson evoked emotional reality: if one has lived at all, then one could see in Aaronson's words the most artful capture of the experience of pain and beauty, and the odd way that they are woven together in life. He was a true master in that regard.

"Terrible movie, though," he continues.

"Complete mistake casting Jakeson. And I'm not much of a fan of Temples as a director."

"I can't say I watched anything else of his," he says. "Wasn't going to waste time after that disaster."

"Can't blame you," I say.

He gestures us on to the next room, and there on the table is a shotgun from the 27th century. One of the last mass produced firearms, and one produced after the banning of private weapon ownership (with innumerable exceptions), it is an intimidating object.

"This is the gun. It's a special sort. Beretta Moses 8. An 8 gauge tactical shotgun, able to shoot twenty two different forms of ammunition, including the standard laser guided pellet ammo. Shoot it and let the computer guide hundreds of explosive particles around corners and obstacles into your enemy who is under the mistaken and soon to be corrected impression of being under cover. Damn near two thousand years old by the time Aaronson used it."

It is a beautiful piece, shiny, all mirrored chrome with black carbon nano-fiber on the stock and forend.

"You'll probably have to pull the trigger with your toe," he says.

I laugh. "I hadn't thought of that. I guess I will." It strikes me as somewhat undignified.

"I'm sorry we don't have any ammunition for you. And I don't know who to contact. But I am sure you can find someone. There's always someone, even if they're retired."

I nod. "I'm sure it will work out."

"Do you know how to use it?"

"I think so."

He explains anyway. "Shells in here. Pump the action to bring a shell up. Safety here. Point the dangerous end at what you want to break. Pull the trigger."

"Seems easy enough," I respond.

"It is."

He pauses for a moment, as if he'd like to say something.

I fill the silence. "It's a beautiful weapon."

"That it is," he says. "You're going to want to keep it locked in the box, though. It's been wired, so the drones will know when you've got it out of the box, and they'll know when it's been fired, too. So, if you're fooling around with it, they'll take it away."

"So, use it to shoot myself is what you're saying."

He nods. "They just might take it away otherwise. You take a practice shot, see if it works, and then they take it away, and you've got no options." He pauses. "And if you go out in public with it out, it'll be gone before you've taken a step."

"I'm not going to try a public shooting, don't worry." We haven't had a mass shooting in…well, probably since the Holt Rebellion. Damn near impossible to accomplish. "I'm just going to shoot myself."

"Glad to hear it," he says, tipping his hat.

He offers me a big black duffle bag, and slides the gun in its case inside. "So you can carry it."

I zip up the bag, and we stand in silence for the moment.

"Thanks for the tour," I say.

"My pleasure, truly. I mentioned we don't get too many visitors out here, everyone's inside all the time. So it's good to have people around."

"Yep. Thanks again."

"Sure."

Nothing is happening. "Want to get some lunch?"

"That would be great," he says. "I know just the place."

A short ride in my pod and we are at a restaurant called Tito's in the downtown area of Cody.

"Tito hasn't been back in a while," he explains, "but it's still a good restaurant."

"Where's Tito?"

"I honestly couldn't tell you. I think…I really don't know."

"Fun."

We take a seat at the bar. The restaurant is completely empty. It is a bit early for lunch, a few minutes before noon, but something tells me there will not be many more visitors to this place. The restaurant is themed like a Wild West saloon, all rough-hewn wood and fake dust everywhere.

"What's good?" I ask.

"Odds and ends, really. Depends what they have." He looks around and finds the bartender, a short robot minding its own business at the other end of the bar. "Hey," he shouts, "the elk special fresh?"

"Yes sir," he says. "Fresh yesterday."

"Excellent. Two elk sandwiches. Fries. Two Budweisers."

"Yes sirree." The robot embellishes his speech like the old timey bartender he's supposed to be.

"Elk?" I say.

"That's right."

"Fresh?"

"Freshly shot. We have an overpopulation of elk out here. So we shoot them every once in a while."

"Neat."

"They make a real good sandwich. Bacon wrapped elk meat with aioli on a baguette. Lettuce, tomato, fried onion rings. It's really the only reason to come here."

"Who shoots them?"

"Well, I do sometimes. There's a few of us. Take a gun out from the museum."

"Oh."

"Yeah, I know, condemnable behavior and whatnot. But honestly, it's better than what the drones do. Somebody's got to cull the population, else they starve to death."

"What do the drones do?"

"They just fly up to them, catch them with their dangly arms, one on the antlers, one around the body, and then twist." He makes a twisting motion with his hands. "The neck is broken and they're dead. I saw one drone twist a little too hard, ripped the head clear off of the elk."

"That's fantastically gross."

"Overpopulation. And the drones apparently knock them out with drugs anyway, so they aren't even awake when it happens. But yeah, I think a clean shot to the head is better than being treated as a twist top beer."

"I'd say."

Our beers arrive and the bartender removes the caps with his dangly arms. If you ever have time, you should look up the story of how Budweiser managed to survive for so many millennia despite its obvious shortcomings.

"Can I ask the obvious question?" I say.

"Why do I live here?"

"Yeah. You're not in your synth chair."

"My wife is."

"Oh. That's why you're here."

"I like the plains, too. But yeah."

"Can you get her to come out?"

"For now. I take her out once a week for a day or two. I go home and I wait for a good pause in her life, and I take her out, and we spend some time together."

"Lovely."

"Yeah."

"Why do you stay?"

"I love her."

"I imagine."

"Have you ever been in love?"

I grimace. "Ten thousand years…"

"So," he says, "what's that, like twelve times."

"That would be the average."

"Then you know it's impossible to give up on someone when you love them. Really love them. It'll probably kill me when I lose her for good."

"It killed me," I say. "That's why I'm here, shopping for what you're selling."

"Loaning," he says, with a smile.

"Of course," I say.

"Interesting."

"But doesn't it bother you," I continue, "being out here." He looks expectantly at me. "I hate it here," I say. "I honestly do. I am completely intolerant of people who stay in all day."

"Why is that?"

"Irrational hatred. It's probably the opposites thing, where, when you see someone living their life in a way completely opposed to what you have chosen to do, you feel insulted by their choice. So you condemn them."

"You are consistently social?"

"Yes. Always living in a city. Always new friends. Or as much as I can. And not because I want to do so all the time. I like my quiet, my peace, my unstructured hours alone."

"I don't mind it here."

"But you're not going into a synth chair."

"Not a chance," he says. "I don't really disagree with you. I'm just not so judgmental."

"Fair enough," I say, smiling casually.

He pauses and looks over to me from his proximate position at the bar. He completes a thorough once over, and smiles to himself.

"What?" I ask.

"You don't strike me as being particularly dead," he says, continuing his smile.

"I'm sorry?"

"You don't really want to die."

"I'm sure I do, actually."

"No, you don't." He takes a deep sip of his beer, finishing it, then waving to the bartender for another one. He swallows, and then returns to his sandwich, picking it up and taking a massive, meaty bite, chewing dramatically. About three quarters of the way through his mastication, he finally acknowledges that I am staring at him. "What?" he says. "It's good news."

"I can't go on living. I don't even want to tell you what I've been through this past year. And I just look around, all I see when I look at people are the dead. Skeletons walking. You aren't even real to me."

"The death's head," he says.

"Uh, yeah."

"So what's happened to you?"

"You really want to know?"

"I do," he says.

"My wife, she was only a hundred and fifty, she killed herself. No ceremony. Then my friend killed himself, and then my ex-wife and my eldest daughter at the same time, and then a month or two ago, the woman I was seeing killed herself. All this year."

"Tough stretch," he replies, taking another sip.

"Tough stretch?"

"Yeah, well, you've been alive ten thousand years, you've got to expect this kind of thing to happen at some point. Odds being what they are." I just nod my head in disbelief. He doesn't understand me. "You know," he continues, "the death's head meditation is actually an insight, not a sign of death. You're treating it like it's a reason for depression, when it actually frees one from the suffering that is reality."

"What are you talking about?"

"You've misinterpreted your philosophy. It's actually providing you with a reason not to kill yourself, when you're taking it as a reason to kill yourself. It's a classic misappropriation of a complicated thought, now twisted to a false end; the proximate cause is usually emotional fragility, whether from misguided sense of exceptionalism, or from some emotional trauma."

"What the fuck?"

"The deaths head meditation is an insight. You know what people are, and then you realize that your belief that people have ever been alive was mistaken, and then you feel okay. Your wives, your children, your friends—they've all been dead the whole time. So there's no need to feel bad."

"Fuck this." I look down at my sandwich.

"We don't have to talk philosophy. How's your sandwich?"

"Great."

We sit silently for a few moments as I fume. Who does he think he is, telling me what I actually believe or what I should actually be thinking or what I am actually thinking? I did not get the damn meditation wrong. It's…I'm seeing the skulls of everyone…

I take a bite. Might as well finish this.

"Good stuff, huh?"

"It's delicious."

It is.

"So are you staying nearby? Catching a flight?"

"I've got to figure out where to get shells first."

"Oh, right. I can't help you much on that front."

"Any recommendations?"

"Search for someone who does custom firearms work. I'm sure there's someone out there that would know how to make a basic shell for your gun."

"Great."

"Hey, I told you that you could use the plasma gun, incinerate your body and the immediate five meters around you. You could do it right now." I nod. "But you won't," he says.

"That's enough," I say. "You don't understand."

"Classic myth. We tell ourselves that our suffering is special and different, when actually it's just as generic as we are."

"Known a few depressed people in your time?"

"I've known myself, for one. And yes, of course, there are others."

"I'm going to stay at the Yellowstone Hotel. On the lakebed."

"Oh."

"What?"

"Have you been there?"

"No."

"Since they rebuilt it after the last eruption, it's just a miserable place. They didn't put much effort into it."

"Wonderful. Well, I'm just going to be searching through archived web pages anyway."

"That's right," he says. I finish eating my sandwich. "We could grab dinner tonight, too."

"Don't you have to check on your wife?"

"No, she went in yesterday, won't be out for at least a week. I'm going hunting tomorrow."

"I could do dinner. Depends on how the day goes."

"Good. I'll see who's around."

"I thought everyone is always inside in their synth chair."

He leans back and takes a deep breath. "That's just not true. Look, I'll tell everyone to come down here. We'll have a party."

I can't tell if he's serious. "No need for that."

"No, no, you are under a false presumption about this part of the world. That it is empty, or filled with people dying or something."

"I was one of three in the shuttle station, and I haven't seen anyone else in this town since this morning."

"You've seen me."

"Got me there."

He pulls out his tablet and taps a few times.

"There, I've just invited everyone to come and join us."

This is the worst surprise possible. I do not want to meet any of these people. I have ignored calls and entreaties since returning from the wedding from Peter, Nigel, Justinus, Oliver, and Henry, who was apparently contacted by three of the previous four and thus pointed on his fruitless quest to check in. Justinus—I'm sure it was him—even convinced Willa Weston to call me under the guise of offering compassion. It's a callous thing for him to do considering the result of the last woman he attempted to heal me with. He even bought me a shuttle flight to join them on Virgin Gorda and to go sailing with them.

I don't want to see anyone right now. I want to have my gun, and to have my shells, to cease this traveling, to sit in my living room and pull the trigger and have nothing like this life to worry about. But in my way are all these brash people who show no interest in understanding me; they plug on ignorantly in their original way of life, unconcerned and unmoved, and pretending that there is no pain, denying its existence so that they do not have to acknowledge their torture.

I just see it now. I see the skeletons, and I don't care if Mr. Street is correct about my misinterpretation. I don't care. I don't want to see the dead anymore.

There's a few subtle "bings" and he pulls out his tablet again. "See, I've got a few people coming."

"I can't," I say. "I hate to be so impolite. You have been most kind to me, and I will be sure the weapon finds its way home to you."

"You're leaving?"

"Yes, of course. I...can't."

"You can't what?"

"I...Look, I'm sorry."

"You can't handle having fun, or being reminded that you can still enjoy life?"

"No, asshole, that's not it."

"Well?"

"Fine, you're right, I don't want to see anyone." I stand, offer a hand. He refuses. "Well, thanks anyway."

I walk out and am greeted by two persons entering the restaurant. They give me a confused glance, attempting to place the stranger in this one horse town. I offer a faux smile and continue on my way.

HAVING settled into this most dreary of hotels, I first turned my attention to locating a gunsmith. This task, unfortunately, required only two minutes of cursory searching, including the time taken to solicit aid from this man and his quick reply. "Yes, come and visit. Bring the gun."

The first possible travel time is tomorrow morning, from Billings, as was suggested, and I will be traveling to an equally unfavorable place in Savannah, Tennessee. I have only agreed to travel to such a location because it is not near the summer, when the cesspool that is that location becomes all the more heated and the stink permeates through to the very fiber of one's being.

Sitting on the couch in my room is the duffle bag filled with the shotgun. It has a strange presence; I feel a reverence for it that I do not feel for anything common. I am also fearful of it, I think, and mildly anxiety disposed by its intimidating suggestion. But it is also this suggestion of my oncoming death and ultimate freedom that I perhaps am so fervently worshiping. My solution is sitting in this bag on a couch. It will end my life of ten thousand years, and I will be grateful for it.

Despite his protestations, I am quite sure that I am correct in my judgment. My personal experience of reality has led me to this conclusion—the phenomenological account of my consciousness, something to which Mr. Street does not have access. He does not know what it is like to be me, while I have the distinct displeasure of enjoying such privilege. In the brief time since I have returned to my room and set down the duffle bag I have thought of ending my life no fewer than twelve times. Because the gun is disappointingly ineffectual in this moment, I look towards the potential weapons around me. I look out the window and I think of jumping, debating whether or not it would work. I notice the tub and think of drowning myself, and look around for something heavy enough to weigh myself down and hold myself underwater. Better yet, have a knife sent up from room service, a large bowie knife, perhaps, and carve a "Z" in my forehead before slitting my wrists a la Cynthia and her damned husband. I inspect the closet and I think of tying sheets to the curtain rod, bending my knees, and welcoming the blackness.

After a quick nap and a few successive hours of watching the television and sitting in abstract boredom, all while moments of plotting are interspersed and rejected, I decide I should find dinner. The hotel restaurant is not recommended, but it is only a brief walk away, and I have not heard a single noise of life since arriving in this place. No one in the lobby, no pods in the lot, no brave souls out on the lakebed, no movement of any kind to speak of.

Timothy Street was correct, this hotel is an unseemly place. It is nano-architecture, which is typically ornate, because why not, the bots are doing all the work and all one has to do is program in a more interesting design. Instead, the walls are drab, the floors the same pseudo-stone material as the walls, the lighting glowing emanating from slits in .the stone, and there is a confusing dearth of windows given the abundance of gorgeous scenery outside. The hotel, as I understand, was only reconstructed because of popular outcry about the lost institution, most of which is now considered to be unbound nostalgia for the place name "Yellowstone," a sentiment testified to by the complete lack of attendance. The spite with which this building was constructed served as an accurate prediction of its future use.

It's not worth anything to go out, so I order room service, take a couple of pills, and fall asleep.

WITHOUT the volcanic impediment, I am thankfully able to fly directly to Savannah, TN. I have been here before, and unlike its charming sister in Georgia, this is one of the least pleasant places to be in the south. It will be unremarkable this time of year; in the summer, it is a sweltering quagmire of diseased mosquitoes, humidity, and a swarming crowd of people who claim to enjoy life on the river. One lives here if they like to fish, hunt, or drink beer while fishing or hunting. It is quite easy and affordable, actually, to find oneself a mansion on the water. But beyond riding on hovercraft and wake boarding, why would you want to do that? And why not somewhere more scenic than a river in the south?

Leaving the pod, I am pleasantly surprised by the activity around me. There are people here! A few people mingling around the station, visitors greeting one another; couples beginning their vacations; it doesn't feel quite so dead here. I receive more than a few stares as I walk through—the only one unaccompanied, and the only one with a sour look on his face.

After finding my rental, I make my way from the small town center (really the shipping warehouse where house robots come in pods and pick up orders for their owners) down along and over the river. The roads become smaller and smaller until the path turns to gravel and the pod comes to an abrupt stop. Looking at the map, I can tell that the address is still another mile down the road.

"We're not there yet," I say.

The pod beeps a response, which generally means "no."

"The road isn't that bumpy, you can handle it."

It beeps again.

"What a wuss," I say.

"I'm not scared, my programming does not allow me to proceed."

"You're not scared?"

"No, sir," says the pod.

"Fine. But register my displeasure with the rental agency."

It beeps again, pleasantly this time.

I step out of the pod and pick up my massive duffle bag. I begin the long, slow walk to the residence of the bullet maker.

The road is muddy, and my pod may have been correct in its hesitation. Potholes and missing terrain throughout. I concentrate on my footing, hopping between puddles in the inverse of my childhood.

Last March, Gwen and I were in Guatemala staying in a hut and walking down a dirt road to the beach. She killed herself the next week after our mostly miserable trip. Not that we fought much or anything. She didn't have much to say beyond a general, passive malaise. It is, I think, the same malaise I feel now. A quiet discontent. I don't want to do anything. I don't want to *be*. It seems a nuisance.

My shoulders burn as I switch hands with the duffle bag and take a deep step into a dark puddle and stumble momentarily. In a previous life, I may have rolled an ankle, but not anymore. I can't even do that anymore. No weakness but that of the mind.

The road is lined with stone fences which look ancient and authentic, but are in fact the product of nanobots organizing raw materials in an intentionally inelegant manner. The wall is overgrown, laced with vines, the trees leaning past the walls and arching over the street to become a canopy shading my way. Every few steps a peek of sunshine pokes through, and my sight dims in the brightness. Through a flash I see a figure ahead, and I am immediately confused.

There is a large man standing beside a number post at the end of a driveway. He is an absolute spectacle, and something I have not seen in centuries. He is fat! Rotund! At least, relatively speaking. He must have at least twenty or thirty extra kilos on him. This is amazing.

"Hello there," he waves.

"Paul?" I say.

"That's me. Paul Farmer. You're Warren."

"Warren Walker." I bow, and he returns.

"Your pod wouldn't make the trip?"

"Nope. Refused."

"Rentals," he says, shaking his head. "Well come on in, let's take a look at what you've got."

Paul's house is a massive compound, all nano-stone manufacturing, designed to look like sandstone, maybe a pueblo style mansion, which in no way fits the setting. We follow the dirt path around to a garage populated by steering wheeled hoverbuggies and mini-karts. Weaving through the mess, he leads me to his shop. The room is filled with monitors and printing machines of all sorts.

There have been no words exchanged between us, as I have not found anything to say just yet. I am overwhelmed by this person.

He silently gestures for my duffle bag, and I hand it to him. As he unzips the bag, he looks up at me, noticing my lack of speech.

"I'm sorry to do this," I say, "but can we address the elephant in the room."

He laughs casually. "What, me?"

"You are a bit rounder than normal."

"Yessir."

"How'd that happen?"

"I lobbied the Federation for about four hundred years for permission to change my body weight."

"Why?"

"Didn't seem natural to be fit. I don't exercise. It didn't seem right."

"Do you feel better now? Now that you're fat?"

"No, not really."

"Oh."

"Yeah," he says. "So what kind of rounds are you looking for?"

"You can make them?"

"Yeah, won't be a problem."

"Well, I don't know anything about guns."

"What do you plan on shooting?"

"Myself."

He laughs. "Is that right?"

"Yeah."

"In the head?"

"I think that's the traditional way."

"Yeah, that'll work. Okay, I'll make a spread shot—it'll blow the back of your head off though, so you won't look too pretty anymore."

"That's fine. I'm not doing a party or anything."

"Oh, that's a shame."

"Ehh, I've been to enough parties."

He nods knowingly, if with cautious disapproval subtly evident. "Okay. This'll take a couple hours. I can print all the parts, but I have to put the powder in by hand. They don't allow automated bullet manufacture anymore. Of course."

"Of course."

He takes the gun over to the scanner so the printer can match the bullets to size.

"Nice gun. Vintage. Beretta Moses 8. I believe Ioan Aaronson preferred this gun when he was out for a hunt."

"Yeah. It's the gun he used to shoot himself."

"What?"

"Yeah, it's the actual gun he used. Supposedly. I got it from a museum in Wyoming."

"Hooo shit. This is it." He looks it over more carefully this time. "He your favorite author or something?"

"One of them. He's the only one whose shotgun I could find."

"So this is the actual gun he used? The one he put into his mouth and pulled the trigger with."

"That's what they told me. I looked up the serial number and it matches from the records I could find."

"Just to be sure?"

"Yeah, it doesn't really matter, but I had time yesterday."

"It does feel different, right? Kind of magical."

"It's got a power to it. For me, at least. I think it's because I know I'm going to end my very long life with it. And I feel good about that."

"You do?"

"I do."

"You're lucky you called me this week. I'm going out soon, too. Scheduling my death party now, and trying to figure out how to go out."

"Oh."

"Yeah, strange fate, huh?"

"I guess so. But you just became fat, didn't you? Didn't that help?"

"Oh sure. I've been fat for like a hundred years. It gave me that hundred years."

"Worked, then, I guess."

"Yeah, they're considering letting other people do it. They've apparently got thousands of applications for fatness. I don't know what they're going to do."

"Crazy," I say.

"You know, it's a crazy thing that they just made everyone beautiful and athletic and physically flawless. I mean, who thought that we would accept that?"

"I did. We all did. Before the transition, being fat or ugly was a tremendous burden. You would be mocked, earn less money, passed over for promotions, and stereotyped as lazy. Not to mention the health issues. So we just took those issues out of the equation. We're all beautiful, now go live."

"It didn't work."

"Well, you say that now, now that this is the standard. You don't really get what the world was like when people were ugly and fat."

"And you do?"

"Yeah, I was alive before the transition."

"No shit." He thinks for a moment. "How? I'm fourteen hundred and thirty five, and I'm bored out of my mind."

"Well, I'm shooting myself soon."

"Are you bored, too?"

"No. Defeated."

"Defeated." He chews the word. "What does that mean?" He grants me a look of genuine annoyance and then actually bites his tongue in his mouth. I return his glance with my own. "Why don't you head upstairs? My partner is up there, hanging out. You guys can go chat."

"You're all set? I can't help with anything?"

"No. Just going to print things. Put 'em together. I'll be up in a minute."

I look around.

"Through that door," he says, "then straight to the back of the house. The great room. Lots of windows."

"Thanks."

THERE's a small pretty woman on the couch.

"Hi," she says, nodding at me after a casual glimpse.

"Warren Walker," I respond.

"Diana."

"Beautiful day out there." The sun floods the room, a round space with seven meter glass walls and a single piece glass dome as a cap. The river flows by beyond the window, quietly, empty. The décor inside does not match the structure, but is quite beautiful nonetheless. It is something like a traditional Japanese inn—all natural wood grain in the spaces that are not windows. Tatami mats on the floor, low couches, gray linen rectangles with low backs and wooden legs and walnut end tables. The non-glass wall is covered in scrolls of calligraphy.

She is drinking a can of beer. It is almost lunchtime, I suppose.

"Got any more of those?" I ask.

"Kitchen. Around the corner to the right."

I head into the kitchen where a robot is loading a dishwasher. He nods at my presence. I tap the counter and say, "three beers, please."

They pop up in a stack.

Returning to the space, I hand her a beer.

"Your can seemed empty," I say.

"How profound," she says. She spins off from where she lays on the couch, and faces me.

"I'm known for my depth."

We tap cans together and take a sip of our new beers. She swings her feet back onto the couch.

"So, Paul's making bullets for you?"

"That's right."

"To shoot yourself with?"

"Uh, yes. That's the plan." I'm not sure how she knew that. Or if it simply was obvious.

"Neat."

"Yeah, I suppose so."

She appears a little more interested now. "Are you unconvinced?"

"No, I'm ready." She studies me. "But people keep telling me I'm not."

"So you doubt?"

"No. I think they're idiots."

"Who don't understand you?"

"Right." It's a bad sign that she finished my thought for me.

"How old are you?" she asks.

"Ten thousand and twenty."

"When's your birthday?"

"Next month."

"Hmm," she says. "You can't make it to ten thousand and twenty-one?"

"Don't particularly want to."

"I see."

She turns her attention away once more. What is going on with her?

"Did you know that your boyfriend is going to die?"

"That's rude," she says. "Partner."

"Partner?"

"Not boyfriend. He's not a boy."

"Anyway…"

"Yes, I know. Since we started dating a year or so ago. He was planning things even well before me."

"And you still wanted to be with him?"

"He's a curiosity. Have you ever dated a fat person?"

"I have not."

"Yeah. It's interesting."

She turns away again and sits pensively. I watch the silence to see how she endures it. I think she enjoys it, and recognizes that I'm comfortable here, too. So she speaks.

"I know that he's going to kill himself. But he's so bored. He was interested in me for a few moments, literally, and then he lost it. Couldn't be shown to care after that, beyond the natural bodily processes. Sex from time to time, company here and there. Not real, though, not with any interest."

"And you've stuck around?"

"Well, he's interesting. And he's almost out. I thought I could stay until the end."

"Sweet of you," I say.

"More selfish of me," she replies.

We sit for a moment once more. "You are interested in being interested, is that right?"

"Yep," she says confidently.

"Are you a collector?"

"A collector?" she asks.

"A collector of experiences? I've known a few in my time. A person who pursues all of the different sorts of experiences one can have in life. Hoverboarding, basejumping, flying, anything different from the norm."

"I didn't know there was a word for it," she replies, quietly disappointed. "But yes, I've done all those things. And I've got a plan laid out. I'm three hundred years old now. I think, by the time I'm your age, I'll have done everything that there is to do on every planet that we have settled. And we'll likely have settled a few new planets in that time. So there'll always be something new."

"You don't want to end up like Paul?"

"He's had a good life, but his interests have run out. I am interested in everything new, and you can always find something new."

"'There is nothing new under the sun,'" I say.

"No, that's stupid. You just need to look."

"Ever read the Bible?"

"Ha! No."

"Any philosophy?" I continue.

"Philosophy?" says Paul, appearing from the workshop below.

"He's asking me if I've ever read any," she continues. "Not really, and not since my time in education. My parents really pushed it and I hated it. So, no thanks."

"Yeah, no thanks," says Paul.

"Okay," I say.

Paul sits down on the couch, lifting his girlfriend's legs and putting them into his plump lap while taking the last beer from its place on the end table. He cracks it open and drinks deeply.

"My neighbor's been telling me to try some philosophy. I read a pamphlet that he gave me. 'The philosophical argument and avoiding suicide.'"

"Milnius," I reply.

"You've read it?"

"I helped him write it, actually," I say.

"And you're going to kill yourself?"

"He killed himself millennia ago. Worked better for me, I guess."

"Well, anyway, it's all about meaninglessness and resisting the desire for the new, for the different, coming to terms with oneself, whatever. I made sure to hide it from Diana here," Paul continues. "It's the complete antithesis of her life, after all."

"Is it really?" she says, curious.

"No, dear, you don't want that. Wait until you're his age, and then you can read it."

"Okay," she says, demurely. She does genuinely like him.

"There are other philosophies of life. Stuff that can help you, supposedly. I'm not one to talk, really, but I did practice my whole life," I say. "Practice the non-practice, you know."

"I have no idea what you're talking about," she says.

"Where'd you do your schooling?" I ask.

"Havana."

"Oof." I'm going to have to call my son again.

"What?" she says. "Don't be rude."

"Yeah," says Paul, "Don't. I'll talk with her."

"Okay. My apologies," I say.

"When will you do it?" asks Diana.

"I don't know. I'm going to head home and put things in order."

"Read Milnius one more time?"

"No, I've read him enough times. Maybe I'll read that book." I point to the book on the end table. *How to Die* by Ai Suzuki.

"Same person gave me that after they gave me the Milnius pamphlet. It's shit, though, just about logistics really."

"Maybe I should read it then. Because I don't know what to do. But I don't think it's so hard to die, not for me. Just pull the trigger and that will be all."

"It is that simple," says Paul.

Chapter 2

I SHOULD PROBABLY write a note. But who would I write a note to? Dear Justinus. I'm glad we met a few months ago and have since that time spent more time together. Tell Oliver to avoid orgasm machines.

Dear Henry, you've been a wonderful son, and I'm glad that you've grown into a wonderful person. I'm sorry we only speak every few decades.

Dear Heather, you've been a wonderful daughter, and though I have no idea what you are doing these days, I bet you are enjoying them. I'm sorry I never met your daughter. I don't even know where you are. I don't know what that says about me. In the olden days, it would say that I was a terrible father. But you probably don't even know where your daughter is, either.

Dear Helen. You're already dead. You asshole.

I'm holding the shotgun in my hands as I sit on my couch.

I wonder what Aaronson wrote as he left the world.

"Meredith," I say, "can you find Aaronson's final note?"

"No," says Meredith. "That's morbid."

"Meredith! Do it."

"He didn't leave one, apparently."

"That seems right."

I pause for a moment.

"Can you find anyone else's?"

"I'll work on it."

I realize that I have no reason to send her on this quest. I have already exhausted my list of people to leave notes for. Even Peter; I called him the other night to say goodbye. He was furious with me. I didn't say I was saying goodbye, or anything of that sort, as he's on his honeymoon, and that would be a particularly grim and selfish thing to do. I just wanted to talk to him again for a few moments, see how things were going, and after my first casual question about the quality of brunch in Mallorca he started his tirade. And then he told me not to talk to him ever again, that he wasn't going to take on the burden of feeling sorry for whatever stupid decision I would make.

It is surprising that I have lived this long, and yet I still end up here alone, without anyone to say goodbye to. In the moment, I think that I should have kept more enduring friends. Or kept in closer contact with my family, or with my former wives, my children, my grandchildren.

But this is the way the world is, and the way my life has always been. We need to break up; children need to grow up and no longer be children, but rather humans, full persons. We need to move on from friends, to keep things different, to try new things, so that you avoid that terrible staleness when you look to a friend and find you have nothing new to say to each other, when everything has been exhausted, even the bond that lies behind the words. We simply cannot live a life of repetition, avoiding the risk of the new for the sake of the familiar. The familiar turns to poison *as the bee mouth sips*. It's a terrible thing, and yet not so terrible, because without that shift we would never be inspired to seek and enjoy the bold and strange.

How did Ioan do this? Part of me wants to study him, or to study anyone in their final moments who went this way. Alone. I don't know how he did it. Was he just sitting in his living room, a shotgun in front of him; and then he grabbed his shotgun, filled it with shells, and then a deep breath, and then the end? Was he more deliberate? Had he planned for weeks? Or was it spontaneous; *the shotgun, already loaded for the next day's hunt, was sitting by the door. On a whim, feeling ready at that moment, he took it in his mouth and pulled the trigger.*

And the toe thing is a nightmare for me. I try it out, slipping off my socks, and grasping the trigger with my toe, the barrel in my mouth. It's an awkward, unfortunate position. Not a dignified way to go at all.

Of course it's not really about the awkwardness. It's about killing yourself. It doesn't need to be accomplished in a beautiful or special way. It just needs to work. And then you're done, you're free of all the shit that you've been running from.

No, I'm not running from something—that would be a weak reason. This is different. It's different for me because I have lived, and I have been through everything that life has to offer, and now I've had my fill and I can move on.

So I can take the gun and load it up with shells and then I can pull the trigger and then I can be done with living. Because I am not running from anything. There is nothing chasing me here. I am only here because I want to be, because it is right for me to be here. I am done.

I just don't know how to do this.

It is my first time, after all.

Maybe I should leave the loaded gun on the table here and take a government pill. Or hang myself. Or leave the pill on the coffee table next to a noose and the gun and just stab myself in the neck. Bleed out on the couch. How wonderfully confusing that would be for the investigators. *Why did he choose the knife? Why did he set out all these options and then choose the most brutal way? Was he trying to say something? I don't get it.*

Who cares, anyway, that I misinterpreted the death's head? Timothy Street. The man living in the middle of nowhere tending to a wife who considers him second to an illusion. Why does he know anything? Why would I worry about his judgment? But he is right, and I know the correct interpretation of that meditation. When you see the skulls on everyone all your sorrow dissipates because you know what they are, just skulls walking around. Because you come to terms with it, then. You know you are the skull, the living skull, along with everyone else, and that's all your life has ever been, and all it ever will be. And that is not sad, because it is freeing. I know what I am. I know what I've always been. Why would I be so confused about anything?

I am ashamed that I misused this, that I inserted it into my own depression. I knew what that passage was about, and yet I forced the thought to fit the feeling. I felt that all of the world was dead and was death, and took it only as an emotional concept, not as an indication of a non-emotional truth.

This is my life as a philosopher, and the work of philosophy. It is so susceptible to our emotional status that we simply conform the thought to our reality—or prefer the thought because it conforms with our reality. Is any great thinker ever sure that he has found the real truth of the universe? Can they truly be convinced that their thought is not just an extension of themselves as they are—a product of the circumstances of their life, disposing them positively or negatively to an event: an optimistic or pessimistic philosophy from the optimist or pessimist; a product of their relationship with women or with men; the person with no social skills and an embarrassing set of genitals "chooses" celibacy; a product of a tortured relationship with parents despises authority; a product of a string of deaths chooses death.

Only in part, *we see now through a glass darkly*. I see the skulls, but these are images, even less than words. I feel the pull towards death, but this—this is only the pull. Humans always feel the pull. Always towards something, and not the truth. Not always what we need. Only what we are pulled toward.

Words never hold the greatest significance, however. They gesture towards the reality we ought to be living. The philosophical has never been perfect, nor will it ever be perfect, nor do I expect it to be. It is susceptible to my manipulation. My unintentional manipulation when I feel burdened by life and confused as to the reason why I might continue onward.

What has brought me here, after all, is the string of deaths. I suppose I am forced to admit that. This renders my choice impure. And it should make me think differently of what I am doing here—but each time I think of it I am only confirmed in my decisions. Cynthia—I am caught up in love and I am mislead, and she shows me what I was to her—the same as Morris, Helen, Addison. I am nothing compared to their exhaustion, to their readiness for death. I did not feel death in this way before Gwen, so it all leads back to her, if I wish to be honest. Her death changed the terms of life because I could not convince her to live, because she counted me as something for a brief while, but all in jest, infinite jest, all pretend for the moment, until she could not pretend anymore and she shot herself in the head. She looked at the world—she looked at me, desperate to keep her, worshiping her very movement in existence, and she counted me as a nothing and went on with her desire in spite of mine.

So it's all Gwen's fault. I can happily assign the blame to her. I remember meeting her the first time and she was so dark and melancholic. An irreverent zest for casting scorn on the most cherished machinations of human society. We're at a party, and she has fun, but in her depths doesn't like the party, is too cool for it, but would never think of herself as too cool, nor would she say anything of that sort. She would just *be* in her own way, never swept up by the others.

She's wearing ripped black glitter mesh leggings and an oversized woven shirt draped over a single shoulder and a half dozen pieces of black leather jewelry. Black on black on black. She looks like a 13th millennia Beta Beta, though she herself was only a reference to Joan Jett, I guess. Gwen was the same though. In spirit.

"I also despise society," I say to her, wearing a particularly stodgy grey mao suit and a bright pink backpack for my drugs. She looks me over and I think she appreciates the feebleness of the conversation starter.

"Is that right?"

"Oh yes. Beneath this bland exterior is a raging storm of countercultural madness."

"Madness?"

"Yes, I'm quite insane."

"Do something crazy, then."

I take her hand and walk briskly and she follows and then begin to run and jump and I lead her over the edge of the balcony. I know she won't let go of my hand, and I know she'll jump, but I do not expect her to respond the way that she does. She closes her eyes as we fall and smiles slightly, and all I notice is how beautiful, contented she looks in flight.

Yes, it's the same thing that I told Oliver to do. It's the same thing I'd seen done the week before, something I'd never done before, because I had no interest in doing it. It gets my heart pumping, but no fear, because there is no justification for fear, you can already see the drones coming for you from the moment you fall. When I saw a friend jump, I told myself I'd save this moment for the most desirable woman I came across. I knew it would work, would bond us. A perfect pickup line.

At the time, as we are being dragged up to the balcony by the drones, while the drone flashes the steep fine we get for jumping, I think that she closed her eyes because she viewed building jumping nonchalantly. That she was so unflappable, so casual, that this brief hint of death would do nothing for her. I realize now that the free fall towards death was a state of bliss for her. At no point would she be so satisfied except as she was able to acknowledge her desire for death, and to find herself tending in that direction.

I cannot say that it was a mistake to love her. Even if she's brought me here.

We went to a party together the next day, at a friend of hers in Boston. She picked me up and we caught the hyperloop in her pod. That's when I learned how old she was, that she was only ninety seven and had just finished her fifth doctorate and was trying to decide what to do with her life. There was nothing that interested her, she said, nothing that she wanted to do or accomplish. What was the point, she said to me, what is there to change in this world?

"No point," I say to her. "Nothing to do but to live."

She smiles at me, amused. I think she finds the answer trite, but it's the best one I can muster. No point at all to living, no point to dying, no point to doing anything in between. Living just seems like the best option out of those three.

We spend the night on her friend's yacht in the harbor and wake up curled around each other. She stares at me as she wakes up and she has tears in her eyes. As I come to, I ask her what's wrong, but she says there's nothing wrong, that she loves me and she hates me for it.

"It can't be your first time," I say.

It's not, but it's new for her to love this way. And, I think, it destroyed her plans even then. I don't think she had much interest in continuing to live, that if she never met me she would have died soon after. I must give her credit for this as she'd already outlived my mother by about twenty years at that point. But the rules had changed and now you were expected to live, and most people took to it, most people would live a few lifetimes even if they were ill made for life.

She told me she didn't want to get married to anyone, but I convinced her to try it out. I said, "what do you have to lose?" and she replied that the only one with anything to lose was me. I laughed her suggestion off. "You are my eighth wife, my hundred-some-odd long term relationship. You are different from them, but I can handle you." She smiles again.

Soon after we were married she began her determined march to death. She asked me if she would get better, or if there was something else she should be doing, but there was nothing that satisfied her. She was confounded by a nagging sense of error—like that feeling you are missing something from your pocket as you step out of the house. There may not be anything missing, technically speaking, but there is a buzzing in your pocket or in your head that you've forgotten something, and it can't be settled until you've answered it. What did I forget? What am I missing? Why don't I feel right?

She first stated her desire for death in the twelfth year of our relationship. She was in tears, which, despite the suggestion of this summation, she rarely was. She hated to leave me and she hated herself for wanting to leave.

"You are the only thing keeping me here," she says.

I try to convince her that there's so much more to life, so much to see and so much to do and so many things to accomplish. She asks what she can accomplish when there is no poverty to end, no hungry to feed, no art to create beyond repetition, no fashion outside of reference, no technology that will save or transform our existence.

I tell her she can make a faster space ship, since it still takes fucking forever to get to the planets outside of our solar system.

"Why does that matter?"

"I don't actually know why it matters. It doesn't. You just travel there and you live the same life that you could be living here. It isn't anything new, except the scenery is different, and maybe you die from an asteroid along the way. You just need to learn how to live here, with nothing else, just the two of us," I tell her. "You can learn to be happy now." I make her read some Buddhism and Stoicism and some Milnius so that she can learn how to live.

"I think I'm just not made for living," she says.

She remains unconvinced, but she does go on living. She works for a while. She actually does design an improved engine; it's been built and is traveling to some far off planet. We didn't attend the ceremony held in her honor—by the time the ship was ready, she'd moved on to being an artist, a painter. Every once in a while she asks me when she should go and I say to her, "Not today."

From my ten thousand years, fifty years does not seem like much. But it is still long when you are actually living it.

You always change as a person, especially when you are married and in love. Through the necessary compromise of relationship you find your interests and passions change. I spent more time inside alone with her than I had in a few lifetimes.

What are women to me? Not everything—but still, the important thing. Not to live for oneself. It's not enough to live for yourself alone. Who cares about yourself alone? But you cannot rely on other people.

She was dead. I should get that now.

I remember our last night together. We laid out on the balcony, on a blanket, and we looked up at the stars—it was a special night in the city, no lights after two in the morning so that those who stay up can see the sky. We stayed up, sharing a bottle of wine or two, and we laid there as the lights went out and the stars revealed themselves. We didn't say anything, but just held each other, feeling small in the face of the universe, feeling an immense contentment and love for each other. It's the kind of moment that makes life worth living, the thing that would make it worthwhile to endure.

So we watched the stars, saying nothing, together. An hour or so later and I've fallen asleep and she shakes me awake, kisses me, and leads me to bed.

She says she loves me.

"I love you always," I say.

She doesn't get in the bed with me, and when I ask, she says she'll be in soon.

In the morning, when I wake up, she is dead.

I don't know how she could do it. I reach for her in my sleep, and find an empty bed. I panic because I know, somehow I know.

Don't be dead, I said. I shouted. Don't be dead. I run out of the room, and I find her, hold her, she's blue, she's very dead, blood, blood and pieces, nothing to do now. I just sit there holding her in my arms. My breathing slows and it's only because I've convinced myself that she's not dead, that it's a dream, it's not happening, that I'm in a strange nightmare.

I step out onto the balcony as they clean up her body, and I look to the sky. It is dusk, very early in the morning, the sun beginning to rise, the birds in the trees of the balconies starting to chirp. No stars now, but still a great beauty. I remember the night before, the stars, the galaxies, the universe. I love them.

That is why I did not want to die then, I think. We'd had such a beautiful moment the evening before, and for that reason, I loved being alive. And it carried through the absurdity of her death, and it was enough for me to see the sky and remember the stars.

I don't know what to do now.

I have avoided calling thus far, but she has stayed in the back of my mind. The jug nun. Rose. She would know. She's been through the end with a great number of people. That's what she does, apparently, for a living.

She is so interesting. I do want to learn more about her, I think. Such a curiosity. Something beautiful in a strange world. Something strange…I don't think it.

"Meredith," I say, "Send a message to Rose."

"Go ahead," she replies.

"Tell her I'm going to the woods. She can track me. Tell her I'll have my gun and that she should join me as soon as she can."

I stand to get dressed. Does one take a coat? I'll take a coat.

Meredith jumps in, "she's already responded. And she's calling you now."

"I'll talk to her when she gets there."

"She says that you're being an idiot and you should stop."

"Tell her to stop me in person."

I get into my pod with my coat and duffle bag full of shotgun and shells.

I think of Justinus. 'I went into the woods because I wished to live deliberately, to front only the essential facts of life, to see if I could not learn what it had teach, and not, when I came to die, discover that I had not lived.' Justinus in his robes in the woods. That day may be one of my favorite experiences from all of my life. Such a ridiculous person.

The pod stops at the end of the service road after a solid forty-five minutes of travel. I hop out and walk along a path near the water's edge. It is quiet here, only the crinkle of assorted wildlife shuffling on with their days. It's cold, crisp; well above freezing, but sharp.

After a few minutes of walking, I find a clearing a little ways in from the water. It is bordered on one side by a steep tree covered hill. This will catch the shot, and I will not have to risk harming anyone else.

I kneel and take the case out of the duffel and the gun out of the case, lining up the shells, and I begin to place them, one by one, into the breech.

"You asshole," she says, appearing from nowhere. "You are not doing this."

I stand up and pump the action, moving a round into the chamber.

She pauses. "No," she says, sternly.

"What?" I say to her, a sly smile.

I take aim at a tree on the edge of the hill, a rotting birch tree peeling its coverings away. I click the trigger and the racket echoes around the trees and across the lake, sending birds in the trees scattering away to quieter climes.

"I had to use it," I say. "Do you want to take a shot?"

"I'm not going to shoot you," she says.

"I don't want you to."

I wish you could have seen her face. She smiles and then reaches out and kisses me.

"You don't want to die?"

"No," I say. "Not today."

I smile, but I am shaking, and she notices this and holds my arms.

"Thank you," she says.

"But you should get a shot off. The drones will come and take this soon."

She gives me a puzzled look.

"How often do you get the chance to shoot Ioan Aaronson's shotgun?"

"Is this his? Okay then." She takes the gun, and with perfect form, finishes off the branch I had previously wounded. We hear the buzz of the drones growing louder.

"Let me get one more in," I say. I shoot one final round into the hillside, sending a plume of dirt upwards. A drone is above me now and its prehensile arm dangles down and grabs the gun. Another takes the case and the rounds.

"Take the duffle, too," I say. "It belongs to Timothy Street in Cody, Wyoming."

The drones beep a response and hover away.

"What a ridiculous thing," she says. "They'll let you get a few shots off, maybe even kill yourself. But no shooting guns into the hillside."

"Against the rules," I say.

She looks over to me and is overcome. She steps near and wraps her arms around my chest, her head against me.

"I'm really glad you came," I say to her, my eyes welling.

"Why'd you make me come out into the woods for this? You could have told me you weren't going to do it."

"What if you hadn't come?" I ask.

"You wouldn't," she says.

"No," I say. "I don't think so, at least. I don't want to go. I still love it here."

"I know," she says. "Keep holding me for a while."

"Yep," I say.

I choke and snivel and sob, the drops falling onto her bare shoulders and rolling down her back onto my arms wrapped around her. They died: Gwen, she is dead. Dead! Dead and gone, never coming back. I'm still here, and life goes on. The world still lies before me, still within me. I just miss her. I miss her every day, every moment that she is not with me. She took a piece of my being in the world away with her and I hate for her it at the same time that I love her insanely and with everything that remains. But that is moot now, it means nothing now. She is nothing now, and life goes on.

After a few moments, I return to myself, and open my eyes and see us standing in the woods. I imagine the way my face is contorted, having been sure to pursue a mirror whenever any extreme emotion strikes me, so that I can know how silly I look.

I don't want to go, I know that now. I know why I came to this point, because I loved so many people who died, who left me, and I felt I was less because of them. I was made to question too much, it cost too much for me. But I had forgotten that life continues, not despite death, but with it.

But now, I will continue on. My life is given to me once more.

"I'm getting snot on you," I say.

She laughs. "It's okay."

I pause in my tears and awkwardly wipe my face with my hand as I remain clutched to her, placing the dampness into my pocket. I take a deep breath and compose myself again.

I hold her at arm's length and look her over, taking her in for the first time since she arrived here. In my weakness I want to kiss her, want to find comfort in her physicality, but I know that isn't what I need right now, nor do I think it would be good for me to commit to such a thing. Not after Cynthia, not after I went headlong into something which I still don't know what it was, whether it was real, or whether it was two broken people engaging in some temporary madness in hopes of ignoring pain.

She leans in and kisses me.

"You weren't sure if you should," she says.

"I wasn't."

"Well, you get that kiss. But let's get you better first."

SHE's lying on my shoulder as we sit in the pod, our hands locked. Quietly, she speaks directions to the vehicle as I sit lost in thought.

"It's funny to me that people care if I die," I say.

She doesn't look to me as she responds, but speaks straight ahead. "People always care when someone dies. There's never a time when no one truly cares if someone lives or dies. I've had the loneliest most miserable people, without friend or blood in the world. You spread the message, someone will cry for them even if they've never met them. Every death is a tragedy."

"You think so?" I say, surprised. "You help them die."

She smiles to herself. "It's a terrible and a beautiful thing."

"Hmh."

"It is the thing which makes the greatest beauty in life possible. And I don't kill anyone who shouldn't die."

"Which is why you didn't want me to die?"

"Exactly. You should never die."

"That's dramatic."

"It's the truth."

"Huh."

"You should never die. I'll see to that."

I don't know what to say after her declaration. I don't want to die right now, but perhaps I could be convinced in a different set of circumstances.

"No one lives any life other than the one they live now. So if it is right to kill yourself now," she says, "then it is always right to kill yourself. If it is not right that you would kill yourself, then it is never right."

"Who said that?"

She lifts her head to face me for a brief moment. "Don't worry about who said it. Do you understand it?"

"Yes."

She doesn't believe me but lets the silence stand.

"I am sorry for crying on you."

"I know."

"But I think it helped me."

"Good. You loved them. Mourn them. And then, once you're done, make them meaningless again."

"It's always meaningless," I say, "No cosmic punishment to speak of."

"It's true, I know you know; now believe it."

"You're very bossy," I say.

"I know. But I know best."

"What did I drag you away from?"

"I was with a client, like I said. He dies two nights from now."

"And you have time for me?" I ask.

"For you, I do." She looks at me again, and thinks about kissing me once more, I think, when she looks down to my lips and slightly licks her own. But she resists, remembering her own declaration. "I want to keep you around, and keep you around me, okay. So you are worth more to me than another client."

I smile at her. "Thanks for that."

"I will earn your trust," she says.

"You came to me now, I don't think you need to do any more."

"I'll do more," she says.

Out of the woods and the houses grow in frequency as we make our way back to the city. The buildings stand taller and taller and we are no longer the only pod, but one of the many, one of the thousands flowing in smooth and synchronous traffic to the center of the city. Now we turn left as the ocean comes into view and head along the piers, moving at barely a crawl as the streets are flooded with the milling of partygoers. The spring festival.

"Are you making me go to a party right now?"

"No, not yet," she says. "But I want you to hear it."

The pod pulls over to a small parking elevator which brings us into an old and dingy rowhouse. In the basement garage now, she takes my face in her hands and smiles and then steps out and over to an elevator at the far end. We ride up five stories and step out onto a roof deck, greeted by salt air and a biting wind. There is a decisive hum, the mixing of people below, as we overlook the festival, hundreds of people on the connected piers walking between tents and huddling under heat lamps eating and drinking and flirting.

"You are here," he says. "I'm so glad you're here." He walks over from his spot on the couch at the far end.

"Justinus!" I turn to Rose.

"I called him," she says.

"You sly bastard," says Justinus. "I thought you were already dead."

"Not at all," I say.

"I really did. I thought this call would be the one. The jug nun buzzes, it was hard to pick up."

"Yeah, I'm sorry."

"Peter's still on his honeymoon," says Rose.

"That's okay," I say. "He's angry with me these days. I imagine you are, too."

"Well, you haven't answered any of my calls." He says, sitting back down. He says it with a quiet intensity, still a smile, but he is deeply angry and sad and betrayed.

"I know that. And I regret it. But I had to figure it out on my own."

"Ms. Death Nun is not helping you plan things," he says.

"No," I say.

"Lovely to see you again Justinus," she says.

"It is lovely to see you, too, actually," he says. "But this man, especially.

He makes my day, I'm just, I am so glad you're alive. I've invested quite a bit in you, I hope you know. If you went, I don't know what I would have done."

"Called me," says Rose.

He looks to her with a smile but still haunted by her knowing answer. "Probably," he says. "Dangerous woman."

"Maybe I can guide you better now," I say. "But I doubt that."

"No, no," he says, "you will help me."

"And me," says Rose. "To live better," she clarifies.

I look at the two of them as they return my glance with expectation. I do not feel up to the challenge in the moment.

"Okay," I say. "I'll be around, we'll have our chats, go to our parties. Eat, drink, and be merry, as best as we can."

"That's right," says Justinus. "Boat trip. We leave on Monday."

"Two days?"

"That's right," he says. "I know you have no plans, and we've got a room for you. Double bed if you'll be joining," he says to Rose, who smiles politely.

"We'll see."

"I'm taking that as a yes," Justinus says as he grins broadly. "I'm having dinner with Aurelius and Theodore, we're planning out the itinerary for the trip. Virgin Islands. I rented the boat months ago, but did nothing about the whole plans thing."

"Sounds right," I say.

"Have you been there?" she asks.

"Of course," I say. "Beautiful place."

"It is," she says, "and it will be good for you."

"That's right," says Justinus.

"I'm going," I say, "I said I'd go."

"Good," he says. "Now promise to answer my calls from now on."

I take out my tablet. "Meredith, accept all calls from Justinus. And make sure that I answer them."

"Done," says Meredith.

"Perfect," he says, looking to Rose. "I'll get us all a drink from downstairs."

"That would be lovely, Justinus," says Rose.

"Rum for me," I say. "Take the edge off this breeze."

We huddle under the heat lamp to wait for our cocktails.

"It will be good for you," she says. "To get out of your house and your self-indulgent mourning and take a swim."

"It does sound nice."

"But before you go," she says, "come to New York with me tomorrow."

"Okay. What will we do?"

"I want you with me, not out of my sight, for at least a few days. Until you are in the sight of your friends."

"I'll go wherever you say."

"Good. You'll come to my temple and you'll see my life, my work. And I want you to meet someone and talk with them for a bit."

This all sounds rather strange and aggressive. "I didn't know you had a temple."

"You'll see."

Justinus returns, a glass of rum and a bottle of champagne.

"Are you ready?" she asks.

"Of course," I say.

SHE has insisted on joining me home, though I attempted to defer and to have her return to her work, she will not let me spend the night alone. We spent the afternoon with Justinus, drinking on the roof deck before the sun set and the chill was too much. Just talking, nothing really. These past few weeks, in my depression, I refused company, as one is wont to do, and Rose will not indulge my solipsistic inclination and forces me to share a space and thus to share my mind. We step into the house and I remove my t-shirt immediately, forgetting that she is still with me—I am exhausted, drained, and desirous of a real sleep.

I turn around and see her kicking off her pants leaving nothing but a bra and a skimpy thong. She notices my eyes and says, "No sex."

"As we agreed," I say, dropping my pants.

"But you need the company."

"I do. I am thankful for it."

"Good. You need anything to sleep?" she asks.

"Maybe a drink. A bit more rum. You want one?"

"A beer for me," she says.

My counter pops up a beer for her reflexively and provides a glass with a single large cube for me to pour my own rum.

"Who are you to me?" I say to her. "What will you be for me?"

"Everything, of course," she says confidently, irresistibly. "You'll come to understand how we complete each other."

I laugh. "Too soon, right?"

She blushes, briefly. "Fine. But you'll see. I have seen so much in my life. And I found you. It took too long, honestly, so I am impatient, I think."

"Are you a seeker?" I ask her.

"No, you know better than that. Not a seeker in general, but for you in particular. I've never been lost. There are so many seekers in this world. You know better than that and I love that about you. I am not searching anymore." She walks to the countertop and takes her beer. "It's funny to me that I just want beer when I'm with you. I don't know what it is."

"I'm just glad you're here," I say. "Though I'm sorry to take you away from whoever you're killing next."

She rolls her eyes. "He's fine, I'm getting updates."

"How long have you been doing this?" I ask.

"Thousands of years."

"Really?"

"I'm happy doing it. It's…I don't know. I don't want to say there's meaning in it, but it's what I needed to do."

"And you don't get tired of it?"

"Never."

"Good. Let's go out to the patio," I say. "I want to see the night and the city again."

"I thought we were going to bed. Isn't it a little cool out there."

"You could add some more clothes."

She gives me a dirty look.

"I'll get a blanket," I say. I grab one off of the cabinet behind the couch and throw it to her. "Go ahead."

I carry the drinks and she is settled in on the daybed on the patio. The air is crisp, close to midnight in March as it is. I feel as though I missed the entire winter lost in myself. I take a seat, dropping the drinks on the side table, nesting my legs in where she lays. She leans over and puts her head on my chest, wraps an arm around me.

"You thought about killing yourself today. Or did you? I don't know that you ever would go through with it."

"I did. I wanted to. But I didn't know what it would look like."

"You're going to live again."

We pause and I look out over the city, up to the scant few stars in the sky, blurred out by the glow of the million citizens and their constant din. I feel as though I was here earlier today, but it does not feel the same now, not now to feel this with Rose with me, to feel it when I know that I will continue living, and I do not have to think of that past moment as the finest moment of the final chapter of my life.

"I'm exhausted," I say. "It was a big day."

"It was. You should sleep."

"You'll carry me to bed?"

"No," she says. "I will not. Haven't you got a sex robot around here somewhere?"

"Yeah, she can't carry me though. You two would have to drag me."

"That might be worth it to see."

"I almost ended my ten thousand years today."

"I know."

"I really thought I would do it, when I had the gun, and the fact that I was, you know, thinking about the end of my life at the time, I really thought this would be it. Today I would die." She squeezes me but continues to listen. "And then I remembered being here with Gwen. On this patio, watching the stars. A year ago. Almost exactly a year ago. And I loved the night before she died, and it's the thing that I clung to after she left that made me want to go on, made me still want to live, even now."

"And?" she asks.

"It's good to be back."

Chapter 3

I am in Manhattan on this quiet Sunday morning standing outside Rose's temple. She did not tell me which temple she owned, and in this way she has buried the lede. This is the Temple of the Trusted, at least before it was sold following the dissolution of the order. On 5th Avenue by 70th, the temple is an absurdity—three hundred fifty meters tall in its exterior, the interior a three hundred meter tall nano stone of black obsidian, pumice, and polished granite. I visited once, a few millennia ago, and I found it utterly breathtaking. Now I stand outside the temple, waiting for Justinus to join me for breakfast outdoors in the park.

It's a warm March morning; it's been a warm winter with only a few fast melting snowstorms, especially this far south.

"This is it?" he says as he walks up the street.

"It's hers, apparently."

"Did you give it to the jug nun last night?"

"No, no I did not," I say. "Platonic cuddling, really. A chaste kiss."

"You rogue. No sex on the first date, that's classic virtue."

"It's what I aspire to. Shall we?"

"Yeah, let's."

He sizes me up as I walk. It's not my typical outfit, dressed as I am in a gray knee length wool cardicoat and baggy black pleated pants. He's wearing a jumpsuit, and given my predilection for these, and his predilection for matching, I sense his disappointment. We walk through an empty Central Park to the boathouse in relative peace and quiet. It is still early—Rose woke earlier than I did, needing to return in time for her busy day of prepping someone for their death. I decided I would ride on the shuttle with her, that I didn't need to sleep more than the ten hours I'd already taken. I'm going to meet her this afternoon and we'll have dinner before Justinus and I leave in the morning for our sailing trip.

When I woke up we were in the bed—not sure if she carried me or if the sex robot helped her—I asked her and she said that a bit of mystery is always a good thing, and she is a constant mystery, which is perhaps what makes her so enthralling. I did feel different in the morning. I did not feel like I wanted to die. There is still a weight on me—my brain has been formed in sadness for so long it will be a while before I can reshape it into what it was pre-Gwen, pre-Morris. But I felt good; not elated in love with her, not hoping today was the day that I would die. I felt nothing significant but an abiding satisfaction, and a deep desire to bury my head in her stomach as she lay next to me.

Justinus and I sit down in the restaurant, still inside, but with a nice view of the lake, the birds taking a dip.

"How are you?" he says.

"I'm good."

"You're good?"

"Yeah, I feel better, I do."

"You look a little better. A little more light in the eyes."

"Yeah, I'm not back all the way, but I'm on my way. I just, not to get too heavy too quickly—"

"—please do."

"I just realized as I was sitting there with the gun in my hands that I didn't really want to do it. Not to do anything else, just that there isn't really a point in me dying."

"No point in dying?"

"No. If I want to end my suffering, then as soon as I let myself stop suffering, I'll stop. They died, but I can be fine when I give myself permission to. The ones who died, maybe they had to go. I don't, and I don't need to drag myself down in their name."

"That's true," he says. "What about me?"

"What about you?" I ask.

"Nothing tragic in my life and I am just barely hanging on. Sorry to make this about me, you're the one who's had the emotional crisis and all. But my problem was not yours."

"I think it's similar actually. Have you attached yourself to something—a conception of yourself that you'd prefer to be, a form of life that you'd rather have, a nagging feeling that your life ought to be other than it is? That's what you should let go of. I forgot for a while—because who the fuck has all of these people die on them in quick succession in a world where people rarely die?—I forgot that there isn't a reason or a rhyme for these circumstances, certainly not one we could understand, and I felt things should be otherwise, as if that feeling had any meaning."

He seems puzzled. "What am I feeling should be otherwise?"

"I don't know, Justinus. You'll have to figure that out."

"I'm completely lost on that front."

"It can be as simple as thinking that you should be less depressed than you are."

"Huh."

"You're smart, you'll get it."

"I've read Milnius, you know. Reread him, I mean, after you mentioned him on our walk."

"Yes."

"The meaningless thing. Meaninglessness. He keeps on saying it."

"Yeah, because most people think they get meaninglessness, but then they get upset when certain things happen, or disappointed, or anything. So you have to repeat it and internalize it to actually get it."

"And you get it?"

"I try. But, you've noticed…" My bacon and cheese omelet arrives along with fresh coffee, courtesy of the friendly dome robot. "You've noticed I'm sure that I failed at it, despite practicing this perspective for almost ten thousand years."

"Not perfect, then."

"No, but still an improvement."

"I see."

"Yeah, let's see if we can't turn you into a lover of the freedom of meaninglessness. I am going to get back into it, I am sure of that."

"I accept your challenge."

He takes a bite of his croissant with jam and a sip of his latte.

"But about this trip," I say.

"Right, right. Not much really to plan, I guess. We land in Jost van Dyke, sail from there that afternoon to Oliver's friend's island, sail from there the next day to Virgin Gorda, from there after a day or two, we head up to the settlement on Anegada—have you been there?"

"No, not since they reconstructed it."

"Right, so the island was so low, mostly lost to the rising ocean, so they built a huge resort and apartment complex on stilts off of the island. It's simply a stunning place, actually, there's like twenty thousand people living there now, great party and dance scene. A friend of mine had a wedding there the last time I did this type of trip. Amazing stuff. Glass and steel and the stilts are nano-diamond, with incredible sparkle."

"I'm looking forward to it."

"You'll enjoy it," he says. "Then back to Charlotte Amalie, Vieques, St. Croix, back to Jost, and then home."

"Lovely," I continue. "So, Oliver, Aurelius, Theodore, you, me."

"Oliver's bringing a date. Peter and Nigel. There are eight cabins, so we have some spare room."

"No date for you?"

"No."

"No prospects?"

He scoffs. "Always prospects."

"Okay then."

"I just didn't want to cloud things. I wanted time for you. Or if you were gone, I wanted time to mourn you. But what about you? Will you bring her?"

"I don't know what she'll do. She can't come the first night. But I have a feeling she'll just show up when she wants to."

SHE's waiting for me outside as I walk up the steps of the temple, dressed in a similar lingerie getup to the one she first visited me in. Stunning. I give her a quick hug, she gives me a quick kiss on the cheek and tells me to come in. Through the main door she leads me off to a side room and grabs a small black slip dress off of a hanger.

"This is for you," she says.

"Oh?" I say.

"Yes. There's a party in there, and a bit of a dress code—hence why I'm dressed like this—and you need to look the part at least a bit."

"Okay," I say. I strip completely and put on the dress and she then hands me a matching pair of silk underwear.

"In case you need to lean over," she says.

"Good."

"You look cute," she says. "Let's go."

She takes my hand and I follow her through the door and another door and through a massive threshold into the main sanctuary. The last time I was here it was filled with the disciples of the trusted. Hundreds of people in lengthy robes sitting in complete silence quietly abiding a government inspection into their organization and practices; now, there are hundreds of people in various stages of undress and sexwear engaging in the full range of sex acts in the glimmer of faux torch light.

"It's an orgy," she says.

"I see that."

"I have lots of followers," she continues.

She notices my eyes wandering through the sea of compromised humanity.

"You can join if you want," she says.

"No, I'm here to see you," I reply, "This is just quite the sight."

"It is. I never partake though. Not for me."

"Oh."

"You're the most action I've had in a long time."

We reach a spot towards the front along the pathway and climb up a few steps to what used to be a pulpit. She scans the crowd and the locates her mark. "That's Avery. He's going to die tomorrow," she explains.

Avery is surrounded by twenty or thirty persons in a tangled mass. I think he is standing, but it is difficult to tell where he ends and where the people entangled with him begin.

"It's important for most people to have sex the day or two before. Morris, not the same—he'd had plenty of sex in his life, too much of it probably."

"He told me he was going to get a blowjob from you," I say.

She laughs. "He didn't. He tried, and I convinced him he didn't actually want one. But with someone like Avery, he has never had that much commitment to sex, so this will be a bit of a new experience for him. He'll be exhausted, and if everything goes as I expect it will, he'll want to die even more tomorrow night."

"Sex doesn't help."

"It doesn't. He's in pretty much the height of human pleasure and he'll find it wanting once he comes down, and he'll return to his disappointed state and he'll want to go."

"Ever had someone change their mind after an orgy?"

"Of course, a few, maybe a few dozen. But I was only surprised once. You do get a few people who have never had truly uninhibited sex before and then they need to go and fuck their way through life for a few centuries. And then they come back."

"Great."

"Life is a funny thing, right?" she says.

"It is the funniest of things."

"We are just crazy creatures." I nod, and she continues. "None of us make sense."

"It would be the absolute worst thing if we did."

"Even worse if the world made sense, too."

"It's true."

"Let's go have a drink."

We walk down from the pulpit and head off to the side of the nave and through another massive gate where a bank of elevators stands. We step into the elevator and she says "to the top" and we scoot upwards.

"I don't love the orgy thing, you know," she says. "But I started to have people following me and then I had a client who needed this, and well, my followers really took to it. They don't stay with me for that long, for the most part, but the offer of weekly unbarred sex as a part of helping people, it really appealed."

"I can see that."

We walk out of the now open elevator doors into a glass atrium on the roof of the temple. It is filled with plants and the heat and humidity suggest the tropical despite the late winter afternoon sky.

"Sex and a good cause," she says, "what could be better?"

"I can see why that's appealing."

Through the palms and ferns to the far end of the atrium is another door. "My office," she explains. The room is spare, poured concrete and white walls, but covered in art, mostly baroque paintings of people dying. A lone desk sits in the middle, spindly legs and a glass top, a keyboard and a few tablets.

"Inspiration?" I ask.

"The paintings?" she says. "Yeah, I guess. I just think they're beautiful, and they're about death, so you know, beautiful death."

"Huh."

"Yeah, well, I haven't updated the design of this office since I first moved in here. A long time ago. But I didn't bring you here to see my office."

"Another door?"

"Open bedroom," she tells her computer, and a section of the wall with a giant painting of Death at a card game slides open, revealing an immense and intricately decorated room with a four poster bed in the center. "Welcome," she says before turning and running and jumping onto the bed. She emerges from the mass of pillows. "This is my room."

"I figured."

"I haven't had anyone here in a long time."

"Shame. It's a nice room."

"Don't say that," she smiles. "It's not your style at all."

"It's a little pretty for me, I guess. But you seem really happy here, which I like."

"I am. Come lay down with me—no funny business—we've got a few hours before they're done downstairs. I want to watch a movie, the new Palsson one."

"I like him…" I say, and she starts to speak, "you know that, of course."

"Yeah."

"You expect me to behave myself in bed with you after we walked through an orgy?"

She shrugs and brings up the movie on the wall with her tablet.

A few hours later, I am awakened by a poke in the back. Rose hands me a cup of coffee. "You fell asleep," she says, which, yes. apparently. "I know you're tired but we've got to go to this meeting. Get yourself ready." She disappears to a bathroom, and I once I can form a thought I follow her to ready myself.

Back in the elevator, we head down a few floors to what I guess are the temporary living quarters of her clients. At one end is a giant window overlooking the temple floor, and a man is standing there appreciating the view.

"Avery Barbous," says Rose.

"Pleasure," I say.

"Delighted," he says.

"I'll leave you two alone," she says.

He gestures towards a couch and he grabs a chair across from me. He is dressed in the lingerie uniform, a complete lace bodysuit with sleeves and little lace gloves, flowing confidently despite the state of undress. He doesn't care.

"What did she want us to talk about?" he says.

"I honestly don't know. She didn't explain?"

"No. I have no idea who you are."

"Oh. Warren Walker. I met Rose a few months ago when she did the death of one of my friends. And then more recently she did the death of my ex-wife and our daughter."

"You've had a lot of people die on you recently."

"I have."

"Is that why you are here?"

"Maybe. I also almost killed myself yesterday. But then I decided not to."

"Huh. Do you think she wants you to convince me not to?"

"I doubt that."

"Good. Because I am out," he says with a broad smile while making a flying motion with his hand.

"Have you guys talked about that?"

"How fucking bad I want to die? Yeah, it's come up."

"Oh."

"She quizzes you all to shit, I guess, it's what I've heard. One of my friends referred me to her. Expensive as all hell—but I'm not spending any money where I'm going. She asked me like two questions though and looked me over and that was all she needed."

"She didn't think I should die. She was rather upset with me."

"Her opinion mattered to you?"

I laugh, "Yeah, I suppose it does. Or it worked out that way."

"The conversation I have with myself is the one that matters," he says. "I can't get past that one."

"I've heard of that before."

"Yeah."

"It was just the people dying for me, I guess."

"Yeah, that happens. Well, supposedly that happens. I'm only like seven hundred so I still have great great grandparents alive, I think. Funny story—I almost slept with my great grandfather, actually, before we got suspicious of how similar we looked, and then we checked. But I haven't had anyone die on me. I can't even imagine what that's like."

"You've had relationships end, though, I imagine."

"Of course. It's like that?"

"Yeah, always losing, but life still gives you more. Seeing that."

"Yeah. I've lost everything. Or, I don't know, not really. I don't want to be here. We're having a pretty interesting conversation right now and I still want to jump out the window here onto that marble floor below. Scare the fuck out of the remnants of the orgy."

"Huh. Are they still going?"

He laughs. "I'm not going to do it, the window doesn't even open, I checked, and we've got a big ass party planned, and something interesting for my death that's a secret. So don't worry. But anyway, the point is that you, you look like a person who is a bit older, which is weird, but you know, someone I could possibly learn from. How old are you?"

"Ten thousand and twenty."

"Fuck. Fuck, man. I can't even imagine."

"Yeah, I've been around for a while."

"No kidding. You've seen everything. You lived before the transition."

"Yeah."

"Neat. And that's cool. But what jumps into my mind right now is not all the questions I would ask you—and, mind you, I wrote three dissertations on the psychological policies of the department of transition in the early years, so I have things to ask you—what comes to mind is how terrible living to your age sounds. I don't—I can't fathom a way that you could be happy right now. Insufferable people, empty parties, unbearable emptiness, the complete absence of a good time. Fuck this, you know what I mean. I can't fucking wait."

"Better off dead, you think?" I ask.

"For me, it will. Guaranteed. If there's a heaven, cool, if there's nothing, cool, if there's reincarnation, so long as I forget this life, forget what I am now, then we're all cool."

"That pain is a terrible thing."

"Maybe," he says.

"I don't think I believe in it."

"Huh. Well maybe you'll get it, maybe not. I don't care, honestly."

"My ex-wife, Addison, one of those who died, was like that. She was about nine thousand years old, though. But her eyes had caved in, the light caved in. She had nothing else, nothing to take from life. Nothing that could satisfy, just the pangs of being."

"Brutal."

"She was worse than you."

He smirks.

"And I didn't want her to die," I continue. "I tried to stop her from dying. A few times. For me, it was only for me."

"She had to die," he says.

"She really did. It was her time. She had a good life." I look over to him. His eyes are not blackened like hers, but they are dimmed. Nothing appeals to them. "Have you had a good life?"

"I've had an amazing life. More than any human could ask for. Fit into seven hundred years, the endless experiences."

"Good."

"Yes, old man, it's been good. And now I'm done."

I nod.

"And you're not. You're different than me."

"Probably what she wanted us to see."

"She's smart stuff."

"I know. Very compelling."

"I think she might be the angel of death," he says.

I laugh quietly, but it does make sense. "She's a good person to be friends with then." He returns my laugh halfheartedly, and then he takes a deep breath. He had interest for a moment, but it wanes immediately, his boredom returning.

"I feel obligated to ask you what it is that you live for."

"Obligated?"

"Yeah," he says, "I don't care what you answer."

"Oh, well. I studied with Charles Milnius—"

"—Fucking Milnius—"

"You know him?"

"His pamphlet."

"Yes, people hate that pamphlet. But he's right, that we can't live for any purpose in this life as it is currently constructed. No point. No need for one."

"Yeah, fuck that."

We pause for a moment, him looking around the room, me watching him as he looks around at everything.

"I'm happy for you," I say. "I'm happy that you can die."

His attention comes back as I say this, and he offers a wry smile. "I'm happy for you, too. But not jealous. Keep on living."

The door opens and the porter robot walks in.

"Rose will meet you on the roof. Please follow me."

A second robot comes in with a tray of something for Avery.

"Enjoy your death."

"Cheers," he says.

"That was a lovely interaction," I say to her.

"I knew you two would click. Perfect inversions."

"He's so young," I say.

She stares at me, concerned that I didn't get it, but she sees in my eyes that I am only playing. "He's completely dead. I've never seen anything like it in someone so young." She walks over to me and takes the hem of my dress into her hands, swishing it side to side. "Almost everyone will try and sleep with me before they go. I don't think I could seduce him no matter what. Only if I promised to kill him after we fucked."

"Black widow."

"Praying mantis," she says.

"Vicious." I want to kiss her as she is standing too close to me.

"You," she says, as she walks away from my designs to the edge of the patio, "are easily seduced."

"I know."

"You shouldn't be so easy."

"You like me though."

"Do I?" she asks, coyly.

We have dinner in the rooftop atrium, brought us to by members of her flock who were previously engaged in their wild orgy. They carry in a procession of food and bottles of wine, many of which are already open.

"From the buffet downstairs," she explains. "Post-orgy buffets are very important."

"Of course," I say.

"The speech will be starting in fifteen minutes," an acolyte says.

"We'll be there shortly," Rose replies.

"Not much time for dinner."

"No. This is busy work, got to eat fast."

"Okay."

"And I've got to spend the night at the party, at least a few more hours until he blacks out."

"That's fine."

"I don't want you to party tonight, though."

"Why?" She doesn't budge. "I can stay here and join the party."

"No. You can't talk to me when I'm working, you're distracting, and I don't want you talking with any of my followers or any of his friends. Someone will try and take advantage of you and you are easily seduced."

"You're saving me for yourself."

"I'm saving you from yourself."

"Myself is fine now."

"No," she smiles. "Not yet."

We eat a hasty dinner and head to the elevator. She brings me to a room in the back with a clear view of the pulpit. There is no one else here, and she explains that she has to go help Avery through his speech. She kisses me on the cheek and turns away and a few seconds later I see her walking towards the pulpit with Avery and a few other women. She moves quickly, as there is much work to be done. She will be busy the rest of the evening.

Avery mounts the pulpit, and the temple is now filled with people standing, no longer the devotees of Rose but what would appear to be the friends and family of the honoree. They are a noisy bunch, certainly they have been drinking and on their way to intoxication for several hours now. Avery looks out over them and smiles.

"So many people here," he says. "Hi everyone."

Not a public speaker, this one.

"I was aided in preparing some lines for tonight. So I hope you'll bear with me as I spit these out." He's going off-script and Rose is cringing a bit, but subtly. "Actually, to be totally honest, I don't want to do any of this stuff. I don't want to do anything anymore. Except die. But whatever, let's get on with it.

"I remember my first and greatest joy and my earliest memory—it was being held by my parents. Something prompted it—I think I fell off a bike or a swing, I don't remember; mostly I remember the embrace of those two, picking me up as I cried. It is a very pure feeling, that shear comfort. That moment…

"That moment is gone, of course, as are all the billions of moments since then. They have been really and truly so good to me. So fulfilling and lovely. I have been married three times to men who I truly loved. I never had children, but I have watched half-siblings come into the world, and felt so much pride at seeing them grow up and succeed. It's been a completely excellent life.

I lived it to the fullest. I know I haven't been around for so long, but it has been enough for me to wring every last moment of pure joy from this life. My life has been wrung dry now, and to get poetic for you, I am a tattered shirt hanging on the line, wrung too many times. A dirty rag. Throw me out, I'm done now.

So I thank you all for this long happy time on earth. I have really lived ten lifetimes, ten beautiful happy lifetimes. I have no need for anything else. I am excited to go. Let's get drunk and party me off into nothing."

He steps down and the applause slowly builds after his non-ending to the speech. He walks immediately over to a table of alcohol and takes a champagne bottle and shakes it until it sprays hosing down what seem to be his immediate family members.

Rose walks up behind him and says something to him. He smiles, and takes, I think, a pill that he receives from her.

It was not the most stirring speech I have ever heard, but it is exactly what I would have expected following my conversation with him. The party is starting so I turn to the door and head to the elevators back up to her bedroom, where she has told me there's a book for me to read while I wait for her to be done.

A few hours later, the wall creeks open and Rose strides purposefully in.

"Drink?" she asks, walking

I look down to my empty glass. "Always. Rum?"

"Of course."

She disappears for a moment and then returns with two rocks glasses of smoky rum served neat. I had struggled to find the counter, and when I did it had a poor selection of rum that I've taking my time to get through. "Where was this hiding?"

"I've got a secret stash."

I look over at her. "What do I know about you?"

"What would you like to know?"

"Everything probably."

"Maybe someday, maybe with a lifetime—an eternity, actually—you could know everything about me."

"We'll start small, then. What's your real name?"

She smiles. "My real name is Rose. But if you mean the name my parents gave me, Persephone. Persephone Walls."

"Goddess of the underworld."

"Yeah."

"Your parents set you up for a love of death."

"I think they just liked the name, actually. The death thing, that was my fault."

"Are they still alive?"

"No, long since passed."

"Sorry to hear that," I say, gently.

"No," she replies. "They died when they were ready, still together after all their years together."

"That's lovely when that happens."

"It is. What else do you want to know?" I perk my eyes at the insistence of her question. "You're testing me," she says. "Probing. I want to pass your test."

"I can't just do that, pass you. You know what I've just done."

She thinks for a moment. "I know you're right, but I'm not her, I'm not any of the people you deal with who you should not trust."

"I make it a point not to trust people who assure me I can trust them."

She sighs. "I didn't say you should trust me. Just that I'm not them," she smiles. "But you're right, I know you're right."

"Fine," I say. "When was your last relationship?"

"Two thousand years ago."

"Wow."

"Everything still works."

I laugh. "Obviously."

"Yeah," she says, wistfully.

"Why have you been alone this whole time?" I ask her.

"Never alone," she says. "But it's what I was for a time. Now, I think, I will be something different."

"And what will you be?"

"With you," she says. "Whatever way you'll have me."

I'm surprised at her insistence. I want her, too, but I do not expect this dependence from her. "Why?"

"Well, I wanted you from the moment I saw you in the church. Purely lustful—seeing you made me want again. But then, when Morris died, I saw you in a different light and needed you more."

I tell her to say more silently.

"You revealed something to me, something I'd forgotten about. I live for death. To help others come to it. So that they come to it beautifully. So I live for beauty, too. That's what I'm about, I don't really know why, but I love the process of giving a good death, of bringing people to the end in the proper way, of making it beautiful and making it good for all of their relatives. And then I see Morris dying and you were a mess, completely destroyed. I haven't seen anyone mourn like that. You might get people crying every once in a while, but it's rare and it's not the way you were doing it. You…I don't really know what was going on with you, but it seemed like you couldn't have hated anything more than him dying in that moment. It was a complete opposition to death. In principle. To the existence of death. And it wasn't selfish—you weren't insisting on keeping Morris alive. I don't know how much you even liked him…"

"…he was a good guy…"

"Yeah, that's it. Right, it's not what he meant to you, but that he was dying. So I'd forgotten about that."

"Life?"

"Wanting to live, maybe?"

"Hmm."

"Yeah, I didn't care about living myself, particularly. So you know why this will work is because we will match each other. You've forgotten about death as a part of life, and I can teach you that. I've forgotten about the living part of life, as embarrassed as I am to say that. You will make me live again."

"Take you out into the world?"

"Yeah. I barely even speak to people anymore. Socially, I mean. I talk to all of these people, but that's work, not living. So you will help me."

"It's so strange to me that people keep asking me for help when I'm at this low point in my life."

"We can all see what you are capable of, and that you're doing better than most of us."

"Maybe."

"I know it," she says.

Chapter 4

The water shuttle lands in Great Harbor on Jost van Dyke, settling softly on the quiet Caribbean waters. Stepping out onto the dock and greeted by the pure white sunlight blinding our northern eyes. There's a robot porter waiting for us, blinking a "Perriman" sign and adding, "This way." We follow him up the main dock, an odd procession, all dressed in matching short navy swim trunks with no shirts and tortoiseshell sunglasses and white leather sandals purchased by Justinus. All except Oliver's new beau, Austinate, who wears a navy smock, shoulder to just over the knee. Down to the right at the fork and down for a ways, dragging our luggage, we reach our designated yacht.

Justinus has rented us a twenty five meter trimaran, a sailboat, but completely autonomous, with none of the hassle of pulling ropes and tacking, but the additional joy of cruising over the water solely on the power of the wind. He came up with the idea, he says, because of our walk in the woods, which has pushed him to get more in touch with nature. I tell him that this is just a made up concept, and is not at all what he needs to do; he smiles at this and replies that then we'll just have a nice week or so of sailing in the Caribbean.

Peter is offering me the silent treatment. His husband, Nigel, however, is still speaking with me, and is generally being an exceptionally pleasant and decent person, which is something I find satisfactory as it means that Peter will be well taken care of. And that he has someone who will tolerate his hyper-rational moodiness.

Walking up the gangplank, I set my bags on the deck and look back towards the shore. The houses blend into the hillside, part of the renovations they accomplished on many of the Caribbean isles in the late 2800s, when they realized that a great number of people, when given the opportunity to live year round on a beautiful tropical island, will choose to live on a beautiful tropical island. You can see the trees, and you can see, faintly, flat areas of green, the camouflaged glass and siding of the apartment buildings that run to the peak. It is difficult to tell that almost half of the island is developed; it blends well enough with the half that is preserved, and I've heard that wildlife entering one's premises is a common occurrence. They did preserve many of the islands, as well, from further development, and even depopulated a few to save for the sake of the natural world. Wild animals do not live forever.

We won't be staying here for very long as we start our sailing trip, heading on to Guana Island where some friends of Justinus' live.

Justinus has mounted part way up the front mast and is scanning the shoreline.

"What are you doing up there?" I say.

"Let's grab a drink," he says.

He descends the mast and departs the boat, pausing only for a moment to ensure that I am following him, which I obediently do, out of curiosity more than anything. He strolls up to a table at the open air bar and takes a seat next to a pair of women who are surprised by his presence.

"I noticed you," he says to one of them.

"Here you are," she says, bemused.

"Can I buy you a drink?"

"Sure. One for her, too."

"This is my friend, Warren," he says. "I'm Justinus."

"We've met before," says the woman across from him.

"Jen," says Justinus, a look of realization sweeping across his face.

"Yep.

"We have met before," Justinus continues, piecing things together.

"Here."

"Like four hundred years ago."

"Yeah," she says.

"Do you still live here?"

"Yeah," she says, "And you never called."

"I was getting married. I'm sorry about that."

She laughs and looks to her friend, "all yours."

"I'm Minerva. I want to hear this story."

"Not much to say," says Justinus. "Though it was a very lovely time."

"One night stand," says Jen, "Though I'm pretty sure you told me you loved me."

"I may have."

"Always the romantic," I say, inserting myself.

"I was having a tough time with getting married again, so I was acting out. My previous marriage, to your ex-wife actually"—he gestures to me—"kind of ruined me. But I made love to this lovely woman and I felt better about marriage. So, thank you."

A robot waiter rolls past.

"Four painkillers please," says Justinus.

"With fresh nutmeg," says Minerva. "You have to request it."

"But we're taking a sailing trip for a week or two, as long as we can last in these cramped quarters, and we'd love for both of you to join us."

"Sure," says Minerva.

"Okay," says Jen.

"Wow," he says, "you are free?"

They laugh and Jen explains, "We were literally sitting here talking about how we need to get off this island for a little while and then you show up with a lovely offer. Plus, you're taking out the Silver Sails, and I love that yacht."

"Good," says Justinus.

"And your friend is enchanting," she says to him.

"He is enchanting, isn't he?"

"I'm a mess right now," I say.

"A hot mess," says Minerva.

Our drinks finally arrive and we each take note of the freshly ground nutmeg balanced on the foam of our cocktails. I wonder how long they've been making painkillers in this place.

"Warren here has just decided not to kill himself," says Justinus.

I offer him a confused look, as it's an odd conversation starter.

"That's wonderful," says Jen. "We were just at a death party last week, in Manhattan for one of our friends, which was a complete disaster."

I think of Rose's temple and have a pang of anxiety. I reassure myself, however, that it can't have been her, as whoever she was supposed to be killing most recently will be dying tonight. So she can't have killed anyone last week.

"Where was this?" I say.

"The Great Hope Mausoleum," says Minerva. "In Tribeca. He was an artist or something most recently."

"We hadn't seen him in like two hundred years. Since he moved from here. He used to be my neighbor."

"We actually met through a mutual friend of his," Minerva offers.

"Yeah, and then he got dour and wanted to become an artist. He said he wanted to put all of his desperation into sculpting, I guess."

"Did he sculpt anything good?" asks Justinus.

Minerva laughs.

"No," says Jen, smiling. Probably a story there.

Austinate appears at our table. "Oliver just spoke with our hosts, and he says we need to get going soon, as they are already partying on the island."

"We've got a couple of new guests coming," says Justinus.

Austinate smiles and bows. “My name is Austinate.”

“Neat name,” says Jen. “Jen.”

“Minerva.”

“We can have our porters bring a bag down. Probably take a half an hour,” Jen says.

“He can wait a half an hour,” says Justinus.

“He can,” Austinate says, floating away. “I’ll tell him.”

“What were we talking about?”

“Sculpting.”

“Let’s not,” says Jen.

“But why was the party so bad?” I say.

“It was just awkward. He paid someone to stab him, and the guy missed, and had to stab him twice.”

“Missed?”

“Missed his heart,” Minerva clarifies. “With a big spear. Ted was like, ‘when’s the last time someone died by spear?’ So he wanted to die by spear.”

“So he gets stabbed the first time, and he’s just looking at the guy. Ted closes his eyes, like it’s a big moment, the moment of his death—he’s desensitized his body, by the way, some combination of drugs—but then he opens his eyes again, and he mutters to the guy, ‘I think you missed.’”

Minerva starts laughing and kicks in, “So the guy yanks the spear out. He’s got the black mask like an ancient executioner, and when he yanks backwards the force shifts his hat and the eye holes get mismatched. So he has to drop the spear and spin his mask around so he can actually see.”

“Meanwhile,” Jen continues, cracking up, “Ted is bleeding out, and that’s not the way he wants to go. He wants his heart slashed so he dies quickly, you know, instantly. So he waits there for a second, and then he grows impatient as the guy struggles with his mask. He’s like, ‘no, no, to the right, no, too far.’”

“We’re all just sitting there in the audience, two thousand of us, watching this struggle in stunned silence.”

“I was positive he was going to call it off and try again later, when they hadn’t fucked it up.”

"No," says Minerva, "He would never do that. He was too stubborn."

"You're right," Jen says, "Plus he really fucking wanted to die."

"Oh my God, his speech," says Minerva.

"He didn't even really give one. He was just like, 'I'm so sick of living. Peace!'"

"That's pretty much it."

"Hmm," says Justinus.

We pause for a moment, and Jen looks to me.

"So you're going to keep living," she says.

"Yeah, that's the plan," I say.

"Yeah, he is," says Justinus.

"Well, that's good for us," says Minerva.

"Good for me, too."

Justinus shakes his cocktail, only ice now. "I'm dry, and that's enough death talk. Should we adjourn to the boat? We've got plenty of rum, plenty of drugs, too."

"Sounds excellent," says Jen.

"It does," says Minerva.

We've been underway for an hour or so cruising over the moderate chop on the windy day. I'm standing at the bow, in a little fenced in perch, watching the islands as we sail past. Justinus sits on the couch with Jen, Minerva, and Nigel, Peter somewhere below.

I take a sip of my drink and lean over the edge, reaching out to touch the water which is still several feet away.

"Oh Fuck!" shouts Justinus. "He's going in."

Oliver walks out from behind the wheel where he's pretending to navigate and yells, "He is not. We are in a fucking rush." Austinate pats him on the back to calm him.

I lean back to safety and give a questioning glance to Justinus, who shrugs; it's unclear why we're in a hurry. I walk back to the couch and lay down at one end, stretching my legs out over Justinus and his companions. "Nigel," I say—he's sitting on the L of the couch facing me—"when will Peter start speaking to me again."

He smiles. "Tonight." He takes a sip of his drink and peers around to make sure his husband is not present. "Or I'm going to make him. He's just being a bit of a baby. Not good with his emotions, you know, and you scared him, and then Justinus here saw you first."

"That was totally random," says Justinus. "You two were still on your honeymoon. Not local. That's why the jug nun called me."

"Jug nun?" asks Jen.

"Long story," I say.

"It is," says Justinus. "Are you two a thing now?"

"I don't know what we are," I say. "I don't know how she does relationships."

"She is insanely compelling," he says.

"Truth."

"Land Ho!" screams Oliver. We pick up a bit of speed, and I'm quite sure now that Oliver has been using the electric motors for an extra boost while we sailed, despite our explicit instructions for him not to do so.

They vacate their seats and head to the rails to watch the shore appear and grab their things. I pull a towel over my eyes and listen to the water slipping by and the wind rounding and I breathe in a clean breath of the Caribbean Sea. I don't think anyone I know is going to die for at least a little while. I don't know that it would affect me in the way that it did—this flurry may have desensitized me to it, which is, I think, actually a good thing, actually something I needed to remind me of what the reality of my existence is. Our existence is. I actually sent a letter to my daughter to check in and see how she was doing and to make sure that she wasn't planning on dying in the near future. She said she was fine and that she did actually know where her daughter was, unlike me.

Guana Island is a privately owned nature preserve and former hotel forming a little community consisting of a mansion and guest houses owned by a few very interesting friends of Justinus and Oliver from who knows when. I have never been here, though I've sailed past, and we're going to be joining for someone's five thousandth birthday party. Birthdays lose their meaning after about thirty-five, but you definitely have to throw a good party for your half-millennium. I had a truly amazing time at mine, and there are still a few hours that are missing from memory and description.

We sail into White Bay greeted with a seductive call by the bleached sand beach. It is almost lunch now, the sun high in the sky, and as we cease our sailing and lose the sea breeze, the heat begins to cling. I hear the anchor clanging and I take it as my cue to get ready. Peter is heading to the back, readying the dingy to drive everyone to shore. But as I look over the water I am sorely tempted to jump in. I think of Addison on that morning a few months ago when she came to see me at the pool. She wanted to see me swim, right, what else could I do? I surface and I see her smiling at me, with just that little glimmer of life left, just for a moment. It couldn't last, of course. It was gone and then she was gone. But what a beautiful time we had together, when we had the time together. And what a beautiful moment that was, just one last time to be each other's joy.

"I'm going in," I say.

"Go for it," says Justinus.

I cannonball into the crystal waters and after circling for a moment to see what the rest of them are doing (not jumping in) I begin a slow stroke to the beach a ways off. I dive and spot a few scattered bits of coral, some fish swimming their lives away, and then return to my nonchalant crawl. Once my feet can touch the ground I stand in the waves and Peter and the crew fly past in the dingy motoring aggressively to the shore, Oliver standing on the bow, the mooring line in his hand. They wave and I return as I wade in.

On the shore are the hosts, I presume, of the party and the owners of the island. She is dark, sunned, curly hair, and is wearing a small silver mail bikini. Her husband's covering outdoes hers, however, bedecked as he is in a small pink thong. Oliver jumps from the sand, and strides gallantly over to the waiting hosts who both open their arms and a three way hug ensues along with several cheek kisses. There is a story here.

I trudge on to the shore after the rest have exchanged bows and kisses and introductions.

"Warren Walker," she says to me, and I recognize her from my last stint in the government. She was the president of the Federation for several decades.

"Daisy Cole. It's been a while," I reply.

"It has." She hugs me and gives me a kiss on the cheek. "My husband," she says, "Ted Wahl. The birthday boy."

"Ted," I say, bowing. He returns.

"Where is everyone else?" says Oliver.

Daisy and Ted laugh. "We were lonely so we told you to rush. They're a few hours out."

"That's not funny," says Oliver.

"It is," says Justinus. "You've been driving us like crazy to get here."

"Let's go up to the house," says Ted. "We can start our party then."

"You think the kids are up?" says Daisy to Ted.

"I imagine."

"Our children are visiting—Sam and Belle. You'll meet them."

"So there are people here," says Oliver, emphatically.

"I guess so," follows Daisy, a little confused.

We follow them up a sandy path which turns to dirt as it winds to the top of the hill where the main house is found. It's an old wood and stucco ranch house, though it sprawls on for quite a ways with different stages up and down and around the slope. It is, of course, not actually wood and stucco, but it does look like something from before my time, a classic island house from the time when an island actually meant a restricted quantity of resources.

They welcome us in to the main room of the house, a colossal great room, wood paneled and trimmed with competing dining tables on either side and an open dance floor in the middle. The far end of the room is two stories of sliding glass, slid back, revealing a deck and a bird's eye view of North Bay and the iridescent sea. It is a stunning view, and one can understand why they have kept this place private for so many centuries.

"Quite the view," I say to Daisy.

"It is. Doesn't get old," she says.

"If any of you want a room, you can grab one," says Ted. "I know you said you'd be sleeping on the boat, but the buildings are all opened, and we've got like forty some odd beds, so you'll have one if you want one."

A woman and man emerge who appear much like Daisy and Ted, respectively.

"Belle, Sam," says Daisy. Sam is wearing a tiny pair of blue swim trunks, though it is particularly reasonable in comparison with his father's. He is blonde, like dad, while Belle, on the other hand, is more like mom, except she is topless and wearing a u-string

"Hi mom," says Belle.

"Mom," follows Sam.

"You can introduce yourselves to everyone. These are our children."

Belle walks straight to Oliver and gives him a hug. I can feel his jaw hit the floor from across the room; he is quite plainly in love with her. I turn to his companion, and Austinate appears equally smitten, while Belle shares Austinate's interest.

Oliver offers a tentative, "Good to see you," and then watches her as she goes down the line, shaking hands and greeting everyone.

As Sam introduces himself to me, I ask, "Who is the big sibling?"

He gives me a questioning look, as no one asks that question anymore, "She's five hundred years older than me. But I'm the mature one."

Nice wit from the man. "Pleasure to meet you," I conclude.

Belle comes to me, and I tell her, "You look exactly like your mother."

"Oof, I know," she replies, "You don't think she's a little prettier than me, though?"

"Well, I used to work with your mother, so I'd deny it if you told her, but I think you win on that front."

She smiles at me. "I'm glad you think so. And I'm sworn to secrecy."

"Who needs a drink?" says Ted, gesturing to a drinks table. But my eyes are instead drawn to the mountain of synth cocaine in the middle on a silver platter, bordered by an assortment of decorative snorting spoons. Seeing my eyes he says, "Or a line?"

"Not just yet," I say. "I'll do the punch."

"It's a tiki drink. Our counter makes an excellent punch. Throws a couple pieces of fruit in your glass, too."

Jen and Minerva, who have been mostly quiet on our trip thus far, step right up to the mountain of synth-cocaine and start snorting successive spoonfuls. Minerva waves over Justinus, and then sees Aurelius and Theodore, and she starts to feed them all little scoops. They are going to be interesting to have on the trip.

I walk out the open doors on to the patio finding a suitable home in a pair of Adirondack chairs hiding under a broad umbrella. As soon as I sit, Belle arrives to sit with me with her own tiki drink.

"Mind if I join you?" she asks.

"It's your home, if I'm not mistaken."

"Not really. Maybe a little. I went away from my parents for a long time, a long time away from here."

"It's funny to meet you," I say. "I was there when your mother announced they were moving to Singapore."

"Is that right? How old are you?"

"Very old," I say. "Transition old."

"Wow," she says. "You do look a bit more dignified than the rest of this bunch."

"I try."

She looks out over the ocean. "It is beautiful here."

"How long has Oliver been in love with you?"

She turns to me now, and gives me a lengthy amused glance, realizing that it was by no means as secret as she pretended and was actually as obvious to everyone as it was to her. "Too long."

"And?"

"I tend to make a mistake and spend the night with him, and then realize that it was a mistake in the morning, or maybe even the next afternoon. I don't know why he thinks we'll work."

I laugh.

"And I hadn't heard from him in a hundred years, so I thought things were going well, that he'd finally gotten over me, but then he shows up here."

"He was in an orgasm machine for the past hundred years. Got out a few months ago."

"Really? Oliver, that's so pathetic."

"I bet it was images of you the whole time."

She seems intrigued, if a bit disgusted. "You don't think he would?"

"I honestly don't know. He showed us movies, but he didn't show his brain feed. But the way he is approaching you now, well...I mean, he made us sail at top speed to be here."

"He would."

"Well, you are stunning. And fun. I can see why he'd want to make it work."

"Are you saying you'd like to make a mistake with me?" she says, smiling.

I laugh. "No, I didn't mean to suggest that. Maybe I did, but no, I want Oliver to like me still. And I'm not in the best place…" I'm talking too much.

"Oh," she says.

"Not that I don't want to, I'm just a bit of a mess at the moment, and I'm trying to avoid falling in love."

"Okay," she says. I think she sees this as a challenge now—at least that is what her mischievous smile is telling me. But before she can say the bad words she's begun, Oliver arrives and sets himself on the ottoman at the end of her chair.

"What are you two up to?" he asks.

"Catching up," she says.

"That's right," I say, playing along. "Remembering."

"You two know each other?"

"Best sex I've ever had," she says. "And then he left me without so much as a note."

"The way I work," I say.

She smiles at me again. "I don't even want to talk to him anymore." With this she stands and leaves, Oliver stranded on the ottoman.

"I didn't know you two had a history," Oliver says.

"We don't." I pat the seat for him to sit next to me, which he does, and sighs. "She's messing with you. You have no will-power around her, huh?"

"I really don't. No self-respect. Nothing. I just die for her."

"Austinate?"

"Austinate is here with me in part because we like each other, but also because I knew we would be seeing Belle and Belle likes three ways with a third androgynous party, and she won't be able to resist the opportunity, at least for the evening."

"Oliver, you rogue. You think she likes the Aristophanes reference?"

He laughs politely. "I don't know. But she doesn't play fair either. You see what she's wearing."

"Suggestive clothes do not provide permission," I laugh.

"That's not what I mean. She's just so comfortable with her body. With her life, too, not just sex. Such casual comfort, such disregard—it's only her own excitement—and it makes her irresistible."

"You didn't message her during your masturbation retreat?"

"No," he laughs, "did she ask where I've been? I know she misses my attention. I didn't think of her at all, the whole time, no pictures to remind me, when I was in there. I thought it would free me of my obsession, but like two days after I get out, I can't stop thinking about her. I'll definitely have to do a memory wipe to get away from her."

"Love's hard."

"It is." He looks over to me with my cocktail. "No drugs for you?"

"Later," I say. "I'll have to stay up all night I imagine."

"You will," he says. "We'll have fun."

"You'll probably run away to screw at some point."

"If everything goes according to plan and pattern, then, yeah, we'll be abandoning you pretty early."

"It's for a good cause, and I appreciate that."

He looks out over the water. "Remind me again why we live in Portland?"

"Yeah, whenever I visit here, I forget why. But whenever I live in a warm place year round I remember why I live in the north."

He laughs. "Hey, I do want to thank you for keeping me alive. Really,

I mean that. I'm still seeing that psychiatrist, but I'm off the meds, and I'm off adrenaline, no need to jump off buildings or run through traffic anymore."

"Were you running through traffic?" I ask, with moderate alarm.

"No, no; not really. But I do feel good about living, better than I have in a long time."

"Are you sure it's me? I've been broken for a while, since we met I'd say."

"It's funny the way it's worked. You've been a bad example, as you say, but the mistakes you were making and the way you were behaving, it was so obviously in error that it clarified all the stupid things I was doing, and all the stupid things I was thinking. So knowing that you would be doing so much better, that you generally were, it still taught me so much."

"I'm glad I could help then."

"I hope that didn't sound harsh."

"It was the right degree of harshness."

"Good."

"I'll do better," I say.

"I know you will."

He smiles and stands to head inside when his attention is piqued. Minerva and Jen have dropped their swimsuits and are engaging in full on sexual activity in the middle of the dance floor where there is no music playing.

"WOOOOO!" shouts Minerva.

"We're having sex!" shouts Jen, confirming the apparent. "Who's coming with us?"

No one says anything, and Minerva loses her smile. "Justinus! Get over here."

He obediently comes to her and they pull off his pants. Aurelius and Theodore join in and Ted says, "down the hall to the right, please." Nigel looks to Peter who shrugs, and they follow down the hall, as well.

"No one else?" asks Minerva, lingering behind, then disappointed. But then she turns and skips down the hall to her orgy.

"That was odd," says Ted.

"We just discovered them," I explain.

"Want to go for a swim?" says Daisy. I look around and realize it is only Ted, Daisy, Sam and I. It's unclear where Oliver, Austinate, and Belle have gone, but perhaps he's already convinced her.

"Sure."

We head outside, led by a motorized countertop rolling down the hill on tank treads. Into the deep woods now, well shaded, down to a beautiful space silently walking. Arriving at a clearing, a tiny beach is revealed, surrounded on both sides by cliffs and stone. It is perfectly secluded and would feel uninhabited and remote were it not for all of the beach chairs and umbrellas neatly dispersed.

I provide a quiet snicker at the setting. I did not realize how much I was due for a vacation like this. "I really have to thank you all for having me here. This is a spectacular place."

"It's a pleasure," says Daisy, while Sam and Ted nod and head to the water.

I take a pair of cocktails, painkillers, from the countertop, and note the freshly ground nutmeg. This is a fancy machine. I hand Daisy her drink and sit down next to her.

"Do you remember back when you last worked for me?"

"Of course. I wouldn't forget that." I never actually worked for her, though she was the president. In an extended sense, perhaps, but she never oversaw any project of mine, nor exercised any direct authority over me. There isn't really any political power to speak of, and there hasn't been for millennia. Decisions are monitored by AI, with counter checks and counter balances, an ever steady eye for corruption and pandering. The system works as perfectly as one could imagine, in that it is efficient, and everyone is afforded a certain degree of opportunity for success and opportunity for an amazing life. And most everyone takes this opportunity and enjoys it, at least for a while. Though I think she feels she deserves some of the credit for ensuring that this system continues, this is hardly the case—nothing changed during her several hundred years in separate terms in the position, and nothing has changed since she has left office.

This may sound like I despise her or something of that sort. I do not; I appreciate that she is the sort of person willing to take on this activity, something which I would never have considered. Not that I would have been considered for the position for that matter. She is just not the kind of person that I am drawn to, something which she has always known about me, and something which inspires her to want to be friends with me.

"Do you miss it?" she asks.

"I do not. Not these days. There are times when I am curious, or when I'll turn on proceedings or read the newest release. But no, I'm happy not doing that. You?"

"The same. I think—have you met Karen Ackerman, the new president, I used to really like her, but she's done some things recently…"

"Cracking down on the Orinoco River Community…" I suggest.

"Like that. I wouldn't have done that."

"I wouldn't have let that happen, either."

"No, right? Do you think they knew something they aren't releasing."

"No. The movement inspector, I know him, he still asks my advice from time to time, and he told me about this after the decision. Because I called him."

"Yeah, it's crazy. I don't know why they are overreaching."

"Too much death," I say. "Ackerman came to him and told him that there was too much death coming out of the group, and that she didn't like it."

"That's not a good reason. More births."

"I know," I say. "I know."

"Get me all worked up, make me want to take office again."

"How could you want to go back when you have a place like this?"

"I know. I don't really want to go back, of course. I've gotten to know my daughter so much more since I've been out, and since I've been here. Ted and Sam, they're like brothers already. Belle and I, we took some more work."

"The fact that you spend as much time together as you do says a lot."

"You think?"

"Oh yeah. I hardly ever see my kids. You know the numbers. One percent of children spend more than a week per year with extended family of any variety."

"And like half of those are in love," she says, with a laugh.

"Yeah."

"So tell me what's been going on with you."

"Not that much. Well, no, a lot, but I don't need to share."

"I'm curious," she says.

"Well my wife killed herself last March with no warning, and she was only a hundred and fifty—"

"She was the young one! I heard about her on the news."

"Yeah."

"That's terrible, Warren. I'm so sorry. Are you okay now?"

"Well, then my friend Morris, then my daughter and third wife went together, and then the women I was seeing surprised me as well with a little suicide, though she left me first. So the day before this one, I was going to kill myself."

"Huh," she says.

"Yeah. But then I was like, ehh, no, I've got living to do."

"Just like that?"

"I'm still messed up, but yeah, I want more life. I don't want to die, I never really wanted to. I was just upset, feeling abandoned. But I still like myself, and like living enough that I don't need to stop."

Belle appears down the path and stops at the counter to grab a drink. She says a quick "hello" to us and throws her u-string to her mother who catches it with a look of disgust and puts it on the chair next to her. Belle takes a deep sip from her straw and then puts her drink back down on the counter and bounds naked to the water.

"She's a bit different," Daisy says.

"I've noticed. But it's good to be strange. Imagine if she were boring, how terrible that would be."

"True. But she doesn't have to throw her underwear at me."

"Maybe there are some lines we should keep."

We watch as she runs out to the water where Sam and Ted are floating and chatting. Ted takes the opportunity to excuse himself and comes our way, and Belle immediately swims over to Sam and wraps her arms around his neck. It is more than a little suggestive.

"Speaking of incest," Daisy chuckles.

"They do seem to like each other."

"More than that," she says, "I think Belle is in love. And Sam thinks she is his sister, and that she looks like his mother, and he has no confusion about it, even when she is clinging to him like that."

Ted arrives in hearing distance. "Are you talking about our incestuous daughter," he says, smiling.

"Yes we are," says Daisy.

"She won't quit."

"That's interesting," I say, "because Oliver is here with an undying crush on Belle."

"Is that right?" says Daisy. "And here I think he always wants to see me because he's asking when we can see each other again. Even got a few letters from him while he was fapping himself for a century."

"Well, he's just like Belle, then," says Sam. "Both bound to love someone who won't love them back."

"Sam is not one for incest," says Daisy.

"He's a bad Freudian," says Ted. Daisy glares at him. "What, she looks just like you?"

"Don't you dare," she says.

"I would never." He laughs, but she is still upset at the faintest suggestion of sexual tension. "I really would never, don't be obtuse."

"Fine," she says. She turns to me. "You would, though, wouldn't you? Why don't you seduce Belle and save her from Oliver and her strange love for her brother."

"No, thanks," I say, watching Belle and Sam floating in the water, still intertwined. He is trying to position his head to the side so that he doesn't have to look in her eyes, and she is, it appears, trying to line up for an accidental kiss. "That seems complicated. Ask Justinus."

"She doesn't want Justinus."

"Especially not after the orgy," Ted follows.

"He's been stained."

"I understand. But she'll just end up with Oliver and his companion."

They both sigh.

I've fallen asleep on the beach after my third painkiller only to wake up when a bird lands on me. Belle has apparently spread fruit all over my body while I was unconscious. She sits a few feet away, laughing as I put the pieces together.

"You got me." A little finch scatters.

"I did," she says smiling.

"Where'd everyone go?"

"They're back up at the house. The other boats have arrived. You've been out for a while."

"Haven't been sleeping well recently, need to catch up."

"Sorry to hear that."

"Eh, I'll be fine."

"I bet you will." She walks over and straddles my lap pinning me to the lounge chair. "Why do you think Oliver loves me?"

"You want to hear again about how stunning you are?"

"Yes."

"And how mysterious and seductive you are?"

"Am I mysterious and seductive? Tell me."

"You know you are."

She leans forward and kisses me. I kiss her back, because in the moment she is all of those things I just said. But I'm not particularly thrilled, and she notices.

"But you don't want me?"

"I do. But, at the moment..."

"A bad time for you?"

"Nothing casual for me. Everything must be slow and deliberate."

She kisses me again quickly and then lays down next to me on the lounge, snuggling in on my shoulder. She notices a piece of pineapple on my chest and she picks it up and throws it off. "Does life ever annoy you?"

"Of course."

"It's getting to me."

"Yeah, it does that."

She sighs and we sit in a silence for a few deep breaths. "This is nice," she says.

"It's beautiful here." She bats some expectant eyes at me. "And it's beautiful to have a beautiful woman in your arms."

"That's more like it," she says with awareness of her demanding quality.

"How many people would you say you are in love with?"

She sighs again. "Counting you, maybe five?"

"And are any of them available?"

"Not the ones I want."

"Life would be a lot less annoying for you if loved the things you could have."

She takes her position back on top of me. "I like the struggle." She holds my arms and kisses me again before licking my lips, and then stands up and begins her walk up. "Don't forget me," she says. "I'll get you before long."

I laugh. She has an incredible energy.

I realize I'm alone on the beach, snickering by myself.

Might as well go for a dip.

My hair is still dripping as I step onto the patio. The great room is filled with new people, maybe thirty or forty arrivals. I have no interest in meeting all of these new persons and learning so many new names. Meeting Belle has been draining enough.

Apparently the orgy has ended as I find that crew on the patio smoking valcigarettes and doing more synth-cocaine. I sit next to Peter. "How was it?"

He nods his head and looks away from me. I forgot he was no longer speaking to me.

"Great fun," says Nigel.

"Where have you been?" asks Justinus.

"Down on the beach."

"You've been down there for a while with Belle. By yourselves."

"Purely innocent, I assure you," I say.

"You didn't have to hop in the ocean to cleanse yourself?" asks Nigel.

"No. I just like swimming."

"He does," says Justinus. "But you shouldn't get involved with her. She is frustrating."

"That's the way she just described life to me."

"That's the way she lives her life," offers Nigel, a bit more knowingly than I would expect from him. Does everyone have history with this woman?

A crowd forms on the patio and Daisy walks to the front and stands on a side table.

"Welcome to all of you. Thank you for coming to celebrate Ted, my wayward but lovable husband's five thousandth birthday. We've been together for thirteen hundred out of the last two thousand years—isn't that remarkable. I don't know why I tolerate you: but I don't know why you tolerate me either. We just fit, don't we?

"But to get to the point of the speech: Ted has selected his daughter to declare the theme for this evening's theme party. Belle, would you do us the honor?"

"As little as possible!" she shouts.

Daisy rolls her eyes and mouths "Are you serious?" Belle smirks and does a juvenile shrug. Mothers and daughters. "As little as possible," Daisy declares.

"That should be easy to do," mutters Justinus, taking off his pants again.

A few rolling waiters appear with tiki drinks on trays and begin to make the rounds.

I've stumbled down the path from the house in a deeply drunken state and begin to search for the kayak. There are no lights, only the moon, but it reflects off the water and everything is sufficiently illuminated for the drunk man on his quest. I hear foot steps behind me. "Who is it?"

"Me."

"Me who?"

"You know who I am."

"Peter?"

"Yeah."

"Hey, there. What's going on?"

"You snuck away."

"I thought you weren't speaking to me."

"I'm tired of the silent treatment."

"And too drunk?"

"I did actually forget that I wasn't speaking to you, but then I remembered halfway down the path, and I decided I would let it go anyway."

"I'm glad to hear it."

"What are you doing, though? Looking for something?" he says.

"The kayak. I'm going to bed."

"Oh. There's a million rooms in the cottages."

"It'll be quieter on the boat."

"True. But let's sit, let's talk," he says.

"No time like the present."

I look around for a seat and I spot the dinghy, the only form of seating available on the beach at this hour. I gesture to it, and Peter offers a confused look followed by a realization and leads the way. I sit on a bench facing him, and I am tilted back as I have the high side in an uncomfortable configuration. He is leaning back in an equal manner, so I cross to where he is sitting and sit on the floor of the raft and gesture for him to do the same. So we are now sitting together drunkenly, side by side.

"I was upset with you," he says.

"I noticed."

"And…"

"I'm sorry," I say. "I should have spoken with you about everything that was happening."

"And you shouldn't kill yourself."

"Yeah."

"Not until I say you can."

"Okay."

"That's all."

He moves to get up, placing a hand on my shoulder to brace himself.

"That's it?" I say. "You love me again?"

"Always loved you. Won't ever stop. We're good."

"That's good."

In the morning, I awake to the poorly closed curtains allowing a piercing sliver of light. It is barely past seven, but it will be a beautiful and quiet time of day so I rise and dress and head outside, donning my designated traveling trunks and sunglasses. I find a spot on the deck on the outer pontoon, looking towards the shore, and I hesitantly remember myself kayaking from the shore very early this morning. I see now that the dinghy has returned, so Justinus and Oliver and Peter and their accompaniments must be onboard by this time. We are, after all, heading elsewhere before lunch, though the boat will take care of that without any help from us.

This is a perfect time, the water delicately slapping the side of the boat as I sit in the complete stillness of the morning before the wind has risen. I hear a noisy tropical bird, and I strain my eyes to the shore not a hundred meters away. I can hear the location, but I cannot quite place it. I hold up my tablet and zoom with the binocular function and as I do, I catch a glimpse of something odd. I drop the tablet to the side and see a person walking across the water. Off with my sunglasses and I squint, rubbing my eyes to confirm it, but yes, there is indeed a person strolling on the bay, and I recognize her. It is Rose, casually striding to me in the morning sun atop the simple lapping of the sea. She offers a half wave, a tentative "hello" unbefitting the image, and not befitting her at all. She is nervous around me, I think. Or she wants me to think that she is. She is dressed in a small white romper, highly structured and short with a gold clasp around her neck for the halter. I have never seen her in white.

As she comes closer, I smile to her, and she returns.

"Don't be afraid?" I ask.

She looks around. "I guess that would be the reference," she replies.

"Mmhmm."

"But it's not what I was going for," she says.

She arrives at the edge of the pontoon and I remove the rope tie from that edge, readying myself to hoist her up, but she instead floats the two meters from the surface up to the final step, accomplishing this with a little mini jump that propels her to the exact height where she places her hand in my waiting palm.

"You have to admit this is a little spooky," I say.

"Oh, well, you know we have technology for everything now." She drops my hand and steps close for an embrace. I wrap my arms around her.

"I don't see any on you," I say, and she defers, doesn't really want to talk about it. "But it is good to see you. What are you doing out here?"

"I'm sorry I came when I wasn't invited."

"You were invited," I say. "And I'm delighted by the surprise. Don't stand on ceremony, love, it's delightful that you're here."

"I wanted to see you again," she says.

"Good," I say. "I told you I'd be back in a week or two, whenever we finished this trek."

"That's too long," she says. "Sorry, I'm being pathetic, but we finished the party for Avery last night, and I decided I wanted to see you now."

"Should we sit down?" I gesture to the center of the boat where there's a large couch on the foredeck.

"Yes, let's," she says, and takes my hand and leads me there.

She sits down and sighs, looking around.

"Nice yacht," she says.

"Justinus rented it for the week. I think he's had this one before."

"I am sorry for barging in."

"Stop, stop. It's excellent that you're here."

"You're sure?"

"Yes."

"Good."

"I am irresistible."

"You do love yourself, we know."

"But why are you actually here?"

"I just wanted to see you."

"Needed a vacation?"

"No…No. I love my job, you know that. I have a couple of weeks off until the next scheduled death. You'll have to meet her, she's very nice, but anyway, I had some time, and I just thought I would rather be here with you." I look at her expectantly, hoping she'll expand further. She obliges: "You are my project, and that isn't as unromantic as it sounds; I do think we'll come to love each other intensely. But you are what I want to work on and redeem and you'll give me something back, too."

"The Morris thing."

"Yes, the Morris thing."

"Well, I like that, being your project, so I approve."

"I knew you would."

"Did you bring anything else to wear?"

"I had a bag delivered last night. Should be in the kitchen, I think."

"You are always so on top of things."

"Morning," I hear behind us. It's Peter, up surprisingly early for the state I saw him in last night.

"Peter. You've met Rose, haven't you?"

"Only from a distance."

"Good to meet you," she says.

"And you. When did you arrive?"

"Just now," I say. "I thought you were sleeping on shore?"

"We all came back at sunrise. They want to get underway soon, get a spot for snorkeling. I'm glad you're here," he says to Rose. "Someone needs to keep an eye on this wayward youth."

"Leaving now?" I say.

"Yeah. If you don't get there early, you don't get a spot on the reef."

"Are you sure everyone is back? It's pretty early."

"Yeah." He pauses. "I'll check. But Justinus set the autopilot so it'll just cruise us over." He disappears below deck.

After a half hour of motoring, we arrive at the dive spot. No signs of movement on our boat, so Rose and I dive into the water, swimming to where a couple of stone pillars jut from the surf and coral lies below. I turn to her as I tread water, noticing her excitement as she takes in the place, dipping her head below the water for brief moments to catch the beauty.

"But there is something I wanted to ask from the other night," I say.

"What's that?"

"What are we?"

"Oh no, did someone try to sleep with you at the party?"

"Not at all," I say.

"I don't believe you."

"You shouldn't. But…"

"What, are we going steady or something?" she says, playfully.

"Mmhmm."

"Yeah, don't worry about it yet," with some stress in her voice. "Why are you worrying about it? You were the one who was talking about not trusting, about not wanting to make mistakes."

"And you're the one who showed up and walked across the water for me."

"I knew you were upset about me coming."

"I'm really not. I'm just saying that it's interesting that you're here, and you're pursuing me, so I must be something to you."

"You are potentially everything to me. Or, the most important thing. Something…you know what I mean."

"I do."

"But we'll build it and we'll be fine."

"I like that idea," I say.

"Good," she says, continuing to swim a little closer to the rocks.

"This is nice."

"Have you ever been to the Caribbean?"

She replies first with an 'are you serious' look, then answers. "Last time was ten years ago, for a death."

I cup the air with my hands and bring it under the water to form a view-finder of sorts and spy some fishies.

I am immediately dunked from behind.

She has positioned her entire body on my shoulders and rides me down below the waves. I break free and grab a leg, dragging her down as she attempts her escape. In my blurry half vision I see her body and her bottom flexing as she kicks and struggles, but I have her, and I bring her into my arms and we surface as I continue to tread and she hangs on to me now.

"You punk," I say.

"You left yourself open. Gotta' be on your toes."

"You're a nut."

"So are you."

"That's true."

Twenty meters below the waves and we are kicking through the artificial reef, a hodgepodge of old shuttles and concrete arches and sculptures. I swim under another structure and locate Rose a little ways away tailing a little sergeant major.

The scuba device is a little mouthpiece with two tubes extending into the water on either side of the mouth for a few inches. One can stay in the water for as long as you like—we have a decompression machine on board—without fear of running out of air. And you can always carry a spare in your pocket if you're worrying about it breaking. Not that this matters anyway. A dive site like this is covered with drones hidden in nooks and crannies in the rocks and waiting under the sand on the shore.

No need to worry about sharks, no need to worry about air, no need to worry about death in any form. This is the sense of security one has in this world. It isn't a false one, either; there is truly no risk of death here. In the distance, looking up to the light, I can see the shark that I've been watching as I swim. If he were to come close to me, a drone would fight him. The drones are extremely hesitant, but the sharks, except for the novices, have learned not to mess with the gangly slowly swimming creatures as they are often joined by fast moving octopi with shocking feet.

Rose points out the shark I've been watching, and I can see her eyes smile. It's a little black tip reef shark, about one and a half meters, again, no threat. They aren't dangerous creatures anyway, and attacks were few and far between even before the time of drones. They just look sinister, and they do, for that matter provide copious amounts of death for the little creatures of the reef.

It is funny that we have left nature behind as creatures that live forever. We no longer kill animals, except for the odd situation like the elk in Montana. The odd situation clarifies, of course, that we have not, in fact, left nature. We are still bound to it and still our lives are determined by it. It just doesn't kill us as frequently as it used to; still, death comes to so many of us, and I cannot forget it. It is a part of life, something I should embrace not by dying but by living with full knowledge of the valuable presence of death.

I spot a shrimp hiding amongst the coral. He peeks out from his cave and I see that he is eating something small, may be a piece of a fish or something of that sort. The average shrimp trades off of the death of the living; it is the only way he stays alive. I smile to myself and turn to find Rose still watching the shark. I point up and she nods.

As we surface I remove my mask and mouthpiece and straighten out my hair.

"You like that shark, huh?"

"I do," she says.

"We should take you cage diving."

"Okay. Have you been?"

"No, no. But I'd take you, get you living."

"I'd like that."

"Are you ready to head back?"

"Yeah, I need breakfast."

"Of course. Let's go."

We arrive at the far end of Virgin Gorda where there are a few scattered resorts connected only by rarely trodden footpaths running over the hills and through the low plains. If one looks due east (just ignore Anguilla) the entire Atlantic Ocean stretches out before you until you reach Africa—it is a beautiful place, and it does feel like the end of the world.

We walk into the lobby area so the auto scan can charge us for the dock fees. As we step into the hotel, the robot concierge provides a friendly chime and a robot arm wave suggesting we come closer, so Justinus and I investigate.

"There is a party this evening, and all guests are invited to attend."

"Oh," I say, "what is it?"

"It is the death party of Lindsay and Jenny James beginning at six PM."

"Oh no, thanks," says Justinus, looking to me.

"No, I'm fine," I say. "I imagine everyone is going?"

"Ninety-percent of residents at the four area hotels have indicated attendance."

"See," I say, "It'll be the place to be."

"I don't want you to push anything," he says.

"No, I'm going to be fine. If I'm not, I'll leave."

"Okay, add us all to the list," says Justinus.

"The party will be at the far beach in Little Bay. Follow the signs on the footpath from the pool."

As we walk back to the boat he checks in on me once more.

"You're sure?"

"Yes, yes, I'll be fine. I need to get back into the world. Imagine if I never attended another death party—where would I be on the social ladder?"

"That's true, but you're not very high on the social ladder anyway."

"It could be worse, though, which, can you even imagine?"

"No, I honestly can't do that."

Oliver is standing on the bow with Austinate, looking stressed.

"Death party tonight," I say.

"Oh really?"

"Yeah, on the island."

"I told them we'd be there," says Justinus.

"But what's going on with you two."

"Belle wants to go home," says Oliver.

"Oh."

"Actually, she's already left. She caught a ride with a random boat leaving a bit ago."

"Wow," I say. "In a hurry."

"She's temperamental. At least we got a night with her," Oliver reassures himself.

"That's right," says Austinate, for further support. "And a wonderful night at that."

"Someday," says Justinus. "You'll get her," he says.

"Where's Rose?" I say.

"She's at the bar, I think. With Peter and Nigel." Oliver looks around, and then points them out. "You can see them." They are about a hundred meters away at a water side bar sitting behind one of the other docks. "We're going to walk over there once Aurelius and Theodore finish their showers and such. Jen and Minerva are napping I guess."

"Okay," I say. "I'm going to do some drugs before we head over, if anyone wants to join."

Austinate nods, and Justinus says, "lead the way."

I walk into the kitchen and grab a couple of little powder bottles, one amphetamine, one painkiller. I haven't been doing too much in the way of drugs these days, but tonight I feel like I am getting back to myself, feel like I can get back on the horse and it won't mean anything. It might be disconcerting for the average person, but I generally avoid drugs when I am feeling down and take more of them when I am feeling better. So my thoughts running to these two powders together in a happy combination is actually a good sign.

I return to the common table on the back of the boat, where the sun is getting lower in the sky casting a sharp angle and brilliant yellow gleam to everything that isn't shaded. The contrast, the sparkle on the water, it is a beautiful thing. Everyone has their sun glasses on, we all look beautiful, and it will be a fun evening, and a good thing to celebrate life with these people as we celebrate the deaths of some others.

I pour out the drugs into a small combined mountain and then start cutting them into lines with the edge of a thin card sized piece of gold that I carry in my drug kit. It is otherwise impossible to find anything to cut drugs with—the counter can't do it, it's a bit awkward to do it with a knife, impossible to do with a tablet. Straws are a bit easier to find, but I've got one of those, too.

Aurelius appears first from one set of stairs, followed shortly by Theodore on the other set. "What do we have here?" says Theodore.

"Evening warmup," says Austinate.

"That is correct."

"We should do a shot of rum," says Aurelius. "Because of where we are." Justinus gives him a dirty look. "What," he continues, "I got yelled at last night for not appreciating the rum around here, and I am doing my best to reform. We're all so committed to self-improvement when we're around Mr. Walker."

I smile. And then do a line. "I am a model of self-improvement."

"The scary part," says Oliver, "is that you really are?"

"It's true," says Justinus.

Austinate looks over to me and nods. I love the brevity.

"I'm glad you and Peter are friends again," says Aurelius. "It was upsetting to see you two avoiding each other."

"We were never going to break up," I say.

"Unless you had died," says Theodore.

"Fair point," I laugh.

"He would have been so upset with you."

"Rightly so," I nod. "Probably would have been upset with myself actually." I raise my shot glass, now that Theodore has passed them all out. "Here's to things we'll never do, and all the people we'll never screw; here's to lives we'll never live, and all the fucks we'll never give; here's to glory long since passed, now's the time to raise your glass;" they all join in on the last line—"Here's to us, we're the best, take your shot, fuck the rest!"

We knock back our drinks and head to the bar to meet up with Peter and Nigel and Rose who are enjoying a quiet glass of wine without us. I can feel the stupid smile on my face, the unfortunate side effect of feeling a little high and having a slight buzz. Rose smiles at me when she sees me and bids me sit next to her at the table. She kisses my forehead as I sit down. We are strangely intimate for never having been.

Justinus and the rest sit at the end of the long table the early arrivals have snagged, though the bar is almost completely empty—most likely people are getting ready in their rooms, or perhaps at some unadvertised early pre-party.

"Death party tonight," says Justinus, and Peter stares at him.

"No, no," I say, "it was my idea. I want to go."

"You do?" asks Nigel.

"I do. No need to drag the rest of you down, and it should be fun."

"It will be fun," says Justinus.

We order a round of drinks and Justinus starts telling the story of how Oliver first met Belle and why he is always in love with her and how he has pursued her for two thousand years and has never made it further than a single night. He has a way of telling stories that I, while I admit I found him rather annoying when we first met some months ago, I have grown to love and I can see why he has so many friends around him all the time. There are even some of these friends who actually love him, they are not only superficial acquaintances or connections to some greater status. I will do my best to keep him alive, and to keep him well adjusted.

Jen and Minerva arrive a few minutes later, looking like they've already started some heavy drug use or drinking immediately after their naps. We make our way over to the party as it edges closer to the time. Rose walks with me at the back of our procession, and we join in with a small parade of people over to the beach.

"I'm glad you are okay to do this," she says.

"It's a good thing for me to get back to."

"It is. It's what I do, after all."

We arrive at the site of the party, all prepared, a few hundred people standing on the sand. There are tables filled with food and drink and beautiful lighting and a little wooden platform leaning up against the beach, halfway in the water. Our group arrives and we start to mingle a bit, socializing, Justinus of course knows someone, but Austinate does, too.

After a little while, a gong sounds and we hush.

Lindsay—at least the person next to me thinks that's who it is—starts to speak.

“Thanks to everyone who came out tonight. It’s time! Love you all.”

Jenny steps up: “What she said”—polite laughter—“We’re ready to go. Our children, our friends, be good, get all that you can. It’s time.’”

They toss the microphone to a robot waiter and then turn to two people, a man and a woman, the woman looks suspiciously like a combination of the two others—this must be their daughter, and maybe their son, or her husband. No tears, though, no overly long hugs or clinging. The daughter lets go of her mothers, she lets them go to death without a moment of hesitation, with a smile, with clear joy.

It’s an imposing thing, and I feel the notch in my throat build and my eyes start to itch. I clutch Rose for a moment, and she turns to me and looks to me. “I’m okay,” I mouth to her, and I am. I think this is beautiful. It’s tinged with sadness for me, but it always is, always has been. I got lost for a while, and I couldn’t see the beauty in any and every ending. I see it again, with Rose I see it again.

They hold hands and walk down to the platform. I take Rose’s hand in mine and smile at her. The wives stand in the middle of the platform as it starts to drift out in the water a little ways, and one says something quietly to the other, they smile, and they kiss one last time, and then another word, I think she says ‘til next time.’ This is it for them, the end of their lives, and I think that they must have made the right choice for them, that there are so many friends and their families here that they must be doing what is good. Sometimes people die, and there is no saving them or restoring them. Addison had died; she was just a shell. Helen was on her way.

Once the platform has floated out a little bit into the water, a safe distance, a loud beeping noise precedes a bright blue flash. It’s an evaporation cloud, an interesting way to go. Generators on the bottom of the platform produce a super high energy field in a sphere which quickly turns everything within it to dust. And dust they are; the orb flickers out and a cloud of dust is visible in the last few glimmers of the sun just as it sets. They have returned.

The momentary pause after the death ensues but is quickly broken by the sounds of the champagne bottles popping and clinking glasses being passed around. We line up to take our glasses from one of the tables and once everyone has them, and has been sipping for a moment, the daughter takes the microphone again. "Thank you all for coming. Here's to my moms!" We cheer and huzzah and then quiet again. "Not much more to say than that. Let's have a great time!"

Okay, then. This family has a true penchant for brevity.

"You would have done this better," I say.

"You're right," she says, stepping into my arms. "You did so well tonight. You really handled this, you know, no tears, no unnecessary sadness."

"Yeah, I'm ready again."

"Good," she says. "Take me dancing?" A dance floor is now illuminated a little ways back from the beach and it is quickly filling up as a jazz trance band starts to toot their horns.

"Sure," I say, "we should always dance."

Awake, and I scan the brightly lit cabin with the sun flooding past the poorly constructed curtains and the gentle lapping sound against the hull. Rose sleeps soundly next to me and I kiss her head but let her sleep as I roll off the bed and head to the bathroom. I look in the mirror and try to unmuss my hair and give a deep stretch and a yawn to greet the day.

I walk up to the deck and Aurelius, Justinus, Theodore, Oliver and Austinate are eating breakfast, and we say good morning and laugh about the night before. They give me a hard time about the extent of my dancing—I'm actually pretty good, but I did dance all night—and about Rose and I making out in a corner of the party behind some palm trees. Back to my youth, back to our youth, like teenagers at the high school dance. I tell them I'm going to grab a bit of sun before breakfast and I walk out to the couch on the bow and I lay down in the early morning sun light with the water still and sparkling.

As we sit in the harbor I am lost in a thought. A bit of early morning profundity; and I think of all that I've been through and if it makes any sense to me. It is the primary challenge to all my philosophical thinking that humans are always an emotional or directed creature, and that the words of our thoughts are always a step removed from what we are. We can practice awareness, but it is hardly ever perfect, and one can easily be swept up. I know what I think, but I am easily distracted such that I cannot live what I think. I forget what I understand. I was swept up in love, swept up in death, death, death, love, death, and then pursued my own death, though I had no real reason for it. I knew better than to think in the way that I did, but I would not accept that because of my conviction that my experience trumped these things I knew, and I thus rewrote what I believed. Now I understand once more that it was just another stream I was caught in, and that I can swim into my old stream of living—or something like it—and it will not change anything except that I will continue to live.

I am not dead, and I am not bored, and I know the ways to prevent my boredom, so it will never be foisted upon me as if it came from something outside of myself; instead I live boldly and with every risk that I can, to love and to socialize, and to embrace all that humanity and the world have to offer, because it is better to be this way.

I have all things. There is no disease or weakness or lack of ability. There is endless opportunity to be something new and different. I have no wants, no need which cannot be met. What would make a reasonable end to life? I have to ask this question of myself—before eternity, what would make it okay for a person to kill themselves? I may one day come across this thing which leads to death, but I certainly have not found it in this life. There are those who have, and I do not begrudge them their choice. But they are not me and I have no reason to die.

I rely on my philosophy, on my theology, on the words that govern my sense of reality. But they are written and will be rewritten based on the whims of my humanity. Neither is prior, neither superior; no one truth, nothing absolute but nothingness; what else can I find, what else can I do, when I happen to be in this place? Did I think it would be different? Did I think it would be as it is? Even with the rumors of eternity before the transition, I could never have understood this life. Not something to be understood, I suppose. We are too small.

My experience was of a great pain and a great tragedy, and I don't dismiss it as nothing though it is nothing when I put it before all things. I loved them and it was good, and now they have died, and though this is not what I have wanted, it is good for them that they died. I still feel their loss, a gaping lack, but I have permission to let it go, to see the lack emptied away. I want to continue on, not to see or do anything, but to continue on. I must say to myself, *those joys have ended; go and find new joy, new life.*

We set out this afternoon sailing north past Saba Rock and Eustatia Island on our way to the Settlement, a few hours to go. As our sails unfurl I stand up and move to take my place on the perch up front. I put my hand on Rose's leg as I walk by; she is reading something, I think something with her work, probably the next client. She is not very good at vacation, but she loves her work so we can let her have it. She is getting a nice tan, though, so she is at least welcoming the sun.

At the edge now, I look out over the ocean, and here there is more sense than words. Take in the open ocean, the mountains rising from the sea floor, these little dots of green and grass dotting the blue: your size in comparison to the world is given to you here, and you begin to know yourself. It may be the truest thought we can have as humans. This, or as I've done a few times, floating freely in space, where the little islands poking out are moons and planets and stars and you are just the speck. There is no real power then, you are just the small thing that is here and walks on these slightly bigger things, and these things are small in the sea of the universe, and the universe to all universes, and everything that is becomes small and nothing when compared with the great sea of nothingness. You are the smallness in the great infinite abyss of existence. Why do you talk about your life? Whether you live or die? What would it matter?

But since you are here, it seems strange to forgo this opportunity. You are now a human, and one with an immensity of joy and beauty and terrible sadness to uncover, and all of it good, if you only acknowledge that it is. If you only let it be what it is, in the chaos of reality, if you just give up your resistance to the crashing waves and the uprising mountains and let them be as they are, as they will be, as they do whatever it is they will do. You are on the boat, sailing, subject, free and bound, always perplexed, adrift in an ocean that will have its way with you and the choices that you have and will make.

Why are you in a rush? I see your sadness, but it still shines in the universe, well beyond you. Why can you see only yourself? I don't want you to die. Perhaps someday you will have a proper reason for the end of your life, but it is not enough when your false sense of true resistance brings you to a misdirected commitment to your own end. Your want of something different, coupled with your denial of the error of your attachments and mental makeup, these are the things that make you think you should die. They are not true, no more so than anything else in this world, and your devotion has no point or purpose to it. Do not choose a higher purpose, but acknowledge the meaninglessness of all of your points and purposes, of all your ends and goals and all your meaning.

This will be the freedom to exist. It is not an easy thing. I have failed at it throughout my life, and I will continue to do so forever. It is not something that one wills themselves into, nor is it something that comes without practice and training. To find yourself truly without the weightiest of cares is a gift rarely given, and then only in part, only imperfectly. So do not think I say this to you lightly, as if you should just understand all the reasons why you should keep on living. You will have to take terrible risks, to lose yourself and your life, and then you may be able to live once you are lost. This will be the freedom to exist.

I will not rely on hope or a dream of the future being better. In the moment I am armed with all I need for my ongoing existence. I will encounter others and love them and love the world when it loves and when it kills, and it will do all of these things.

One day death will come, and you and I will welcome it. There is nothing in this universe that will last forever, and I will be no different.

In this moment is life, not the past or the future. So we will live.

At sea, Saturday Evening, January 5

I like the latitude of 37degrees better than my bitter native 42degrees. We have sauntered all this calm day at one or two knots the hour, and nobody on board well pleased but I, and why should I be pleased? I have nothing to record. I have read little. I have done nothing. What then? Need we be such barren scoundrels that the whole beauty of heaven, the main, and man, cannot entertain us unless we too must needs hold a candle and daub God's world with a smutch of our own insignificance. Not I, for one. I will be pleased, though I do not deserve it.

Ralph Waldo Emerson[16]

Coda

The report came in today that we are unable to locate any more fuel for the principal reactor, the universe having completely exhausted itself. Our titanium planet's molten core will no longer burn, and there will be no heat, no electricity. A returning mass-miner shuttle may extend our timespan for a few weeks, but the end is truly here.

I see myself, standing with Rose, at the door. We look out into the vast blackness of space, no stars or nebulas nor any single bit of light. No more black holes or neutron stars to mine. We are the last bit of humanity, and we stand in the embrace of nothingness. There is no fear, however, as this is where we have always been, always in this moment, always on the edge of existence and non-existence, and always ready, too.

Appendix

Not dead yet: A response to "On the goodness of dying." © Milnius Group, 2970.

The plain decision making of the follower of Wittgenstein, the famous and well-loved Hans Svendsen, provides a new philosophical challenge to those who struggle onwards for the purposes of life. Svendsen's short final lecture, "*Principia moribunda*," is now the most discussed and most widely read and watched piece of philosophy in human history and this for good reason. The good reason is found in Svendsen's conclusion where he suggests that the answer to the question of life is "no," that we should choose death over life because it is an inevitability that we will choose death at some point. Our final choice is the choice we always should be inclined to make, the right choice, so to speak, the end to which we are directed and may mistakenly select to delay but for only a brief time in the span of history before we conclude our march to death.

The philosopher—at least those who actually understand philosophy—has always had a keen interest in the question of suicide. They have possessed this interest because they ask the fundamental question of the purpose of life, and in so doing, they must ask whether or not it is right even to live such a life as this, whether it serves a point, whether even if pointless it might be better to continue living. This question was much easier when life lasted, on average, between sixty-five and eighty-five years, with the possibility of sudden death from disease or external forces ever present, as even if one were not sure about the correct answer death would arrive in short order and provide a conclusion. Svendsen was over six hundred years old when he arrived at his "realization" about the "good" end of life, and at the time of his death last year he was one of two billion of the first generation to have eternal life to have chosen death, by no means a small or inconsequential number. He evidences the complications of a longer life, as do the rest of the dying, all of whom show us that the conclusion, even if reached from a methodologically alternative pattern than Svendsen's claim of evidentiary fact, is nonetheless the conclusion for a great multitude of persons.

I write to provide a philosophical alternative and response to Svendsen's articulation of the problem. He repeats a classic error from the history of philosophy, one particularly proper to the English and the analytics—though he is not English—who demonstrate consistently the general lack of awareness of the possibilities of human alteration and training. Philosophy is intended to change a mind and this can happen more than once.

I do not write to condemn those who choose suicide. I have no confusion about this subject, and make no such claim to knowledge of an absolute good which would allow for a shout of "wrong!" at the person who claims suicide. I will not predict the outcome of life, of my life, of all lives, and I do not seek a prohibition on the offering of philosophical justifications for suicide. I imagine we will see many more of these.

Instead, I ask the question whether or not there is something missing from the practice of those who go to suicide, something missing which could be included and developed as a valued component, something to alter perspective and bring into new life. What Svendsen misses is the lack of objectivity in making a claim of the objective necessity of death. Even if it were objective, if this were a thing, we are not bound by objectivity, and if it suits us to continue living we can mock the objective and see it from the standpoint which does not need to rely on reason or the rational but rather sees from the standpoint of meaninglessness. The reason for this is the reasonable or rational is simply a standpoint in itself and not the true standpoint, i.e., what could it mean to be the true standpoint in the universe of existing and non-existing things?

The complaint against suicide is thus that it is not necessary. It is not objective because there is no objectivity about such matters, as Wittgenstein's assertion still holds through Svendsen's objections, but also even if we were to approach from an objective standpoint, the experience described by Svendsen can be overcome and the perception changed. The choice of living is not found in a willing towards life but in the preparation to analyze and interpret the varied events of life which one encounters on a daily basis in a manner which does not lead to one's death. It is not merely passive, but responsive. The ability to embrace monotony and to find the greatest of joys, and not false joys, but true sincere joys, within the monotony, this is the method whereby one defeats the inclination to suicide and comes to live a renewed life.

Svendsen's experience and the desiring of death

What makes a person desire death? We have the footage of much of Svendsen's final year and we see the classic indications of suicide approaching as the direct result of his conclusions about these experiences. In particular, we see that he no longer finds anything to be a source of joy, and there is a hollowness to his eyes and a shallowness to his interactions with his partner, Tomas de Montevideo. Their mutual experience is of great instruction on this point. They love each other to such an extent that the prospect of no longer loving each other as a result of boredom and monotony is a proper reason for death, i.e., life is not worth living if in this life a love like this cannot persist. They are deeply attached but find no joy in each other from their interactions; there is no remaining interest in sexual activity; no remaining interest in quality time spent together; no interest in a date night; no interest in any of the things in life which bonded them previously.

A study completed by the Department of Transition indicates that the primary causes of suicide are two main categories, a lack of contentment with or acceptance of oneself, and the experience of boredom. Svendsen experiences both of these: he is bored with life and with his partner, and as a result, he is not satisfied with himself. He knows himself to be one who loves Tomas. He knows that he ought to do this, but he knows that he will not be able to continue to do this in a satisfactory way because he no longer receives joy from his interactions with this person, because the little things that once amused now frustrate and annoy after two hundred years together. He can choose to leave Tomas, but he still loves him, and does not want to leave him, and to leave him would change his identity as one who loves

Tomas, and this he does not want to do. He, instead wishes to persist as one who loves Tomas or to die as one who loves Tomas, and thus to possess this identity in the static place of death.

You will note that I am not talking about his philosophical writing but what some still persist in calling his "personal life." The personal life is the true domain of the philosopher, and the only area that philosophers should direct their attention towards in the evaluation of another's philosophy is precisely this personal life which is the domain of the manifestation of thought and understanding. If a person fails in their personal life, then they either do not understand their own philosophy, or they have a deficient philosophy, one which cannot provide any proper guidance on life or living. I use "fail" in a general and vague sense, of course, but there are innumerable failures which are possible, and they do not have to be considered moral or cosmic to be significant.

Svendsen fails in his thought because of the patently clear contradiction between his Wittgensteinian silence towards the ethical and metaphysical which is placed alongside his maintenance of an identity based in part on a love relationship. The relationship is thus given the status of metaphysical, and he holds an ethics of his life derived in part from his continued attachment to this person in contradiction of the required silence towards the ethical. There is nothing in his philosophy to support these actions—his philosophy is silent, while his actions speak the truth of his actual philosophy in contradiction of his silence. He is not silent on the ethical, but lives a clear ethics, and this clear ethics is the thing which leads to his choice of suicide.

Thus Svendsen's claim that the conclusion of a logic like Wittgenstein's is in suicide and death is rendered moot because it has not addressed the lifestyle which has manifested itself in the conclusion of suicide and death. If Svendsen does not make such attachment, if he instead remains silent about that which he "must" in his life, he will have no reason for saying that he "must" go to his death, and no reason for the condemnation of Wittgenstein's weakness in not going to death himself. If, instead, the evaluation of attachments and practices formed a coherent and central strategy of Svendsen's thought, his decision does not follow but demonstrates his inconsistency.

The varied lifestyle and the recapturing of wonder and novelty

The shortcomings of the approach offered by Svendsen are the product of an underdeveloped attitude towards the processes of interpretation of stimuli and phenomena. This is a piece completely unexamined by Svendsen in his own work. He does, in fact, write an extensive excursus[17] on the practices of logic in relation to the interpretation of external reality, but he does this in an analysis of Wittgenstein not his own thought, and he does not provide a constructive methodology for the alteration of the interpretation. Further, the methodology does not provide an account of the lived experience of this sort of process, i.e., he certainly discusses the interior workings of the human and the various thought processes which are possible, but does not discuss what the experience is for an actual person—himself, perhaps—and thus does not show what it might mean to live this intellectual excursion. The intellectual is not a piece to be separated from the practical, not at least without devastating consequence in the form of a life disconnected from suitable examination.

The process, then, must be outlined as to how a person might come to implement an alteration of perception such that monotony and boredom do not come to rule one's life. This alteration is necessary because of the fact of living—in the course of living, a person comes to experience monotony and it corresponds to depression and dissatisfaction with life. I take a key finding from those identified as "mystics" in previous generations, those who are able to see the world imbued with the presence of God in a moving and constantly beautiful and uplifting manner. I do not recommend the same elation which is at times associated with such practice, but I also caution against the sober hesitance to avoid these sorts of alterations. One may object that seeing things differently is not "true" or not "objective." These objections are rendered meaningless, however; if the objective leads to death, is it objective? Is it objectively true that death is inevitable, as Svendsen argued? The answer, of course, is no. The subjective, then, is this really subjective? Or is that which makes life possible that which is to be followed, leaving the meaningless and ignorant questions of what is objective or subjective behind in the dust, trampled upon, and in their proper place, buried in the dirt?

The common answer to the problem of boredom is to attempt to live a varied lifestyle, i.e., in the experience of new things one can escape the problem of monotony. This may appear to be a straightforward answer, and there are many things that one can encounter as "new" in the course of their lives. I call this person the "collector," i.e., the collector of experiences. This lifestyle becomes difficult when the experience of experiencing the new itself becomes monotonous, as it inevitably does, as all things do without the training necessary to render the new itself a non-attachment experience.

Can you see the sunrise every day and still recognize that it is beautiful and appreciate it? One must have some aspect within that can appreciate it always and forever if one wishes to stay alive always and forever. It is the most basic thing in some regard, to love the sun, and if you do not love the sun when it rises and sets then your life will no longer be subject to the ups and downs that make a life a life. You should regress, then, regress in a special, limited sense and become like a child internally, with the mind of a child see all the world as you saw when you were younger. You saw the sun rise and it was not the first time that you saw it when you first appreciated its beauty and wondered at it, but in that experience of seeing the sun rise and wondering at it you have found something new and amazing.

The objection arises: it is natural that we should grow to see things as monotonous, and the sun rising is no different. Why should we feel something special towards the sun when we see it all the time, every day? Would we not be forced to perpetrate a falsehood in imagining it to remain significant or in some way interesting?

The answer, first, is that there is nothing "natural." Do not make any claims to the natural, as one cannot do this without knowing the purpose of nature, of which nothing can be said even if there is one. The entire category of nature or "the natural" is foolish and impossible. The claim that humans naturally do anything does not matter. What matters, again, is whether one lives or dies, and if one dies from following this "natural" route isn't that an action against nature? Death is part of life, of course, I do not want to set these in opposition, but I do not want to insist on death as an always present and quickly arriving aspect of life—I do not grant the conclusion Svendsen offers.

So we need to revert to something within ourselves and find the child-like perspective, not at the time of the first experience of the sun but rather the first experience of the sun as source of wonder and something to be cherished. It is in this momentous experience that one finds the ability to re-enjoy and thus rejoice in the everyday features of life, and to do so continuously and throughout one's existence. One remembers all of the experience—perhaps a rising heart rate, a sense of connection with others, a feeling of awe, and one practices such to elicit these responses in oneself. This is not done by forcing oneself to have certain feelings, but by holding beliefs and practicing responses from which the rote response will be to reflexively experience this reaction. If one doubts that this set of reactions is natural, then one should doubt what it would be to be natural. If one doubts that this is how one truly feels, then one should doubt oneself and the supposedly unquestionable nature of what it might mean to be oneself. But if one wishes to continue living and to counter boredom, then this form of a basic appreciation for the everyday events of life is a necessary portion of one's life. One must be open; open to continuing to exist; open to the sun; open to life.

The answer to Svendsen as a form of life

One must therefore adopt an altered form of life including the practices which will allow one to avoid the sense of monotony and distance from oneself. This involves the maintenance of the appreciation for the things which one appreciates—remembering what it is to enjoy something and to be able to continue enjoying the same thing for the rest of one's existence. This involves practices like moderation, i.e., not doing something to such an extent it becomes burdensome, but also not avoiding any such thing for any extended period of time. One should show persistence and satisfaction in the enjoyment of whatever one has enjoyed.

This is an expansive, whole-life project. Whatever one masturbates to, one must persist in masturbating to that thing. What one does for fun with friends, where one travels to, where one chooses to eat at a restaurant, where one lives, in all these things, one should not be afraid of the monotony but work to fight against the creeping dissatisfaction one may feel in their experience of these things as a repeated practice.

How many times can one go to a party and still enjoy it? I am just past eight hundred years old, and I have been to approximately twenty thousand parties in the course of these eight hundred years. I have never enjoyed parties, particularly, except with certain exceptional combinations of events, so I did not have a high bar to maintain in terms of my level of joy. If I fail to enjoy parties, however, I fail to find enjoyment in a key feature of human social life. If I fail to find enjoyment in this key feature of human social life, I may fail to find a necessary outlet for the social inclination found in humanity. I may attempt to rewrite this social inclination, but if I do not wish to take on a hermetic lifestyle, I must persist in my tolerance of going to parties, and I must do so for another eight hundred years and as many years after that as I continue to live. The party example may seem frivolous, but it is indicative of a full range of mundane human activities which become acidic to the person who is unable to find or maintain joy. When a mundanity is no longer fresh but poison, then the person will start to find death of particular appeal.

Meaningless life and the identification of areas of attachment and meaning

In my recent work *On meaninglessness: Life and death in life eternal*, I argued that the only possibility for enduring existence is found in coming to terms with the complete lack of meaning for our lives. This is, in part, a product of the fact that we can now live forever—the brevity of life actually provided it with greater meaning or possibility of meaning, or at least the impression or belief that it was actually meaningful could be said to persist. Svendsen, though he does not express this in what he has written, is disappointed in the lack of meaning for his life. In particular he is disappointed that he is not able to maintain his love relationship and to have it stand up against the weight of the universe. The idea that you and the one you love stand together against the cosmic forces of all existence is a powerful and commonplace sense. Love is certainly the most powerful and significant force in our lives, and this is a good thing. But we cannot forget the meaningless which stands intermixed with love—our being in love does not mean that this love becomes eternal, and it does not mean that we can become the static creature like that God who supposedly is Love. One cannot live for love simply so called. Instead, we are powerless to avoid change and decay because we are material and the law of matter is the law of change until the end of time. They will die or you will die. Perhaps your love will die, or your children, your friends, all those that you love, all of them will die in all the various ways of dying this world holds. We do not stand against the universe, but rather we are a part of it and we will always change as it does, always become something different. Now I am one human, next I will be another, and then I will be a third. I am in one form now, sometime in the future I will be in a new form, perhaps as dust, then grass, then burnt in a wildfire and rise into the sky, settling as ash, shipped on a trash buggy into a distant star, becoming a star, radiating free, landing on a planet in some distant universe, becoming food and eaten by another living species and becoming a living being once more. I should not even say we are limited to the material—what is the limit of possibility? Has what I am changed in the meantime? Is this thing still me? What would even be the meaning of that question, to speak that answer precisely? Would it matter anyway? Was I ever a true "thing" anyway?

I certainly do not know the answer to these questions, and anyone with a suitable epistemological hesitancy is forced to acknowledge the necessity of a certain form of agnosticism. This is not a permanent agnosticism, or an absolute silence, because, as is the case with Svendsen, claiming silence does not allow one to actually live a life of silence. Every action of life is a spoken word and a claim of purpose or activity to the universe. We assert a form of meaning in our lives with every decision made and action taken, and this contradiction of what we know about our lives can create a tension; or we can acknowledge this and embrace meaninglessness as we live with meaning in our lives. This is a dual standpoint—both/and, neither/nor—which by possessing such combination grants true freedom. One can fall in love but one knows that the one whom he loves is mortal and subject to change, as this one is, as their love is, and all of this is the truth, which is also subject to change. When the love dies the attachment formed will cause pain but it will one day fall to the side, so long as one remembers that there was never anything there to begin with. It was always a meaningless thing filled with great meaning to us but never meaning anything in the face of the great depth of the universe.

Some accuse this meaninglessness of taking away the goodness or beauty of life to which we must respond most harshly. Nothing that makes life possible takes away its goodness or beauty—and we must ask whether that goodness or beauty as traditionally spoken of ever existed in the first place. I know this philosophy sounds severe, but it can save you from the pain of believing in something which will always come to an end, will always come up short, and in the forgetting of this limit is the greatest of risks for our human lives.

Becoming a different person

There is a great risk in not liking oneself. This is something plainly said and repeated, but the effect of not liking oneself is that you come to desire your own death. You do not want to be the one that you are, and if you do not understand the capacity for change, then you give up hope for a good life in which you actually enjoy yourself. If you cannot hear the sound of your own voice, if you cannot listen to your jokes and hear your feeble attempts at attracting sexual partners. If you cannot weather rejection from friends and loved ones and from disapproving family members disappointed in the choices you have made. Worst of all, if you have disappointed yourself and not forgiven yourself, not given up your expectation that all of your actions should have tended in a different direction, that life should be different for you than it currently is; if these things happen to you, you will choose to die.

Coming to terms with oneself and all that one is and has been is an essential feature of coming to live. It must be possible to relive every single moment of one's life and not cringe in horror or avert your eyes in regret. You must accept what you have done, that it was perhaps mistaken, that you can make mistakes and that these things do not truly mean anything, that it was only you at that time and perhaps now you are something different. Or you are not something different, but you understand what you are, that you are flawed, weak, human, and that this does not mean that you should hate yourself, because you are only what you are, and you are a human, and you have always been such.

Still, you should separate yourself from this past person. You are not bound to act in the way that your former self acted, and if you have made terrible errors in your time on this earth you ought to give yourself permission to remove them from your point of view. The past has passed on, it is no longer your concern, out of your power in every significant way except that you should not repeat your same errors. You will, but again, put those errors behind you, no consternation or grieving over the past, just an openness to the future.

In coming to like oneself, there are two more things that I would add. When I have proposed these ideas in the past I have routinely heard criticisms that they are unphilosophical, as if that was a serious charge. I ignore those charges because these two aspects are crucial to staying alive. First, you should not be concerned with what anyone thinks of you, at least not as a source of self-worth. The judgments of others mean nothing against you, except when they are true, in which case you should alter your behavior and correct your error, and then put it behind you. If someone insults or otherwise rejects you, or judges you wanting or lacking in some key regard; if someone finds they do not want to love you, or they do not want to even spend a night with you in casual sexual activity, this means nothing. It does not change what you are.

So, you should not be concerned with what others think of you, and as a result you should be odd. You should be a strange person, willing to engage in weirdness and oddness and reject the ignorant and stupid and otherwise significant portions of society worthy of critique. You should be weird. I cannot say this enough. If you are not odd, if you do not garner a curious glance from time to time, then you are not doing things correctly, i.e, you are almost certainly still concerned with the concerns of others, something which is deeply problematic.

The reason you are not concerned with the thoughts of others is for exactly the same reason that you should come to accept yourself. If you do not like yourself because you rely on the judgment of others for what you ought to be and what you ought to do, then you will die. You will internalize the judgment of others and all of their disapproving perceptions will become your own. You will think as you imagine they do about you, and you will judge yourself and condemn your failures as somehow something intrinsic to what you are even though they are not and they are meaningless. You are your own, and your love for yourself is needed only for the self that you are as you live and breathe in this present time.

Some conclusions which can be drawn

Let go. Let go of your assertions, of all that you would have life be, of all that you would have yourself be, of all that you feel the universe should be. Let go. It is the pursuit of meaning according to our own plan that causes us to disconnect from what is given to us in every moment of our existence. The sun is rising, it is beautiful, the sun sets, it is even more beautiful. Let go until you can see this.

You may say, but I have things to do. Plans for dinner or brunch or perhaps you simply have plans to sleep, whatever they may be. Plans to be famous or to be loved or to be perfectly detached and a perfect human. You have plans, don't you, they tug at you when you watch the sun rise and when you watch it set, they take you away from this place under the sun as it rises and falls.

Those things are all meaningless, even as they are our joy, even as they are the things which provide interest or manifest interest in the things of the world. They are all meaningless, and we enjoy them best when we understand them to be empty. Empty yourself of what you would wish to be meaningful in your life, and only receive what is given to you, receive what is both meaningful and empty, meaningful in its emptiness.

Do not seek a reason to live. Do not go out searching. You don't get to answer "why?" The answer is in the sun when it rises and the sun when it sets. The answer is in the stars that come out at night and the grass that tickles our feet. They are always given, always giving, but you deny, deny, deny, you close yourself off to what they might give you when you could be open. I wonder at this life so much, I love it, this life, this life in death, this life and death together. Won't you stand with me in this golden hour that lasts forever?

Endnotes

1. Tolystoy, Leo. *Anna Karenina.* Translated by Marian Schwartz. Yale University Press: New Haven, CT. 2014. P. 461.
2. NRSV Philippians 4:4
3. NIV Ecclesiastes 3:1-2, 3:15, 3:20
4. NIV John 14:1-2
5. NRSV 1 Corinthians 1:20
6. Nietzsche, Frederick. *The Gay Science with a Prelude in Rhymes and an Appendix of Songs.* Translated by Walter Kaufman. Vintage: New York. 1974. P. 273.
7. This paper is quite obviously an extended reference to the work of his esteemed greatness Jacques Derrida, namely his speech, "Specters of Marx." Derrida, Jacques. "Spectres of Marx." Translated by Peggy Kamuf. Published in *The Derrida Reader: Writing Performances.* Ed. Julian Wolfreys. University of Edinburgh Press: Edinburgh. 1998. Pp. 140-168.
8. The Derrida Reader, p. 142
9. Cited in Nishitani Keiji, *Religion and Nothingness.* Translated with an introduction by Jan van Bragt. University of California Press: Berkeley. 1982. P. 51.
10. Ibid.
11. Ibid.
12. Ibid.
13. Marcus Aurelius, *Meditations.* Translated by George Long.
14. Wittgenstein, Ludwig. "A Lecture on Ethics." *The Philosophical review*, Vol.74 (1). 1965. pp.3-12
15. Ibid.
16. *The Heart of Emerson's Journals*, p. 63
17. Svendsen, Hans. *This is a hand: coming to certainty in Wittgenstein's world.* Random House: New York, 2777 CE.

Made in the USA
Middletown, DE
03 January 2021